PRAISE FOR WENDY JAMES

'Australia's Queen of the Domestic Thriller . . .'
—Angela Savage, *Books and Writing*, ABC Radio

'A master of suburban suspense' —Cameron Woodhead, *The Age*

The Golden Child
'. . . an engaging and intimate read that will appeal to fans of Liane
Moriarty and Jodi Picoult, with nods to Lionel Shriver and Christos
Tsiolkas' *The Slap* . . . 4 Stars' —*Bookseller + Publisher*

'Brilliant. Such a clever plot, and such real characters, and so very, very
well written' —Danielle Hawkins, author

'What a fantastic read . . . another triumph' —Angela Savage, author

'This book is utterly brilliant. I just don't even know where to start with
a review—it was compelling, it was tragic, it was clever, it was frightening, it was heartbreaking, it was shocking and it gave me shivers and it
made me question myself as a parent'
—Nicola Moriarty, author, Goodreads

The Lost Girls
'A wonderful, unputdownable story by a great Australian author'
—Liane Moriarty, *Australian Women's Weekly*

'. . . the novel is nothing less than compelling . . . *The Lost Girls* grabs
hold of you and doesn't let go—the sort of book you find yourself still
reading long after you intended to put it down. In short, everything
you want a novel of this kind to be' —*Weekend Australian*

'Wendy James has again demonstrated her flair for suspenseful diver-
sion, buttressed by her not inconsiderable literary talent'
—*Australian Book Review*

'James' character development is flawless, building up a picture of each
of the characters subtly, as they duck and weave around one
another . . . this book is a rich, dense novel, that goes so much deeper
than whodunit . . . this is as much literary fiction as it is a crime
novel, driven, above all, by character growth, deep themes, and exqui-
site writing' —Magdalena Ball, *Compulsive Reader*

'Within its suspenseful narrative, *The Mistake* has important things to say about how we think about motherhood, how the media views women, and how, when it comes to "the natural relationship between mother and daughter", few can be neutral'
—Linda Funnell, Newtown Review of Books

'As in the public narratives we devour with tea and toast in the morning, there is nothing to convict Jodie upon except our own judgment of her character; we relish or condemn her according to our sense of moral distance from her. We take part as armchair jurors, comfortable in our own safety, never suspecting that buried secrets of our own may one day be uncovered'
—Naomi Milthorpe *Canberra Times*

'. . . an amazing book that had me hooked from start to finish'
—Helen McKenna, author, Great Aussie Reads

'Brilliant, haunting and disturbing, with a twist that will leave you gasping, this is both a subtle and closely-observed portrayal of a family under stress, and a gripping thriller that leaves you guessing to the very end' —Sophie Masson, author, Goodreads

'It's sneakily challenging, disconcerting, compelling, car crash fascinating, and probably one of the best fictional reminders I've had in a while that public and media opinion should never be mistaken for the justice system, regardless of the ultimate outcome'
—Karen Chisholm, AustCrimefiction.org

'It's hands down one of the best endings I've read in a book, possibly ever' —1girl2manybooks.wordpress.com/

Where Have You Been?
Where Have You Been? is a novel you'll not want to put down'
—*Bookseller + Publisher*

'The narrative's power and cumulative suspense call to mind Alfred Hitchcock's *Vertigo*' —Sara Dowse, *Sydney Morning Herald*

'Wendy James's third novel is structured like a symphony . . . Skilful structuring, fine, flexible writing and suspense that comes to a satisfying, if not limitingly cut-and-dried conclusion, make

this social-realist novel as hard to put down as any thriller'
—Katharine England, Adelaide *Advertiser*

Why She Loves Him
'Emotionally astute, vivid and eloquent, underpinned by eroticism, James's fiction traces the contours of her characters' lives as they grapple with responsibility, freedom, and love, propelled by multifarious desires. These fresh, sensuous stories are by turns witty, perceptive and coruscating, many with a delicious wry twist'
—Felicity Plunkett, critic

'. . . absolutely amazing . . . There is something for everyone in this fantastic book' —*Bookseller + Publisher*

'From single page tales to the long sequence that ends the book, James's sure hand leads us through sometimes harrowing, sometimes redemptive moments in her beautifully rounded characters' lives'
—*Who* magazine

'. . . a penetrating picture of our life and times . . . a knockout'
—Sara Dowse, *Canberra Times*

'What quiet confidence, what an honest setting down of things as they are, nothing extenuating . . . This is a gifted story-teller and these are unusually arresting stories' —Robert Lumsden, *Adelaide Review*

Out of the Silence
'This is a work of intelligence and talent informed by a deeply humane sensitivity . . . If Wendy James aspires to be our national novelist, she is on her way. In equal measures intellectual and sensual, *Out of the Silence* is a brilliantly cut literary gem sparkling from every angle'
—*Sydney Morning Herald*

THE
GOLDEN

A NOVEL
CHILD

WENDY JAMES

Skyhorse Publishing

First North American Edition 2018
First Published 2017 in Australia by HarperCollins

This is a work of fiction. Names, places, characters, and incidents are either the products of the author's imagination or used fictitiously.

Skyhorse Publishing books may be purchased in bulk at special discounts for sales promotion, corporate gifts, fund-raising, or educational purposes. Special editions can also be created to specifications. For details, contact the Special Sales Department, Skyhorse Publishing, 307 West 36th Street, 11th Floor, New York, NY 10018 or info@skyhorsepublishing.com.

Visit our website at www.skyhorsepublishing.com.
Visit the author's website at www.wendyjames.com.au.

10 9 8 7 6 5 4 3 2 1

Library of Congress Cataloging-in-Publication Data is available on file.

Jacket design by Erin Seaward-Hiatt
Jacket photo credit: iStock

Print ISBN: 978-1-5107-3791-4
Ebook ISBN: 978-1-5107-3793-8

Printed in the United States of America

For all the teenage girls in my life—past and present.

And in memory of Emma James (1971–2015).
Hoping you've found calmer waters, little sister.

'She sat beside her daughter a long time, watching the soft placid signs of her breathing, thinking how innocent the child looked, how free of the dark, terrible instincts that were in her; then all at once she felt these things were not true, that the things the child had done could only exist in her own imagination; but she pulled herself up sternly and said, "I'm imagining nothing. It is all true."'

William March, *The Bad Seed*

PROLOGUE

IT COULD HAVE BEEN A WHOLE LOT WORSE.

Through it all, Beth holds on hard to that thought. She's such a glass half-full girl, Beth, though it's been something of a struggle lately.

For one thing, it could have happened in New Jersey. She hates to think what might have unfolded had they not been back in Australia. Oh, she can see it, how even in the rarefied air of their particular Garden State village—wealthy, middle class, predominantly liberal—the whole situation would have been far more public. There'd have been no containment, no way to damp down the conflagration. There'd have been no old connections leaned on, no past favours to call in, no possible way to keep things quiet.

In her worst nightmares, it would have been a full-on media circus, with both perpetrator and victim in the spotlight: the story syndicated in umpteen newspapers; experts on child psychology enlisted to speak on every prime-time talk show—deliberating on possible causes, offering up their professional insights into the case, pontificating on everything from the sorry state of contemporary childhood to the pernicious influence of the internet, from the increase in malignant narcissism and sociopathy to irresponsibly overindulgent parenting.

And their parenting, *her* parenting—that's the thing that

would have become the hot issue. Her family would have been put under the microscope. She can imagine the interviews—hadn't she seen them in so many other cases?—with so-called 'friends of the family', with teachers, coaches, people who'd served her in the grocery store, even her hairdresser. *There was always something odd about them,* they'd say. *Those parents gave that girl everything, did everything for her. She didn't know how good she had it, didn't know right from wrong.* And they'd have asked the questions she's asked herself endlessly, to no avail: *How could this have happened? What went wrong?*

She imagines public agitation for new laws—petitions, even—that would ensure both child and parents could be charged, convicted and punished. They would have been forced to listen to the solemn utterances of some public figure—a senator, say, or district attorney—assuring a fearful, appalled citizenry that, regardless of the final outcome, the matter would be taken seriously, that it would be investigated to the full extent of the law. And Beth can see, terrifying even in her overheated imagination, the crowd that would have gathered outside her front gate, once their name had become public property. The press, concerned locals, curious passers-by—relatively benign; and then the out-and-out toxic—all the nutty vigilante types with their placards and banners, calling for the immediate reinstatement of the death penalty for minors.

And the virtual world. Oh, the virtual world would have been nightmarish—the links, the comments, the never-ending barrage of unfiltered public opinion. Perhaps Beth's online self would have been identified and her little blog community—her haven—would have been breached. She would have finally received enough views to think about sponsors, might even have inspired a Twitter trend—but for all the wrong reasons.

Back home in Australia, these things are approached more cautiously—in a more civilised manner, as her mother would, and indeed has, put it. Here, it has all been ... not precisely brushed under the carpet, but discretion has been, and will continue to be, maintained. Though the hushing up—because that's what it is—has been as much for Sophie's sake as Charlotte's. What parent would want the details of such an act looming over their child's future? Slightly to one side of all the surface concern and sympathy, Beth suspects there is a level of judgement, too: what child, other than one who is already psychologically suspect, emotionally damaged, would submit so readily to such bullying? Looked at coolly, realistically, isn't Sophie's desperate act indisputable proof of that child's mental instability, just as much as it is evidence of her own daughter's wickedness?

Beth is well aware that public discretion is only a politesse, a ramshackle facade, and perhaps only a temporary stay at that. Privately, the news will have spread like wildfire among the school community, and beyond. Of course all the people she knows, and so many others that she doesn't, will be avidly discussing what has happened.

She's grateful, too—she's so much more than grateful; there's no word that expresses the magnitude of her feelings—that Sophie is still alive. And her gratitude that Sophie is alive is, she knows, the one thing that should overwhelm all the other sensations—fear, anger, defensiveness—that are threatening to engulf her. It's a matter for considerable thanksgiving on her part (on all their parts) that the child is still breathing.

But despite all the positives—these not so small mercies—Beth's finding it hard to maintain her usual optimistic outlook. From where she's standing, the glass is looking ominously empty.

DizzyLizzy.com

Who is Lizzy?

Lizzy is an Aussie gal, formerly a journo, now a mother of two and 'trailing spouse', transported from the sunny shores of Sydney town to the colder climes of *Somewhere*, USA, via *Elsewhere*, Canada, and *Overdaire*, Ireland. She's mostly enjoying the experience—even if it has left her feeling a little disoriented.

Writing this blog is a way to ensure that Lizzy's communications skills stay honed. It also keeps her sane.

The Parental Bogeyman Goes Trick-Or-Treating

Surely, C insists, she's old enough to go trick-or-treating without me. After all, she'll be twelve in a few weeks. And twelve is a teenager, practically a grown-up. We're on our front porch (where so many of these boundary-setting negotiations seem to take place), just about to join a small troop of neighbourhood kids as they head out into our tree-lined suburban street in search of treats.

Up until this year, Halloween has been a family affair: sometimes a school friend might join us, but usually it's just been our little trio—C, her older sister, L, and me. D stays home, ready to appease any visiting demons with candy. This arrangement suits me—I've always found Halloween slightly disturbing, one of America's stranger traditions. I mean, why would anyone choose to send their babies out alone on the one night of the year when the Hellmouth, as they call it in the Buffyverse, is most likely to be wide open? And frankly—those grinning pumpkins freak me out. That orange glow makes every house, even my own, seem sinister.

But this year is different: L is trick-or-treating with a friend, and C and I have planned to join up with the neighbourhood kids. It's different in other ways too. Instead of the usual cutesy parent-approved outfit, this year C has devised her own Halloween costume. She's a zombie: which means her face is plastered white, her undead eyes have been blackened, and there are frighteningly lifelike gashes of red at her temple and around her mouth. She's rather terrifying to behold.

'It's lame, you coming,' she says. 'Everyone else gets to go on their own, without their parents. Every year. And they've all survived.'

'So far,' I say darkly, trying hard not to think of all the possible ways they might not survive.

The look she gives me is murderous (admittedly her emotional range is limited), and she stamps down the stairs and out the gate. I follow slowly, clutching my pumpkin-shaped bucket, my devil's ears headband, the little red tail that clips onto my jeans pocket.

I Google on my phone as I walk: At what age should children trick-or-treat without an adult? One mother with the same worries as me—and a few others I hadn't considered—volunteers online that she reluctantly let her eleven-year-old out alone, conceding that the constantly hovering parent may be the biggest bogeyman of all. I swallow my anxiety. By the time I meet C, who has joined the small tribe of monsters gathered at the park across the road, I'm almost ready to give in.

One of my neighbours, a grade-school teacher with three kids, all younger than C, waits with them in the gloom. Her T-shirt is embossed with a luminous skeleton; her hairclips are shaped like witches' hats. 'Are you going with them?' I ask, hopeful.

'Oh, no.' She looks shocked. 'They'd hate that. Parents worry too much.'

I nod, give a weak smile, think about abductions, LSD-laced Twinkies, paedophiles. Guns.

'Actually,' her son, a boy aged around ten who is dressed as Captain America, pipes up, 'some really gruesome stuff has happened to kids at Halloween.'

'Oh?' I try not to sound too interested.

'We had to write about the meaning of Halloween at school, and I found this cool site with all the Halloween murders on it. There's heaps and heaps,' he smiles with ghoulish enthusiasm. 'One time all these girls were kidnapped, and there was this kid that was shot. But the best one was this dad who actually poisoned his own kid. He put cyanide in all the kids' Pixy Stix, but his son was the only one who died, which was actually what he wanted because then he could get the life insurance.' Captain America shudders with delight.

His mother beams. 'Jackson just loves his history.' She pats him on the head proudly.

'So,' says C, clearly reassured by this conversational turn, 'you're not coming, right? I can go on my own?'

I mutter, look vague.

The captain's mother gives a cheery wave. 'Off you go, then. Be good.' She offers me a smile, heads back across the road.

I wait until she's tripping up the stairs to her orange-lit porch, then pick up my bucket, clip on my tail, straighten my ears. Parental bogeyman? There are worse disguises.

52 ♥

EXPATTERINGS:
@AnchoreDownInAlaska says:
I always thought Hellmouth was what happened after they'd eaten all those sweets ☺

@BlueSue says:
I'm afraid that the horror that is Halloween is fast becoming ubiquitous in Australia. Our house was egged last year when we refused to join in. It's just another nail in the coffin of our free and independent nation. In another fifty years, we'll be the fifty-first state.

@GirlFromIpanema says:
Halloween is for the fainthearted. You should see what goes down in Brazil during the Day of the Dead ☺

THE GOLDEN CHILD'S TEN LESSONS FOR SUCCESS

ABOUT: I'm a girl who knows how to get what she wants and likes to share ☺ What more do you need to know?

LESSON ONE: SWEET REVENGE

In my first year of grade school, there was this girl, M, who told me I had beautiful hair, who said she was my best friend, who shared her hummingbird cake with me every day for a week. Every day for a week we played together in the lunch break, we sat in a special corner of the courtyard and went through our favourite books, both of us pretending we could read. Her book was Brown Bear, Brown Bear, which I thought was the dumbest story ever. My book was Green Eggs and Ham. I had memorised all the words and could read it just like my dad. I did all the expressions, the same voices that Daddy did. The girl laughed and laughed and said I read it better than the teacher. She said I had beautiful hair. She said that I was the prettiest girl in the class as well as the smartest and that she wanted to be my best friend.

But when we came back after the weekend M ignored me. She shared her cake with another girl. The two girls sat in our special corner and laughed at me, sitting alone on the losers bench. My teeth were too big, they said. I looked like a rabbit. I was ugly and stupid.

The next day I opened her lunch box when she was in class and put dog shit in her sandwich.

Lesson? Don't let anyone mess with you.

But if they do—act.

COMMENTS

@RANDOMREADER says:

I thought this was gonna be about the movie, not dogshit sandwiches. But hey, whatever. You go, Goldie!

PART ONE

BETH

SHE'S JUST SETTLED DOWN TO RESPOND TO COMMENTS ON yesterday's blogpost—one on husbands and affairs (not that Beth has ever had to worry on that account)—when Dan calls her with the news. There's no lead-up, no warning: 'I've got news, Bethie,' Dan says, his voice a little slower than usual, full of portent. 'They're sending me to Newcastle.' He doesn't wait for her response. 'There's to be some sort of merger—a takeover really—with DRP, that new engineering outfit. You know, that one I was telling you about. Those amazing young blokes, straight out of uni, set it up, and they've got some incredible projects already. And it's in Newie. Isn't that the most brilliant thing?' Dan's voice has gradually sped up, his excitement palpable, but now it slows again. 'It couldn't be better, could it? Home.' She can hear the wistfulness, the barely disguised pleading.

'Oh. Newcastle. Not Sydney?' Beth knows that this isn't what he wants to hear, that it isn't what she should have said, but it's the best she can do. She knows that Dan will know what she isn't saying, what she's thinking: *Your home, not mine.*

'Yeah.' Dan's voice is instantly flatter, more cautious. 'I know you were hoping we'd be able to go straight back to Sydney, but it's not really that far—only two hours on the freeway. A bit more on the train. And you know how much it's changed. It's

11

not so—or not *just*—industrial. It's different to when I was growing up. Things are happening. And we'll be able to live close to the beach there, which would be out of the question in Sydney. It's a good place, Beth. You said yourself, last time we were home, that Sydney was crazy. All the traffic; all the people. And it will be great for the kids to be close . . .' He pauses, quickly changes tack. 'To be close to the ocean.' She knows what he'd begun to say, what he didn't say: that it would be great for the kids to be close to family. Meaning, of course, his family, not hers.

Beth takes a deep breath, tries to sound brighter, asks the million-dollar question: 'So, when do we go?'

She spends the next hour writing, and then trashing, a blog-post announcing the news of their departure, studiously avoiding thinking too hard about what a move to Newcastle might really mean, and keeping her disappointment under control.

She knows her discontent is unreasonable and, to Dan, inexplicable. After all, they've discussed it numerous times, and she's told him she'd be willing to go anywhere if it meant going home, that it didn't have to be Sydney. She'd imagined Perth, Melbourne, maybe even Adelaide, but it had never occurred to her that Newcastle was a possibility. And it isn't so much Newcastle itself that worries her—it's a sizeable city, and a beautiful one in its own way—but the proximity to Dan's family, specifically his mother, Margie.

However hard she tries, Beth has never been able to rid herself of the sense that Margie disapproves of her. That she thinks Beth isn't quite right for her only son. That she's just that little bit too middle class, private school, North Shore, *Protestant*. That it's somehow Beth's fault that Dan moved so far away. If it wasn't for you and your ambition, the imagined accusation runs, Dan would have been content to stay near his mother in Newcastle.

Margie's disapproval is well controlled, there's not much Beth can put her finger on—just the occasional, and quickly suppressed, expression, the mildly barbed words that when mulled over later appear completely innocent of malice. Perhaps Margie's behaviour is entirely unconscious, or perhaps it isn't really directed at Beth personally; perhaps it was always going to be impossible for Margie to be enthusiastic about her only son's wife, whoever she might be.

Beth has never said anything; how could she possibly complain when her own mother has made nothing but the most cursory effort to disguise her disapproval of Dan? But somehow her mother doesn't count: Francine's disapproval is fairly universal—she doesn't really approve of Beth, either. But Margie, Margie is different. Margie is—or so everybody says—lovely. Warm, generous, broad-minded, salt-of-the-earth Margie. If Margie doesn't like you then most probably you aren't worth liking.

If she's honest with herself, Beth has to admit that it isn't just the prospect of being closer to Margie that worries her—but what she thinks of as the Margie effect. The way Dan becomes a little less hers, a little less *theirs*, when he's around his mother. The way he tends to defer, to acquiesce, to Margie's . . . not demands, no one would ever accuse her of being demanding, but to her opinions, her ideas about him. The way Dan seems almost apologetic about his career, his expanded horizons and, on occasion, his wife and daughters. Truth is, when they're around Margie, Beth feels vaguely sidelined.

Regardless, the return to Australia is necessary: Beth has been desperate to get back before the girls get any older, before they become irrevocably, unchangeably, American; before the relocation is too traumatic, the differences—more marked the longer they live in the States—too ingrained. She can already see it happening; sometimes they feel slightly alien, their child-hood experiences, their concerns, their *accents*, so very different to her own. One day soon they'll be embarrassed by their moth-er's Australianness, will do their utmost—even more than the required snapping of apron strings—to differentiate themselves from her.

By the time Beth goes to pick up the girls from school, all the positive aspects of their impending return have begun to filter through, quashing her initial anxiety. She waits impa-tiently in the schoolyard, bursting to tell them. Desperate to share the news, she confides in one of the other waiting moth-ers, just an acquaintance really, and not one of her particular friends.

'You're going to Australia?' the woman, Karen, says in a tone of mild horror. 'Are you sure that's good news?' She still seems a little uncertain when Beth laughingly assures her that going back to Australia is definitely good news, and that they won't be heading back to a life of deprivation, but to home and family and considerable creature comforts in a civilised and beautiful coastal city.

'Oh, Janey will be just devastated,' Karen says, 'I don't know what she'll do without Charlie. I don't know what any of the girls will do. She's such a *force*, you know. They'll be lost. What do your girls think?'

At this, Beth has to admit a little guiltily that the girls don't know, that she's only just found out herself. Karen gives an unreadable moue—whether out of concern or disapproval isn't clear—but she doesn't say anything more, interrupted by the noisy approach of her twin sons. Immediately caught up in the maelstrom of children's demands and desires, the women's conversation ends in the usual abrupt schoolyard way, with farewells and apologies neither given nor looked for.

Beth's girls arrive soon after. Lucy first, cheerful, but ready for home; Charlie later, more reluctantly. Charlie, as always, is surrounded by friends, and only slowly extricates herself, making her way over to her mother, walking slowly, calling back over her shoulder, smiling and giggling, unwilling to finish the conversation.

She launches immediately into a frantic entreaty for a weekend sleepover for four or maybe even five—*Please, Mum*—of her best friends, ignoring her older sister's prior claim to conversation. 'I haven't quite decided whether Stella or Carly should come, but definitely Evie, Liza, Belle and Rosie—' But Beth is impatient, full of her own news, and shushes them both, pulling them towards her. 'Hold on, Charlie. I've got something very exciting to tell you.' Lucy looks intrigued, but Charlie pouts. 'Oh, but Mum, this sleepover is really important. I need to know now. I've been planning—'

Beth interrupts. 'I've got some great news, girls.' She has their attention, finally. 'We're going home to Australia.' Lucy looks momentarily surprised and then, as if sensing her mother's pleasure, grins widely, grips her mother's hand, breathes an exultant *Yes!* But Charlie is another matter. Her expression, momentarily blank, becomes steely in a heartbeat. Her eyes narrow, and she glares at her mother. 'Actually, that's your home, *Mom.*' She emphasises the vowel. 'Not mine. I wasn't even born there. This is *my* home.' She throws out the words, her voice suddenly hard-edged, then clamps her mouth shut and turns away, brushing aside her mother's hand. Ignoring the bemused glances of her schoolmates, Charlie stalks through the school-yard, out the gate, and begins the short walk home alone.

Beth and Lucy follow, subdued, all their initial excitement dampened. Beth tries to respond to Lucy's obvious efforts to lighten the mood, but there is no dispelling the guilt. She should have broken the news differently: gently and in private. She should have considered the effect. She should have waited. She should have known.

Unusually, there are no afternoon activities scheduled and, once home, Charlie goes straight to her room and slams the door. She doesn't emerge until dinner time, despite Beth's anxious tapping at the door throughout the afternoon, her blatant attempts to placate her. 'I've made cookies. Darling?'

'Go away, Mom.'

'But Charlie . . .'

'Just go away.'

Eventually she sends Lucy in to check.

'Charlie's okay,' she reports, after being closeted with her younger sister for a good ten minutes. 'She's just upset about leaving here.' She shrugs. 'She'll get over it.'

'And what about you?' Beth realises with a pang that she's been so worried about Charlie that she hasn't given Lucy's feelings a second thought. It occurs to her that her elder daughter's calm demeanour might be deceptive.

Lucy gives her a valiant smile. 'Oh, I don't know. I don't really want to go, I guess. I'm going to miss . . .' She throws out an arm as if to encapsulate, well, everything—her whole life, Beth guesses. 'I love it here, but it was always going to happen, wasn't it? We've been warned our entire lives. So there's not really much point in complaining, is there?' Lucy's smile wavers momentarily; she brushes at her cheek, wiping away a rogue tear.

Beth feels her heart lurch, puts her arm around her daughter. 'God, you're a good egg, Lucy. I should have realised how hard this would be for you. I was just so excited, I didn't think . . .'

'Are you really excited, Mum? I thought you wanted to go back to Sydney. Newcastle's so different.'

Beth admires her daughter's careful understatement. 'I know. It's not Sydney. But it's probably not so different from the Sydney I grew up in, when I come to think of it. Sydney's so big now—much, much bigger than here. And busy. And expensive. Newcastle's a bit more small-townish—but the big city's just a train ride away. Just like here.' Beth knows she is reassuring herself as much as Lucy.

'But it's so . . .'

'So what?'

'Oh, I don't know. Newcastle has never seemed like somewhere we'd live. Where Nanny is . . . it's okay, I guess, but it's . . . Well, the houses are so tiny. And crowded in. And the people all seem a bit . . . poor or something. I mean, it's not like here.'

'Oh, darling.' Beth almost laughs at her daughter's effort to be diplomatic. Margie still lives in the same small cottage in the inner-city suburb of Newcastle where Dan grew up. While the suburb, like so much of the once-industrial city, is slowly gentrifying, it is certainly very different to their leafy middle-class enclave in America, where the only dirt and grime her children are ever exposed to is the occasional pile of dog shit left on the sidewalk by some irresponsible dog-walker. Beth hurries to reassure her daughter.

'We won't actually be living where Nanny is. There are much, much prettier suburbs. With bigger houses. And Dad says we can live close to the beach . . . Remember that beach we went to last time? There are some lovely places around there. Honestly.' She sounds so much more certain than she feels.

Beth isn't entirely convinced she's satisfied her daughter, who bombards her with questions, most of them impossible to answer. 'So, where are we going to go to school, Mum? Do you think . . . do you think I'll fit in? I won't be too different? Too . . . American? Do they even like Americans? What if they don't like me?' Her daughter's eyes are wide, her forehead crinkled in a way that reminds Beth of Dan's when he's anxious. She strokes the absurdly furrowed brow, plants a kiss and bites back the tears that threaten whenever she's faced with her elder daughter's lack of confidence—so different to Charlie, but so painfully familiar. She makes her voice as cheerful and encouraging as possible.

'Oh, Lucy. You'll always make friends. It might take a little bit of time to settle, but wherever you go, darling, there'll always be someone. Someone who thinks you're special.'

DizzyLizzy.com

Yellow Brick Road

I tell the girls the Big News: we're going home. Very soon.

First comes the anger. Then the tears. Then the blind panic. And that's just me.

The girls, of course, are far more laid-back.

'Hey, Mum.' L looks up from her homework. 'Do they do math in Australia?' She sounds so hopeful that I don't answer right away. Let her enjoy the sum-free moment.

'I'm afraid they do, darling. Yes.' Her face falls.

'They call it maths, though,' I offer.

'How about geography?'

'Afraid so.'

'Athletics?'

'Yes—but it's called PE in Australia.'

'What about history?'

'Uh-huh. But it wouldn't be American history.'

'So, what sort of history? Would it be, like, Australian history?'

'There'd be a bit of world history, but I guess there'd be a fair bit of Australian too.'

'Oh.' She pauses, thinks for a bit. 'I guess that would be about when Christopher Columbus discovered it and all that?'

So, yeah. As well as the packing and the cleaning and the interminable filling out of forms, all the endless things that have to be done before we move our little household from one hemisphere to another, we've clearly got our work cut out on the educational front.

Sigh.

46 ♥

EXPATTERINGS:

@BlueSue says:

And so it begins . . . I hate to be a wet blanket, Lizzy, but sometimes moving home isn't all it's cracked up to be. Coming back to Australia was a complete disaster for our family. Both of the kids ended up moving back to the UK as soon as they'd finished school—and they've never really come back. It's one of the great regrets of my life that we ever left Melbourne to begin with. Anyway, I wish you the best of luck on your journey 'home'. You're going to need it!

> **@DizzyLizzy** replied:
> Hey, @BlueSue—I'm sure it might be a bit complicated when it comes to settling the kids, but they're pretty tough cookies, both of them, and I think they'll be okay. Really glad to be heading home, but wouldn't swap the last fifteen years for the world!

> **@AnchoreDownInAlaska** replied:
> Just remember that children are resilient, Lizzy. What's the bet that in twelve months time they'll have made a new life!

@OzMumInTokyo says:
Oh, Lizzy, I'm so happy for you! But promise me you won't stop writing! I can't do without my daily fix of DizzyLizzy <3<3<3

> **@DizzyLizzy** replied:
> Of course I won't stop writing, ozmum! I'm sure being an ex-expat will provide plenty of blog-able moments!

@GirlFromIpanema says:
My youngest daughter asked me if we had the same numbers in Australia. I told her that they went backwards—so 100=1; 99=2; 98=3 etc. It was all fun until she asked me to make up an Australian times-table chart for her.

RANDOM FACT № 1

THE OLEANDER

The oleander is one of the most poisonous of commonly grown garden plants. Ingestion of this plant can affect the gastrointestinal system, the heart, and the central nervous system. The gastrointestinal effects can consist of nausea and vomiting, excess salivation, abdominal pain, diarrhea that may or may not contain blood and, especially in horses, colic. Cardiac reactions consist of irregular heart rate, sometimes characterized by a racing heart at first that then slows to below normal further along in the reaction. Extremities may become pale and cold due to poor or irregular circulation. The effect on the central nervous system may show itself in symptoms such as drowsiness, tremors or shaking of the muscles, seizures, collapse, and even coma that can lead to death.

   (Wikipedia)

COMMENTS

@HAPPYGARDENER says:

I'm just wondering if oleanders grow in cold climates? I live in Devon, England, and was thinking of planting an oleander hedge. The flowers are so pretty.

   @RANDOMREADER replied:

   I don't think this is a gardening website, honey;)

BETH

HER FIRST INKLING COMES DURING A MILDLY HYSTERICAL game of telephone between parents at school pick-up, a constantly morphing tale: an ambulance was sighted out the front just after lunch, or was it just before recess? Paramedics had rushed in; someone had been carried out on a stretcher. It was a sixth grade boy, someone says, hurt in a fall. Or has a kindergartener broken a leg? No one knows the truth of the matter, but all feel guiltily relieved, happy to be left in the dark for a little while longer—because knowledge would presume some sort of connection, and tales of ambulances in schoolyards are something all mothers are glad not to be connected to. A collective prayer is sent out for the safety of the hurt child, and personal thanks given: *Not my child. Thank you . . .*

When the bell rings and the noisy mob of children swarm onto the playground, the question of what actually happened falls away in the tide of demands and demonstrations—Charlie complaining that the apple her mother packed for lunch was covered in revolting little brown spots; Lucy requesting that they hurry as she has to get to the town library; Charlie embarking on a story about Mr Cannon's secret pipe-smoking habit (too gross), his hairy ears (even grosser); Lucy exclaiming over her forgotten hat, a journey back to the classroom required.

So in the muddle of departure and then the business—total chaos, really—of the afternoon and evening, Beth simply forgets to ask if they have any idea what has gone on.

And chaos is no overstatement. The countdown for their return to Australia has begun in earnest. Beth has started on the endless, but weirdly satisfying job of culling their belongings—and every corner of the house is filled with seemingly random piles of stuff-to-throw and stuff-to-take. The mess is remarkable. It is remarkable, too, how easy it is to divest yourself of your belongings. All those things Beth had imagined she'd keep around her forever—things that are imbued, or so she'd thought, with meaning, representing her life here, her past, *their* past: the colonial ladder-back chairs they bought for a steal and so lovingly restored when they first arrived; the maple Art Deco dressing table Dan gave her for her fortieth birthday; the chintzy club lounge they'd planned to have recovered. So much of it now seems old and worn, past it, and despite the fact that every object contains a myriad of memories of their family life, none seems worth transporting across the sea. None of it seems necessary.

Beth wonders if the growing pile of cast-offs is some sort of metaphor for her attitude to leaving; sometimes she feels that she is just as easily casting aside the life she's lived—more than a decade spent in America—as irrelevant, now that it's almost over. She'd imagined she'd been fully engaged, but now she wonders whether the whole of her life in New Jersey has been a life suspended, a life spent waiting. But the girls, too, who have embarked on their own lesser culls, are no less ruthless, both of them tossing without a second thought things that Beth knows they once considered precious.

It isn't until the phone call comes—the three of them

having eaten their thrown-together dinner (scrambled eggs, sausages, toast) and settled down to watch an old episode of *Doctor Who*—that Beth recalls the ambulance, the whispered schoolyard rumours. Too late. If only she'd had some sort of hint, had a response ready.

Naturally, the call comes not from a friendly source, but from Sarah Fuller, who is the mother of one of the girls in Charlie's class, Macey. Macey is a tall, pale girl, asthmatic, shy, slightly awkward. She isn't a particular friend of Charlie, but they share a violin teacher and have been pushed together for concert duets a few times, with Macey (who can always be relied upon to play in time, if not in tune) relegated to the second part. All through grade school Sarah has made her disapproval of Beth clear (though what she's done to earn this disapproval is a complete mystery), and Beth dislikes her intensely.

'Hi, Beth? Sarah Fuller?' The woman speaks with an irritating uplift, as if her every statement requires assent.

'Hello, Sarah.' Beth assumes that the woman is calling about a class bake sale she's promised to contribute to the following week. 'The bake sale's next week, right? Tuesday? I haven't forgotten. I thought I'd do my Anzac cookies again—they seemed popular last time.'

'I'm not actually ringing about the bake sale.'

'Oh?'

'So . . . I take it you haven't heard, then?'

'Heard about what?'

'About what happened at school today? The girls haven't told you? I thought one of them would have let you know?'

'Oh, you mean that ambulance? I heard there was something when I got there this afternoon, but then we got caught up, all the packing . . . and I forgot to ask.'

Her occasional conversations with Sarah always leave Beth in this same position, apologetic and feeling slightly deficient, though she can never really work out what it is exactly that she lacks.

'Oh, well. I'm surprised the girls didn't tell you what was going on.' Beth senses something else in the other woman's voice now, a tamped-down excitement.

'You know how it is—we've been distracted, busy. Have you heard we're heading back to Australia?'

Sarah ignores the question. 'Well, I'm real sorry to have to be the one to break the news.' It is difficult to imagine her sounding less sorry.

'Break the news? What do you mean? What's happened?' Beth's heart begins to race uncomfortably.

'It was Arya Stannard. You know, she's new in the sixth grade? In the other class? Mrs Reardon's class? She's only a little girl, dark-haired.'

'Oh, dear. What happened?' Beth can't picture this Arya at all, is certain she's never heard of her, is mildly glad that, whatever it is that's happened, they're not discussing some child she knows or can picture.

'She was . . .' There is a long pause, a dramatically indrawn breath. 'She was poisoned.'

'Poisoned? Oh my God! How? Is she okay?'

Again the pause.

'She seems to be fine. Luckily, they got her to hospital in time. The principal was very good.'

'What sort of poison? Was it a cleaning product or something?' Beth imagines the caretaker or perhaps the gardener leaving some solvent or fertiliser around, but can't imagine how a sixth-grader would be so silly as to ingest it.

'It was an oleander leaf. She chewed on it?'

'An oleander leaf? Good lord. Why?'

'For a dare, apparently.'

'For a dare? For goodness sake, who would dare her to do such a thing?'

Another pause, lengthier, and then a voice filled with satisfaction.

'Well, here's the thing, Elizabeth.' She enunciates all four syllables in a sweet sing-song. 'It was some type of initiation test; you know the sort of thing? And Macey seems to think it was your girl's idea. Your Charlie's.'

When the woman, smugly satisfied she has done her duty, rings off, Beth doesn't wait for the information to settle, she doesn't wait to discuss it with Dan, or even to think about it. She calls for Charlie to come immediately and asks her straight out what happened to Arya.

Charlie shrugs, pleads ignorance. 'Arya? What do you mean? Nothing happened to her.'

'At school today. She was taken to hospital in an ambulance.'

'Really? Wow! Someone said there was an ambulance but we didn't know why. Arya was fine at lunch. What happened? Did she break her arm in gym or something?' Charlotte's surprise seems genuine, her concern authentic.

'Apparently she was poisoned—something to do with eating oleander.'

'Oleander? What's that?' Charlie's face is blank.

'It's a leaf, Charlie. A poisonous leaf.'

'Oh.' Charlie's eyes open wide. 'Oh, no.'

'So you do know what happened? Mrs Fuller just rang up. Macey's mum. She said that Macey told her it was your fault, that it was your idea that Arya eat the leaf. That it was a dare.'

'It wasn't like that at all. I didn't deliberately dare her to eat a poisonous plant!' Charlie's face is red, her jaw taut. It is rare, Beth realises, that she sees her daughter in any way discomposed. Over the last year or so she has developed an almost adult control of her emotions; she can't even remember the last time she saw Charlie cry.

'So what happened?'

Charlie takes a deep breath. 'It was a sort of test, for the gang. She just had to put some . . . weird stuff in her mouth. Just plants and other random things. We didn't make her swallow anything. And none of it was meant to be *poisonous*. It was just a game.'

'Just a game? Mrs Fuller seems to think it was an initiation to be in your gang. That doesn't sound very kind, Charlie.'

Charlie rolls her eyes. 'It's just what we do. It's nothing. We've all had to do it.'

'And was it really your idea?'

'I don't know.' Charlie has begun to look exasperated, defensive rather than worried. 'I don't actually know who thought it up. It could have been any of us. We've done it before, heaps of times. It's just . . . it isn't anything serious. Half the girls in the year are part of the gang anyway.'

'And who's not? Are there people you don't let in? If they won't play your game?'

'It doesn't work that way, Mum.' Impatient now. 'Some girls have different friends. I mean, Taylor Roberts and Georgia Barry aren't part of the gang—but they're idiots. And there's Tina and Maria—but they don't care.'

Tina and Maria are the only two Hispanic girls in the class, and while there is no overt exclusion—Beth knows they have been invited to numerous parties over the years—the two girls still stick together, tend not to join in. But surely there is a great gulf between exclusion and difference: Tina and Maria's mothers remain aloof from most of the other mothers, too. It seems patronising, wrongheaded, to insist that her daughter play with certain children simply in the name of ethnic diversity.

'And the leaf? Where did it come from? I'm sure there aren't any oleanders at the school.' Beth thinks of the miniature oleander she potted last year and carefully nurtured to a late-season flowering as a reminder of her more tropical origins and is immediately apprehensive. '*You* didn't take the leaf in, did you? It wasn't from our garden?' Even as she speaks she realises the unlikelihood of its being from anywhere else—oleanders aren't common in New Jersey.

'I did take some leaves, but I don't even know what an oleander is. We just had all these random things, truly. Evie brought a chilli, Liza brought someone's old toothbrush, Belle brought in a tube of wasabi. Rosie brought in some dog biscuits. Someone else gave her some dirt. I just had this bag of leaves.' Charlie swipes at her eyes, her lips quiver, turn down at the sides.

'But where did the bag of leaves come from?'

'I don't know. I think . . . I'm not sure. I think I just found them.'

'What? How can you just find a bag of leaves?'

'I just thought they were ordinary leaves.' Charlie sounds slightly breathless; she won't meet her mother's eyes.

'Well, where did you get them? Tell me the truth. I just want to know.'

'Actually, it was Lucy. Lucy told me to.'

'Charlie. How can you say that? I did not.' Lucy speaks quietly from the doorway. She moves towards them, her expression serious.

Charlie turns to her. 'You did so. You were out in the garden, drawing. And when I told you about the game you said I should make her eat leaves. And then you gave me those skinny ones. I thought they were . . . what are the ones koalas eat? Gum leaves.'

'I didn't, Mum. I promise. I was out there doing that botany project. I'd collected a whole heap of leaves to draw and I said Charlie could have them. She didn't tell me anything about what she wanted them for. If she had I would've told her it was a dumb idea. And I wouldn't have given her *any* of the leaves. Especially not the oleander. I can remember you telling us they were poisonous when you planted it.'

Charlie glares at her sister. 'Lucy, you— '

Beth interrupts. 'Look, it doesn't matter. You're not in trouble. Either of you. I just wanted to know what happened.'

Charlie looks relieved. 'I honestly didn't know what the leaves *were*. Any of them. I didn't have a clue they were ollie whatevers.'

And then Lucy asks the question that Charlie hasn't asked, the question that Charlie should have asked. 'So, is she okay, Mum? The girl who ate that leaf? She's all right, isn't she? I'd hate to think she was sick from one of our leaves, even if it was an accident.'

Beth lies curled up in bed, waiting for Dan, her flannelette pjs on, lamp dimmed, the thriller she's reading opened invitingly on her bedside table. But she's too tired to read more than a few pages, and is already half asleep by the time he gets home. It's past twelve, and Dan is irritable and unresponsive when she says she needs to tell him something.

'Can't it wait? I'm exhausted. If it was that urgent why didn't you call me at work?' She wishes she had, or wishes she'd waited until morning. She is sleepily content, and somehow it doesn't seem all that significant now, just a silly schoolgirl prank. She tells him anyway, just the bare facts, without any editorialising, as he undresses.

'Jesus Christ.' Dan drops his tie at his feet, doesn't bend to retrieve it. Just stands, his long, pale arms dangling loosely, mouth open, eyes wide. 'Those stupid girls. She could have died. What were they thinking, sticking things in their mouths? At that age! They're almost thirteen, for fuck's sake. Not six.'

'I think the point is they weren't thinking. And the girl's okay, according to what's-her-face, Macey's mum. Totally fine.'

'Well, thank Christ for that.' He crawls in beside her. Beth snuggles against him, listening to his heartbeat, breathing in his familiar tangy scent.

'Should we be more worried, do you think? It isn't great, is it?' Dan's voice is low but his anxiety is clear. She tries to reassure him.

'There's no harm done. She'll learn a lesson from it. They all will.'

'I guess. But maybe there is some sort of problem . . . maybe it's something we need to discuss with Charlie.'

'Oh, I don't know that there's anything to worry about. It's just typical peer-group silliness, surely? She'll know not to do it again. Charlie's fine—she's better than fine, don't you think? She doesn't actually seem to have *any* problems.'

'But don't you think that's a bit odd in itself? Don't most kids have some sort of . . . issues? Uncertainties? Doubts? Do you think there might be something that we're missing?'

'Missing how? She gets on with her teachers, she works hard, she's popular.'

'But being *so* popular. Maybe she's *too* popular . . . That can be a problem, can't it?'

'You think that's a problem? Honestly.' Beth giggles. 'How

neurotic is that? Half the time you're worrying that Lucy only has a few friends and now Charlie's too popular.'

'Were you one of the popular kids at school?'

'Well, no, but I wasn't that *un*popular, if you know what I mean. I was sort of in the middle. Like Lucy, I guess.'

'I remember when I was a kid, the popular kids weren't always the nicest kids.'

'But that's just—'

He interrupts. 'And what's she doing running a bloody initiation for her gang, anyway? Did you ask her that? It sounds kind of . . . horrible. Punitive. Not the sort of thing I like to hear about. As if she's some sort of little—what do they call them?—a nasty little Queen Bee.'

'I really don't think it's anything we need to worry about. It's not some kind of secret society, you know. And she's not one of those mean little girls; everyone genuinely likes her. It really *is* everyone, you know—the kids and the teachers, too. Someone's got to be at the top of the pile. She's . . . she's just different to us. She's one of those girls—the ones we all wanted to be. Well, me anyway. I know it's hard to believe, but I think she's kind of . . . extraordinary.' Beth can hear the little thrill of pride in her voice, doesn't try to disguise it around Dan.

'Yeah. I know all that. She *is* special. It's just . . . I hope she's using her power for good, that's all.' He sighs and turns towards her, closing his eyes. She watches his face relax. He opens his eyes, gives a slow smile. 'And I don't know why you think it's so odd that our daughter should be extraordinary. I'm pretty extraordinary too, you know.'

'At some things.'

'At lots of things.' His hand moves down her shoulder, cups her breast. 'At this sort of thing, anyway.'

DizzyLizzy.com

Where Did They Come From?

Do you ever wonder where your kids came from? I mean, I've done the research—and I'm pretty sure I understand all the biological stuff. Which is handy. But who they are: therein lies a mystery. I suppose I understand my elder girl, L, pretty well—but only because she's a bit like me. She's quiet, dreamy, a bit uncertain, easily crushed by an offhand remark, a thoughtless gesture. But there are ways that she's different, too: she's calmer, kinder, more thoughtful than I can ever remember being. She's interested in the world around her, good at school work, and she's bright—but she's not particularly competitive. She does her best, but it doesn't faze her if others do better. She seems to have worked out the whole friendship thing without too much angst: she has one or two close friends and that's enough. She's just thoroughly together—in a way that makes me tear up whenever I see it in action.

Then there's C. She's a completely different kettle of fish. She's nothing like me—and nothing like her father, either. She's one of those impossibly bright and shiny girls. She really *is* good at everything. Her academics are outrageously high; she's captain of the hockey and the soccer and the swim teams; public speaking comes naturally. You guessed it: she's a regular teacher's pet.

But the thing is, she's popular too. Every morning when I leave her at school, a gaggle of girls rushes out to greet her; at birthday parties you can see the mood lift when she arrives. Sometimes, when we're at some school or sporting do and she's winning an award or commendation, D and I look at one another, proudly yes, but also with some astonishment, and I know we're both wondering the same thing.

58 ♥

EXPATTERINGS:
@AnchoreDownInAlaska says:
LOL. You obviously worked out the biological stuff earlier than me! I don't think I really got it until #4 son arrived;)

@OzMumInTokyo says:

Do they get on, Lizzy?

> **@DizzyLizzy** replied:
>
> They really do! Don't know how I'd cope with fighters.

@ExpatMum says:

I love this post!! They are such a mystery: I'm amazed and awed every day. Keep on doing a great job ☺

@BlueSue says:

Our youngest was a real type A, too; she always won everything—all the academics, all the sports. But during her final years of high school she had a major breakdown; apparently she was pushing herself too hard. She's fine now—after years of therapy, she has her perfectionism under control. But it's definitely something to watch out for. And you need to be careful, too, that the quieter one doesn't miss out.

BETH

After drop-off the next day—and it is just a drop-off, there is no exiting the car, no chatting to any of the other mothers—Beth rings the principal.

'Mrs Mahony. How can I help you?' Mrs Guterman's voice is as low and pleasant, as always.

'Oh, Mrs Guterman. It's about the young girl who got sick yesterday. Arya. I was ringing to ask how she is.' Beth's voice seems suddenly very Australian.

'Oh, yes. Arya.' She pronounces it Ah-yah, not Ar-i-a as Beth had done. 'She's fine. I spoke to her mother this morning and she was discharged from hospital last night with no apparent ill effects. They gave her charcoal, I believe, and the relief was immediate. It was only a short-lived discomfort, along with a moment of panic on our part when she showed us all the things she'd . . . tasted. One of the teachers recognised the leaf and knew its properties.'

'Oh, I'm so glad. I was so worried.' Beth is powerless to stop herself gushing. 'I don't know if you know, but apparently it had something to do with Charlie and her group.'

'The initiation rite? Yes, we're aware of that.'

'And we think perhaps Charlie may have brought the leaf in from home. We have a little oleander that I planted last year . . . But she tells me she had no idea that the leaf was

34

poisonous, or even what sort of leaf it was, of course.' Her words sound defensive even to herself.

'Of course she didn't. Nobody thinks that Charlie—that any of them, for that matter—knew that.' She pauses, 'But we are extremely concerned about this initiation business.' Mrs Guterman's voice has hardened, cooled.

'Oh, I'm sure it's nothing; just something they thought would be fun. You know, girls that age.' Beth tries for airy unconcern, but only manages bluster.

'Yes. No doubt that was the intent, and they probably got it from some book or movie and it was all in fun. Nevertheless, initiations and the sort of exclusivity inherent in those rites are not something we encourage at Brookdale.'

'No, I'm sure they're not. And it's really not something we endorse, as a fam—'

'This is something we need to take very seriously. I'll be seeing the girls involved this morning, and talking to them about some of the issues.'

'Oh, yes. That seems sensible. I'm glad that—'

'And there will be—for the ringleaders, including Charlie— some sort of disciplinary action. They won't be punished in the usual sense, but they will have to give up some of their time. I would like to make them truly understand the way their behaviour affects others.'

Beth feels her stomach sink as if it were her, and not her daughter, who is in trouble. 'But I'm sure they do understand. I know Charlie got quite a fright when she found out what had happened. I'm sure they all did. And I'm sure the incident won't ever be repeated. And we'll certainly—'

Mrs Guterman again interrupts, but her voice is gentle. 'Mrs Mahony, you're possibly not aware of how much influence your

Charlie has over the other girls. She's a delightful child in so many ways and she's smart and well-behaved. But your daughter has an exceptionally forceful personality. In fact she's quite the strongest and most powerful among a cohort of girls who are all very intelligent and determined. We—the staff and I, that is—have been watching her carefully, and up until now her influence has always been . . . benign, even positive, I would say. But there have been a number of things lately—incidents in the classroom, as well as in the playground, some reported by other students—and now these rites of entry into what is effectively her group, and in every way that's important, that group *is* undoubtedly under Charlie's control. I think it's time to talk to her. I'm going to be speaking to all the girls involved later this morning, and then I'd like Charlie to see Mrs Lopez, the counsellor here. I've scheduled appointments with her for the next few lunchtimes.'

'I see.' Beth feels cold and then hot suddenly, the blood rushing to her face. 'Will the other girls be seeing Mrs Lopez too?'

'Not at this stage.'

'Oh. You know, Charlie's never . . . she's never been in any sort of trouble.'

'Oh, she's not in *trouble*. It's not that we don't think she's a very good girl. In most ways she's exemplary—her academics, her work ethic, her organisational skills. She's a wonderful child to have in the class. And she's the same at home, I'm sure. We just want to work towards keeping her on track. Moving her forward.'

'Well, I guess it's sensible.' Dully.

'I realise you and your family are moving back to Australia

in the new year, and this will all seem very long ago and far away in no time at all.' Mrs Guterman sounds almost chipper now, reassuring. 'She'll be going straight into the next year of school there, won't she?'

'Yes. It'll be the Christmas holidays when we move, and then school starts again in late January. She'll be going into the first year of high school. Year seven. We don't have a separate middle school.'

'So it's probably an ideal time to work on this. An opportunity to fill some gaps. And perhaps you would consider organising additional counselling during the break, before school goes back.'

'More counselling? Do you really think that's necessary?'

'Sometimes it's helpful during these . . . transitional periods. Even if it's just a precautionary measure. You don't want any more of these incidents.'

'But surely this was just a—'

Mrs Guterman's voice is firm. 'At least then we'll know we've all done everything in our power to ensure that nothing like this happens again.'

When Beth relates the conversation to Dan later, none of it seems as painful, as humiliating, as it did at the time.

'I don't know what you're so up in arms about, Beth. Mrs Guterman's just doing her job.'

'Doing her job? I'd say she's overdoing it, wouldn't you? Charlie's just a little girl—all that stuff about her controlling the others. It made her sound like some scheming little . . . Machiavelli.'

'I think you're reading too much into it. The principal's just covering her arse—isn't that what she more or less said? They need to be seen to be doing the right thing. Stop worrying. A bit of counselling's not going to hurt her, is it? And you've spoken to Charlie about it, haven't you?'

'I have. She was a bit put out that she'd be losing her lunchtimes, but apparently they're sent off to the counsellor for every little thing, so she wasn't too worried.'

'I didn't think she would be. And have you spoken to her about the whole initiation thing?'

'I've made it clear that we disapprove, but I haven't really said too much about it. I expect she'll probably get enough of that at school. I thought me adding my bit might be overwhelming right now.'

'Maybe there are some other things we need to talk to her about.'

'What sort of things?'

'Oh, I don't know. Nothing major. Maybe some suggestions about how you should treat your friends.' He gives a soft snort, adds, 'And your enemies.'

'Now *that* sounds Machiavellian.'

'I was thinking more Sun Tzu, actually.'

'But seriously—do you really think we need to explain that stuff to her?'

'Maybe. Why?'

'I think she knows it already. I don't think there's much that Charlie doesn't understand. She'll have worked it out all by herself. I asked her what was going on; she explained the situation. I told her that what she did was silly—and dangerous. I really think we've said as much as we need to say. She's learned her lesson.'

'Okay, Beth. Whatever . . .' Dan yawns and turns away from her, obviously reluctant to argue, ready for sleep. 'Whatever you reckon. You're the mother, after all.'

The girl recovers; the friendship, such as it is, resumes. Charlie sees the counsellor, pays her penalty. When Beth asks, Charlie only shrugs and says that Mrs Lopez is okay; that she's figured out a few things.

The lesson, clearly, has been learned; there is nothing more to be said.

BETH

THE MOVE ITSELF ISN'T THE MOST PAINFUL PART, THOUGH it's bad enough. For the entire month before they are due to fly out, tempers fray, especially in the case of Charlie, who continues to make her resistance to the whole lame idea of moving to Newcastle perfectly clear. She is uncompromisingly peevish; even Beth's somewhat extravagant Christmas festivities fail to improve her mood.

On the Saturday before their departure, Beth hosts a farewell outing for Charlie and Lucy, taking a small group of girls to lunch and then to the movies. The usually stoic Lucy sheds a few tears as she farewells her friends, in particular her BFF, the romantically named Viola, a tall taciturn girl who excels, rather unromantically, at field hockey. Charlie remains oddly cool during each protracted farewell; her goodbye hugs are perfunctory and she barely responds to the excess of devotion offered her.

When Beth asks her, when she goes in to kiss her goodnight, whether she is okay, Charlie looks at her blankly.

'Yeah. Why?'

'I thought you'd be more upset. Leaving all the girls, all your gang . . .' Beth pauses, adds gently, 'You can be sad if you want to, Charlie. It's okay.'

'Oh, that. Yeah, I guess I'll miss them. But not that much.'

She shrugs. 'I guess we haven't been getting on that well lately. Not since the thing with Arya, really.'

'Really? But I thought that had all been cleared up. I'm sorry, darling, I didn't realise. What's been happening?'

'Oh, nothing in particular. It's just . . . I don't know. It's like, since then, and maybe because I'm moving or whatever, we're just not as close anymore. It's not that bad or anything.'

Beth is suddenly hopeful. 'So you're feeling better about moving?'

Charlie scowls. 'No. I'm not feeling better about moving. I like it here. This is home. Sydney would have been okay, I guess. But Newcastle . . . it's just stupid. It's not even a proper city, is it?' Her air of indifference has deserted her, and she looks suddenly miserable, her eyes filling.

'Oh, darling.' Beth can't bear the thought that her daughter's determined calm has been a mask for who knows what sort of pain. Her heart contracts. She gives Charlie a hug, and for the first time in what seems like months, Charlie responds, wrapping her arms around her mother, letting herself be pulled tight.

'I know it's hard. But it'll all be okay. You'll see. In a year's time, Newcastle will feel like home. You'll have so many new friends. It's going to be a wonderful adventure, you know.'

In reality, Beth has to work hard to keep her own anxiety at bay. All the reservations she's had about Newcastle seem to be consolidating, rather than dissipating. If they had been going straight back to Sydney, where she imagines she might be able to pick up where she left off in terms of career and friends, she would feel differently. But to relocate to a small and no doubt insular city, where she knows virtually no one, where she'll have to start all over again, makes her suddenly realise how much she's going to miss *this* life.

Beth knows she's sometimes discounted her existence here, has felt as if she's put some part of herself on hold, but now that she's leaving it's clear that she has in fact managed to make a good life. In the ten years she's been here she's established her-self—she has good friends, a social network; people know who she is. She suspects the transition back is going to be far harder than she's anticipated. An adventure, yes, as she keeps telling the girls, but the appeal seems to fade as the time for their departure draws closer.

But here, now, comforting her fearful daughter, there is no room for doubt.

'It's going to be a huge adventure, sweetheart,' she repeats. 'And you're going to enjoy every minute of it.'

Charlie pulls out of the hug, wipes her eyes and sniffs.

'You really think so?'

'I do.' Beth sounds confident, assured. 'I really know so.'

So Long, Farewell, Auf Wiedersehen, Adieu . . .

'So, you're heading back to Austria? Y'don't really have much of an accent. Been here a while, have you?' The removalist, who is a tall man, with very well-defined, possibly steroidally enhanced muscles, looks over my head at the mess of half-packed boxes strewn around the living room. He doesn't appear to need an answer from me, but I give him one anyway.

'It's *Australia.* We're from Australia, not Austria.'

'Uh-huh. Y'know, ma'am, the packing is included in the cost of the removal, so you're going to have to unpack all these boxes for us, so we can repack properly. It's for the insurance.' He sounds slightly apologetic. He takes his cap off and scratches his shiny head, still looking beyond me.

'Oh. Okay. Well, we can do that, I guess. But we're going to *Australia, not* Austria. You know, kangaroos? The Sydney Harbour Bridge?' I imagine us arriving in Newcastle only to discover that all our worldly goods are somewhere in the middle of the Atlantic.

'Oh, right. Aust-*rail*-ia.' He looks down at me for the first time, gives a slow smile. His teeth are small and yellow and pointy. 'You Europeans get about a bit, don't you? But Australia? That's gonna be a *real* different experience. It's dangerous. You know, like Africa.' He gives me a wise look. 'They've got some crazy wildlife. Snakes. Spiders.' He pauses for a moment, thinking. 'And I hear they've got some pretty vicious sharks Downunder.'

'*Ja.*' My nod is abrupt, Germanic. 'Ve'll try our best not to get eaten.'
43 ♥

EXPATTERINGS:
@SunLover says:
Hahaha! Lucky it is Australia and not Austria. At least you're heading back to sunshine. We went back to London after many years in California, and I couldn't stand it. Only lasted 6 months.

@OzMumInTokyo says:
LMAO. Again. Xx

@AnchoreDownInAlaska says:
Oh, what bliss. Someone to pack all those boxes. What I wouldn't give. Muscles are a bonus!

@ExpatMum says:
Hey Lizzy—just caught up with your news! You will still be blogging though, won't you? I think all your experiences around resettling will be excellent blog fodder! I hope you can make it to the next expat convention—planned for Philadelphia in May.

@BlueSue says:
It never ceases to amaze me how the most powerful nation in the world can have the most ignorant population. I once had an American friend who insisted that Australia was annexed by the Nazis during WWII. I fear the US is in terminal decline, and from what I can see China doesn't offer much of an alternative. Best wishes to you and your family on your journey home, Lizzy.

BETH

SHE HAD IMAGINED IT WOULD ALL BE GRIST TO HER WRITING
mill, but once back in Australia it seems there are so many
things about the move that just aren't for public consumption. The numerous, always unexpected, negatives; all the
problems, some large, others small, that she just doesn't want
to air publicly, even though her blog is virtually anonymous.
There are the minor inconveniences—all the things forgotten, gone missing: naturally Beth is in charge of the logistics,
of making sure everything runs smoothly. Then there's the
emotional fallout: the sudden, inexplicable tension between
her and Dan. He's clearly nervous about the new job, about
moving back home, but he won't discuss it. The girls, Charlie
in particular, are tetchy, easily upset, uncharacteristically
argumentative.

And then there's the small matter of her own mother. News
of the impending move may have instantly brought all her anxiety about Margie to the fore, but somehow she's managed to
avoid thinking about what close proximity to her own mother
would mean.

Perhaps she simply, conveniently, forgot how fraught the relationship with her mother could be. Short and tightly scheduled
annual visits have meant that for the past twelve or so years, her
mother's input into her life has been limited, contained.

Francine hasn't been given many opportunities to find fault in Beth—her life choices, her children, her spouse—other than in the most petty, but easily shrugged off ways: Beth's failure to cut her carrots lengthwise (so slapdash); her preference for cheap iodised table salt (so old-fashioned—but that's America, I suppose); her wardrobe (so many flat heels, darling. What if you have to go out?); her decision to wear her hair curly (straight would be so much tidier, surely?); her relationship with her children (all that scheduling. You're not one of those—what do they call them? Rollercoaster? No, *helicopter* parents, are you?); Dan's numerous deficiencies (I suppose it's all these years of driving on the wrong side of the road, dear). Small things, and bearable—there are none of the more traumatic emotional dramas that were commonplace when she lived closer.

A similar limit on time spent with her mother-in-law meant that Margie, too, has generally revealed only her loveliest self to them. During their brief visits to Newcastle she was so busy ferrying them back and forth to the beach, taking them on picnics, or showing them off to this aunt or that cousin, that Beth only occasionally felt the chill wind of Margie's disappointment.

In retrospect, those tightly scheduled week-long holidays were perfect—each visit ended with only goodwill on every side. And more to the point, they ended. Something about fish and visitors, isn't that the saying?

But prolonged contact with both mothers . . . this is something else again. Despite all her protestations to the girls and on her blog about how wonderful it is going to be, back in the bosom of their respective families, how beautiful to have grandmothers, aunts, uncles and even cousins on the same continent, Beth has a feeling that continued contact is going to be far more problematic, and that it won't be long before they experience (as @BlueSue would no doubt put it) *issues.*

Beth's initial experience with her mother is instructive. On arrival, the four of them go straight from Sydney airport to her mother's apartment in Manly. As always, they are made welcome in the most generous way: their bedrooms are beautifully arranged with flowers and towels; the pantry and fridge are stocked and at their disposal. Though Francine isn't all that keen on cooking, she's arranged delicious meals, at home and in restaurants, for the durtion of their stay. None of them is expected to lift a finger, and they are as comfortable as they would be in any five-star hotel. But Francine only manages to maintain her attitude of magnanimous welcome for the first two days, and by the third—their last—she has unleashed her waspish inner critic, clearly unable to contain herself.

Beth and her mother go for a walk along the Esplanade late in the afternoon, just the two of them, while the girls watch television and Dan sleeps. They call in at Francine's latest favourite coffee shop, all bushranger beards and Birkenstocks, with impossibly uncomfortable seating and a menu that is completely sugar-free. They find an outside table and sit in the shade, chatting about all the things that are exciting about the move: the new house, the possibilities for schooling, Dan's job. Then: 'Darling,' her mother says. She waits, takes an exaggerated breath, gives her daughter a steady look. Beth recognises that particular crooning inflection, that pause, that concerned expression; knows what's coming is going to be painful.

'Darling,' Francine says again, peering at Beth over the top of her latte, 'I don't want to interfere, and I don't want to be a—what's the phrase?—a damp squib, but don't you think it's time you started to do something about your own career? You've wasted so much time, yet I'm sure it's not too late.'

Beth's colour begins to rise the moment her mother starts speaking, and by the time she utters the word 'wasted', her head is buzzing so loudly she barely hears the end of the sentence.

'Mum, I don't know how you can say I've wasted time.' Beth has to count to ten in order to continue. She closes her eyes, takes a deep breath. 'I've had no choice—you know that. I wasn't allowed to work in the US.' She takes another breath, works hard to keep the defensiveness out of her voice. 'And anyway, even if I had been, I don't think I would have done anything differently. I have two children—and that *is* actually work, you know, especially when you're living in a foreign—'

Her mother interrupts, waving her hand impatiently in a gesture so unpleasantly familiar that Beth has to bite her lip to stop the reflexive quivering. 'Oh, God, sweetie. Don't be so sensitive.' She sighs. 'Of course I know that it's all been about the children, and that it's terribly hard, and that the choices are never easy. I did have to make those choices myself, you know, back in the dark ages, and without any sort of child-care. You and your sister had to be latchkey kids—there wasn't an alternative. But you've got so much more going for you than I ever had. I had to basically invent a career for myself after your father died. I wasn't a trained accountant, for Christ's sake. I was just lucky to have connections. But you . . . you've had the education, the experience, you've got the contacts. Or you did. You have to get back into the real world, darling—for your own sake. That's all I'm saying. Your sister has four kids, but that hasn't stopped *her* from working, not for one minute. I don't understand why you have this desire to sacrifice yourself, when you have so much, *so much*, going for you.'

Susie, Beth's obstetrician elder sister, has a medical specialist husband, a combined annual income in the high six figures, a nanny and a retinue of staff. She can afford to outsource every menial task. And her children—though Beth would never say it; she barely lets herself think it—suffer in ways that wouldn't be visible to someone like her mother, who can never see beyond their good looks, their remarkable scholastic achievements, their cultivated manners.

'You know, Mum, I *have* actually done what I wanted—just like Susie—as well as what I've needed to do.' She is pleased to hear that her voice is steady.

Her mother waves this comment away too. 'Of course you've done the *right* thing all these years, I'm not disputing that. But surely it's your turn now? Now that you're back home it's time for you to get a life.'

'I have a life.' Beth feels a slight prickling at the back of her eyes. She swallows, wills it away.

'You're taking this the wrong way, Beth. I just mean you're back in Australia now, the girls will both be in high school, you'll be living in a . . . big enough place where your skills will be needed. You should make the most of it.'

'I know all that . . . And yes, once we're settled I'm going to start thinking about it. But it's not as easy as it used to be to find my sort of work, you know that.'

'But the longer you leave it, the more difficult it gets.'

'It's not like I've completely lost touch—there's my blog—'

'Your blog? Oh heavens, that nonsense. Who on earth reads that stuff? There's simply too much information on the internet—all those people with all those *opinions*.'

'Mum.' Beth speaks through gritted teeth, angry now. 'It might not be something that interests you, but my blog does actually mean something in the real world. Hundreds of people read it every day. From all over the world. It's won prizes. And it's meant I've had pieces published—'

'No, no, no.' Her mother smacks her hand on the table. 'Just calm down and listen to me for a moment. I've gone about this the wrong way, as usual, but there *was* something I wanted to tell you—an opportunity you might want to look into.'

Her mother has been pointing out these opportunities for years: there has always been something that was just that little bit better than whatever it was Beth happened to be doing, always something magical hovering just around the corner, something that would turn her duckling daughter into the swan who would properly reflect her mother's efforts.

'Drew Carmichael.' Her mother looks smug.

Drew, the son of one of her mother's oldest friends, Sylvia, and the brother of Beth's own childhood best friend, Julie, is a lawyer with a perfect pedigree. According to her mother, Drew is the one Beth let slip through her fingers, the one she gave up, stupidly, for Dan. No matter how frequently Beth reminds her that she and Drew only went out for a couple of months back in their early twenties, and that it was an unmitigated disaster, Francine still insists that Drew would have made the perfect spouse. And son-in-law. No matter that the charismatic, handsome, somewhat vain Drew was clearly casting about for a wife from a more elevated social and political—and to be frank, physical—sphere than Beth's own.

'Oh, God. What about Drew Carmichael?'

'Don't roll your eyes, dear. You're too old to behave like a teenager. Now, don't tell me you don't know about Drew.'

'Mum, I've been out of Australia for almost fifteen years. I have no idea what's happened to Drew Carmichael. I mean, I know he married that lingerie model, Angela What's-her-face, but that's about it. He's not even a friend on Facebook.' Although, of course she does know all about Angela What's-her-face; who in the blogging world doesn't?

'A senator's daughter; just right for Drew, don't you think? And they're still happily married. They have three children: twin daughters—I think they're a few years younger than Charlotte—and a little boy. They're a real power couple. Angela's a lovely girl; she runs one of those online mummy websites now.'

'You do know that she's actually a blogger? That website of hers, Motherkind, it started out as a blog like mine.'

'Oh, it's a little bit different to what you're doing, surely? Angela's a professional. And Sylvia tells me she's making an absolute fortune out of all those young mothers and their anxieties. Such a clever girl!'

'Mum—'

'Anyway,' Francine waves away Beth's objections, 'that's not what's important, darling. The thing is, Drew, as you'd expect, has made his name too. He's still practising law, of course, but some fancy specialty—communications law, would that be it? It's extremely lucrative, anyway. And the big news is that he's just been preselected as the Liberal candidate for—oh, it's somewhere up that way. Some lake? MacLachlan?'

'Lake Macquarie?'

'That might be it. I believe it's practically Newcastle, anyway. There was some scandal with an independent up there, and apparently the Liberals have a chance at the next election. And Drew's the perfect candidate—he can get on with anyone.'

'Of course.' This time Beth's eye-roll is deliberate. 'But what's that got to do with me?'

'Well, he moved the family up there last year; of course Angela can work from home. He's been commuting back and forth—they kept the house in Double Bay—but his mother said he'll be opening an office in the next few months, so he's established well before the next election. He'll have to run the campaign locally, obviously.'

'And?'

'Well, it's just the most perfect opportunity for you. He's going to be needing additional staff, isn't he? Sylvia mentioned something about a press secretary. Now, isn't that right up your alley?'

'Oh, Mum. Honestly, I'm not ready for—'

'It would be perfect. And what better way to get to know the right sort of people?'

'But I don't want—'

'I've given his mother your contacts, and she's going to pass them on to him. Apparently he's got himself onto the board of that lovely school the girls are going to—is it Hunter Ladies' College? He could be helpful there, too.'

'I told you we haven't decided about schools. Dan's thinking of sending the girls to his old school. Margie still works in the library there, so—'

'Oh, don't be ridiculous, Elizabeth.' Her mother gestures for the bill. 'The girls don't want their grandmother breathing down their neck at high school. I couldn't think of anything worse.'

'Well, she's sixty-six. So I guess she'll be retiring—'

'Anyway, surely you won't be sending them to a *Catholic* school. From everything I hear, they're still so backward. And all those *paedophiles.*' She draws the word out unpleasantly, gives a little shudder. 'And the girls aren't even Catholic, are they?'

'Mum, we're still—'

'What would your father think? And Grandma. It was bad enough you marrying . . . but we don't want the girls . . . My God! Mother would roll in her grave. And you can't go public—there's a dreadful surf culture in Newcastle, and you certainly don't want the girls to get caught up in that. I've spoken to a few people, and there really are no other decent private schools up there, so you don't have any choice at all. Unless they board, of course. Which would be fabulous for the girls, especially Charlotte, but I can't imagine that would be your cup of tea.' Her mother's smile is mocking. 'You have to admit, it would have been so much easier if you'd come back to Sydney, darling.'

Beth, too frustrated to respond, sits and watches as her mother gets ready to leave and counts out the necessary coins.

'Anyway, there's plenty of time to discuss all that. But make sure you get in touch with Drew, won't you? You're home, and the girls will be out of the nest before you know it. It's time to concentrate on yourself.'

Beth is relieved to leave for Newcastle the following day—though she knows that in so many ways it will be out of the frying pan into the fire. They are to spend two days with Margie before moving into a short-term rental—a small but comfortable flat in the city—that Dan's company is paying for. They will have a month there before they move into the house that they bought rather impulsively—they'd fallen in love with it over the internet, and Dan had finalised the deal during his week-long orientation the month before their departure.

Although Margie couldn't be more welcoming, and is so

pleased—*thrilled!*—to have them come home to Newcastle, she is finding it hard to contain her disapproval of many of Beth and Dan's decisions, with their choice of house right at the top of the list. It's a three-storey Victorian brick house—romantically gabled, sprawling, and very rundown—in an exclusive suburb near the city centre, and only a short walk to the beach. Margie, who has lived all her life in the working-class suburb of Mayfield, has obviously assumed that Dan would return to his roots. The fact that he's chosen to settle elsewhere is something of a blow, a betrayal of sorts. And naturally, in Margie's eyes, Beth, the middle-class daughter-in-law, is to blame.

The day of their arrival, the five of them—Dan and Beth, the two girls and Margie—pile into the diminutive hire car and Dan drives them to look first at the rental unit and then the house. Despite Beth's insistence that she sit in the front, Margie chooses to sit in the back, crushed between the two girls, as they take the scenic route beside the harbour foreshore and then along the winding road that follows the coast, before finally puttering into the city. Margie is not particularly enthusiastic about the rental property, a rather unexciting apartment near the harbour, furnished sparsely and unimaginatively, but comfortable enough to do them for the next few weeks. 'It'll be lovely for a while, I guess. It's real city living.' But she is positively aghast at both the site and the structure of the house, which is high on The Hill, not far from the imposing Anglican Cathedral.

The house had obviously been quite grand once, but has been a rental for decades, and is desperately in need of renovating. Beth loves it immediately, just as Dan assured her she would, all her doubts banished the moment she steps onto the tessellated tiles of the entry hall and sees the gracefully sweeping staircase with its polished mahogany balustrade. She almost weeps when she walks into the enormous first-floor sitting room and sees the spectacular view over the city's waterfront and out past the lighthouse to the ocean.

'So you're really going to be living up here, then, love?' Margie asks Dan as she marches, purse-lipped and determinedly unimpressed, through the dusty maze of high-ceilinged rooms. 'Up on The Hill? Your dad would be surprised. The world's a funny place, isn't it?'

Dan, as always, either doesn't notice or chooses to laugh in the face of his mother's negativity. 'Oh, I dunno, Mum, I kind of like it up here. Nobs' Hill. Isn't it where everyone in Newcastle wanted to live when we were kids?'

'Well, I can't say it ever appealed to me, Daniel. But then I was a miner's daughter, I suppose. And wife.' Dryly. 'It's all very . . . grand, I suppose, but there's so much to be done. It's going to cost a fortune to get it liveable. And it's very inconvenient, isn't it? There's no grocery store within walking distance. There's nowhere to park a car, and there's no real yard. I don't think that's good for the girls. I know they're getting older, but it's always good to be able to go outside into a yard that's big enough to run around in. And I'm sure Beth would appreciate a proper garden.

'And that furniture!' This in reference to the furnishings they've bought from the previous owner and intend to keep until the planned renovations are done.

'Oh, the furniture's not that bad for the time being. Not while there's so much to be done inside. And I think it'll be lovely to not have to worry about a garden for a while, Margie. The girls can go to the park—or the beach for that matter—if they want to run around.' Beth keeps her voice light and determinedly cheerful. 'There's so much to do, anyway—getting the girls sorted at school, and their sport and music and all the rest of it. And the more we're out and about the better; it's a good way to get a proper feel for the place'

'I imagine Dan already *has* a proper feel for the place. He did live here for the first twenty-five years of his life, after all. And that reminds me,' Beth knows exactly what's coming; it's the one subject she's been hoping to avoid since they arrived, 'have you decided what you're doing about schools?'

Beth glances at Dan, hoping he will deflect the question somehow, but he won't meet her eye. Charlie, who has been listening closely to the conversation, answers. 'Aren't we going to that school you showed us on the net—the one you said was just down the road from here? Hunter Ladies' College? Don't we have an interview tomorrow?' She glares at her parents. 'You haven't changed your minds, have you? There's no way I'm going to any of those other places.'

Margie's voice is grave. 'A school is more than first impressions, Charlie—it's not a decision to be made lightly. Or,' she adds pointedly, 'by children.' She doesn't wait for a response but moves briskly to the next room, Dan and the girls trailing behind her.

Beth lingers in the lounge room, watching as a brave little tug-boat pilots an enormous container ship into the harbour. Right now she could do with some help negotiating the treacherous waters of mother–daughter-in-law relationships, mother–daughter relationships, life itself. It would be lovely to have some quick, clever vessel guide you in the murky waters of your own life—to push you this way and that, ensure your progress is smooth, help you find a place to lower your anchor. To make sure that you're heading towards a safe berth, calm waters.

Schooldaze

'Oh. My. God. It's just like Hogwarts,' says L, her eyes wide.

'It's awesome.'

The school we're checking out (and it's exclusively girls, much to L & C's disgust) *is* awesome. It's on an acre of land in the heart of the city, close to the harbour. It's all sandstone and turrets and vaulted ceilings and grassy quadrangles and ancient fig trees, and the girls can't quite believe they'll be going here.

'Do you think they have houses like Gryffindor and Hufflepuff? I wonder how you get chosen?'

Oh, school houses. That's an aspect of Aussie life that I haven't thought about for years.

'Do you think they play quidditch?' C zooms around us on her imaginary broomstick, whooping.

The school is in summer recess—only the admin staff and the headmistress (not principal!) are here, and we're alone in the park-like playground. After our interview, Dr H, who is everything the head of such a school should be—tall and thin and quite austere—said that we were welcome to have a little wander through the school grounds, to get a feel for the place before we make our decision, and that's what we're doing.

When we reach the northernmost boundary we sit on a stone bench beside an elegant wrought-iron gate that opens onto the street. A shiny brass plate tells us that the gate was donated to the school by Mr and Mrs S-J in 1925, in memory of their daughter, Millicent (1896–1916), a former student who was killed in the Middle East during the Great War.

L gazes at it for a long time, her expression thoughtful. 'So there were women soldiers, way back then?'

'No. She was probably a nurse.'

'A nurse? And she died?' L looks surprised. 'How would that've happened? Would she have been bombed?'

C, who is possibly regretting her earlier bout of enthusiasm, interrupts before I get a chance to explain. 'Did you see the high school uniforms, Mum? In the photos? They're totally gross. Those checked skirts—

they're down to your ankles, almost. And that giant pin? What *is* that? It's like a hundred years ago. We're going to look ridiculous.'

'They aren't that long—and they're called kilts. They're Scottish.'

'Anyway, we're only going to look as ridiculous as everyone else,' says L, bless her practical older sister heart, 'so it won't really matter.'

That's the charm of Australian schools: you might be forced to dress up like some nineteenth-century Highlander's wet dream—but then, so is everyone else.

42 ♥

EXPATTERINGS:

@OzMumInTokyo says:

Oh, that poor young nurse. Those poor parents. So, so sad. XX

@AnchoreDownInAlaska says:

School uniforms. Yay! No comparing brands or competing. One aspect of life here that I really hate.

@BlueSue says:

But what about kids expressing their individuality, Lizzy? Clothes are such an important element in sorting out who you are, especially as a teen. In my experience, uniforms only suppress this. But then I guess that's what the private school ethos is all about.

@GirlFromIpanema says:

Private schools?? School uniforms?? Kilts?? OMG, Lizzy. Your girls are doomed. Doomed, I say;)

THE GOLDEN CHILD'S TEN LESSONS FOR SUCCESS

LESSON TWO: YOU <u>CAN</u> ALWAYS GET WHAT YOU WANT

This is maybe the most important lesson of all. Because yolo. Or, just in case you live under a rock: *You Only Live Once.* They talk about God, and about the afterlife, and how we need to be good to be rewarded in heaven, but most likely that's just bull. This is probably the only chance you've got, so what's the point of waiting for some reward that you're never actually going to get?

It's no different to those stupid promises your parents make that you know they'll never keep: one day, when we're millionaires, we'll do this, buy you that, take you there. You know it's never going to happen.

How much of a waste would it be to live only once, not getting what you want—not even trying to get what you want—in the hope that what you'll get in heaven (when you're actually dead) will somehow make up for what you've missed out on here.

Sounds like shit to me.

Get what you want when you want it—that's my motto.

And do what you have to do to get it.

COMMENTS

@RANDOMREADER says:

What, no gardening tips this month, GC? Disappointing.

SOPHIE

SHE'S BEEN AT HUNTER LADIES' COLLEGE—OR HLC AS IT'S known locally—for more than three years now, yet somehow Sophie still feels like a new girl. She's never quite lost that sense of disorientation—of never really being certain that she's in the right place with the right people, doing the right thing.

But she's not even close to being the newest girl in the class. Since Sophie's arrival, eight girls have left and nine have taken their place. Two of the girls who left—Tess and Maya—represented the sum total of her friends at HLC, and Sophie is finding it hard, maybe impossible, to replace them. Their friendship began tentatively enough: the other two were very close, had known each other since preschool, went to gymnastics together, played violin in the same string group; their parents were old friends who spent weekends away up the coast. But early in year five they took her in, and the three of them formed their own tight little group. By year six they were inseparable, spent all their lunchtimes together, as well as their spare time—there were sleepovers, play-dates, visits to the movies and even a few parent-free trips to the mall.

The three of them were initially bound by their weirdness. While they weren't exactly the *least* popular girls, they were regarded by most of the others as mildly irritating. None of them were pretty or sporty, and all three of them were talented in ways that most of the other girls considered lame. But their friendship kept them safe. Without each other they might have been picked on; together they were left in peace. Their friendship was real enough, though; they knew everything there was to know about one another—favourite colours, TV shows, books; their opinions of classmates, parents, teachers; the boys they knew outside school; even the occupations of their future husbands, the names of their future children . . .

So Sophie was devastated when both girls announced they were leaving midway through year six—Maya heading to Melbourne and Tess to boarding school in Sydney—and though there were promises made to keep in touch, cards with many hearts and crosses exchanged, a flurry of hugs and even a few random tears, they haven't met up once since their departure. To begin with there was a bit of virtual interaction: text messages and emails, but these gradually dried up. Sophie has remained a little hurt, but she understands that it was inevitable. After all, she barely talks to Ruby, her BFF from Scone, at all these days. They've both moved on. It's the way things work.

She couldn't care less about the other girls who left at the end of last year. None of them were her friends—even Jemima Hobcroft, who once told her (in the quietest whisper, so that no one else would hear) that she thought she played the piano awesomely. The remainder of the class are pretty much bitches—at least when it comes to Sophie. Those who aren't actively nasty are nasty by omission: they simply don't notice her, don't include her, don't care. One or two aren't so bad: Mimi Leroux, whose mum has just had a baby, too, occasionally compares notes on the relative cuteness of their new brothers, and Matty Matherson sometimes talks to her in choir, but this friendliness never extends into lunchtimes or invitations to play. Even the new girls who came to the orientation days at the end of year six quickly worked out that Sophie is on some sort of class blacklist. That she is one of half a dozen girls who—for whatever dumb reason—are to be avoided.

Anticipating the painfulness of sitting alone at lunchtimes—or worse, being forced to sit with the other class lepers, who form an unhappy clique of their own—and maintaining the pretence that it is done by choice, Sophie has had her mum arrange all her additional music tutoring during lunch breaks. With music and theory lessons, and then ensemble and choir, free time should be a rarity. On those days when empty lunchtimes loom, now she's in year seven she can join Miss Foley's reading club, which is a haven for the more bookish freaks and misfits. And if there are times when there's really nowhere to go, like this first week back, when there are no lunchtime activities, there's always the reading nook in the library.

When Charlotte Mahony arrives during the period three maths class—she's spent the morning doing the placement test the rest of them sat last year—Mrs Taylor chooses Indiana Olsen-Goring (or Indiana Oh-so-Boring, as Tessa nicknamed her back in year five) to look after her, even though the headmistress, Dr Holding, has already asked Sophie, calling her into the office to arrange the pairing when Sophie delivered the roll after pastoral. All the other new girls were paired with a buddy during last year's orientation, but Charlotte has only just arrived in Newcastle (she's come all the way from America!) and needs someone to show her the ropes.

'Oh, I am sorry, dear,' Mrs Taylor says when Sophie explains that it was meant to be her job. 'I'm afraid it's too late now. And I thought *Indiana* was the perfect buddy for our new classmate, seeing that she's just come from America.' Mrs Taylor gives a loud and slightly mucosal snort of laughter, and the class joins in, not laughing at her pathetic joke, of course, but at the woman herself, who has the reputation of being the ugliest teacher in the school, with her fat cheeks and her googly blue eyes and her huge nose that hooks right under like a parrot beak. Even Sophie, who knows that looks aren't important, and is always predisposed to see the best in people, has to admit that Mrs Taylor is odd looking. She's a very good teacher—she ran the maths enrichment program back in primary—and is usually kind to Sophie, so she's willing to forgive her this oversight. After all, a new girl isn't really such a big deal.

Big deal or not, Sophie has to swallow her disappointment when the new girl arrives halfway through the lesson, accompanied by a smug-looking Indiana. Charlotte Mahony is amazingly pretty—her hair, in two neat plaits with navy ribbons tied in bows at the end, is the colour of sunshine; her eyes are the brightest shade of blue, wide and clear; she has a cute little gap between her two front teeth; and there are even dimples in her cheeks when she smiles, which she seems to do constantly. She has a sprinkling of freckles across her nose—not the horrid fat splodges that Sophie has been cursed with (or, as her mother likes to put it, *kissed* with) all over her face and legs and arms, so that sometimes, if she squints hard at herself in the mirror, she could be a very brown person, instead of a very pale person with spots. If you discount the not-red hair, Charlotte Mahony is much closer to Sophie's idea of Anne Shirley than the actress in the TV version of *Anne of Green Gables*. Her accent might be American and not Canadian—but who can tell?

Oh, she likes everything about the new girl—especially the fact that she's new, and doesn't know that Sophie is currently (because who knows when this will change?) a social outcast. Every new girl provides an opportunity for friendship, for new beginnings, and Sophie gazes at Charlotte longingly as she follows Indiana across the classroom. Their desks are in line with hers and Sophie gives Charlotte a shy smile as the girl pulls out her chair. Charlotte beams back and mouths *Hello*, before turning back to her desk, unpacking her bag.

Sophie's heart gives a little pitter-pat. A smile, a greeting—oh, miracles!—a possible new friend.

The Haunting of Hill House

'Did you two hear the ghost last night?'

'*What ghost*?' I suspect my daughters' in-unison shrieks can be heard right across the valley.

'There's a ghost, apparently. The real estate agent warned us when we moved in. Any house this old is bound to have a ghost or two.'

I glare at D and shake my head, but he's having too much fun to notice.

'What sort of a ghost is it?' asks the ever practical C.

'What sort?'

'You know. Is it a kid or a grown-up?'

'And how did they die? Were they murdered? Or did they just die of old age?'

It's obvious that D hasn't thought this through. 'I've no idea. I'm sure it wasn't anything serious like murder, though.'

'Why?'

'Well, the real estate people would have told us, wouldn't they?'

'Why?'

'Because they have to.'

'Oh. So what does this ghost do?'

'Oh, you know,' D waves his arms about, 'ghosty things.'

'Dad. Seriously. Like, does it just make noises? Does it move things? What?'

He has to think for a moment. 'It's just footsteps, apparently. Up and down the stairs all night.'

'Up and down all night?' I can't resist. 'That sounds like your mother and her bladder.' Now D glares at me.

'Actually,' L's eyes are wide, 'I *did* hear something weird last night. It wasn't on the stairs, though.'

It's time for me to intervene. 'I'm sure you didn't really. Dad's only kidding.'

'I did. It sounded like a baby crying.'

'Oh, that. I heard it too, darling. It's just some strange bird. Maybe an owl?'

'Are you sure? It was pretty loud. And it went on and on.'

'Actually,' C is looking worried now, 'I've heard that too. Heaps of times. It's really freaky.'

'Hey, it's okay. There's no ghost. Really. I was only joking.' D's attempt to reassure them comes too late—they're not even listening.

'Well, I'm not sleeping in my room tonight.'

'Me neither.'

'I HATE my room. It's totally freaky.'

'All those paintings of dead animals—and that wallpaper. It gives me the creeps.'

Then, what I've been waiting for ever since D mentioned the G-word: '*Muuuuum,*' the two girls shriek. 'Can we sleep with you?'

44 ♥

EXPATTERINGS:
@GirlFromIpanema says:
Could it be the ghost of grandma's bladder?

@OzMumInTokyo says:
But there isn't really a ghost, is there? I'd be sleeping with you too ☺

@SunLover says:
So the house is old, is it, Lizzy? Bet it's cold! We lived in a really big old place in Sydney once and it was unbearable in winter! Nothing we could do to get warm. Spent half of winter wrapped in a blanket.

> **@DizzyLizzy** replied:
> Tbh, I'm freezing my tits off, @SunLover. It's a shock, after central heating L
>
> **@AnchoreDownInAlaska** replied:
> No sympathy from me, Lizzy ☺ I'm sure your winter temps are way higher than our summer!

@BlueSue says:
Old houses can be so romantic—and so hard to live in. We're still renovating the Federation cottage we bought when we first

moved back. Somehow it never seems to end—you fix one thing and another needs doing. Looking back, we should have bought a nice new brick home, with a fitted kitchen and ensuite bathroom and a manageable garden. So much easier to maintain and keep warm—though we thought they were terribly boring back then. Ah well, you live and learn!

@TheExorcist says:

If you're experiencing a haunting or have a resident spirit that needs resettling, contact theexorcist@happyghosts.com for a free consultation.

BETH

THERE MAY NOT BE AN ACTUAL GHOST, BUT THEIR FIRST
weeks in the new house are still somewhat horrifying. They
were in holiday mode when they first moved in. Up until then
everything had been easy; even their stay at Margie's had
been surprisingly pleasant, without incident. And the weeks
in the apartment had been an idyll in retrospect: they spent
hours wandering the inner city and the foreshore, went surf-
ing almost every day (the beach was only a block away!), ate
out every second night—Newcastle being a gourmet's para-
dise, apparently. Dan's workload was only light thus far,
and he was constantly cheerful. Even the first few weeks of
the school term felt oddly free of the usual pressures: there
was little homework, no ongoing issues with friends and
teachers—everything was new and exciting. But the move
into the house signals a return to reality.

Despite its charming appearance, living in the old place is
anything but. Not only are the rooms cold and dark—even in
late summer—they're dingy. Nothing seems to work properly.
Their (solitary) toilet flushes only on occasion, and then
half-heartedly; hot water runs out after a single shower; the
ancient dishwasher covers all the dishes with a fine layer of silt;
the reverse-cycle heating barely takes the edge off the cold.

The kitchen cupboard doors don't close properly, and once night falls, all horizontal surfaces (and some vertical ones) teem with tiny brown cockroaches. The furniture, which had seemed in reasonable condition when Dan viewed the house, is beyond salvaging—springs have sprung in every mattress, chairs have missing legs, the lounge suite cushions don't fit the lounge. And everything smells faintly of cat piss.

There's nothing that's unfamiliar to Beth—the house is no more dilapidated than those she'd rented when she was a student—but the girls have never lived in a house that's so ramshackle. Their West Bloomfield house was built in the middle of the nineteenth century—so it was old by Australian standards, and older than this—but it had been completely refurbished: kitchens and bathrooms had been renovated, the rooms painted and re-carpeted, the windows restored and double glazed. Inside, it was like a new house. But the mansion on The Hill is showing all the wear and tear of its one hundred and thirty years. It'll be fine once the renovations are done, but there's so much to do. Beth has made a start on the painting, but the roof needs repairing, they need new carpet, built-ins, the kitchen and bathroom have to be replaced and a second toilet and shower installed in the enormous laundry. It takes so much time. She still hasn't managed to arrange all the quotes, let alone finalise installation dates.

Both girls find reasons to complain, but Charlie makes her disgust clear at every opportunity. 'It's just revolting, Mum. It's so *dirty*. It's like there's a thousand years of grime on everything you touch. Look.' The four of them are squeezed into the kitchen nook—a little nineteen fifties built-in table and bench that seemed cute until they actually had to sit at it eating breakfast. Charlie runs her finger along the wall, and it comes away coated in a thin film of grease. 'And the furniture. It's foul. It stinks like . . . dirty socks.'

'You could always stop breathing.'

Dan's joke falls flat.

'That's actually *not funny*, Dad.' Charlie's voice is icy. 'You know, even if I had any friends, which I don't, I couldn't invite them back here. It's embarrassing. Why did you have to buy such an old house? Aren't there any new houses around here? And when are we getting new furniture? You said it wouldn't be long. Why couldn't we just stay in the apartment until all the renovations are done? I can't sleep on that bed any more—it's lumpy, and the smell is making me *sick*. And there are spider webs on everything. This is like living in the slums.'

'Slums? Oh, come on, Charlie. Get real.' Dan tousles his daughter's hair, but she pulls away. 'It's not that bad, you know. It's not like we're in some mud hut in Africa.'

She rolls her eyes at this. 'That's a stupid comparison.' Charlie is clearly ready to work herself up into a self-righteous rage, but Dan interrupts, his voice suddenly stern.

'You girls are very, very lucky. You know that this is temporary, that we'll be doing renovations, getting new furniture, as soon as we can. In the meantime, the house is perfectly comfortable. It's nothing like living in a slum. Perhaps you need to be sent somewhere where there are real slums, where people don't have fresh running water or hot meals or comfortable beds to sleep in.'

He sounds so much like his mother when he starts on these lectures, and his effect on the girls is similar to Margie's— Lucy looks dejected and slightly guilty, Charlie immediately defensive. Beth intervenes, changes the subject before the conversation gets any more heated. 'Speaking of friends, Charlie, I've arranged a sort of a play-date for you.'

'A play-date? What do you mean? I'm too old for you to arrange play-dates.'

'Well, it's not really a play-date. It's all of us . . .' a smile here at Dan, '. . . us girls, anyway. You know that woman I met in the playground last week? The one I told you about. Her daughter Sophie's in your class. She's invited us over for afternoon tea. I thought it might be fun.'

'Sophie? She's that girl who plays the piano, isn't she? The fat one?'

'Charlie!' Her sister looks shocked.

'Well, she is.' Charlie looks amused all of a sudden. 'I wasn't being mean, Lucy. Just calling a—what does Grandma Francie call it?—just calling a spade a spade.'

'Oh, Jesus.' Dan looks at his daughter, aghast. 'Please don't start quoting Francine at us.'

'But Sophie *is* fat, isn't she?' Charlie challenges her older sister. Lucy looks uncomfortable.

'Well, maybe she's not skinny.' Lucy looks at her mother. 'But she's awesome at the piano, Mum. I've never heard anything so amazing. She's just about finished all the music grades, the music teacher said, and she's won all these huge prizes. She's like a child genius.'

'So I've heard.' Beth is desperate to regain control of the conversation. 'Anyway, her mum, Andi, seems really nice, and she asked if we'd like to come for afternoon tea, so I said yes. We're going over on Thursday. Charlie, you and Sophie can walk back to her place after school, and then Lucy and I will come after her dance class. This will be our first Newcastle visit! Won't it be lovely?'

Lucy gives her mother an uncertain smile. 'Sounds like fun.'

Charlie looks down at her toast, drags a finger through the thick peanut butter.

'Charlie?'

She shrugs. 'Yeah. Whatever. But Mum. And Dad. And you too, Lucy.' She puts a buttery finger in her mouth, looks around the table with an expression that Beth can't quite read.

'What?'

'There's something I've been wanting to tell you all. It's important.'

'What is it?'

'It's that I want to be Charlotte from now on. Not Charlie, Charlotte.'

THE GOLDEN CHILD'S TEN LESSONS FOR SUCCESS

LESSON THREE: HOW TO WIN FRIENDS AND INFLUENCE YOUR TEACHERS

I found a copy of this dusty old book in the back of a cupboard in my bedroom: 'How to Win Friends and Influence People.'

Anyway, I dunno why, but for some weird reason I decided to read it—and it turns out it's a pretty awesome book. There's a section on how to make people like you, and what he says is kinda cool. These are the main points:

Become genuinely interested in other people.

Smile.

Remember that a person's name is, to that person, the sweetest and most important sound in any language.

Be a good listener. Encourage others to talk about themselves.

Talk in terms of the other person's interests.

Make the other person feel important—and do it sincerely.

All these things work. I know because I've tried them all.

But there's one more important thing that Mr Dale Carnegie (who wrote the book) left out. One that's guaranteed to build up, not so much your popularity, but your strength.

You need to choose an enemy. Choose carefully and fight dirty.

And don't worry about the collateral damage ☺

COMMENTS

@DCFAN says:

Please contact info@carnegiesociety.com if you're interested in becoming a member of the Carnegie Society, or if you'd like to attend our annual conference in Warrensburg, MO.

CHARLOTTE

SHE'S CHARLOTTE HERE, NOT CHARLIE.

A fresh start, that's how her mother sells it. A new beginning. As if she thinks Charlotte needs one. And Charlotte has smiled and agreed that the whole thing is going to be a ton of fun: new country, new friends, oh, yes! Fun fun fun! Agreeing is easier than arguing about the meaning of the words her mother uses, easier than asking her why exactly she *needs* a new beginning, or a fresh start. Her mother will only, Charlotte knows, look alarmed and then a little sad. She'll say that it is just an expression, that she doesn't mean anything particular by it. It is just words, she'll say, and then change the subject.

Just words. Charlotte knows that there's no such thing, knows that even the most basic expression can contain a whole lot of meanings, and a shitload of power. It was *just words* when in that last week at Brookdale more than half of her gang told her that their parents had said they weren't allowed to associate with her anymore, which she knew was complete bullshit because most of them had been involved anyway—and their parents knew it. It was *just words* when the boy who had given her a Valentine earlier in the year—Caleb Jackson, the coolest and best looking and smartest boy in the seventh grade— asked her if she was some kind of kid psycho, and then announced to the other seventh grade boys standing behind

74

him in the lunch queue that they'd all better watch out when she grew up because she'd probably end up a serial killer like those monster women on the crime channel. It was *just words* when Mrs Lopez, the school counsellor, whose Latino accent was so thick that most of her words were unintelligible, told her slowly and carefully that it was *afortunado* that she was leaving: if it had been up to her she would have had her expelled for playing such a dangerous game. Additionally (just in case Charlotte hadn't quite got the point), she would have recommended an extended visit to some sort of *institución*; that in her experience, intensive *terapia* was the only way that *niños malos* like her could be made to understand the consequences of their actions.

But Charlotte's own words—and there had been a torrent of them—about what had happened: her explanation to the teachers that she'd had no idea that the leaf was poisonous; that it hadn't even been her idea that the stupid girl eat that particular leaf, or any leaf for that matter; that all the other girls had been involved too, urging Arya to eat all the hideous things they'd brought for her to sample; that it was just a game, and that at some point they'd all done the same thing—were utterly devoid of any sort of power. Nobody listened (except, she had to concede, her mother); nobody heard—everyone had their own version of the tale all worked out: Charlie was the leader of the clique, the initiation ceremony was her idea, she had brought the poisonous leaf and she had forced Arya to eat it. The other girls, poor misguided darlings, had just gone along with it; the other girls had no idea what was going on, no idea what she, big bad scary Charlie, had planned.

Nothing Charlotte said was going to change anybody's mind: in one fell swoop she went from being Miss Popular, teacher's pet and all-round parents' favourite, to being the meanest girl in the sixth grade.

Here, in this new school, in this new class, she is going to be more careful. Charlotte is going to make friends slowly and cautiously, is going to watch and see where the power lies in this particular set of girls. She isn't going to be put in the position, ever again, of being blamed for something that isn't her fault. This fresh start, new beginning, new leaf, whatever—this is what it means: Charlotte won't be letting anyone have that sort of power over her ever again. Not the teachers, not the parents, not the other students. No one.

On her first day, the headmistress, who seems okay—far warmer and less intimidating than Mrs Guterman, though also less impressive—buddies her up with another girl in her class, Indiana. Indiana is a tall, graceful girl who wears her long brown hair in a thick, high plait and arranges her feet in dance positions when standing still for any length of time. She seems friendly enough, though maybe a little quiet for Charlotte, and is satisfyingly impressed by the new girl from America. Because among these girls, almost all of them Aussie born and bred, Charlotte's American-ness (slightly exaggerated, naturally) gives her instant prestige. Some new girls have to fight to get to the top, but Charlotte knows she has an advantage, and she intends to use it.

It doesn't take her long to sort out how things work, what the pecking order is. The set-up is pretty clear after her first two recesses. HLC is a smallish school: in her year there are only two classes, a little under fifty girls. The popular group, into which Charlotte is immediately welcomed, is far smaller than its counterpart at the Brookdale Academy. There are about eight girls who form the core, with another half-dozen who belong only marginally, drifting back and forth between other groups. There is no clearly defined Most Popular Girl; instead there are three who more or less share the honour of being highly sought after, and who are engaged in a covert and sometimes nasty battle for supremacy.

All three girls—Amelia, Grace and Harriet—are immediately well disposed towards Charlotte, vying for her attention, offering her the seats next to them during lunch and recess, as well as in class. All three of them are instantly trusting and confiding, supplying her with all the information, and ammunition, that she needs.

After her first week, Charlotte has already received two thirteenth birthday party invitations: one from Amelia, and the other from a quirky girl in her art class, Matilda. Matilda is not one of the popular gang—who are primarily the pretty, academically talented group, mostly very wealthy—but one of a smaller gang of arty girls, the ones who draw, do drama, play instruments; girls who would probably end up being goths or emos at a different sort of school. She gets on well with Matilda, and has fun at her party, but is quickly made aware that the two groups are mutually exclusive. Matilda's gang calls Harriet and co the Three Stooges; the Stooges call Matilda's gang the Cutters. And it's hinted that to make it into either gang, she'll have to make a choice. By the end of her third week, two of the Cutters have invited her for sleepovers and one of the Stooges has invited her to spend a weekend on her father's cruiser. By the end of her first month, Charlotte has made her choice. She's gone for security rather than excitement. And they can't be the Three Stooges if it's a gang of four: Harriet, Grace, Amelia and now Charlotte.

The other girls in the year, who are neither cool nor

popular, are harder to categorise. Some of them are nondescript, the same girls who are invisible at every school; girls who, Charlotte supposes, will probably be invisible all their lives. These girls, who are neither pretty enough nor clever enough nor confident enough to make themselves attractive to either teachers or students, form loose and endlessly changing coalitions. The girls who are physically unattractive, those who are ridiculously immature, the girls who are dumb, the ones who are somehow damaged or disturbed. Finally, there are the loners: girls who are simply off any sort of scale of looks, of smarts, of freak-ness, girls who don't want or need or are simply incapable of making friends. Most of the loners appear happy enough to be alone and their status is explicable and justified. They fit logically into the year seven social ecosystem.

But there's one girl, Sophie, whose status perplexes her. Sophie has multiple defects: she's fat, asthmatic, shy; her auburn hair is untidily curly, she's not pretty (her nose is too big, her eyes too widely spaced); she's awkward physically and socially—but her exclusion is not about this. Or not just. It's weird, but it seems that her loser status is more about her immense musical talent than the more obvious things. Charlotte has been told that because Sophie is a genius at the piano, she has no interest in anything else, not even in making friends. Somehow Charlotte doubts this; there was that hopeful smile on her first day, and there were a couple of other times since—once in music class when Charlotte was forced to take a seat alone and Sophie made obvious overtures towards her—when her shy friendliness, her desire to connect, was embarrassingly clear. Charlotte suspects that Sophie's lunchtime music sessions have more to do with her lack of prospective lunch partners than the obsessive focus that the other girls despise.

The teachers have been harder to work out. Charlotte is careful always to appear keen and interested, even when she's not. She is conscientious in class and never joins in illicit iPad conversations or games, avoids whispered conversations and gossip. She intends to develop just the right reputation here. Mostly, it's working out. Some teachers, like her maths and science teachers, have warmed to her immediately, but others have been harder to impress. Some, like Mr Pollard who takes PE, are generally indifferent to all the year seven girls, but one, her young English and Drama teacher, Miss Foley, seems impervious to her charms. She has even tried to give her demerits, once because Charlotte misheard her, and another time because Charlotte had mistakenly worn the wrong sports shirt. The woman's attitude is baffling. English is Charlotte's best subject, and one that she clearly excels in: her reading age is far beyond her actual years; her writing is sophisticated and fluent, exceptional even in this class of bright and privileged girls. She's used to being the English teacher's pet.

Still, Charlotte's first weeks at the college go well. She has firm friends, she is already establishing a reputation among her peers and her teachers as reliable and smart and helpful. She may not be the most popular girl in the class yet, but she's popular enough.

Things can only get better.

PART TWO

ANDI

THE WORST THING, IT SEEMS TO ANDI, IS THAT THERE *WERE* no early signs. There were none of the things that parents are warned to look out for: no evidence of depression, no episodes of self-harm, no negative self-talk. There had been no indication at all that whatever it was that Sophie had been hoping for—attention? *oblivion?*—was being sought. However Andi looks at it, whatever angle she takes, she can see no clear trajectory leading them inevitably to this point. No. That's the thing—it wasn't inevitable. The whole fucking tragic mess could have been avoided.

There are things that, added up, taken together, might have led to the moment, but Andi likes to think that it would have taken only one small change—if she hadn't fallen asleep that afternoon, if she'd called Sophie down to watch television with her, even if she'd just checked on her daughter once during that disastrous drowsy hour, the whole thing would never have happened. Perhaps then that particular moment would have passed; the desire (fleeting, surely) would have been replaced by others, more imperative.

It's the sort of possibility that she rarely came across during her years in legal aid, where other families' fucked-up, sorry disasters of lives were never decided in a split second, but had been inexorably making their way to that particular destination for years—since their miserable fucked-up child-hoods, generally. The drink-driving incident or domestic violence or drug conviction that sent them her way was just another toxic drop in a cup that was already filled to the brim with poison. But there had been no build-up of the sort, she would swear to it, in her own little family.

There are other moments that she would change too, given the chance. That initial schoolyard meeting with Beth—she'd gladly excise that event from her life, if she could, because chances are, if she hadn't spoken to Beth on that particular day, the two women would probably never have become such friends. Andi's visits to the school have grown increasingly infrequent. She no longer does drop-offs or pick-ups, now Sophie's old enough to walk or catch the bus, and since Gus arrived she attends only those events that are absolutely essential—concerts, parent teacher interviews—sometimes not even then. And when she does attend, Andi has neither the time nor the inclination to socialise.

Part of her is aware that she probably should have made more of an effort, that the schoolyard is one way to meet other mothers, and that forging connections with a few parents might have helped smooth things socially for Sophie, if only indirectly. But Andi has never been one to join gangs or cliques. Of course she'd done her bit early on, had volunteered in the canteen and the library back in Scone, but in the years that Sophie has been at HLC, she has never really been involved in any of the numerous school activities. Maybe she should have made more of an effort, but during this precious time off with Gus, she has been happy just doing her own thing.

New motherhood has suited her that way. Not for Andi the confected intimacy, the faux concern, the intense

competitiveness that lurks beneath the hugs and organic cupcakes of mothers' groups. She'd made an attempt when Sophie
was a baby, but it hadn't lasted long. She had been impatient
with the other mothers and their anxieties, always faintly
annoyed by the fussing, the complaints, the tensions and the
absurd comparisons: whose baby was sleeping through, whose
was feeding to schedule, whose was more clingy. Though she
had found Sophie—and now Gus—entirely fascinating, the
public examination of every detail of their routines seemed
intensely boring. No, Andi isn't really a mothers' group kind of
mother; she owned up to it this time round and simply refused
to put herself in that position. She had Steve, she had her children, she had her wider family and a few good friends, and
that was all she needed.

But the two women *had* met. Andi had been in the HLC
playground, waiting for Sophie's late return after an excursion. She hadn't noticed Beth particularly, had been busily
concerned with keeping Gus quiet and avoiding eye contact
with the huddle of lycra-clad gym mummies on one side of the
playground and staying out of the way of the pacing power-suited mobile-clutching career mums on the other. She'd
been crouched beside the pram, bobbing up and down, making silly noises and pulling faces in a vain attempt to stop Gus's
hungry grizzles from escalating into full-scale screaming. The
last thing she wanted was to have to breastfeed among this
lot—to have them witness (with pity or, worse, plain incompre-
hension) the additional rolls of flesh she'd accumulated during
her pregnancy. It might just have been a paranoid delusion,
but it seemed to Andi that all the women were stick thin, with
not an ounce of unwanted flesh between them. She was sure
that, taken singly, most of them were likely to be reasonable

people—all of the women she'd met in the time they'd been in Newcastle were fine, normal enough, even friendly in a distant sort of way. Ridiculous then that Andi, one of those power-suited mums herself in a not-so-long-ago former life, and who told her daughter repeatedly that looks weren't important—that she should ignore the gibes of girls who thought that their future hinged on their bust-to-waist ratios, the length and glossiness of their ponytails, the smooth hairlessness of their tanned legs, the maintenance of their *box gaps,* for Christ's sake—ridiculous that in this context she should be so instantly self-conscious about her postpartum self, almost ashamed of the additional bulk around her middle, the bountiful excess of her breasts.

Andi knew her adult accomplishments were considerable, but in some horrendously Pavlovian way, just being in a school playground brought back all her adolescent uncertainty. All those things that mattered when she was sixteen—looks, clothes, friends—felt like they were important again. Other things, deeper things, turned to dust—it was all about smooth surfaces, outward appearances. And her self-consciousness wasn't just a matter of self-esteem: what a sight it would be to greet poor Sophie—her fat, frowsy mum breastfeeding in the playground. Her daughter didn't need her sense of being different from her well-groomed, uber-confident peers to be so embarrasingly confirmed.

Gus's squawks had become slightly more intense, and she was contemplating pulling him out of the pram and finding a shady spot when a woman sat down beside her, her attention all on the baby, and crooned. 'Hello, you gorgeous thing. Are you giving your mum a hard time? Don't do that, little one.' The woman bent over the pram, gave a sweet smile, and Gus stopped his grizzling almost immediately. His eyes widened, his frown cleared and he smiled gummily at the stranger, distracted momentarily from whatever discomfort he was suffering. Andi turned to thank her, but the woman's attention was still on Gus; she murmured some nonsense to him, his smile became wider, and he made that sound that approximated a laugh— somewhere between a cry and a whistle.

She was quite gorgeous herself, this woman; not in the expensively well-groomed way of so many of the mothers at the school, but gorgeous in a natural un-made-up way: her hair a mass of dark blonde curls, tied back messily, falling in ringlets around her face, her skin fair and freckled, her eyes hazel under dark heavy brows, her mouth wide in a narrow face. She was dressed badly—or what Andi knew was considered bad in these parts—in faded jeans and a black T-shirt, a pair of worn joggers, an old cotton cardigan wrapped around her waist. She was obviously renovating or engaged in some sort of manual labour—there were splashes of paint on her shoes, dirt on her knees, dust on her shirt. Gus was still smiling up at her, patently smitten by the curls and the colours and the smooth, soothing murmur of her voice, and Andi—watching her—could quite understand why.

Eventually the woman turned away from the now content baby, and smiled at Andi. 'My God,' she sighed, 'he's just so delicious. I think I'm totally over the whole baby thing—but, oh man, I get so clucky when they're that age.'

'Truly?' Andi spoke without thinking. 'I've never really been clucky. And definitely not over other people's children.' She regretted the words as soon as they were out, but more than that she regretted her tone—spiky, deliberately unimpressed and basically unfriendly. She had been on the defensive, keen to show that despite appearances she wasn't just some plump, dowdy, nobody housewife, but she realised almost immediately that her defensiveness wasn't required, had been taken as an attack. The woman took a startled breath, then sat perfectly still as a blush worked its way up her neck.

'O-kay . . .' She gave Andi an anxious smile, got to her feet.

'Oh, God.' Andi put her hand lightly on the woman's arm, suddenly desperate to stop her going, to salvage the moment. 'Look, I'm so sorry. I didn't mean to be so rude. I'm just . . . I'm just a bit over it, over the whole thing, at the moment. I fed him before I left, and the thought of having to feed him here was just kind of . . . mind-boggling. I'm more grateful than I can say for your amusing him. He was about to start whinging seriously.' The woman still looked uncertain, as if she was about to move away. Andi patted the seat beside her, pleaded: 'Please don't go. He's going to cry if you go. And, actually, I might too.'

The woman seemed surprised, and slightly bemused, and sat down beside her. She gazed steadily into the pram, making a series of silly faces at Gus, and spoke softly, not making eye contact with Andi. 'Well, I think you're brave to even consider breastfeeding in this schoolyard. I can imagine Dr Holding might come out and ask you to leave for making such an . . . unseemly exhibition of yourself.'

Andi laughed, a loud raucous burst that had several of the other mothers looking their way. 'Oh, my God. You're spot on. She's terrifying. I have a feeling she thought I was pretty unseemly just being pregnant. I'm surprised they let me pick Sophie up. I don't usually come,' she added. 'She usually catches the bus. Or walks. It's just this excursion.'

The woman turned to her, all the stiffness gone, the smile

relaxed and friendly again. 'So you're Sophie's mum? Isn't she the incredible little pianist who played at assembly on Monday?'

'That's the one.'

'My God. She's amazing. You must be so proud.'

Andi laughed the compliment away. 'I am. Also surprised. And who's your daughter?'

'I'm Charlie's mum.'

'Charlie? I don't think I know . . .'

'Sorry, it's Charlotte. Charlotte Mahony. She's always been Charlie, but apparently she's not keen on that anymore. And yes, she just started at the beginning of the term.'

'Oh, Charlotte. The new girl. Sophie's mentioned her. You've come from America?'

'We have.' The woman held out her hand, gave her sweet smile. 'I'm Beth. Beth Mahony.'

Andi took her hand without a second thought, held it firmly, though it was an odd gesture in the playground, in this environment, between women. 'And I'm Andi Pennington. Andrea, if you want to be formal, but nobody ever does. I'm very pleased to meet you.'

She rang Beth early in the day, while Gus was having his morning sleep, just after Sophie left for school. She hadn't even checked with Sophie first, was looking forward to presenting it as a *fait accompli*, a surprise.

Beth wasn't at all hesitant, immediately agreeing that it was a great idea to get the girls together.

'Oh, that sounds lovely,' she said, obviously pleased, 'Wednesday's are great. Charlotte's got nothing on. It's mad—we've only just arrived, and it's already so full on. I can barely keep up. And we're still in utter chaos. I'm lucky to find my own head some days.'

'We're still unpacking boxes, and it's been almost three years, so I know what it's like. And I was wondering,' this was entirely spontaneous, 'why don't you come early to pick her up? We can have coffee, even a drink.'

So perhaps that was it. Maybe that was the moment when all of their fates were decided: Sophie's and Charlotte's and, intimately, inextricably, her own and Beth's. And then the others, too: Dan and Stephen, Lucy and even little Gus. At this meeting—a juncture, surely—it was as if the directions and patterns of their various lives were changed and reset. From then on they were all moving along the one particular path. And after this moment, this meeting, perhaps it was too late to take another.

SOPHIE

SHE TRIES NOT TO EXPECT TOO MUCH—AFTER ALL, IT'S JUST a few hours—but it's hard to contain her enthusiasm, her feeling that this first visit might be the start of something special.

She mentions the visit to Charlotte, in English, the day before. A big mistake, she realises, even as she's making it.

She has to twist around to talk to Charlotte, who is at the desk behind her, which she shares with Amelia Carrington. Sophie ignores the scowl that Amelia is very obviously directing at her, and takes a breath. 'My mum says you're coming over tomorrow after school, and your mum and your sister. For afternoon tea.'

'Yeah, Mum said.' Charlotte gives a tight smile and looks back down at her work. Amelia snorts. The conversation is clearly over.

Sophie swallows her disappointment and turns to the front again, gets back to work.

Later, in the locker room, Charlotte seeks her out. 'Hey, Sophie,' she says. 'I'm sorry about before, it's just I could see Miss Foley was about to turn around and I didn't want to get into trouble. I'm really looking forward to it.' Her smile is big and warm and friendly, a smile that reaches her eyes.

Sophie returns it eagerly. 'I'm really glad. It's going to be fun.'

It doesn't begin well. The two girls are in different afternoon classes, so they have arranged to meet just inside the Honeysuckle Gate. Sophie leans against the cool brick wall, watching the passing stream of girls and parents, barely able to suppress her excitement. But Charlotte takes her time, first standing in a huddle with Harriet and Amelia, the three girls laughing, just metres away from where she's waiting. Sophie is standing in plain view, but Charlotte doesn't wave or smile or make any indication that she's seen her. The other girls eventually leave, rushing past Sophie and through the gate, heading to the bus stop—and then Charlotte begins a conversation with a girl in the year above them. A few more girls join them and Charlotte is one of the last to leave, only wandering over to Sophie when almost all the others have gone.

Charlotte gives a brief smile when Sophie greets her and barely responds to her enthusiastic recital of plans for the afternoon: 'So, I thought we could call in at the Cupcake Cafe on the way home. Mum's given me enough money for two each. We can eat one on the way and take one back home with us. There's enough money to get one for your sister, too, but we don't have to worry about Gus, my little brother, because he isn't eating solids yet, and I'm pretty sure Mum won't let him eat cake until he's eighteen anyway. I know it means going the long way, and we have to get to the top of that mountain,' Sophie indicates the incline they are about to tackle, 'but I think it's worth it for the sake of cake, don't you?' She giggles at her inadvertent rhyme and chants it again: *Sake of cake, sake of cake,* but Charlotte only sighs and slings her violin case over her shoulder. 'A mountain climb. Awesome.' Her voice is flat, expressionless, without any of the airy American lilt that Sophie so admires. The two girls trudge up the hill in silence, Sophie subdued, suddenly suspicious that Charlotte isn't as pleased about the afternoon as she is, is perhaps only accompanying her under duress.

After they get the cakes—Crème Brûlée and Triple Choc Ripple for Sophie, Vanilla Crunch and Strawberry Sundae for Charlotte—and the walk is easier, all downhill, Charlotte relaxes. First there are the cakes to be exclaimed over, between greedy mouthfuls—how much better they are than they'd anticipated, if that was even possible—which segues into a conversation about the hideous and completely inedible savoury muffins they were forced to make in cooking, which leads to a discussion of the bizarre habits of the cooking teacher herself, which leads to a general critique of the other teachers and, inevitably, their classmates.

Sophie answers Charlotte's many questions about the other girls in their year—how long they've been at the college, where they live, where they belong in the class hierarchy—and somehow finds herself discussing her own pariah status, and actually laughing about it. 'They've always thought I was weird, because of the piano, and because I'm hopeless at sport. That's why I got that stupid nickname—Slowphie. But I think they're kinda annoyed that I'm really smart too. And now because all my friends have left, I'm like some kinda freak. Mum says it'll change eventually, but I don't know that it ever will.'

'So why don't you change schools, too?' Charlotte sounds genuinely interested and sympathetic.

'I'm only here because I got a music scholarship, and the school has the best music program in Newcastle, so Mum and Dad really want me to stay. And I do really like the music here. There's nowhere else that's as good; I'd have to go to Sydney.

But I s'pose if things get really bad . . . The thing is I kinda like everything else about the school. I like all the teachers. The way they do things. I just need to find some more girls who are as freaky as me.' She carefully avoids looking at Charlotte as she says this, not wanting her to think she's fishing, but Charlotte has gone off on her own tangent anyway.

'You know, it *is* kinda strange. Back at my old school no one thought it was weird to have some amazing talent. I mean it was actually a good thing. Like there was this musical genius in my class, and she actually went off to *the* big music school in New York. I can't remember what it's called, but it's like the best in the world. And that was when she was only in the fourth grade, which is totally awesome. And pretty much *everyone* wanted to be her friend.'

By the time they reach Sophie's house they are giggling so hard about the week's most hysterical moments—the sports mistress farting; Miss Foley's broken bra strap—that even her mother's cross enquiry, 'Where have you been? I've been calling you. It shouldn't have taken you this long,' can't dampen Sophie's enthusiasm. However mad her mum is about her late arrival home, her failure to text or to answer her phone, none of it matters: Charlotte is here.

THE GOLDEN CHILD'S TEN LESSONS FOR SUCCESS

LESSON FOUR: WHO COUNTS AND WHY IT'S IMPORTANT

If you want to get somewhere, be someone, one of the most important things to do is to keep the people who don't count out of your life and keep the ones who do count in.

So who counts?

Most parents, teachers, coaches and other adults who have some power over you—they count. But not always. Mostly, the popular kids at school count, and the unpopular kids don't.

Every now and then you discover that a member of your own family—like a sibling or a grandparent or even a parent—doesn't count.

Sometimes it can be tricky to work out who's what. But once it's clear—you must be ruthless.

Because just like your parents are always saying: the company you keep reflects on who you are. Or who you want to be. And if you surround yourself with people who don't count, in the end you won't count either.

And remember: even those who don't count can be used.

COMMENTS:

Contact thecount@numeracysolutions.com and solve your numeracy problems today!

CHARLOTTE

IT DOESN'T REALLY HAPPEN VERY OFTEN ANYMORE, THE TWO of them together, just chilling. When they were little they'd shared a room, and most of their activities were shared, too. But now, as teenagers, they're too busy and their interests have diverged. There's some activity almost every afternoon—for Charlotte, anyway: music, drama, hockey, dance. On weekends she is usually flat out doing assessments, and if not, she and Lucy hole up in their separate bedrooms to watch endless reruns of whatever TV series they're currently hooked on. At least, that's what Charlotte does, and she assumes that Lucy occupies herself the same way. Really, though, she has no idea. Even before they moved here, maybe since Lucy became a teenager, her sister's life had become oddly mysterious, distant from her own.

But this particular Sunday it's raining, and for once Mum's made no plans—there's no walk they really must do, or market they need to go to, or boring historic site they really have to visit. There's been some sort of phone issue all week and now the internet's gone completely. At first Charlotte is furious, she's been waiting all week to catch up on a particular episode of *Supernatural,* but the slow pleasures of a device-free rainy day gradually reveal themselves. She and Lucy watch the network cartoons in the morning—for the first time in years—then sit around the lounge room reading actual paper books for a few hours, and now they've left both parents happily engrossed in the Sunday papers and have come up to Lucy's bedroom to go through the pile of old board games that they haven't so much as looked at since they moved here. They play their old favourite, Junior Monopoly, try Mastermind, which has somehow become amazingly easily, and Yahtzee, which seems ridiculously boring, try two-handed UNO, which is hopeless and then have a hilarious round or two of Trouble.

Games exhausted, they listen to music and fossick through the still unopened boxes for something else to do. This particular bedroom has become Lucy's by default—Charlotte declared it too scary; it is even bigger and darker than her own, with densely patterned wallpaper, mahogany-stained dados and skirting boards. The furniture, an enormous oak wardrobe and a rickety cast-iron double bed, is even dingier than the furniture in Charlotte's room.

Charlotte finds a pile of musty old children's books hidden right at the back of the wardrobe, educational Ladybird books from the sixties, which must have been left by the previous owner. They flick through them for a while, laughing at the old-fashioned illustrations and instructions, the odd wording and bad outfits and awkward expressions. They undertake a few of the very simple (and less obviously dangerous) electrical experiments from the *Magnets, Bulbs and Batteries* book, and then try to lever some of the heavier objects in the room, including the ridiculously immovable wardrobe, according to the instructions provided in *Levers, Pulleys and Engines*. They find some old clothesline and attempt a makeshift pulley, which is a little too successfully attached to the bed frame, and leads to complaints from irritated parents.

Eventually the girls collapse onto the bed, dusty, exhausted and slightly hysterical. They sprawl, one at each end, feet tangled in the middle, and chat in a way that Charlotte can't remember doing for a long time, if ever.

Most of the conversation involves school stuff: the differences between HLC and their school in New Jersey, the weirdness of the house system, the uniforms, the tradition and, OMG, all the religion! It then moves easily into gossip about the teachers and, of course, other students. Charlotte, suddenly curious about her older sister's perspective, asks Lucy whether she's found a group of girls she likes here.

'I guess. There's really only one or two girls I can be bothered with, though. Or maybe it's just that there's only one or two girls who can be bothered with me.' Lucy gives a short laugh, looks over at Charlotte. 'But you're already Miss Popular, aren't you? Didn't take you long.'

'It's not really something that I can control, Lucy.' When it comes to discussing this sort of stuff with her sister, Charlotte always feels simultaneously guilty and defensive. And awkward. 'It just . . . it just happens.'

'Right.'

'It's true. It's not like I actually *do* anything.' She is aware of Lucy's relatively lowly position in the social hierarchy, but has never really considered whether it is something her sister worries about. Somehow she's always imagined that Lucy is above such concerns.

'I'm not trying to be mean, Charlie. It's only an . . . observation.' Her sister's smile is reassuring. 'I just don't care about all that stuff. Being popular. Or hanging with the coolest girls.'

'Anyway, it's not like there's anything wrong with Harriet

and Grace and Amelia? Just 'cause they're pretty and popular doesn't mean that they're bad, does it? Or stupid? I mean, they're nice, and they're practically the smartest girls in the class.' She draws herself up, adds haughtily, 'We all are.'

Lucy shrugs, clearly unmoved. 'No. Nothing's wrong with them, exactly . . . I guess they're just not my type.'

'So, if you were in my year, who would you want to be friends with?'

Lucy's answer comes quickly. 'You know, I actually think Sophie's *really* nice. She's smart and interesting. I know she's not someone the cool girls want to be friends with, but if I was in your year, I wouldn't care, she'd be my—'

Charlotte interrupts, suddenly enraged. 'Actually, Miss Perfect, there's a reason no one wants to be Sophie's friend—she's a complete retard.'

Lucy's eyes widen with surprise or hurt, Charlotte can't tell which, and doesn't much care.

'Maybe she's a bit awkward or something, but from what I've seen Sophie's really sweet.' Lucy's voice is uncharacteristically loud, indignant.

'She's fat and she's weird. And she's not the sort of person I want to hang with. It's not that hard to understand.'

'I get it, Charlie. I really do. You only like the pretty, rich girls.'

'What would you know, anyway? You haven't got a clue what goes on in our year.'

'Yeah, right. I suppose I live under a rock.'

'You're such a douche—'

Lucy gives her sister a warning look, then gazes beyond her to the doorway and produces a beatific smile. 'What do you think, Dad? Don't you think Sophie's a really nice girl?' Their father is leaning against the doorjamb, his arms folded, face stern.

'I do. And she's certainly not a retard. Or fat. Or weird.' His voice is cool. 'Lucy's right, you shouldn't be making friendships based on whether people are popular. Being popular is the least important thing. I didn't realise you were so—superficial.'

'But I didn't mean—'

He interrupts. 'I heard what you said, Charlotte. And I'm disappointed.'

ANDI

ANDI IS SURPRISED AT JUST HOW EAGER SHE IS TO PURSUE this new friendship. Her initial overture was for Sophie's benefit—she hoped to encourage a friendship between the two girls—but she enjoyed herself more than she expected that first afternoon, was buoyed by the chat, the casual confidences, the unexpected bursts of laughter. It was a while, she realised, since she'd had this sort of girly fun.

There was a time, long ago, back when she was a career woman, a clever young solicitor accruing billable hours at an astonishing rate, heading for the bar exam, before she met Steve, and long, long before she had Sophie, that Andi had made time for friends, time for fun.

When she met Steve she was at what she knows now to be her career pinnacle. At the time she thought she'd be going a lot further; she had no intention of following any sort of old-fashioned, if still dominant, female trajectory. She wasn't looking for an out—a bloke, babies, a mortgage, all that. No. Andi was going to do it differently to her mother, who'd retired from primary-school teaching when she'd married her builder husband and insisted she'd never regretted it—though Andi could only see boredom and restlessness in her mother's volunteer work and endless committees. She was going to do it differently to her two much older sisters too, both of whom never even finished school, let alone went to university, but married young, and quickly filled their nests with an appalling number of chicks (or so it had seemed to the young and disdainful Andi). Andi, as she'd understood ever since Mrs Rice in year two told her she was the cleverest—if not the prettiest—of the Marshall girls, was meant for Better Things.

And so for a goodly number of years she was consumed with chasing those better things. She hadn't stopped to think about what they really were, or what she actually wanted; it was more a case of what she didn't want—a life like her parents' or siblings'. She'd studied hard, and then worked hard. She'd moved as far away from her lower middle-class background as she could without actually leaving the city she'd grown up in or actively disowning her family.

And then came Steve.

They met, strangely enough, at a nightclub in the Cross. It wasn't the usual scenario; neither of them was there in the hope of picking up. In fact Andi was there reluctantly, out of duty—it was a work outing—and she'd planned to leave as early as was polite. But gradually she gave herself up to the evening—from the raucous exuberance of the strip show to the loud surreality of the nightclub, it was all a laugh, and for once she drank enough to unwind and embraced the experience of losing herself. She was sitting out a dance at the end of the night, nursing a drink and dreamily watching the writhing bodies on the dance floor, when a contingent of local police entered the club for a routine Friday-night visit. They looked frightening, Gestapo-like in their blue overalls, high-laced boots and heavy belts, their faces blank. Andi was surprised by her fellow patrons' nonchalance—most barely gave the cops a second glance—and the police themselves, despite their initially intimidating presence, were remarkably relaxed. She handed over her licence without demur to a solemn young constable. He looked at her photo carefully and then back at her, his expression deadpan.

'Are you sure this is your ID? Not somebody else's? A cousin? Or your older sister's, say?' he asked eventually in a voice that was low and monotonal.

'What do you mean?'

'Well, for one, you don't look old enough to be thirty-two, and for another, it's not a real good photo, is it? Doesn't do you justice.' She baulked momentarily, before she noticed his liquid eyes looking at her hopefully. It wasn't the most straightforward of pick-ups, but pick-up line it definitely was.

Andi thought later that it could so easily have backfired— she could have taken offence, kicked up a stink, complained to his superiors. At the very least she might have told him to go fuck himself. She was a lawyer, for Christ's sake; she had a typical lawyerly disdain for the cops—but something about him appealed and she responded in a way that was atypical of her thirty-two-year-old wisecracking professional self, smiling back at him, answering politely: 'I'm afraid it is me. I take the worst photographs in the world. But thank you. I think.' He must have understood the risk he was taking, because he looked instantly relieved, smiling broadly. The smile lightened his heavy face considerably, and she noticed that beneath the uniform he was a good-looking man: shortish, dark-skinned, powerfully built.

He made as if to hand back her licence, but paused and looked at it again. 'You know, I'm not sure that I am satisfied. I think I should probably follow up on this. Check that this is actually your correct address.'

She laughed then, amazed by his brazen behaviour. She held out her hand for the licence.

'You can visit whenever you like, and you'll definitely find me there, but why don't I make it easier for you. How about I give you my phone number? That way you can make sure I'm in when you call.'

He raised his eyebrows, took a small notebook out of his pocket.

'Oh, you don't need to write it down. She flicked through her wallet, handed him her business card, with her name and work number: *Andrea Marshall, Solicitor at Law, Winston Chalmers and Associates.*

He read the card, a grin splitting his face. 'You work for that prick?'

'I do.'

He snorted, shook his head, handed back her licence, pocketed the card.

'Well, I've always wanted to consort with the enemy. What do you say I give you a call in the morning? It's the end of my shift tonight. We could . . . go for a walk. Buy an ice-cream. Trade secrets. Commit a little espionage. I'm in Bondi, just up the road.'

'You do that. I'll be looking forward to it,' she said.

The risk was greater than Andi had known. She soon found out that Steve's behaviour was wildly out of character. He admitted to her, lying in bed later that week, that he wasn't that sort of bloke at all, was generally hopeless with women, had never before behaved so boldly, either in or out of uniform. But somehow he had been unable to resist, he confessed, awed and slightly confused about the rapid sequence of events. It had happened almost without him thinking about it. 'As if I was

104

bewitched. It was as if you'd put some sort of evil lawyer spell on me. The words just came out.'

She laughed. 'And then coming over to my place the next day—I guess you couldn't help it? That was powerful lawyer magic too?' she asked.

'Oh no. That was entirely conscious. I wanted to check if you were real and not some kind of hallucination—I always have these insane dreams when I'm on night shift, and at first I assumed the whole thing was just one of those. And then when I found your card in my wallet, I thought I'd better come and check you out.'

Steve was as unlike her as it was possible to be, and a long way from being the sort of man she usually hooked up with or had ever imagined marrying. Whenever she'd thought about it—though she'd always had a take-it-or-leave-it attitude to marriage—she had seen herself with another lawyer: a city boy, fast-talking, energetic, ambitious. But Senior Constable Stephen Pennington was from a background that was entirely foreign to her. He'd been brought up in a series of country towns, his father a Uniting Church minister, his mother long dead. He was serious, earnest, alarmingly literal, sometimes dour. He had studied theology after high school, intending to follow in his father's footsteps, but lost his faith mid-degree and joined the cops instead. He had found his calling in the police service, transferring his zeal to the upkeep of law and order. Oddly, for a cop, in Andi's experience anyway, Stephen's idea of good and evil was never murky. He was clear about what was right and what was wrong, about how justice should be meted out, in a way that the utterly secular Andi never could be. And though she could never hope to understand it, his ideals, his unwavering faith in order and righteousness, somehow appealed to her.

Despite all their surface differences, the attraction between them was startlingly simple. And irreducible. They recognised each other. She had known him immediately—and he her.

At Steve's insistence they married (there was no way his father would tolerate him living in sin) six months after that first meeting. And just on a year later, Sophie was born.

Marrying Steve probably kept Andi closer to her own family than she would have been otherwise. Most of the men she'd been out with up until that time came from very different worlds to her own: most of them were middle class, some of them from private schools. They were generally lawyers, too. The relationships were all clearly finite and she made little effort to introduce any of them to her parents and siblings. But Steve insisted on meeting all her family pretty much immediately, and despite his odd background and his off-centre personality, was quickly made welcome. Indeed, he seemed more comfortable in her family than she was herself, enjoying the boozy card nights, the endless barbecues, even watching the cricket with her brothers-in-law. When they moved to Scone her mother was most upset, not because she'd miss Andi— although she would—but because Steve wouldn't be around every couple of weekends to mow the lawn and have a cuppa. Steve was the perfect son-in-law.

And their marriage was remarkably happy. During the long years of trying to conceive a second child—the miscarriages, the rounds of IVF—Steve never gave up. He never said he'd had enough, or suggested, as so many had, that Andi was too old. And he never complained about the emotional stress: Andi's constantly crappy moods, her tears, her complaints about the physical discomfort, the intermittent despair, the inevitable depression. He set his shoulder to the wheel, as he always did, and kept on. 'It'll happen, Andi,' he said when things were at their worst, when she began to feel that the desire to have a second baby had become something else, bordering on obsessive, unhealthy and all-consuming—when *she* was ready to give up. Somehow he always managed to reassure her. 'As long as the doctors think we're in with a chance, I think we should keep trying. We've come this far . . .'

Home-based freelancing seemed like the perfect solution when they first arrived in Newcastle. Andi had built up plenty of connections, and it was practical on so many levels—so much easier to fit in with Sophie's schedule, the IVF, Steve's shifts, pregnancy—and it wasn't until the last weeks before the baby's arrival, that calm before the storm, that Andi realised how few people she knew. She had made a few half-hearted attempts to befriend some of the school mothers when they'd first arrived, there were a couple of coffee dates, other mothers sounding her out, and she doing the same, of course, but these went nowhere, which was probably her fault as much as theirs, she realised.

Andi had become fussy and impatient, and difficult to please when it came to other people—or more particularly, other women. She couldn't bear women who talked about themselves too much, or too little, or who were only interested in their children. She couldn't stand women who rattled off their husband's accomplishments and boasted about their incomes. Women who were too intense and who got too intimate too quickly made her uncomfortable—and then those who never opened up, even after successive conversations, were just plain exasperating. Or maybe it was none of those things. Andi sometimes thinks that she'd like to be a kid again. In her memory, childhood friendships were simpler, based on instinct, surely—*you smell good!*—rather than intellectual and social compatibility. But then, her daughter's friendships have never been quite that easy—were fraught even as a small child. Perhaps it is just the modern world—everyone expecting more, and somehow ending up with less.

It isn't that Andi despairs of ever making real friends in Newcastle, but it is something she's put on the back burner. She's watched Steve and Sophie settle into their respective routines, but her own routines have been temporary, uncertain, and she's been so preoccupied she's forgotten just how much she enjoys, how much she needs, really, other women's company. But now, with Beth so fortuitously arrived, it's time to make an effort.

Over that first afternoon any initial awkwardness between the two women quickly dissolves. The question of whether it is to be tea or wine isn't even broached—Beth has brought a bottle of a good local white with her, and as Gus has already had his afternoon feed, and won't need another until early morning, Andi can indulge with minimal guilt. She can relax altogether—she's got dinner ready early, Gus is contentedly swatting at his floor mobile and the three girls are upstairs in Sophie's room doing God knows what, something iPad-related, she guesses, leaving the two women to chat. At first the conversational balls hit the net a little too frequently, or bounce outside the lines, but it isn't long before a deceptively light discussion about the school and its particular dynamics mutates into an intense confessional rally, and in no time at all they seem to have covered everything important: children, parents, marriage, work, motherhood.

Andi admits to Beth—and Beth is the first person she's said this to, she's barely managed to admit it to herself, really—how much she's dreading having to start working again.

'I know it sounds stupid. I work from home, anyway, so it's not like it's all that difficult. I can pick my own hours. But I'll still have to put Gus in care—and I don't think I can bear it. It really is ridiculous. I mean, I was so desperate to get back to work with Sophie. I had her in care from six weeks . . . It must be my . . . er . . . advanced maternal age.'

Beth is curious—she's had the opposite experience, been out of the workforce since she left Australia and is wondering what to do now she's back home.

'It's not that I'm not happy being back, I really am. But here it's so clear that I'm not doing anything. In the US it was okay. I was foreign, I didn't have a green card, so I *couldn't* work. Maybe it's the whole thing of having too many choices.'

'And somehow they don't necessarily make you happy, either.'

'I know. I feel like I was almost happier when I had no choice. Maybe I could have another baby. Maybe that'd solve the problem.' She looks enviously at Gus.

'It really does seem like bliss, staying home with Gus. Just giving in to the whole mummy thing. With Sophie, I hated it. She was hard work, wouldn't feed or sleep. I couldn't wait to get back to my real life. It was as if everything I liked about myself had disappeared; as if I'd turned into this big soggy blancmange.' She laughs. 'And you know what, I actually look like a big blancmange this time, but for some reason it's okay. Steve thinks I've gone a bit mad.'

'But it's a good madness, right? Oh God, I am kind of jealous. I loved it when they were babies. Especially nursing.'

'Really?'

'I did.' Beth looks wistful for a moment. 'I really liked that whole animal thing of motherhood. I'd have had more, only Dan wasn't up for it. And now, of course, I'm too old.'

'I don't know about the animal thing, but I'm definitely enjoying it more this time round. Although I am feeling my age. The broken sleep seems way harder to cope with. But you know the old cliché—I wouldn't swap them. Whatever trouble they are, it's all worth it.'

On this, as in so many things, they agree: whatever trouble children bring—morning sickness, ruined bodies, hard labours, leaking breasts, late nights, career dilemmas—it is all, always, whatever the cost, worth it.

When Beth lets slip that she has a blog, Andi has to fight against a somewhat irrational prejudice, although she's never read Beth's blog, never heard of her. Mummy-blogging had seemed a brilliant thing initially—at last, a forum where ordinary women could voice their conflicting experiences, could vent about the combination of boredom, ecstasy and terror that was mothering. But it changed over the years. The blogs proliferated insanely, some went 'professional', and it now seems to Andi that the whole thing has transformed into yet another competitive arena. All the posturing, all the arguing about the right way to parent—it just isn't Andi's scene. To her it all seems very old-fashioned, very retro, like those manuals, periodically republished as humorous oddities, on how to be a good wife.

'Wow!' Andi tries to sound impressed. 'Do you have a lot of readers?'

Beth shrugs. 'Not really. I'm pretty small fry—maybe a few hundred a week. Regulars. If one of the big websites shares one of my posts, which happens every now and then, I get more traffic—maybe in the thousands—but it only ever lasts for a day or so. Not many of them stick around. It's not enough of an audience for advertising, and that's the only way to make money. It's really just a hobby, a way of keeping my hand in, in some small way. I always hoped that I'd go back to journalism when the kids got older. But the internet's kind of made that impossible anyway. There are no jobs. It's ironic, isn't it—I've been enthusiastically making myself redundant.'

'I think we're all in the same boat, really. I've kept working, but in a way I've been on cruise control for years. I could get a job in a big firm, I guess, do something interesting, move up the ladder. I can really only do the most basic stuff from home—it's pretty boring. But there are all these women in their early thirties without kids, so ambitious, so competitive. Argh. I don't think I can play that game anymore.' Her shudder is only slightly exaggerated. 'Although I'm sure I was no different when I was that age. I'm embarrassed to think of all the middle-aged mumsy has-beens I sneered at back then.'

Beth laughs. 'Oh, God, me too. And now look at me . . .'

Andi takes her iPad to bed that night, and reads the DizzyLizzy blogposts, going back into the archives, scrolling through months of posts, and then years—and then it is suddenly it's past one in the morning and Gus has woken for a feed, and she feels a little grimy, like some sort of online stalker. But despite her initial qualms, she quite likes Beth's online alter ego. Lizzy isn't didactic or authoritative, disingenuous or self-congratulatory. She isn't a humble-bragger or a pain-in-the-arse know-it-all. Beth's online persona meshes with the actual flesh-and-blood woman Andi has met—smart, insightful, wryly humorous. Her virtual life seems just as chaotic and uncertain as Andi's own. And, appealingly, just as real.

SOPHIE

IT BEGINS INNOCENTLY ENOUGH. THE TWO OF THEM barricaded into Sophie's bedroom, late in the afternoon, bored, all other possibilities for entertainment, real and virtual, exhausted. There's nothing left to do but take selfies of themselves making stupid faces. They move on from faces to close-ups of eyes, from eyes to noses, from noses to lips. Their photo session culminates in a mass of weirdly angled close-range shots of various body parts: arms, hands, fingers, toes, soles of feet, kneecaps, crooks of elbows. They post the wildest, least recognisable shots on Charlotte's Instagram account, without any accompanying descriptions, then laugh themselves silly as the likes come thick and fast, along with bewildered, off-the-wall comments from her followers: *What sort of flower is this? It's so pretty!* someone says about an artistic shot of the creases on Charlotte's elbow. A girl in year ten asks about the hill and valley shot of Sophie's knocked-together knees: *Is this in Japan?*

'Okay, so what about our butts, then? Or our boobs?' Naturally, it's Charlotte's idea.

'No way.' Sophie shakes her head violently, but can't help giggling at the thought.

'We could make them look totally bizarre. Nobody would ever know. Come on, it'll be cool.'

'No way,' Sophie says again. 'If anyone found out we'd be . . .'

'But that's the thing. Nobody *will* ever find out. Nobody's got a clue what these photos actually are. Come on, Sophie!' Charlotte is impatient, excited. Irresistible. 'If you don't want to, I'll go first. You take a shot of my boobs. I'll push them up like this.' Charlotte pulls her school uniform off without hesitation, then whips off her little lacy bra and pushes her tiny breasts together. Sophie gazes at her friend's tanned, angular body enviously, then looks away quickly, embarrassed, but Charlotte is entirely unselfconscious. She thrusts her iPad at Sophie. 'Here. Take some photos from different angles. We'll post the funniest ones.' Her discomfort quickly overtaken by her desire to keep the game going, keep Charlotte happy, Sophie takes a dozen shots, from close in and far away, none of them even vaguely recognisable as any body part. The girls squeal over the pictures, select one that, after some clever Photoshopping, looks like a teacup and saucer with a crazed patina, and post it. Charlotte pulls her clothes back on then turns the iPad on Sophie.

'Okay. Let's do your butt.'

'My butt? No way. That's gross.' Sophie feels slightly sick. 'No one wants to see that.'

Charlotte's eyes narrow. 'Come on, Sophie. You just took shots of my tits. Now it's your turn.' Her voice is cold.

Sophie doesn't want to, but there's no way out. She can't upset Charlotte, not now, not when they're getting on so well. She turns away from her friend, unbuttons her uniform, shrugs it slowly over her shoulders and wriggles it over her hips, her legs, taking her time. She looks down at her body, despairs at her shapeless breasts in their dingy overstretched bra, the pasty corrugations of flesh from her chest to her pudgy thighs. She finds it almost impossible not to wrap her arms around herself, to offer her exposed body some sort of protection.

'What do you want me to do?' Sophie's voice is breathy and high. Charlotte is leaning back on the bed, the iPad held out in front of her, focused, intent.

'Just pull your undies over a bit and show me some skin, girl.' She looks up from the iPad, gives a brief, mischievous grin.

'Really? Can't you take something else?'

'No way, José. If you don't give me some butt, I'll put up a video of you like this.'

'Like what?'

'In your underwear.'

'What? Like this? Have you been recording me? No way! Charlotte.' Sophie panics, lunges for the iPad, but Charlotte scrambles off the bed, laughing, the iPad still held firmly in front of her.

'Come on, Sophie. Fair's fair.'

It's not fair, but Sophie pulls back her shameful undies (too small, faded and threadbare, the elastic gone limp) and reveals a square of porcelain skin, marred by a constellation of tiny red pimples. Charlotte comes close up, takes a series of shots.

By the time they edit the shot and post it, Sophie's uniform and good cheer have been restored, and she LOLs as genuinely as Charlotte at the comments.

Hey that's amazing @CharlotteMah. My doona is exactly that material. I love the red polka dots!!!

And when Lucy knocks on the door to let them know that she and Beth have arrived to pick up Charlotte, Sophie doesn't even mind that Charlotte shows her older sister the original shots as well as the Photoshopped versions. After all, it's been so much fun. Charlotte's her friend. And Lucy, too.

DizzyLizzy.com

Mummy-fied

I test the idea on the girls first. It's one that's been floating around in my head for a while, long before we arrived back in the land of Oz.

I put it to them gently—very gently—as we're driving home from hockey training. 'I've been thinking, now that you girls are both in high school, I should probably think about getting a job.' My voice is pleasantly neutral; my eyes are on the road.

'But you always say that being a full-time mum is work.'

'And who'd drive us to hockey?'

Later, over dinner, I make the suggestion, just as casually, a mere suggestion, to D.

'Get a job? But you've got one.'

'I mean a *real* job.'

'But you're always saying that mothering *is* a real job.'

'Well, it is, but—'

'And anyway, you've got to finish the painting.'

I sound out the girls again, as we're heading to the beach on Friday afternoon.

'You know how I mentioned getting a job the other day?' This time I make eye contact. 'Well, I think it'd be really good for everyone—it'll give Dad the opportunity to help out a bit, do more stuff with you girls.'

'Would Dad have to cook dinner?'

'I guess so. Sometimes.'

'Then no way. All he can make is frozen pies. In the microwave. We'll end up really fat.'

'Or starved.'

'Please don't.'

They hold on hard to my hands, clearly afraid.

I talk to D again. It's ten o'clock at night, and I'm standing in front of the wardrobe mirror, trying on potential work outfits. D's sitting up in bed with a cup of black tea, doing something important on his laptop. I put on one of my favourites, a tight-fitting cream dress—a Hervé Léger knock-off I bought for a wedding a couple of years back. It may not be the real thing, but it was still expensive. And it looks good. I pair it with a plum silk jacket to give it an appropriately office-y feel.

I put on lipstick. Heels. Pile my hair into a fashionably messy bun.

I strike a pose—hand on hip, head on the side—do my best not to teeter in my barely worn Jimmy Choos.

'So. What do you think?' D looks up and I give him my best office-seductress look.

He blinks, looks confused. 'What the hell are you doing? It's bedtime.'

'You know, I really miss having to get dressed for work.' I make my voice wistful, raise my eyebrows meaningfully. 'Don't you?'

'Perhaps you haven't noticed, but I do get dressed for work. Every single morning. I can't say it does anything for me.'

'That's not what I meant. I thought you—'

'It's a bit too late for sex games, honey—I've got a meeting in the morning. And anyway,' he adds, 'I hate that dress.'

'What do you mean?'

'It's the fabric. You look like you've been wrapped in bandages.' He snorts.

'That's the point.'

'Yeah, well you sort of remind me of a mummy.' He yawns, closes his laptop.

I give it one last go. I'm with the girls in the local shopping mall. We've spent two hours here, and according to them the shopping expedition has been lame. Meaning: I've bought nothing but the things they need, and nothing that they actually *want*.

'Oh, Mum,' says C. 'This skirt.' She crushes the completely unsuitable and hideously expensive suede miniskirt to her chest. 'I just *love* it.' She turns begging eyes on me. '*Please*. I'll do anything.'

'Sorry, sweetie. Money doesn't grow on trees.' C rolls her eyes, sighs. Shares a bitter look with her older sister.

'But, you know, if I had a job, it'd be a bit different.' Suddenly I have their undivided attention. 'It wouldn't be a money *tree*, exactly. But certainly a . . . seedling.'

'If you got a job could I get a new iPhone?'

'And could I go on that China trip in year nine?'

'Oh my God, Mum,' says C, 'what sort of example are you setting? Who wants to be a stay at home mum? You should *totally* get a job.'

51 ♥

EXPATTERINGS:
@OzMumInTokyo says:
Oh, it's so exciting, Lizzy! So did you find anything?? XOX

> **@DizzyLizzy** replied:
> Not yet—there isn't really that much around for forty-somethings who've been out of the workforce for fifteen years. Might've left my run too late L
> **@OzMumInTokyo** replied:
> No way! You'll be snapped up in no time. Xxx

@HausFrau says:
Who are you kidding? You can tell yourself whatever you like, but age IS a huge barrier to employment. Who wants a middle-aged woman with family responsibilities when they can get a fresh-faced twenty-something who's willing to work a ninety-hour week, sleep with the boss and clamber up that greasy pole? Good luck with that!

> **@BlueSue** replied:
> I hate to agree with such a snarky comment, but @HausFrau has a point. When I went back into the workforce after years as a SAHM, I had to accept a nursing position that was so far below my former experience (and income bracket) that it was a joke. My self-esteem took such a massive dive that I don't think it was worth it. Take it from me, it's a tough old world out there, Lizzy.
> **@GirlFromIpanema** replied:
> I'm not so sure you hate to agree, @BlueSue. But whatever rocks your boat. Total rubbish, btw, Lizzy. You go girl!!!!

@AnchoreDownInAlaska says:
Mummy-fied!!! LOL. Love it!

@TrailingWife says:
Hi Lizzy! Great to hear you've made it home safe and sound and pretty much sane ☺ TrailingWife.com are planning a blog round-up over the next couple of months, asking home-comers like yourself to list the ten things they most miss about their expat homes. We'd love to have your contribution. Contact linda@TrailingWife.com for details.

BETH

BACK IN NEW JERSEY, BETH HAD FELT AS IF SHE WAS ON TOP of everything. The house, the cooking, the bills, all the complex details of the girls' lives, emotional and physical—it had taken considerable effort, but she had it finely tuned, perfectly calibrated. But here, everything feels slightly out of control. They've been in the house for more than four months and are somehow still living out of boxes, the place is a mess, all their paperwork is out of sync. For the first time in her married life she's been late paying the bills—their mobiles have been disconnected twice, and she's had threatening letters from the gas company.

Worse, for the first time since their births, Beth feels excluded from her daughters' lives. There have been parties, play-dates, parent–teacher meetings, and she's even made a point of going to Monday assembly whenever she can, but something has changed now both girls are in high school, something fundamental. Even though they are into their second term, she still has no clue about the classroom dynamics, how they spend their lunchtimes, their day-to-day experiences. She has barely had any conversations with other parents in the girls' classes—while she meets Lucy and Charlotte just inside the school gates, the other high schoolers seem to walk or catch buses—so that until her recent, providential meeting with the lovely Andi, there have been none of the deceptively casual afternoon conversations with other mothers that Beth has always depended on for information and gossip. She knows that it is probably a normal development—an inevitable part of the girls growing up, growing away, becoming women—but the truth is she misses her babies. Misses them needing her.

And Beth's own life feels strangely uncertain, too. She is entirely without local friends, and doesn't quite know how to find them. There's Andi, of course, and she's hopeful about her, but that relationship is still in its early stages—casual, easy; the confidences general, not particular. Increasingly, the blog is her principal social outlet: there she can continue to be that smart, gently funny, *connected* self that she's constructed over the last few years. Beth likes to think that her virtual persona is just as authentic as her 'real life' self. Or almost: Lizzy is perhaps just a touch more laid-back than Beth, she seems to be able to brush aside, laugh about, all the petty, and not so petty, annoyances of her life in a way that Beth never can.

At least the girls are okay. Or they seem to be—although if she thinks too hard about them she's likely to break out in a cold sweat. They may not have become the nightmare adolescents she has dreaded—neither of them is particularly rebellious, or not yet; neither seems to be suffering from depression or anxiety; there are no signs of eating disorders, self-mutilation, self-loathing; they haven't suddenly become hyper-sexualised or boy-crazy. Neither of them has announced that they're gay or bi or transgender. Still, both girls seem to be moving further and further from her: they keep their thoughts to themselves and, increasingly, their actual physical selves—both of them spending more time in their bedrooms and with their various devices than with each other or their parents.

And maybe it is early days, but she still doesn't have a solid sense of their friends—what they're like, who their parents are. She has to rely, as she supposes so many other busy middle-class parents do, on the school being an effective filter. It is a school established for the children of families like theirs, after all—well-off, respectable, ambitious for their children—otherwise they wouldn't be there.

So Beth has begun doing exactly what her mother suggested: thinking about herself. She's started wondering whether it might be time for her to get serious about working again. Whatever she said to her mother, or told herself, the decision to *not* work wasn't a natural one for Beth. Sometimes it seems as if a rotten joke has been played on her, as on so many women she knows: all those years spent struggling to achieve career success, material gain—time at university, the two years working on her masters, the willingness to start right at the bottom of the ladder as a receptionist at a women's magazine, to work through all the departments (marketing, sales, PR) before finally ending up in a place she wanted to be. All that dressing-for-success, going to the right parties, making the right connections, schmoozing with her superiors—licking arse, basically. There were a few years of doing precisely what she wanted, and doing it well, and then, *bang!*—she met Dan at the wedding of mutual friends (they were both in the bridal party; such a cliché!), they fell in love and married, and in the blink of an eye she was pregnant and agreeing to a twelve-month stay in Canada. For *his* work. 'I'll have the baby to occupy me, Dan,' she had reassured him. 'It won't matter that I'm not working—and anyway, there'll be things I can do if I want. I can work online; I can freelance.' She doesn't regret it, not really—what she said to her mother is true: she loves her life, loves the fact that she's been able to be there for the girls. And she knows the girls have benefited from it—they are both happy, bright, well-adjusted. Normal.

It was okay when they were in the US, where she couldn't work anyway, but now she is back in Australia, she feels differently. She feels somehow lessened, wasted, judged. She knows that she made the right decision, the only decision, but she has begun to wonder whether she'll ever get to be that other person again, whether there'll even be a career to go back to. The current of technology has kept rushing forward without her, and her once cosy little anchorage is almost unrecognisable, has practically been washed away. So this possibility of working with Drew Carmichael that her mother told her about: there's no ignoring it. It is an opportunity, and if her quick recce of the local employment market is any indication, right now it's the only one Beth has.

What she doesn't expect is that Dan's reaction will be so reflexively negative. When she mentions, over breakfast one morning, her mother's suggestion that she get in touch with Drew, that there's the possibility of a job, Dan makes his opposition clear. 'You're not really thinking about starting work now, are you?' he asks. 'There's no point—you can't make any sort of commitment, not yet.' He sounds annoyed. 'We really need you around to get the girls settled. Sort out all the house stuff.' It's true—there are so many other things she needs to do—but Beth has a sudden, unexpected burst of resentment at this too-easy dismissal, which she knows is probably motivated by Dan's instant realisation that if Beth is working, more will be expected of him.

'What about your mother? Surely she could help out with the girls. They could go to her place a couple of afternoons a week, couldn't they? Isn't that part of the reason we moved here—so we'd have some support?' They'd discussed it before they moved back—how great it would be to have his mother close by—and Dan had assured her that Margie was over the moon, that she couldn't wait to see more of the girls. It was supposed to be an enticement—a reason to be happy about the move to Newcastle. But since they've been back it's been a different story; Dan is reluctant to ask his mother to do anything.

'You think Mum should run the girls around after she's finished her own work day? Do you really think that's fair? She's already done her share of parenting. Look, I know she'll be more than happy to babysit when we really need her to, and I know she's enjoying having the girls, having all of us, in her life, but you can't really expect that she's going to want to mind them, or ferry them around to all their after-school activities. And anyway, you know how much they do, and you can barely manage it yourself. You can't ask Mum to do it.' *You can't ask Mum to do it.* It's becoming a familiar refrain.

'I wasn't going to ask her to do everything, Dan, or even anything much. I just thought it might be worthwhile giving Drew a ring, to see what . . . possibilities there might be. I'd really like to get back into the workforce, now we're home. Do something other than the girls and the house. Something useful.'

'Look, I don't want to sound like a dictator, but wouldn't it be better if you left it for a while longer? Wait till things are settled?' Dan slurps down his coffee in a way that really annoys her, too fast, noisily, then wipes his hand across his mouth. 'And Drew Carmichael? Okay, I know he's an old family friend and all that, but I think it'd be a bit much to ask Mum to give up her time for that tosser. I honestly wouldn't think about asking for her help if you get a job with him. It'd be like asking her to look after the kids while you work for Satan.' He laughs, but uneasily, as if sensing Beth's anger.

She is furious that his mother's opinion of Drew matters so much to him. There have been too many instances since they've been home, times when his loyalty to his mother, his fear of somehow offending her, has come close to being a betrayal of Beth, of *them*. She notices how he always makes a point of chipping the girls (Charlotte usually) over their perceived device addiction (*Why not read a book, go outside and play?*) when Margie is around; how enthusiastic he is about his mother's cooking (*World's best mashed potatoes, Ma!*), her superior housekeeping skills, her knowledge of politics, history, literature, religion; how he asks (and defers to) her opinion about virtually everything. He's completely oblivious to his mother's subtle exclusionary tactics, her apparently playful habit of making Beth's background, her lack of working-class credentials, conspicuous and somehow inferior, inauthentic (*Dinner? Oh, you mean* tea, *love*). She could make something of it now, she's just about reached that point, but decides to leave it. It's all so petty, really.

She takes a deep breath and changes tack. 'Okay—I guess you're right. I'll wait. And I'm sure Drew's too busy to play catchups at the moment, anyhow.' She gives him a breezy smile.

He looks relieved. 'I don't want to burst your bubble, but I just can't see how you could make it work—not right now. You've just told me that Charlotte wants to try out for rep hockey. That's going to take a big chunk of your time, isn't it? All those early mornings and then the trips away. It'd be a logistical nightmare.'

Dan's attitude to her working seems paradoxical: he doesn't want his wife to work for a conservative politician because it might offend his mother's finely wrought class sensibilities, yet it's okay for Beth to spend her days driving their appallingly privileged daughters hither and thither, ensuring they're given every possible opportunity—sporting, academic, creative. It is too absurd. And that her own desire to work, to contribute something to the world beyond her immediate domestic sphere, should be seen as some sort of an indulgence is outrageous, surely.

So Beth makes the phone call surreptitiously and doesn't tell Dan that she's arranged to meet Drew for lunch. She doesn't hide things from him often; in fact she can't remember the last time she told him an untruth. But she doesn't want to have to make excuses, to lie about her intentions. It's better to keep Dan completely in the dark for now. If anything eventuates she will offer it up as a *fait accompli*, deal with the fallout then.

The secret nature of their meeting adds a pleasant zing. She dresses well, business-y, but with just a little extra appeal: short skirt, tights, heels, a shirt that hints at her cleavage. She straightens her curls, applies make-up that's cleverly *au naturel*. Perfumes her pressure points.

And for once she likes what she sees in the mirror: she looks striking. And professional. It has been a long time since Beth has seen this particular woman, a long time since she's *been* her—so long she's almost forgotten she exists.

She arrives early at the small and surprisingly hip cafe in a lakeside suburb that is itself far more hip than Beth expected. She recognises Drew immediately, though she isn't sure she would have had she not looked him up online beforehand. As a young man he wore his curly hair long, and dressed, as they all did, in regulation student wear—jeans and T-shirts, joggers. He'd never been edgy, or out there, or in any way bohemian, but now, in his dress pants, his sockless boat shoes, his obviously expensive shirt, casually open at the collar, he looks terrifyingly establishment: middle class, middle aged, successful. His hairline has receded a little, but his hair is still plentiful: his once dark blond curls have somehow transformed into that dense silver that only Hollywood actors and politicians seem to possess. There is no evidence of jowls; in fact his jaw seems to be even squarer than Beth remembers. His eyes are still the scalding blue of memory, but are set now in a nest of highly attractive wrinkles. He exudes confidence, charm. Money.

Drew is obviously well known at the cafe: several waitresses vie for his attention, flirt, offer him his usual table, which he declines when he notices Beth seated in the corner, waiting. She stands up as he approaches, and he strides towards her, his face breaking into a wide (and impressively white) smile that is surprisingly familiar. Her own response is familiar too—she'd experienced that same slightly quickened heartbeat when he was her best friend's unattainable older brother, and then later during their short-lived romance.

'Elizabeth. How are you?' She is expecting a polite air kiss, but he wraps his arms around her in a hug. He holds her away from him, his hands firm on her shoulders, looks into her eyes and beams. 'You're still the same gorgeous Beth I remember. Actually, you barely look any different to when you were six and running around playing aloha with my little sister.'

She laughs at the memory, slightly embarrassed, as he surely intends: that particular game having been played wearing nothing but raffia skirts and painted-on bras. It was the sort of game that no self-respecting six-year-old would ever think of playing now—and she imagines any parents who allowed it would be in all sorts of trouble.

She draws back, gently pulling herself free. 'I think I may have changed just a little. That was forty years ago.'

He grins. 'I guess there've been certain improvements. You're quite a lot . . . taller.'

She laughs. 'Well, *you're* still the same, Drew.'

He joins in her laughter, looking slightly sheepish. 'What can I say? But seriously, you are looking good. Very good. And that's going to help us both, I reckon.'

'What do you mean?'

'It's lovely to catch up, of course, but I assume we're here for the same reason. I'm looking for staff and you're looking for work.'

'Well, yes and no. I'm not entirely sure yet.'

'I thought Francine told my mother that you were?'

'Well, you know how it is. Maybe.' It's Beth's turn to look sheepish. 'But I would have rung anyway, just to catch up.'

He grins. 'Of course you would. But when you found out I was getting ready for the election, that I might be needing a press secretary . . .'

'I suppose it might have been an added inducement.' She is slightly startled by the slickness of her own response, but it is obviously the right thing to say. Drew nods appreciatively, pulling his chair close to hers.

'Look. I know you've worked for newspapers and magazines, and I'm pretty sure this is the kind of job you'd be good at. You might have been out of the workforce for a while, but I have a feeling you're exactly what I'm after. You're presentable—more than presentable—and you're smart. I've had a read through that bloggy thing you write. What is it? Busylizzy?'

'Dizzylizzy.' This surprises her. 'How did you . . . ? It's meant to be anonymous.'

'You must have told Julie about it. I rang her up to see what she knew about your life, what you've been doing for the last ten years or so.'

'I guess I must have.' She can't remember telling Julie, who lives in Singapore now, and who she's only in occasional contact with, but imagines that her mother—despite her uncertainty about the respectability of the enterprise and patently disregarding Beth's desire to keep it low-key—has spread the word.

'So, yeah. I had a read through your blog, and it told me a few interesting things about you. You're quick, you communicate well, you have an engaging voice. More style; less opinion. In that sense you're a bit different to a lot of the mummy-bloggers out there. And believe me, I'm an expert. You know Angela's site of course.' The smile he gives is wry, but she can hear the little note of pride.

'Oh, of course. She's done so well; it's amazing. But I don't really aspire to that sort of—'

'No, Motherkind's in a different league altogether. It's big business now. But still, yours gives a pretty good indication of your talent for fabrication.'

'What do you mean, fabrication?'

'Well, I'm assuming that the picture of your life that you paint on the blog isn't your real life. Don't get me wrong, it resembles real life, it's an excellent little window into a domestic world and all that, but there's something slightly unreal about it. It's like one of those Potemkin villages or whatever they were called—you know it's too good to be true.'

'Oh?' She isn't sure whether this is praise or insult.

'I dunno. It's hard to pinpoint. I mean, you're obviously not one of those ridiculous Stepford women with their perfect lives, and it's not all slow-cooker recipes and bloody crochet patterns, but it's still a bit too tidy, a little too contrived. Maybe it's too . . . positive or something. Even when you're being ironic.' He grins again, obviously enjoying her discomfort.

'It's not always upbeat, though. Perhaps you haven't read . . . There are a few darker posts. I did one on domestic violence just a few months ago.' Beth can feel herself bristling.

'No. It's not that. I've read those. Maybe it's just that even the darker bits are . . . well, they're so careful. You're always covering yourself. Your *true* self, I mean. It's like they've been spun.'

'Spun?' She still doesn't quite get what he's saying, and isn't sure whether she should be flattered by his attentive reading or appalled by the analysis.

'You know: like sugar into fairy floss; straw into gold. And in my business I reckon that's a good thing, it's a good talent to have. It can be difficult to find people who understand that. Almost impossible to find people like you who do it almost instinctively.'

'You're saying that you can tell from my blog that I'm good at *spin*?'

'Yep. And, more importantly, that you're comfortable with it. You have to be if you're going to work with me.'

'Why?'

'Well, I'm a politician. Or I'm going to be.'

'Are you saying I'd have to lie?'

'Nothing that straightforward. It's more that I can't always tell the whole truth. It has to be shaped for public consumption. Come on, you worked in PR for years. You know what I'm talking about.'

'I guess.'

'Anyway, as it happens there is a job—and if you want it, it's yours. It's probably way lower down the ladder than you're used to,' he adds. 'You'd just be doing our social media to begin with. I know you're good at that. When you've built up a few useful connections, we'll find you more to do. And obviously when the election actually gets into full swing, the whole thing'll ramp up. I'm thinking if it works out you can have the official media officer job. What do you reckon? Are you up for it?'

Later she will wonder why his perception that she is good at lying doesn't worry her more, but at this moment, all caution thrown to the wind, Beth gives Drew her most affirming smile and tells him without any sort of uncertainty that she's in.

ANDI

IT ISN'T THAT SHE DREADS THESE OCCASIONS, BUT SHE CAN'T say she really enjoys them. As always before one of Sophie's performances, Andi feels slightly unwell. The sensation begins that morning as a slight fluttering, and by the evening it morphs into a dull weight—like a cloud of butterflies has turned to lead and settled in her gut. It isn't as if she has absorbed her daughter's emotions. When it comes to the piano, Sophie never displays any sign of nerves. She is calmly cheerful about the prospect of playing to an audience, however large, however important. She remains assured, unflappable, cool. Even Andi's very obvious anxiety doesn't seem to rattle her.

Andi is especially nervous about this particular performance. The Hunter Annual Arts Showcase is one of the most important events on the school calendar, held in the concert hall at the Conservatorium, and open to all the local schools, public and private. The college board makes a point of attending, as does the mayor, along with numerous other local big-wigs. It is traditional for a report of the occasion—with accompanying photos—to be published in the *Advocate*'s social pages. While Sophie's scholarship isn't dependent on these sorts of events, there is still subtle pressure for her to do well, to show that the investment has been worthwhile; this in addition to displaying the school's superiority to anything the public system has to offer. In her earlier life, Andi would have scorned such blatant displays of privilege, but the brute reality of Sophie's talent has forced her to modify her (admittedly rather fuzzy) socialist principles. It seems there's no end to the compromises wrought by marriage and motherhood.

This night Andi has additional worries. Steve is staying home with Gus, who is naturally proving difficult to settle. Although desperate to make her escape, Andi has to feed him just moments before they are due to leave to get him to sleep. She had planned to pick up Beth and the girls on the way but has had to cancel, promising instead to meet them there. To make things worse, Gus dribbles milk all down her dress, and she is forced to quickly find an alternative—not an easy task in her current pneumatic state.

'Oh, fuck. This is ridiculous.' She throws a pretty but currently unzip-up-able skirt hard at the wall. 'Why don't you go instead, Steve? I don't know why I ever bothered thinking I'd be able to do this.' Rage is better than tears, she thinks, but only just.

Steve is lying on the bed with his hands linked behind his head. He surveys the scene calmly, as if amused by the spectacle. Sophie, who has also remained serene throughout the drama, looks diligently through her mother's wardrobe and pulls out a black elastic-waisted skirt. 'Why don't you wear this one, Mum,' she says, 'and you can wear it with the blue shirt? You always look really good in this.'

It's true this particular combination looked okay—when she was nine months pregnant. Andi frowns, ready to snap, but a surreptitious gesture from Steve stops her. He doesn't need to say anything; she knows: this is Sophie's night, not hers. She pauses, takes a deep breath, holds out her hand: 'That's perfect, darling. I don't know why I didn't think of it myself.'

The evening improves once they arrive at the Conservatorium. Andi locates Beth and her two girls almost immediately, while Sophie makes her way backstage. Despite having to greet various school worthies, she is able to relax slightly under the combined effects of a glass of champagne and Beth's easy conversation, and by the time they take their seats in the grand hall she is almost enjoying herself, the butterflies still present, but less intrusive. And when Sophie finally begins the evening's entertainment—her two solo performances bookend the program—the relief is immediate. Sophie's performance is phenomenal, transfixing, transporting. As ever, when her daughter plays, Andi can hear muted sighs of delight and surprise echoing through the audience. And, as ever, though she's never stopped wondering about the random nature of Sophie's talent, she allows herself a quiet moment of self-congratulation. It may be Sophie's night, but there certainly are some rewards for being the mother of the star act.

Afterwards, while Beth and the two girls wait with Andi in the post-show throng, Beth is barely able to contain her enthusiasm. 'Oh my God! Andi. She's just amazing! You must be so proud.'

'I am.' Andi's smile is a little tremulous. 'I get so nervous, though. Every single time,' she confides. 'Though I shouldn't. She never hits a wrong note.'

'No,' Beth agrees. 'You shouldn't. She's totally professional. I've never heard anything like it. I've heard her play at school once or twice, but tonight was remarkable. So, tell me, where did she get her talent? Are you some sort of musical genius, too?'

Andi laughs. 'No way. I was always desperate to learn an instrument, but my mum wouldn't let me. We weren't really that sort of family . . .' She shrugs. 'Anyway, I was determined that Sophie would at least have the opportunity. When she started, I thought it'd be one of those things that we'd all be over by the time she was ten. But by ten . . . Well, you heard. Steve and I still can't believe it.'

'I'm impressed! Sophie was definitely the highlight of the show. Why didn't someone warn me? What did you girls think?'

'She's so good!' Lucy enthuses. Then, in a sweet echo of her mother, she smiles shyly at Andi. 'You must be so proud.'

'And what did you think, Charlotte?' Beth smiles encouragingly at her younger daughter, who has been oddly subdued the entire evening and is standing a little apart from them now, looking bored. 'She's completely amazing.' The girl's words are expressionless, almost mechanical.

'And she's your friend, darling. Fancy knowing such a prodigy!' Beth's voice has taken on a slightly teasing tone, but Charlotte doesn't respond.

'So, are there lots of girls from your class here, sweetheart? I imagine the year sevens are out in force tonight. I thought I saw Amelia earlier, and that other girl, Harriet, is it? And isn't that girl who played the flute one of your friends? And that girl who sang the Strauss, don't you know her from somewhere? Maybe we could go and say hi, if they're still here. You could introduce me to their parents.' Andi admires Beth's persistence, her lack of caution.

'Do we have to wait?' Charlotte ignores her mother's enquiry. 'Can't we go?'

'Oh, but don't you want to congratulate Sophie? I want to say hello.' Beth's irritation is clear.

'And I'm sure she'd love to see you all, to thank you for coming,' Andi adds, keeping her voice casual.

'I'm actually not feeling well, Mum.' Charlotte's voice is dull, and Andi notices that she's careful not to look at her mother. That she's careful not to look anywhere in particular. 'Do we have to wait for Sophie? It's late, and I really just want to go home.'

CHARLOTTE

IT WAS A HUGE MISTAKE; SHE REALISED THAT ALMOST AS SOON as she agreed to spend that first afternoon at Sophie's. Charlotte should have just said no to her mother, right from the start; it wouldn't have been that complicated—not in the beginning. The thing is, in the beginning she hadn't properly understood. Sure, she had a fair idea that Sophie wasn't cool—that was obvious from day one—but she hadn't realised what a humungous social blunder it was going to be, hanging out with Sophie, even outside school; how it would change the way the other girls regarded her. In the end it had almost ruined Charlotte's chances with the big three, Harriet, Amelia and Grace, just at the point when her inclusion in their group was practically a done deal.

It's not that there's anything all that awful about Sophie herself, when she actually thinks about it. The first few times their mothers arranged play-dates had been fun. Of course, they're no longer called play-dates, but really, that's what they are, and not all that different to the ones arranged when they were toddlers: the mums surreptitiously checking out one another's levels of respectability, coordinating the drop-offs and pick-ups, the activities, the food. The two girls got on pretty well, found plenty of things to talk about and to do. It turned out that they'd read lots of the same books, enjoyed the same movies and were obsessed with the same lame YouTube clips. She was actually pleased, that first afternoon, when her mother agreed to have a drink with Sophie's mum at pick-up, prolonging her stay.

But now that Charlotte is no longer conspicuously new, now that she has established herself better at school, now that she almost has a real gang and feels like she's working her way back to the centre of things, she doesn't need (and doesn't want) a Sophie hanging about like a bad smell. Now that she understands Sophie's position better, Charlotte is embarrassed about their relationship and resents the fact that their mothers' continuing friendship means that she has to spend time with such an obvious loser. And if that isn't hard enough, Sophie's unshakeable assumption that this means they are *actual* friends, the way she expects some acknowledgement of this at school, and in front of everyone, is becoming increasingly difficult to manage.

Charlotte is conscious that she has no reputation to protect her here. Back at Brookdale, if she'd chosen to hang out with someone like Sophie for an afternoon, it wouldn't have changed anything about how she, Charlotte, was regarded by the rest of her clique. It would have been seen as a quirk on her part, or perhaps some clever strategy, and while the standing of the loser might have been raised temporarily, there's no way Charlotte's would have gone down. It just wasn't possible. But here, where she is still working hard to establish herself, it has the opposite effect. Sophie has nothing to gain from hanging with her, but Charlotte has everything to lose.

None of the other girls has said anything about it yet, but she's seen them exchanging glances when Sophie goes out of her way to greet Charlotte in class, or when she brings over a slice of brownie that her mother has sent, or when she mentions something, anything, that shows they are in some way connected. Having to hang with Andi at the Arts Showcase was a total humiliation. Against Sophie's pariah status her gift means nothing—as Amelia has pointed out, piano is the most pointless musical talent you can have, right? It's not as if it will ever make her famous—it's not like being able to sing or, even better, dance. No one can understand what all the fuss is about. Niamh O'Reilly, who left to go to the performing arts high school, was shortlisted for *The Voice,* and nobody could understand why the school hadn't offered *her* the scholarship. In fact, playing the piano is just another social disability in the eyes of Sophie's peers, and on top of being an actual freak, Sophie is nerdy, unattractive, physically incompetent and socially inept. And she's stupidly sensitive: her round eyes widen and fill with gluey tears if anyone so much as sneezes at her.

Even so, it's hard to actually dislike her. Outside school her enthusiasm doesn't seem quite so daggy, and she has a mad and sometimes wicked sense of humour that isn't evident in the classroom. But all the ways she is okay to be with out of school have to be measured against the ways that publicly acknowledging her as a friend are likely to lessen Charlotte's own status. Charlotte has to do something to distance herself before the others discover the extent of their association. She has to make it clear to the other girls that Sophie isn't really her friend, that she isn't even a distant ally.

And even more importantly, she has to make it clear to Sophie.

Sophie comes up to her one Tuesday morning in the locker room, all sunny eagerness, panting with excitement. If she had a tail she would be wagging it like a puppy. Charlotte tries hard to put her off, looks studiously elsewhere as she approaches, and then turns her back, but Sophie doesn't take the hint, she walks right around until they're practically face to face. There is no way, short of literally running away, that Charlotte can avoid talking to her.

'Mum says you're coming home with me this afternoon?' Sophie's voice is high-pitched and carrying.

'Yep.' Charlotte keeps her face deadpan and her voice low, hoping that Sophie might follow suit.

'And you're all coming over in a couple of weeks for dinner. Mum's making a baked alaska for dessert. She wants to do something American for you guys. It's either that or pumpkin pie. Have you ever had that? It sounds totally yuck.'

Charlotte can hear the sniggers behind her back.

'Uh-huh.' Her voice has dropped to almost a whisper, but Sophie's seems even louder.

'So, will we meet after school? I think we've got different classes last period?'

'Whatever.' Charlotte gives a cool shrug.

'Oh. Okay.' Finally Sophie's voice has lost a little of its volume; she sounds uncertain, slightly deflated. 'Well, I'll just wait near the Honeysuckle Gate again, I guess.'

'Okay.' She turns away decisively, clearly ending the conversation.

Sophie hesitates for a moment. 'Okay. So, do you want to go get some of those cupcakes again? I've got money.'

Charlotte can't bear it any longer, wants her gone right now, but Sophie hangs about for a long breathless moment, waiting for her response. When Charlotte refuses to turn back to her, pulling her textbooks out of her locker ferociously, then slamming it shut, the other girl takes the hint and drifts off slowly down the hall.

When she is finally out of sight, Charlotte hefts the books to her chest and looks across the row of lockers to where Harriet and Amelia are waiting for her. They have watched the whole exchange and stand there smirking. Harriet purses her lips. 'So, you're getting all close with *Slowphie*, are you?'

Her denial is automatic. 'Not really.'

'From what old Slowphs was saying, it sounds like you two are going on a . . . play-date. And then going for dinner, too. *Baked alaska. Have you had that? Oh, yuuuuummmmy.*'

Charlotte ignores Amelia's high-pitched mimicry and Harriet's sniggers, shrugs. 'Well, her mum and my mum, they organised it.' Adds, her voice as cool and unconcerned as she can make it, 'It's not my idea of fun but there's not much I can do about it.'

Harriet gives a small, pitying smile. 'Her mum's that totally weird-looking one, right? Short, curly hair. With the baby? My dad thought she was a lezzo—she looks a bit like a man.'

Charlotte quite likes Andi, but she doesn't hesitate, snorts. 'Yeah. She does kinda look like a man. But a really daggy one from the eighties: all baggy pants and big tops.'

Amelia screws up her nose. 'I heard they live in one of those old terraces in Arnott Place. Slowphie's dad's a policeman, isn't he? I guess policemen don't get paid all that well.'

Charlotte shrugs again, feigning ignorance, lack of interest. 'I honestly don't know that much about them.' Then, eagerly: 'Actually, her mum's doing some sort of work for my mum—it's just business. That's all.' It is a total lie, but a perfect, irrefutable defence. 'Anyway, it's not like we're actual *friends* or anything.'

'You wouldn't want to be. Not with Slowphie. *Ugh.*' Harriet is laughing, but somehow it feels like Charlotte has been given a warning. Or an ultimatum.

BETH

DESPITE HIS INITIAL OPPOSITION, DAN GIVES IN FAR MORE gracefully than she expected. She waits until Drew makes her a formal offer, and then carefully sets the scene for her announcement: lunch, just the two of them, at a busy foreshore hotel. They've tried, over the years, to do as all the marriage guidance manuals suggest and have a date night, or day, at least once a month. This is the first they've managed during their time in Newcastle—thus far all their weekends have been insanely busy, and Dan's work schedule completely full.

The setting couldn't be more conducive to good cheer and relaxation: they're sitting at a table overlooking the glittering water, watching the life of the busy harbour on this sunny autumn day; a bottle of wine, good food. Dan gazes at the harbour scene for a long moment, then turns to her. 'Brilliant idea, Beth. I'd forgotten how much I love it here. I know it's not Sydney, but maybe it's just as beautiful in its own way.' It's true: there is something quite unique about the contrast between the picturesque—the lighthouse perched charmingly at the end of the isthmus, the vivid blue of the channel, the big ships lumbering through the water—and the almost post-apocalyptic landscape on the other side of the bay—the looming silos, the gleaming mountains of coal, the surreal angled skyline of cranes and belts and trucks.

Beth waits until they've eaten to tell him the details of the contract: two days a week to start, eight till four; the reasonable but unexciting pay. 'I haven't signed anything yet,' she says, slightly nervous, though Dan hasn't said a word. 'I wanted to wait and hear what you think. I'll only be working Monday and Wednesday, and the girls don't have anything before five. They can go to your mum's if she's okay with that—it's only a few hours. And if not, apparently they can stay at school and study. I know the money's not that great, but it's a beginning. I'd really like to do it, but I need you to be okay with it, too.'

He frowns. 'I don't understand why you didn't tell me. That you were having a formal interview.'

'Well, it was actually pretty casual,' the lie comes easily. 'We just talked about it over the phone. And then at lunch. And you were so opposed to the whole thing, when I first mentioned it.'

He shrugs. 'Yeah. Sorry. I'm not sure what that was about. I was probably having a bad day. This has all been harder than I thought. The move, the new job. Mum. Everything.'

'So, it's okay?' It is hard to believe—the easy acceptance, the apology, the fact that Dan admits that he has some problems with his mother. It feels like a moment of conciliation, some-how. 'You really don't mind?'

He takes hold of her hand across the table. 'Drew Carmichael is an utter wanker. I'm never going to change my mind about that, Beth. But if working for him is going to make you happy, then I'm happy.'

The girls' response is less reassuring. She tells them both in the car, on the way to Lucy's violin lesson. 'I didn't realise you knew a politician, Mum. Wow.' Lucy is clearly impressed. 'That sounds pretty exciting. What'll you be doing?'

'To start with I'll just be working in the office. Answering phones, taking messages, talking to people. Doing stuff on the net. Later on, I'll probably write things—press releases, that sort of stuff.'

'So what happens after school on the days you're working? Can we just walk home and wait?' This question from Charlotte.

'Afraid not.' Beth keeps her voice casual. 'You know Dad and I don't want you at home alone. You can go to Nanny's for a couple of hours. Apparently one of the school buses goes right past her house. It'll be a great opportunity for you girls to get to know her better.'

'But Mum, that's totally stupid.' She can't see Charlotte's face in the mirror, but her outrage is clear. 'I'm almost thirteen. And Lucy's fourteen. What do you think we're going to do?'

'I don't think you're going to do anything. I just don't think it's healthy for you two to spend all that time by yourselves.'

'And going to Nanny's is healthier how, exactly? We'll probably just watch TV there, anyway.'

'No, we won't. You know Nanny hates us sitting in front of the TV.'

'Then she'll make us do housework or cook or something. It's stupid.'

'We can just do our homework, Charlie.'

'But I don't like doing my homework as soon as I get home.'

Beth intervenes. 'Look, there's no point arguing about it. You're going.'

'But we're not babies. A few hours on our own twice a week isn't going to kill us.'

'And it's not going to kill you to go to your grandmother's either, Charlotte.'

'I seriously don't want to go there, Mum. I'd rather go almost anywhere else.'

'Why? What's the problem? I know she can be a bit fussy . . . she'll make you do your homework, and probably some chores, but that's not going to hurt.'

'It *is* going to hurt, actually, Mother.' Charlotte's tone is suddenly scathing. 'I'm surprised you haven't noticed.'

'Noticed what?'

'That she doesn't really like me.'

Lucy turns to her younger sister, her voice surprisingly stern: 'She does so. You're being silly. Nanny loves everyone.'

'Not everyone. Nanny loves you, because you suck up to her.'

'I do not!'

'It's not like I actually care. It's just a pain. Anyway, she loves you and she loves Dad. She kinda just puts up with me and Mum, though.'

Lucy looks over at Beth. 'That's not true. You're making things up. Nanny loves us all. I know she does. You shouldn't say things like that.'

'It's okay, Luce.' Charlotte sounds disdainful. 'You know what? I don't actually like Nanny much either.'

DizzyLizzy.com

The Real World

I knew it was going to work the moment I walked into the busy office, felt the excitement, the vibe of people who were intent and full of purpose.

In fact, I'd known it from the moment I stepped out of the house, power-suited, hair up, heels on, face done. Right then I felt ten, even fifteen years younger. In all the years of intense full-time mothering, somehow I'd forgotten the singular pleasure of working outside home, of having a separate existence, another raison d'être. I hadn't realised how much I missed it.

And so, in that centrally heated, ergonomic-everything eyrie, with its wall-to-wall glass and views across the valley, where everyone was on a mission, and nobody was grizzling about homework or dinner or asking me where they might find their hockey shin-guards, I felt as if I'd re-entered the world. The real world.

And then, three hours into my first busy day, madly Googling after assuring my boss that *of course* I could do a prezi, no problem!—a sudden revelation. All those things: dinner, the hockey shin-guards, the washing, the vacuuming, the whining—power suit or not—they were all still out there, just waiting for me . . .

So, here I am, back in the real world. It's a busy place.

37 ♥

EXPATTERINGS:
@OzMumInTokyo says:
Haha! Still, it sounds fabulous, Lizzy, shin-guards and all!!!
I'm *sooooo* envious;);) I need to get back to Aus before this mummying thing is the ONLY thing I'm fit for. XOX

    @GirlFromIpanema replied:
    You just need to get those damn bandages off, girl!
    @BlueSue replied:
    And so what if it is the only thing you're 'fit for', @ozmum? It's a
    privilege bringing up your kids, and being able to do it full-time
    is as good as it gets. I always regretted having to go back to
    work long before I was ready. I'm pretty sure my kids suffered,

and I know I did. I think you'll find the novelty of work wears off pretty quickly—and the nine-to-five becomes humdrum in no time at all. No one ever wished on their deathbed that they'd spent more time at the office.

@GirlFromIpanema replied:

Pretty sure no one ever wished they'd spent fifty years of their life cooking and cleaning for no thanks and no pay, either, @ BlueSue.

@AliceBTickled says:

Just discovered your blog, Lizzy. Love it! I'm a long-term trailing spouse too—twenty years this December. So much of what you write rings true for me.

@ShelaghO'D says:

I'm starting back at work next week after only five years away, and I'm terrified! Great to hear your week went well. I'll be posting my experiences too: anirishlass.com

THE GOLDEN CHILD'S TEN LESSONS FOR SUCCESS

LESSON FIVE: ENEMIES AND FRIENDS

Most proverbs are crap. I mean, who would want two birds in the bush, anyway? No moss on your stone? Who cares? Like, it's moss, right? And because the two wrongs are negative, then they do so make a right. I know my math.

But 'The enemy of your enemy is your friend.' That's a proverb that makes all kinds of sense.

Sometimes it can be hard to work out exactly who your enemy's enemies might be. But you can bet your ass that there's someone else out there who doesn't like them.

Or won't.

COMMENTS

@RANDOMREADER says:

Two birds in the bush? Gotta say I kinda like that one ;)

@PROVERBEXPERT says:

Need to know the origins of your favorite proverbs? Visit proverbsource.com for accurate proverbial information

CHARLOTTE

Was it her idea? Or was it one of the others? When she thinks about it later, Charlotte can't remember who suggested it first. She can, however, remember exactly how the subject came up. The four of them, Amelia, Grace, Harriet and Charlotte, were all at her place; they'd taken the big laptop up to her bedroom and were watching an episode of *Doctor Who*, illegally downloaded: the one that features the terrifying Weeping Angels. They had freaked themselves out completely: sitting with the lights out, curtains drawn, the shadows around them deepening and lengthening. Plenty of scope there to imagine some eerie presence in the dim corners and oddly angled recesses of her room: the huge timber wardrobe looming in, the horrible paintings on the walls— gloomy old portraits, landscapes, still lifes—all adding to the freakiness. It culminated in a frenzy of half-pleasurable fear when Grace and Amelia decided simultaneously to enact the part of the angels—moving slowly, one inch at a time, across the room towards Charlotte and Harriet, who huddled together on the bed, squealing, before diving under the covers and begging them to stop. The four of them giggled themselves silly, high on creaming soda and Tim Tams—contraband smuggled in by Amelia, whose mother had no idea that these things were verboten in the Mahony household—and then did it all again.

'Hey,' one of them said when they were spent, had flung themselves head to rump on the bed, a sweaty tangle of bodies and bedclothes, 'why don't we do it for real? Dress up and everything. It can't be that hard.'

There were endless hours of YouTube tutorials they could watch to find out how to do the make-up, create the costumes. It looked complicated, and perhaps expensive, but not impossible. Still, it wasn't going to be something they could embark on spontaneously. They were going to need assistance from parents in the form of sponsored shopping trips, help with make-up and sewing. More than that, they needed a reason—at least *they* didn't need one, would be happy to do it just for the fun of it ('Yes, let's walk down Darby Street in costume, scaring the crap out of everyone,' said Amelia), but parents, they knew, would only cough up if it was for a legitimate occasion. A birthday, then. And Harriet's was next. Doctor Who was a brilliant theme. Or was thirteen too old for themed birthdays? But didn't Daniela Russell in year eight have a Divergent party just a few months before which was a huge hit—even some year ten boys crashed it. Maybe Amelia's brother Jake could come and bring some of his mates—one of them, Rowan Arnold, looked a bit like Matt Smith. He'd be an awesome Doctor. And Janna Rice—she'd make an awesome River Song with all that wavy hair. Harriet's mum would be able to source a Tardis cake, or maybe make one herself (she'd done a tutu cake for Harriet's little sister last year, but it had turned out more like a spaceship, tbh), and surely there were Doctor Who lollies and maybe even cups and plates and . . .

But the four of them would be totally awesome as the angels.

They'd keep it secret, make a surprise entrance, a really big deal—get everyone in the room fully spooked. Oh, and they could play that game: what was it, that lame kids' game? Statues? It would be the best party *evah*. They were almost writhing with excitement just thinking about it. It was the idea of the century. Amazeballs.

Then one of them—Charlotte honestly can't remember who: it might have been her, or it might just have easily been Harriet; it was her birthday, after all—one of them had the brilliant idea of doing a practice run first.

'Why don't we do a rehearsal? You know, test it out on some-one, see if we can scare them?'

'We could wear maybe just masks and get vampire teeth, and no, not the dress-up—that'd be too complicated, but we could do the . . . moves? Like in Statues?'

'It'd be sort of like a dance, wouldn't it? Maybe I could cho-reograph it properly?' This from Grace, always looking for ways to connect her extra-curriculars with her social life.

'We can do it at school. But just to one person, so it doesn't get out.'

Squeals from all four of them: *Yes. Yes. LOL. Yes.*

Then, *Who?*

This part they hadn't even had to discuss: the answer was blindingly obvious, had come to all four of them at once, as if they were no longer individuals, but some sort of hydra-headed multi-limbed beast. This, Charlotte doesn't have to even try to remember. They'd spoken her name in a single breath:

'SLOWPHIE!'

Oh, it had been a good idea, such a great idea. The best.

SOPHIE

Even if Charlotte won't talk to her at school (and Sophie is getting used to the idea that they aren't ever going to be at-school friends), things are usually fine when they are forced into one another's company in their own homes. Charlotte might be cool and distant initially, but after the first half hour or so she warms up and they find something to do together—playing Minecraft or Wii, watching some weird YouTube video. Last time Charlotte came to her place, they spent ages watching one of the senior girls, Gemma Radisson, who set up a YouTube channel that features tutorials on applying special-effects gore. They started out watching her clips for a laugh, though no one would ever think of laughing at Gemma at school. She is a pretty scary sort of girl, stocky and athletic, with a deep and scratchy voice, but the tutorials were surprisingly impressive and the two girls had spent the afternoon giving each other highly life-like slit throats and gaping facial wounds—the blood made from a combination of jam and oil—much to their mothers' disgust.

But this afternoon, Harriet George, who is one of Charlotte's gang from school, has arrived unexpectedly early at the Mahonys' for a sleepover. Harriet, whose father is a local real estate developer, is one of the girls that Sophie likes least. She is tall, sporting, and though her academics are barely passable, for some reason she is kept in the top class. Her reputation among teachers and parents, and even some of the girls, is of a friendly, conscientious, civic-minded girl, chiefly focused on her sport, but this is not what Sophie has observed. In reality she is one of the most poisonous girls in Sophie's year, a subtle, smiling bully. When Sophie first arrived at the college in year four, Harriet was the one who started the rumours that she had some sort of physical disability. And Harriet was the one who coined the nickname *Slowphie*, when she came last in her heat of the fifty metres at the primary athletics carnival.

This particular afternoon, Harriet manages to give a sterling impression of being polite and friendly to Sophie in front of Beth and her own mother, but as soon as the girls are left to themselves, she drags Charlotte upstairs to the bedroom, leaving Sophie with Lucy in the family room.

Lucy looks up from her iPad and smiles sympathetically, but Sophie keeps her gaze on the television screen, knowing that any expression of pity will have her own eyes filling up. She can't help laughing, though, when Lucy says, 'I expect Harriet Kardashian needs to show Charlie her new bra or her gold glitter toenail polish or something equally earth shattering.' Lucy's expression has somehow taken on the vacuity of Harriet's: her small face suddenly extended, jaw dropped, her eyes widened—even her voice sounds like Harriet's, with its affected breathy drawl. The resemblance is uncanny, and Sophie is intrigued. Lucy is usually so reserved, almost shy compared to Charlotte, who, though younger, is definitely the more out there of the two sisters. Sophie has never imagined such a brightly sparkling malice beneath Lucy's benign exterior.

She has noticed, though, that Lucy hasn't made quite the same impression at her new school as her younger sister. Her position isn't anything like Sophie's—she's never seen Lucy skulking in the library during lunch break, for instance—but she isn't popular by any stretch of the imagination, hanging out with a small group of girls who are all relatively marginal to the year nine social scene: not the brains or the pretty girls or the sporty girls or the rich girls—just girls who stay comfortably under the radar.

Lucy grins at Sophie's obvious surprise and then looks quickly back down at her iPad, her fingers flying as she types.

'What are you doing?' Sophie asks shyly.

'Nothing, really. Just commenting.'

'Are you on Facebook? I'm not allowed on Facebook till I'm fifteen.'

'I wouldn't worry. Facebook is only for old ladies these days.'

'What then?' Sophie's experience of social media is limited. She has Snapchat on her iPad, but there isn't really anyone she wants to send pictures or messages to anyway. She follows thirty people on Instagram—friends from her old school, Tess and Maya, her piano teacher and a couple of musicians that she listens to—but she only has half a dozen followers herself. And as with all things virtual, she rapidly lost interest after signing up.

'Just different things. Hey, are you actually watching that?' Lucy gestures towards the TV screen from the depths of her corduroy beanbag.

'Not really.'

'Then come over here and I'll show you.'

Lucy gives her a tour of her own social networking sites. She doesn't have Facebook, but she seems to have every other account in existence: Pinterest, Instagram, Tumblr, Twitter, MeowChat, kik. Mostly, she confesses to the fascinated Sophie, as she moves easily from one app to another, she uses them to see what other people are up to. She isn't actually that interested in posting things herself. 'Sometimes I comment, but mostly I just stalk,' she says, grinning. 'I haven't really got that much to say. I just like listening to other people's conversations.'

She shows Sophie ASKfm, her current favourite. She explains the rules—how the questions are posed randomly by the app itself, or by followers; the way comments and questions can be posted anonymously. She browses through the accounts of girls she follows—girls in various years at the college, most of them familiar to Sophie by name at least—clicking through links from one account to another. Sophie can immediately see the attraction of this particular site for someone like Lucy, and for someone like her: girls who are more interested in observing than taking part in the action. Sophie is astounded by how much the girls reveal about themselves (*tmi!*) online, sometimes continuing conversations and arguments that have obvious real-life origins, and sometimes having discussions she knows they would never, ever have face to face. Sometimes they comment anonymously, but sometimes—shockingly—not. So much of the online action is surprising—such transparent fishing for compliments from girls who Sophie has never imagined would be so needy, comments that are subtly malicious, others overtly bitchy. Girls are constantly asked what they think of others, and then bizarrely—it is so potentially humiliating—ask what others think of them. More often than not getting far more than they bargained for. Their comments are sometimes barely literate and crazily random, swinging between crude and cutesy in a single sentence.

Reading the ASKfm posts is a bit like watching a car crash, sick-making and compulsive in equal measure. Even someone like Sophie can join in anonymously, can have some sort of an impact on girls who barely know she exists in the real world. Being a nobody at school is painful and lonely, but to be anonymous online has a particular appeal, and the prospect of actually participating is tantalising.

Sophie is an almost instant convert to ASKfm. Soon she's spending all her spare time, and occasionally time she should be spending practising or doing homework, on her iPad or her laptop. It's easy, with her mother so distracted with the baby, and her father always busy, to get away with it: nobody's taking too much notice of her. She learns to make the concentrated and casually clever comments that seem to come so easily to some of the others. She has a fantasy that in this virtual world, with its strict structure, its particular etiquette, those girls who have nothing to do with her at school will come to realise that she is more interesting than they imagine. Perhaps this is somewhere she can shine, show another, a more conventional, self. Perhaps they will eventually realise that she is someone they should get to know better in real life, that she is someone worthwhile.

And for a while, it works. Initially most of her conversations are with her old friends from Scone and from outside school, kids she knows from music camp, but her network soon expands. She is amazed by how many girls from her year, some who will barely acknowledge her existence in real life, are willing to follow her online, and excited to see just how many of them will actually comment on even the most banal computer-generated questions. She plucks up courage and comments occasionally on their pages too, sometimes using her name, sometimes posting anonymously.

But somehow, none of what happens online seems to translate to anything at school. It's as if there's some sort of unspoken rule that states that what goes on in the virtual world doesn't count in any real-life scenario. So a friendly *tbh I think you're really amazing* on ASKfm from, say, @MattyMat, doesn't prompt any friendly overture from the real Matilda Matherson at school the next day. It appears that the online world can reveal the inner nice guy as well as the far more prevalent inner monster.

ask.fm/sophiepen

SIGN UP   LOG IN

What are you having for dinner? **BridieS**
Chops and mash and peaz

Thoughts on meeee? **MayaR**
Cool beautiful funny. Wish you were here:(

Fave movie? **LucyMah**
Hunger Games, duh

Best teacher? **CharlotteMah**
Don't know. Maybe Mrs W? She has reaaally good fashion sense. Lmao

Ha ha. Good one **MattyMat**
It's true:)

PAP of when you were a baby **LucyMah**
What's PAP mean?

Post a pic ☺ **LucyMah**
Can't find one:(

Thank god. Bet you were a really UGLY baby **anon**
Probs. Haha.

Stop trying to hang around @CharlotteMah **anon**
I don't!

You shouldent try to be what your not **anon**
That's true. But tbh I don't

Tbh whose the hottest in year 7 **anon**
Don't care

Has anyone ever told you your nose is really big **anon**
Who is this?

Hey Slowphie you should stop trying to talk to @CharlotteMah and @AmeliaCar in class, no offence but they don't really want to b ur friends. No offence juz tryin to help **anon**
Not really a help:(

Hey Slowphie your the hottest girl at hlc. I know that you want to know who I am, but I can't let you know that because if people found out shit would go down, what I'm basically trying to say is that I've fallen for you **anon**
Who is this?

Wouldent you like to no **anon**

Hey, anon—stop being so mean. And @SophiePen, you're really gorgeous. **LucyMah**
lol. I'm not, but thnx

Hey Slowphie—you should try and lose some weight. Just saying to be helpful **anon**
Leave me alone, whoever you are.

SOPHIE

IT HAPPENED TO HER ONCE BEFORE, BUT THAT WAS IN YEAR five, and then her tormentor was Holly Bridgewater, who's since been sent to boarding school in Sydney. Holly was year captain, and seemed to be captain of everything else too: netball, debating, dance, football. And for no reason that Sophie has ever been able to work out, she'd had it in for Sophie from the day she arrived. It began on her very first day at the college, when, noticing Sophie wiping away miserable tears, Holly whispered loudly in the ear of some other girl, clearly and pointedly, about how red Sophie's face was, how puffy her eyes had gone. After that, Sophie tried hard to avoid her, but it was almost impossible when she was still essentially alone, before she had really met up with Tess and Maya and found in them two loyal friends and an effective buffer against the sort of persecution that Holly was already so expert at.

And Holly refused to be avoided. At first it was only little things. She would ignore any comment made by Sophie, pretend she couldn't see her, snigger at her efforts in PE. She would roll her eyes any time Sophie was asked to perform either in class or, as happened frequently enough, in front of a larger audience at assembly—and then cough or sneeze loudly while she was playing. Mostly the nastiness was contained: the other girls were rarely involved, or only as accomplices, some-times unwittingly. It was always surreptitious, and utterly deniable. It never got to the stage where anyone other than Sophie herself noticed anything calculated. There was no point dobbing, no point complaining; it was all too subtle for that. But it ensured Sophie was kept out of the action. Even if the other girls weren't aware of it, Holly's dislike of Sophie spread into an intuited shunning by the rest of the year—including those girls who weren't even part of Holly's inner circle. The implicit politics of that particular year were spectacularly sim-ple: if Holly didn't like you, nobody liked you.

By the end of the year, things had escalated. The torment-ing became more overt and, on one occasion, physical. Sophie was hurrying along the deserted junior hallway one morning, running an errand for a teacher, when Holly suddenly appeared around the corner. She headed straight for Sophie, barging into her with her heavy schoolbag as they passed one another.

Sophie skidded, then slipped and sprawled, her legs splayed at an embarrassing angle on the waxy floor. The other girl stood above her, waiting for her to get to her feet. 'Sorry,' she panted, 'I didn't see you there.' She giggled at the ridiculous-ness of it, and held out her hand as if offering to help Sophie to her feet. Sophie grabbed hold, not thinking beyond the ges-ture, and to begin with the girl pulled as Sophie pushed, but she let go at the crucial moment, just as Sophie was almost upright. Sophie crashed back down again, this time falling heavily, hitting her hip. 'OMG, you weigh a ton!'

Sophie bit her lip, blinked to stop the tears from welling. She pushed herself up onto her hands and knees and then crouched for a moment, too nervous to get up while Holly still loomed. Holly stared down at her hard for a long moment, as if considering what to do, and then smiled. 'You're *actually* quite ugly, did you know that?' She spoke kindly, as if trying to comfort Sophie. 'I mean, I knew you were fat, but I've never really seen your face this close . . . Your nose is really huge and your eyes are weird—it's like you've got . . . what is it? Downs syndrome or something? And your freckles—*ugh*. There are so many of them, and they're so *brown*. Maybe you could have some sort of operation. But you're not going to be able to do anything about your eyes.' She sighed and held out her hand again. 'I'll have another go,' she said, 'but you should do something about your weight. It's *actually* irresponsible, you know—being fat. My mum always says that people like you are totally selfish: you're going to end up sick and cost the rest of us a whole lot of money. Which is totally not fair.'

Sophie ignored her, pulled herself upright, and continued down the hallway as if nothing had happened.

That was the finale of Holly's victimisation program. Other than some residual sneering she pretty much left Sophie alone after the hallway incident. Perhaps she had worries of her own: a few months later her parents divorced, and the following year she left the school, much to Sophie's relief.

Still, for a long while after that, Sophie avoided being alone in the corridor and out of sight of teachers. She told no one; it was somehow too humiliating—not just the fall itself, or Holly's gibes, but her own behaviour. Her own lack of anger, her passivity, the way she cowered, terrified, was excruciating to recall.

But now, in year seven, she's finally stopped noticing whether the hallways are empty or isolated. So when she sees the four girls—Charlotte, Amelia, Harriet and Grace—heading towards her as she's rushing to her music lesson, it doesn't occur to her that this could mean anything sinister. She moves towards them innocently, directs a tentative smile towards Charlotte, who surprises her by smiling back uninhibitedly. Sophie had already greeted her that morning in maths class, and, as usual, was confused by Charlotte's lack of response; she'd feigned deafness, turned away and spoken loudly to someone else. Sophie has consciously decided not to be hurt, thinking that perhaps her friend's coolness that morning wasn't deliberate, and sees this as a good opportunity to greet her again—just a casual hi. She calls out cheerfully, but there's no response.

Instead, the four girls stop as she approaches. They stand absolutely still for a moment and then, as if by design, each of them moves equidistantly across the hallway. Sophie pauses, confused and suddenly nervous. The four of them look beyond her, their faces expressionless. Then they step slowly, in unison, towards her: left foot, pause; right foot, pause.

Sophie looks behind her, seeking help, but there's no one. She could run, but the thought of their laughter paralyses her. The four girls keep moving in sync, eyes distant, faces stern, taking slow, fluid steps across the waxed surface of the floor, coming inexorably closer. 'Hi there,' Sophie says again, her smile quite uncertain now. She can hear how anxious she sounds, her voice high-pitched and sticky. Her mouth feels unaccountably dry. She backs towards the wall as if for safety.

The four girls pause, ignore her, continuing to stare straight ahead for a long moment as if she's invisible. Then they're on the move again: left foot, pause; right foot, pause. They are coming towards her on a slight angle now, pushing Sophie further against the wall, blocking any possible means of escape.

They halt in formation when they are only a few feet away and then stand motionless for another long moment, still looking beyond her. But this time Amelia deviates from the blankness: her face twitches and she makes strange little hic-coughing sounds as if swallowing down laughter. The tension broken slightly, Sophie takes the opportunity to speak: 'Are you guys practising for a play or something?' She tries to keep her words casual, her voice even, but she can hear it shaking.

'Did you hear something, my angel sisters?' Charlotte's voice is monotonal, chant-like. She maintains her blank expression. 'I heard a strange noise.'

'Perhaps a mouse?' Amelia offers.

Squee squeeeee. Little mousie.

They come out of character then and laugh, overpowered by the humour of their joke. *Squee squee.*

Sophie tries to take advantage of their momentary distraction, goes to walk through them, but they are immediately alert, re-forming in a solid line and marching towards her, still in the slow step–pause routine, blocking her forward movement wherever she goes.

'I have to go to my piano lesson.'

'She says she has to go to her piano lesson.' Charlotte's voice has lost its incantatory solemnity, has become arch, playful.

'Imagine that—a mousie who can play piano.'

They erupt into laughter again. *Squee squee.*

Sophie wonders whether she should push through them or run back the way she has come and walk the long way through the playground. Or maybe even miss her lesson altogether. She is late now anyway; another few minutes and she'll be too late.

'How badly does the little mouse want to go, d'you think?' The laughter in Charlotte's voice has gone, replaced by something hard and cold, and the other girls' faces are grim. Sophie looks beyond them, hoping desperately to see someone else approaching, but the corridor is empty.

'There's no one coming, little mouse.' Charlotte's voice has become menacing: low, sinuous, almost a growl. 'No one's going to save you.' Sophie lunges to the right; all four follow, blocking her way. She lunges to the left and they are there too. She tries pushing through them, crashing into Harriet and Amelia, beyond caring now, terrified, desperate to get away. They retaliate violently, following Charlotte's lead; barge into her repeatedly, forcing Sophie back, back, and then back again, until she is right up against the wall. She drops her music bag and the books and manuscripts spill out, scattering across the floor.

The four stand in front of her, panting, their faces red.

'Mousies really shouldn't try to play rough, should they?' Charlotte's voice is syrupy, her smile sweet. 'They should stick to piano.' At this, they burst into wild laughter, take hold of each other's hands, and race off down the hallway, trampling over her music deliberately as they go.

Sophie stays leaning against the wall, waiting for her heart to stop racing, her breath to return to normal, swallowing her sobs. She's glad it's over, whatever it was; relieved that nobody has seen. When she can move, she gathers up her music, some of it torn and all of it battered, and shoves it back into her bag, continues her journey, her steps slow, to the music room.

When she arrives she is surprised to find she is only ten minutes late. Madame Abramova, impatiently waiting, comments on her tardiness, the state of her music, the griminess of her hands, but notices nothing else. 'The eisteddfod is only weeks away. What are you thinking, you silly girl? It is unacceptable that you waste my time when I have so many other students,' she says in her harsh, humourless way. Sophie tells her that she is sorry, that she has been held up in class, that she won't do it again.

ANDI

THE FIRST FEW MONTHS AFTER GUS'S BIRTH WERE HARD FOR Sophie—and some of the difficulty, Andi knows, was of Andi's own making. She had been prepared for sibling jealousy, had known that it might not be easy for Sophie—an only child for so long—to adjust to sharing her parents, in particular her mother. Andi had been warned by her mother, and by a multitude of child-rearing manuals, that the road ahead might be a bumpy one; that unconditional love between siblings wasn't the norm.

What she hadn't expected was that the problem wouldn't come from Sophie, but from herself; from Andi's own attitude, her own feelings of resentment. The day they brought Gus back from the hospital, Andi carried him straight upstairs to her bedroom. She put the sleeping baby down in the readied bassinet—Gus was, in those first few weeks, a sound sleeper, as a result of his mild jaundice. She took a long shower and crawled into bed, almost tearfully grateful for the comfort of her familiar mattress, pillow, blankets; for the smell of home. She was physically spent, both from the unexpectedly drawn-out labour—which had gone on for a good ten hours longer than her first—and from the emotional intensity of the previous few days. He was here at last—this beloved second child, a son— almost ten years after they had first started trying. She could hardly believe that he had arrived safely, intact—as beautiful and as perfect as any baby ever. And right then, released from the hospital, and with a few weeks of cosseting from a quietly jubilant Steve, and the promise of a month-long visit from her own mother, she was looking forward to following her basic primal urge, to crawl into bed and sleep and nurse and sleep and nurse.

It was very different to her experience with Sophie. She remembered those first few days with Sophie being particularly gruelling. She had been numb with the shock of it all: the feeding had been impossible; Sophie had been kept in the nursery in a humidicrib for the first two days, until her oxygen levels normalised. It had all been fraught, medicalised. Andi had been swamped by simultaneous feelings of failure and anxiety, had not experienced until much later (weeks or even months after they were home, when things were running relatively smoothly) anything close to the wash of uncomplicated maternal love that she was already feeling for Gus. She would have been happy to be completely alone with him, to feel his soft uncertain suck, to watch the fluttering of his lips as he slept, to have his little fingers wrap around hers, to trace each vein in his translucent skin, to gaze into those slate-grey eyes that seemed to see everything and nothing. She would be content to do only this; wanted nothing more.

Perhaps if she had experienced the feeling before, she would have been prepared. As it was, the extreme resentment she felt at having to share her time with anyone other than Gus, even Sophie, came as a complete surprise. Sophie had also returned home that first day, having spent the previous couple of nights in Sydney with Andi's parents. Although she ran directly up the stairs after greeting her father, she had waited shyly at the bedroom door rather than walking straight in to her mother, who was sitting up in bed feeding the baby. Andi welcomed her with a smile, but was shocked by the coolness of her feelings towards the daughter who only days before had been most beloved: Sophie seemed suddenly unappealing—a bit grubby and unkempt, her mouth open, nose running, her breath slightly laboured. Worse, she seemed to pose a vague threat to the new and precious life Andi held in her arms.

As if sensing her mother's transformed regard, Sophie stood there, watching them silently. 'Can I sit up on the bed with you and the baby, Mummy?' she asked eventually, her voice soft. 'Can I hold him?' Her big dark eyes were filled with longing.

Andi's response was not as welcoming as it should have been—she frowned and put her fingers to her lips. 'Wait a moment, Soph,' she said. 'You can come in, but just sit on the bed and watch quietly for a bit. He's feeding now and I don't want to disturb him.' Sophie crept over to the bed and perched carefully on the edge. She inched towards her mother, then leaned close to her baby brother, still breathing heavily, her cheeks pink. Andi had to ask her to move back a little, to give them both some space, some light. Sophie did as she was asked, but then slowly worked her way forward again until she was almost on top of them, leaning across the bed towards Andi and Gus, gazing at the nursing child as if mesmerised. As she gazed, a drip of snot formed on the end of her nose and then dropped, splat, on Andi's breast, just millimetres from Gus's furiously working mouth. Sophie opened her mouth to apologise, her hand moving instinctively to wipe the mucus away, but Andi rounded on her, unexpectedly furious.

'Oh, Sophie, you're just hopeless. I asked you to give us some space. You're too old to let your nose drip like that. Go away and blow it properly.' And then, her voice ice cold: 'Sometimes you are just completely repulsive.'

Her daughter's face immediately flushed red, the bright colour moving down her throat and suffusing her chest. Her eyes brimmed with tears.

'I'm sorry, Mummy,' she said, swallowing a sob. She gazed at her mother blindly, wordlessly, for a moment, and then fled, thumping along the hall and clattering down the stairs.

It was an appalling thing to say, cruel and insensitive at any time, but worse at that particular moment. Andi was ashamed. It just happened, she told Steve later, without warning, and was no doubt to do with hormones, was followed by a bout of silent crying. She explained all this to Sophie, later, but despite Andi's apologies, her entreaties, her efforts to make it up to her, it was days before Sophie relaxed around her mother and Gus, almost a month before she again asked to hold him. She spent more and more time alone in her bedroom, before and after school, and the door tended to be firmly closed. Andi knew that on some, perhaps inarticulable, level, her daughter had been badly hurt.

She and Steve did everything in their power to alleviate Sophie's feelings of loss, of marginalisation. They took her to movies, cafes, on numerous shopping trips, even a concert. Andi made sure Sophie was included in cuddles with Gus; she had her help with nappy changes, bath time, pushing the pram.

Yet another part of her welcomed Sophie's distance, enjoyed the luxury of the time she was able to spend alone with Gus, with only his needs and wants to worry about. She knew she was taking advantage of Sophie's slight withdrawal, but her daughter's lack of demands was something of a relief. There were no doubt things happening in Sophie's school life that she should take an interest in—the friend situation was clearly difficult, with Tess and Maya gone. But Sophie was busy with her music anyway, and Andi was hopeful that with all the opportunities available in high school—drama group, art appreciation, film club—Sophie would find her tribe. And then Charlotte had arrived, and a friendship seemed to be developing between the two girls. Regardless, whenever she asked, Sophie assured her that things were fine at school, and Andi took her daughter at her word.

What was the saying? Never trouble trouble until trouble troubles you.

ask.fm/sophiepen

`SIGN UP` `LOG IN`

Thoughts on me **HelenBurns**
Really good cellist. Best voice at camp. Funny 'n awesome

When you played piano at assembly today I was frothing your so hot **anon**
LOL. Ty

Fave character in a book **MattyMat**
Charlotte from Charlotte's Web

Thoughts on @CharlotteMah **HarrietGeo**
Smart funny pretty cool nice. Love her accent!

Thoughts on @Nellshep **BridieS**
Seems pretty nice but don't really know her tbh

Thoughts on @Jadelon **MattyMat**
Don't really know her, seems really nice, haven't really talked but would like to.

@Jadelon would rather suck Mr Steens cock than talk to you **anon**
Who is this?

Are you gay? **anon**
No

If so you should totally stay in the closet **anon**
Not gay

Do you want to lick @CharlotteMah? **anon**
Do you mean like? haha

No. I mean LICK HER CUNT **anon**
Gross. Who is this?

Dont know you but tbh your the ugliest girl in school **anon**
Get lost

Pap of your butt—need to get sick kwik 4 day off school lmfao **anon**
haha

I'd take a handful of sleeping pills if I was as ugly as you **anon**
Who is this?

ANDI

IT'S THE FIRST TIME THEY'VE HAD PEOPLE TO DINNER, OTHER than family, since they moved here. Which is bizarre, Andi supposes, or at least she suspects that most people would find it bizarre. It's not like they're hermits, or that there's anything badly wrong with them, socially speaking. They're pretty normal people. She just hasn't had the time—or, if she's honest, the inclination. Steve has made some vague suggestions, over the months, that they invite this colleague or that from the station, but nothing has eventuated. It seems the entire time they've been here, Andi's either been too busy, too sick, too pregnant—and, since Gus, too royally stuffed—to make the effort.

Steve has just come off night shift, so it's up to Andi to prepare the meal and get the house, a disaster even by Andi's pretty low standards, in some sort of order. She's decided to keep things simple—lasagne and salad, gourmet ice-cream rather than the mooted pumpkin pie—but of course, with a baby in the house, nothing runs quite to plan. Gus, naturally, has chosen this particular day to be difficult, requiring twice his normal number of feeds and determinedly not settling for his two sleeps. When she tries to enlist Sophie—*Can you just entertain him for five minutes?*—her daughter is worse than useless, all her attention focused on her iPad, jiggling the bouncer half-heartedly with one foot and ignoring her brother's whinging.

'Oh, come on, Sophie,' Andi says, exasperated, when the whinging turns into a full-scale meltdown and she is forced to abandon the kitchen at a crucial moment to soothe him. 'You don't get asked to help out that much. You could have made a proper effort. Now I'm going to have to do the white sauce again. Jesus.'

The look Sophie gives her is grave, her words oddly defiant. 'It's not like I asked for any of this, you know.'

'Any of what? Having people over for dinner? I thought you'd be pleased that Charlotte's coming over.'

'Not that. Or not *just* that.'

'What then?' Andi is impatient. Not only does the white sauce need to be redone, she'll probably have to make a trip to the shops to get more flour, and she hasn't even started on the bathroom. She thinks resentfully of Steve, peacefully asleep upstairs. She really doesn't have time for adolescent angst.

'Oh, nothing.' Sophie shrugs. 'Don't worry. It isn't important.'

Andi makes an effort. 'Come on, Soph. What is it? Is there something going on at school? Are you and Charlotte fighting?'

Sophie snorts. 'We're not exactly on *fighting* terms, Mum.'

She takes the comment at face value. 'Well, that's good.' Gus snuffles at her breast, making his desire for a feed clear. Andi gives up and sinks down on the lounge beside Sophie. She sighs and unbuttons her bra, watches as he latches on. When she looks up, Sophie is looking at them both, an odd smile flickering. 'So, what's the problem?'

'Nothing.'

'Sophie?'

'Nothing.' Sophie is quiet, but adamant. She stands up. 'Can I go now? I've got practice to do.'

Andi worries momentarily that she's missed something, but doesn't have the energy to dig any further. She gives her daughter a quick smile, turns back to Gus.

By the time the Mahonys arrive, the house isn't really clean, but isn't entirely uncivilised—the toilet has been given a cursory scrub, bedroom doors have been firmly closed on mess, random clutter has been shoved into cupboards—and the lasagne is bubbling away. Gus has been fed and bathed and is finally content in his bouncer, cooing like a baby from a nappy ad. Steve has had two beers already and is bright-eyed and as ready for socialising as he ever gets. Sophie doesn't emerge from her practice session in the family room until the doorbell rings, but then she seems cheerful enough. After the preliminary hellos she takes the Mahony girls up to her bedroom, the three of them armed with the requisite laptops, iPads and iPhones and a big bowl of chips. The parents get on with the serious business of drinks and small talk.

The men adjourn to the lounge room, ostensibly to keep an eye on Gus, while the women stay in the kitchen.

'Good to see the traditional division of labour is being adhered to.' Beth pours them both a glass of champagne and then perches on a stool while Andi prepares the salad.

'I know.' Andi sighs. 'I just give up. You know, when we had Sophie, we made such an effort to keep everything fair.'

'Fair?' Beth raises her eyebrows. 'Go on.'

'We actually had this chart.' Andi laughs, remembering those long-ago days before she resigned herself to an ever-present sense of unfairness. 'Everything counted: nappy changes, feeding, laundry, cooking. But what it meant was that Steve would have to come home and do everything that needed doing until Sophie's bedtime. Bathing, changing nappies, rocking her to sleep. That was how much more I was doing when we actually measured it. Even counting his hours at work. So he ended up putting up his hand for twelve-hour shifts. And then, of course, it was impossible.' She slices down so vehemently on a cucumber that it shoots off the chopping board and lands on the floor. Beth laughs. 'The whole thing is impossible, isn't it? I think you just get used to the impossibility. And then get over it. Though I imagine it must be a bit shocking, having to get used to it all over again.'

'Shocking? That's an understatement.'

'Especially when Sophie's just hit such an easy stage.'

Andi pauses in her chopping. 'It *is* easy, isn't it? I mean, I've heard such awful things about this age, and I've been waiting. But Sophie . . . well, touch wood, but really, I thought there'd be more stuff going on by now.'

'More stuff?'

'Well, all that attitude business you hear about. It can't be that much fun having a new baby brother. I couldn't have imagined anything worse when I was her age than my mum having a baby, but Sophie's been pretty good about it.'

'Does she help out? With Gus, I mean?'

'She does when I ask her, but to be honest I try not to. It doesn't seem fair to expect her to do too much.' When she puts it that way, Sophie's distance from her mother and brother sounds like a deliberate strategy on Andi's part. 'And anyway, there's only the two of them, so really it's not that hard.'

'It's a cinch, right?' She can hear the laughter in Beth's voice.

'Yep. You're right.' She takes a gulp of champagne, laughs back. 'It's a total fucking cinch.'

They all sit together for the meal: the girls at one end of the table, adults at the other, Gus banished to a dim corner of the dining room, asleep in his pram. The two Mahony girls eagerly join in the adult conversation. Andi is struck by their confidence, Charlotte's in particular, their lack of self-consciousness in stating their opinions, adding their own observations. Their expectation that what they're saying is of value. Sophie watches it all, subdued, but not, Andi thinks, unhappy. The discussion moves from school gossip to town gossip to family gossip, the two women finding common ground in complaints (in Andi's case slightly confected) about their mothers and their constant interference, physical and emotional.

'Oh, come on, Andi.' Steve misunderstands the social nature of her betrayal, is quick to defend his mother-in-law, whom he likes. 'I don't think you're being fair. Your mum's been excellent since you had Gus. You can't really complain. She spent a whole month with you, and she's been up every couple of weekends.'

Andi rolls her eyes. 'How come you can't behave like a proper son-in-law and complain about my mother? What's wrong with you?' Only the two women laugh. Dan says earnestly, 'Talking of mothers, I'd forgotten how good it can be, how much easier it is, having family about. Having Mum around has been one of the best things about being back home.' Beth chokes on her drink, but only Andi seems to notice. Dan continues enthusiastically. 'I don't know if Beth has told you that the girls are going over to Mum's the afternoons she's at work. It makes it so easy—we could never have done it in America.'

'We could never have done it in America because I couldn't work in America.' Beth's voice is dry, unimpressed.

'And it's actually really lame, Dad.' Charlotte's interjection is a little louder than necessary. 'We don't need to be babysat. We could actually just go straight home after school. It's annoying going to Nanny's.'

'It's not that bad, Charlie. She lets us do what we want pretty much.' Lucy chides her sister gently and Charlotte's eyes widen. 'But that's only because you actually want to do the things Nanny wants you to do. I don't really want to bake cakes. *Or* learn how to knit.'

Dan's look is indulgent, his tone wry. 'You're just put out because she doesn't have the internet. Isn't that it, Charlie? You have to put your beloved devices down for a few hours.'

'*Charlotte*, Dad, not Charlie. And anyway it's not just that. It's just . . . it's a waste of time being there.'

'Going to Nanny's is a waste of time, eh? What I'd like to know is what you're spending all your time doing on those gadgets anyway. I'm sure it's not anything useful like homework. What is it? Are you talking to boys?'

'Yeah. Like we actually know any boys. Maybe you haven't noticed, but you sent us to a *girls'* school, Dad.' Her tone is scathing.

Dan turns to Sophie. 'Maybe you can explain it to me, Sophie. I guess you're the same. Do you want to tell me what you girls spend all your time doing on your iPads?'

Sophie looks down at her meal and mutters something unintelligible. Andi is annoyed by her daughter's lack of manners.

'Sophie, you were asked something. You need to look at people when you're talking to them. Answer Dan properly, please.'

Sophie continues to stare down at her plate. Eventually she looks up at Dan and gives a wide smile that doesn't quite reach her eyes. 'I only know what *I* do, and that's mainly homework. I have absolutely no clue what *other* girls do on the internet.' Her eyes have narrowed, the smile has gone. 'Maybe they watch online porn. Or YouTube clips of small animals being tortured.'

'Sophie!' Steve sounds shocked and his expression signals a warning, but the other adults laugh. The Mahony girls both look vaguely embarrassed, as if Sophie has farted at the table. Sophie picks up her fork again, then pauses. She takes a deep breath and looks at Charlotte, her dark eyes unblinking, her voice low and now utterly devoid of humour. 'For all I know they're the types of girls who hang out on social media all night, leaving nasty comments about the kids who aren't quite as popular as them.'

There's one in every class.

She's the one with the fat face and the big butt and the gross flabby stomach that hangs over her skirt. A whole carton of laxatives wouldn't help this bitch. (Beware boys: she ain't got no box gap.)

She's the one who pants when she walks up the steps to the stage. If she has to run in PE she goes so red in the face you think her head is going to explode. #fattyalert

She's the one who's good at something lame like playing the piano. #loser

She's the one who says that the librarian is cool, and that she's happy just to chill there at lunchtime with her Jane Austen book. #gay

She's the one who shows you a photo of her baby brother and expects you to say how adorable he is when really he's cross-eyed and looks like a retard. #fucktard

She's the one who every year invites the popular group to her birthday party and is surprised when none of us turn up. #freak

She wants so bad to be part of it all—to be one of US—and we have to tell her how by just wanting it so bad she's showing exactly why she can never belong . . . #killyourselfslut

Slowphie in her school uniform

Slowphie playing netball. rofl!

Hey—why don't you show us some skin, Slowphie . . .

And ta da! Here's a vid of Slowphie *getting out* of her school uniform. OMG!

Wtf, maybe you don't want to see this, u should keep a bucket handy. Lol.

Hey Slowphie, why don't you die? #endthemisery #forthegoodofhumanity

COMMENTS CLOSED

ask.fm/charlottemah

SIGN UP   LOG IN

Did you see the slowphie website? **HarrietGeo**
Wtf?

www.Slowphie.com **HarrietGeo**
OMG!!!! LMFAO!!!

Did you do it? **HarrietGeo**
Don't be a twat. Hey @AmeliaCar was it you?

No way. That's seriously freaking mean. I'm deleting all my accounts now
AmeliaCar
Way overkillL

She's right. Totally mean. Nothing to laugh about @HarrietGeo and
@CharlotteMah **LucyMah**
@LucyMah your just an old woman

This is some sick shit and your some sick idiotic assholes **MattyMat**
Go fuck yourself.

What's next? Kittens? Old ladies? Babies? **anon**
Go get fucked

Heard your a psycho bitch from way back **anon**
Yeah? Well who the shit are you?

Oleander poisoning ring any bells? **anon**

ACCOUNT CLOSED

SOPHIE

It hardly bears imagining.

If you asked her, the child—because she's still a child, freshly minted, really—would say she's old, too old, that she's carrying the weight of the world on her frail shoulders, that too much is asked, too much expected. Oh, not school work, not music, not the chores she does at home—these are easy tasks, they barely require an effort. Lately they're the only things that set her free from the rest of it, set her free from herself. Because that's the hard part. It's not the doing, it's the becoming, the *being*, that she's finding so difficult.

It wasn't always this way. Once, not so very long ago, it was only last year, although sometimes it feels like a hundred, a thousand years, a lifetime ago—once it had been easy. *Being* required no thought, no active participation. She just *was*. She went to school, she played or she didn't play, she was happy or unhappy, she had friends or she sat alone. It was easy; it was second nature for her to be good, to do her work. Sometimes in the playground it was harder—there were always patterns she was unaware of, undercurrents she didn't understand; sometimes it felt like there were dance steps that everybody else had learned when she wasn't there. But mostly it didn't matter—some days were good, some bad, some ordinary, but there was a solid pulse, a central rhythm to her life, something substantial that she recognised as her *self*, that made sense. But now, nothing feels certain, nothing feels secure—least of all herself.

There have been endless talks at school—about adolescence, about the changes that can be expected. The physical growth of breasts, hair, periods, the fat that will, that already is, accumulating around her thighs, her belly, doesn't worry her too much, though she knows other people (girls, mothers, teachers, maybe even her dad) think it does or think it should. They've explained too—ad infinitum really; she probably knows enough to set up a counselling service herself—about all the emotional changes that are happening. How she is likely to experience mood swings; that she might feel she is on a rollercoaster, up one minute and down the next. And she has, if she thinks back over the last six months or so, experienced everything they predicted. She can remember the excitement when Gus arrived, how she felt almost giddy with love, the joy of seeing him. And then there was the misery and rage, uncharacteristic, unexpected, that she suddenly felt towards her parents—her father's stolid implacability, her mother's irritability, her distance. She still adores her baby brother, but she's sick of the constant attention given to him, the unnoticed sidelining of her own needs. She's sick of all the adults in her life, her teachers as well as her parents. They don't notice anything that's going on in her life, all they care about is themselves.

And she'd started off the year with such high hopes. She'd imagined, at the beginning of year seven, even though Maya and Tess had gone, that things would change for the better: there would be new arrivals, everyone would have matured. Everything would be better. But it wasn't. It was all the same as it had been before Maya and Tess, and she'd gone back to the old misery, the old loneliness—of keeping busy at lunchtimes, of not knowing who her friends were. This time it was worse— because she knew how much better it could be.

And then Charlotte had come, and for a while it had all looked bright again. How she'd hoped. They'd had fun together, she knew that they had. And Charlotte had liked her. But Charlotte couldn't resist the lure of being popular— Sophie understood that; who would choose the alternative? And being popular meant leaving Sophie behind. More than leaving her, it meant showing the world that she wanted noth- ing to do with her. It had been a blow, and the bullying had been shocking, but even *that* was bearable. She'd still had other things: odd moments of fun in class; times when she'd enjoyed being around her family; her music, books, her fanta- sies of the future.

And then that website. The numbness set in the moment she saw it. She had followed the link, emailed to her from an address she'd never heard of, completely innocently: *Concerned friend,* the email had read. Some concern. As she read, it was as if she was swallowing something sick-making, some poison concocted from words; she could feel the familiar bubble forming in her stomach, feel it roiling away. But when she saw the pictures further down the site, and the clip of her that had been taken in her own bedroom, practically naked, in the process of undressing, her body revealed in all its ugli- ness, there was an immediate end to the churning. Instead it was as if everything had drained away, as if all the warmth of her, blood and flesh, all the living matter, had been replaced by ice. By something cold and hard and unfeeling. Something dead.

It was her own fault, she supposes. They'd all been warned about what could happen on the internet by teachers, parents; there'd been films, booklets, visits from experts, police. She should have expected it. She should have realised what would happen if she opened herself up to it. She was an obvious target, a sitting duck. She should have been prepared for it, steeled herself. She should have toughened herself up. But how? What she didn't know about, what nobody had ever really explained, was how it worked. How there was no escape. How, even though it was making you sick, you couldn't stop reading it, watching it. How it followed you wherever you went. How it worked its way inside you and swallowed you up. How it eventually *became* you.

What she hadn't understood was how this would gradually destroy, one by one, all the things that made her herself—and leave only this great, vast void. She is surprised now that, when she bothers to look, she is still able to see herself in the mirror, amazed that she looks the same, looks normal, that there is nothing in her face, nothing in her eyes, to tell everyone, to give it away. When she moves her lips the right way she still smiles, her eyes crinkle up at the corners just as they always have, a dimple still appears in her right cheek. She is astonished that there is no outward indication of the fact that she has gone missing—there's no bright *Empty* sign flickering across her forehead.

But in truth she has been stripped down until she can't see the point anymore, not of any of it. She can still solve any equation the maths teacher throws at her without raising a sweat. She can play the piano as beautifully as ever—but she has lost the feeling. Making music doesn't fill the world with sweetness the way it used to. There is no love in her—not a flicker for her parents, not even for her baby brother. And maybe it's a relief. Because at last, at long last, she doesn't care whether the girls at school want to be her friends or not. She doesn't care what they think about her, or say about her, or even write about her.

None of that matters anymore. There is nothing to look forward to, nothing to hope for.

Why don't you die? whoever was responsible had written. *End the misery.*

Well, why not?

ANDI

IT'S SOMETHING ANDI WILL DREAM ABOUT FOR THE REST OF her life, a moment that she will find herself reliving over and over again, years into the future. This scene will be the one that lingers, the one that will stay with her as no other moment, before or since, of happiness or pain, ever will.

Late afternoon on a Saturday. Almost evening. The house dim and cooling quickly as it always does at this time of year. Gus has fallen asleep in the pram on the way home from an afternoon walk, and though she knows that she will pay for it later—no 7.30 bedtime for this baby tonight—Andi wheels him into a corner of the room, checks he is safely strapped in and warmly covered and leaves him to it. She takes the opportunity to lie down in front of the TV and snooze for half an hour. Saturday is takeaway night, so there is no meal to prepare, nothing else she should be doing . . . bliss. The house is an uncharacteristic oasis of quiet as she dozes off: Steve in the study, reading; Sophie in her bedroom doing God knows what.

Andi falls asleep quickly and wakens with a jolt when one of next door's dogs starts barking. She must have had just the right amount of sleep because she feels, not that horrible wave of thick exhaustion that usually overwhelms her if she falls into a deep slumber during the day, but amazingly alert, full of an unaccustomed (for this hour, anyway) energy. And she is starving. She checks the pram, where Gus is still miraculously out to it, and then wanders through the house, looking for the rest of her little family, flicking on lights as she moves from room to room.

'Hey,' Andi calls out, her voice low so as not to disturb Gus, 'where is everyone? What's happening?' There is a brief muffled response from Steve (everything is muffled in this house), who is obviously still in the study, but not a peep from Sophie. She clomps up the stairs, not in any sort of hurry, slightly disoriented in the half-dark. Flings open her daughter's bedroom door without bothering to knock. 'Sophie. Soph,' she calls, 'what do you reckon, how about we have Indian tonight? We could even . . .'

The words freeze on her lips. She has expected to see what she always sees—Sophie sprawled in the middle of her bed, clutching her iPad, blankets piled up around her, and her bed a sort of island surrounded by a mess of books and papers and music and clothing. Sophie's horizontal storage unit, as Steve likes to call it.

Instead, her daughter's room is impossibly tidy. Her bed is made, the floor around it entirely bare, clothes and papers packed away. Even her desk is clear: her school books piled tidily, pens and pencils neatly upright in their holder.

Sophie lies sleeping in the centre of that perfectly made bed, wearing her new black velvet eisteddfod dress, her auburn curls fanned out on her pillow, her hands folded on her chest. Her daughter, pale and motionless, like a latter-day Sleeping Beauty.

Other moments Andi won't be able to recall—they'll be lost in the fog of shock, buried deep. She won't really remember, though she'll know because Steve will tell her—and because what else would she have done? What else would any mother do?—that she immediately tried to rouse the still child, a gentle hand on her shoulder at first, a whispered *Soph?* She'll know that her failure to rouse her was synchronous with her noticing the empty pill bottle placed carefully (and oh so considerately!) on the bedside table. She'll know, too, that her next attempt to rouse her was more insistent, that she shook her daughter, tentatively at first and then more roughly. She will know that by this time, as the reality of what she was seeing began to filter through, as panic set in, that she had begun to yell, to scream for help, all the while shaking, lifting, pulling frantically at her unresponsive daughter.

She will know, because Steve will tell her it was the first thing he saw when he entered the room, that in her terror she made an attempt to resuscitate her daughter, that when he entered the chamber of horror Andi was attempting mouth to mouth— true love's kiss—that she was trying to force oxygen into lungs that were still breathing, and Steve had to pull her away, make her leave—*Get the phone,* he told her, *call an ambulance.* Somehow she managed to leave the bedroom and descend the treacherous flight of stairs. That she made it to the bottom without tripping or stumbling was a miracle in itself. That she found the phone and made the call, dialled triple zero, managed to give a coherent account of the situation—name, address, age, calamity—was another sort of miracle. Years, days, moments later when the paramedics arrived with their flashing lights and their calm authority and Steve relinquished their daughter's limp form into their care, lowering her onto a stretcher to be carried away, she clutched at Sophie, clutched first at her daughter's immobile face, then her arms, her hands and finally her feet, as they fed her pale, still body into the waiting van.

Steve had to prise Andi's hands away, so that they could shut the door.

But Andi remembers none of this. She will never recall anything beyond that first moment when she knew, in her head as well as her heart, when she understood beyond the evidence of her eyes, that Sophie's peaceful repose was no normal sleep.

That like Sleeping Beauty, her daughter might slumber for a hundred years, and without a miracle she might never wake at all.

PART THREE

ANDI

WHY DIDN'T YOU KNOW?

It's the million-dollar question. The one everyone's so carefully not asking her: the police, other parents, teachers, doctors, her family, even Steve. It was her responsibility, after all. She's the mother—she's supposed to have her finger constantly on the pulse of every member of her family's emotional and physical needs. It was down to her, her job to know these things. And so, too, her fault.

Why didn't you know?

There are other questions, too. A relentless barrage of unanswerable questions that come at her as she sits, hour after hour, day after endless day, stroking her daughter's pale and unresponsive hand, her eyes glued to Sophie's face, alert to all the machines and monitors and tubes that prove to her that even if she isn't showing any signs of consciousness, her daughter is still alive, and that therefore there is hope.

So much she doesn't know.

Why didn't she know about Sophie's unhappiness? She knew, she had always known, that Sophie's social life was challenging: even in infants' school her daughter was a bit of a square peg in a round hole. Her musical talent, the focus that arrived seemingly from nowhere and singled her out from a very young age, despite Andi and Steve's efforts to keep it low-key, normalise it.

But it was in no way normal. Both she and Steve were awed and humbled by their daughter's prodigious talent. Her teachers were impressed, but of course they had seen children with similar talents and their matter-of-fact acceptance of it made things easier. It might last, it might not, but in the meantime they had a responsibility to support her efforts, to provide whatever she needed.

So there was the obvious singularity of her talent, but there were other differences too—for Sophie, fitting in, being just like all the other kids, was never going to happen. Because Sophie was too *everything*: as well as being too talented, she was too clever, too sensitive, too modest, too good. And too plump. She was slow at running, clumsy at ball games, afraid of being hurt, hampered by occasional asthma. Despite her confidence playing the piano—and even as a seven-year-old her self-assurance at the piano, alone on stage for an eisteddfod or concert, was beyond her parents' understanding—her confidence among her peers was fragile, easily shattered.

Andi recognised this in her daughter, accepted her outsider status as inevitable, as a part of being Sophie. Andi would pick up the pieces, sure, when there were problems or dramas—when Sophie came home crying after a bad day at school, when she wasn't invited to a party that she desperately wanted to attend—but Andi never gave her daughter strategies for survival, never involved counsellors or psychologists, never wanted to make a song and dance about it. She assumed that the situation would improve, that Sophie would work it out eventually. She assumed it was no big deal.

She trusted that what they said about resilience was all true: whatever doesn't break you makes you stronger. But maybe Sophie just broke.

Why didn't she see depression and despair in her daughter's eyes? How did she miss the hints that must have been dropped over the last few months, clues to what was going on and how Sophie was feeling? Where were the tummy aches, the missed school days, the uneaten lunches, the crying jags? Professionally, Andi has always considered herself a good observer, someone with the ability to look beneath the surface, reach her own conclusions. How could she have been so complacent, how could she have relied on evidence she should have known was contrived?

Yet even with the benefit of hindsight Andi still can't see that there were any significant signs. Was she just too vague, too spaced out by those new mother hormones to notice? And what would she have done—honestly—if she had been aware that something was happening, that Sophie was being bullied? What has she ever done? Sophie would have known from experience that there wasn't much point discussing it; that her mother would avoid making any sort of fuss, that Andi's advice would only be a variation on the advice she's always given: try to toughen up, try to ride it out, try to ignore them. It was advice given out of love, surely, but wasn't there an element of impatience too, of wanting her daughter to grow up, to sort it out for herself?

What did she not hear? Were there odd conversations that she dismissed mid-sentence because she was too busy, too tired, too distracted by the all-consuming duties of new motherhood? Had Sophie tried to confide and had she rejected her overtures? Andi knows that by some measures she has been slack.

But Sophie is so good, so uncomplaining, so conscientious— her marks consistently high, her behaviour exemplary. Andi actually missed the first year seven parent–teacher night—Gus had had one of his rare bad days and she was dead on her feet. Steve was on shift, miles up the valley, and he couldn't get back to mind Gus, or to go. What will they tell us anyway, she'd asked Steve over the phone. Sophie was performing well in all her subjects and had no problems with discipline.

Steve was doubtful. Maybe it was a good idea to meet the new teachers, he suggested; sometimes they'll tell you things in person that they don't want to discuss on paper. But ultimately it was Andi's call—she was Sophie's mother. And mothers always know best. Except when they don't.

She has since gone through Sophie's most recent report, desperate for any sort of hint, reading between the lines for any suggestion that things weren't as they should have been. But there is nothing there either. *Sophie works hard, Sophie always gets her work in on time, Sophie is a lovely girl. Sophie's work is always of the highest standard.* The only minor negative in pages full of praise: *Sophie is sometimes unwilling to contribute to class discussions. But as this is due to a lack of confidence, rather than subject knowledge, I feel certain this will change as Sophie gets older.*

She assumed that everything was okay because Sophie told her that it was. It was convenient to accept her daughter's assurances. Andi needed peace, quiet, time to concentrate on Gus—and that's what Sophie, always so accommodating, never any trouble, gave her.

And then, there it is—the horrifying possibility. The one that's been staring her in the face the whole time, the one that's almost unbearable for any mother to look at: what if Andi's contribution was something more than just a case of not noticing? What if the effect of Gus's birth, of Andi's redirected focus, was more profound than any of them realised? Andi assumed that the distance between her daughter and herself was an ordinary thing, a necessary part of growing up; that Gus's arrival probably made little difference at a time when apron strings were designed to be stretched. But what if Sophie had felt usurped, discarded? She feels sick when she remembers how the two of them have observed out loud, more than once, how much easier a baby Gus is than Sophie, how much less fraught the whole experience has been the second time round. They didn't mean anything by it, of course they didn't. But what if Sophie, always sensitive, took it to heart? What if her daughter felt less precious? What if she felt unloved? Oh, God, what if?

Andi sits and sits and waits and waits, barely conscious of anything but the soft pinging of the monitors, the flickering lights, the slow rise and fall of her daughter's chest. Oh, there are no answers, no reasons, no excuses. All she has is hope—but that's as faint as Sophie's breath, as tangled as her fluttering lashes.

DizzyLizzy.com

Secret Women's Business?

We used to laugh about it sometimes, me and my girlfriends, the ones with busy corporate husbands, the way we had no idea what it was they actually *did* to bring in the bacon. Easy enough to understand what a doctor does, or a teacher, or even a lawyer, but some of the others—the analysts, technicians, consultants—man, were we clueless.

'F— knows what Terry does,' my friend S once admitted over drinks. 'He's something in management. I think. Or maybe it's IT now. When I met him he was a lawyer and I was a lawyer, and I had a handle on it— but now?' She shrugged. 'Who knows.' She drained her champagne, poured another.

'Then again,' she added drily, 'I have a feeling that he's just as clueless about what I do.'

'What *you* do?' For a moment I thought I'd missed something important, that she'd started working again without telling me about it.

'I mean what I do at home all day—you know, with the kids, the house, running the whole show. It's probably just as big a mystery to him.'

At the time it seemed like she'd hit on something profound. And maybe she had.

But now that I'm working too, certain things have changed. I remain, I have to say, pretty clueless about what D does. He's an engineer so he engineers things, right? And I reckon he's probably pretty clueless about what it is that I do in my job too. If he asks, I tell him that I talk to people, make phone calls, write stuff.

But, I'm relieved to report, our household has now entered the twenty-first century, and what goes on at the coalface is no longer secret women's business. You know, all the nuts and bolts of running a household: how the washing machine works, what the girls eat for lunch, where the dishwasher tabs are kept, where a clean sports uniform might be found . . . all that vital information has finally been shared.

And let me tell you, like any long-held secret, it was a relief to get it off my chest.

29 ♥

EXPATTERINGS:
@OzMumInTokyo says:
Oh, Lizzy. More envy from me. We're definitely in the dark ages here. *Sigh.* XO

@BlueSue says:
Good for you, Lizzy. We've never quite got there—though I have to say my DH tries. I've managed to get him to help with the washing now that he's retired, as well as the occasional bit of gardening, which would have been impossible when he was working. I hope that the next generation has better luck. I wonder sometimes if boys' mothers need to work extra hard, though. I have a feeling that, despite feminism, women still favour their male children in that regard.

> **@GirlFromIpanema** replied:
> Yeah, if there's a problem, it's gotta be women's fault, right? *Faaaaark.*

BETH

It is one of those days. First, the office is in crisis mode. There has been negative press about Drew in one of the Sydney dailies—a pre-election state leadership spill is brewing and some comment he made years ago about the current premier has resurfaced. Beth has forgotten all about these sorts of work days: when the overarching mood is unpleasant, everyone prickly and short-tempered; when the worst aspects of all seem to be on public display. Until today her time at work has been almost only pleasure—most of the staff are smart and friendly, and quite beyond her expectations, a real camaraderie has developed between her and Drew. It's not just the easy rapport that comes with familiarity, all those shared memories of people and places, although no doubt that also plays a part. Beth's surprised to find she really likes—and trusts—him. And the day's events reinforce her respect. In the end, against the wishes of all his advisors, and the party, Drew decides to lie low, to say nothing. He offers no qualifications; no excuses.

Beth plays only a very peripheral role in the day's drama—answering calls and running errands, ordering lunches and coffees when requested, but even so she feels exhausted and oddly despondent. It has been a long time since events outside the family have had any sort of an emotional impact, and she isn't sure that she really welcomes the experience.

After work she picks up the girls from Margie's, and things go from bad to worse. She is running late, naturally, although Margie assures her (of course) that it doesn't matter. 'I'd half planned to go to zumba this evening, but it's on again on Thursday.' Margie understands perfectly, she's been a working mother herself, these things happen. As always there is no possible response—any apology will be swept aside, magnanimously, as unnecessary. Beth apologises anyway, and tries not to prolong the farewells, to hurry the girls to the car, but Charlotte, excited, holds them up, insisting that she read Beth a note from the sports mistress first: she's been asked to try out for the rowing team after the holidays. 'Rowing?' Margie frowns. 'Good heavens. I don't think your parents are going to have time for that, Charlie.'

'It's Charlotte. I don't see why not, Nanny. A heap of other girls do it. And *their* parents work.' Charlotte's voice is haughty, dismissive.

'Yes, why not, Margie?' Beth can't think of anything worse, really, but her hackles rise immediately at her mother-in-law's unasked-for opinion.

'Well, of course I've never had anything to do with rowing— only the private schools do it—but I do know it's a huge commitment. The teams train very early in the morning. Before five, I believe. And then they have regattas all over the place. Every weekend. I suspect it's all hideously expensive. You and Dan have enough on your plates right now, it seems to me. And I think Charlotte probably has enough to do, too.'

'I guess that's something for Dan and me to discuss.' If

Margie notices that Beth's smile is forced, her voice danger-ously polite, it doesn't deter her.

'You're right, it is none of my business. But you know, Beth, it is okay to say no to the girls every now and then. In the long run, it'll actually do them good.' She smiles benignly, handing Beth a portion of the banana loaf she and Lucy made that afternoon.

In the car, Charlotte is scathing. 'You see. I told you Nanny doesn't like me. It doesn't matter what I tell her, she has to be negative about it. I told her about Harriet's Doctor Who party, and about us dressing up as the angels, and she just said it was an awful lot of expense for no good purpose. And that modern parents have more money than sense.'

'That's not really what she said. She was actually talking about the Tardis cake—you told her it cost three hundred dollars.'

'Oh, whatever. You would say that. But do you see what I mean, Mum? And do we really have to spend *whole days* with her during the holidays? Can't we just stay home?'

'We've discussed this already, I have to work. Anyway, I'm sure it's not personal. And maybe Nanny actually has a point about the rowing, darling.' It hurts her physically to say it.

'What do you mean, she has a point? Are you saying I can't do rowing? That's totally not fair and you know it.'

She isn't sure that she does. In many ways, Margie is right: they very rarely say no to the girls' requests. Beth knows this is something Dan's become increasingly uncomfortable about since they've been under his mother's critical eye. He's men-tioned once or twice that saying no is something they need to make a point of doing, on principle—to teach the girls about values, about their own privilege. But almost everything they ask for, everything they want, seems perfectly reasonable. They *need* phones to stay safe, to be in contact; they *need* iPads and laptops for school. Why shouldn't they learn music, dance? Why shouldn't they play a variety of sports? And it's not that she *fears* saying no, as Margie—and, she expects, her own mother—seems to imagine; surely she just wants her girls to be as engaged and active as possible, to be contributing and success-ful members of their community? It's yet another of the paradoxes of modern middle-class parenting that Beth can't bring herself to think about too deeply.

And there is no time to think about it at present. Right now she can think of nothing worse than the prospect of getting up before five several days a week to take her daughter to rowing. Right now she has to go home and make dinner, take an inter-est in everyone's day, organise the washing, lunches, homework, bedtime—when what she really wants to do is curl up in her pyjamas, pour a glass of champagne and watch reruns of *Friends*.

'We'll talk to your father about it, Charlotte. Later.'

But as it turns out, the rowing conversation never happens.

Beth diverts to Woolworths to get a few things she needs for the night's dinner and tomorrow's lunches (but of course she then remembers all the other things they are out of—mayon-naise, ketchup, conditioner, toilet bleach, coffee pods) and dashes in, leaving the girls in the car. She is standing in the queue (why does the queue Beth chooses always seem to take the longest?), her too-full, too-heavy basket hurting her arm, half tempted to just dump the lot and run, when she receives a tentative tap on her shoulder. Out of context, it takes Beth a moment to recognise the receptionist from the girls' school, a short, heavy woman sporting the most hilariously unsuitable name, Carla Caress.

'I thought it was you, Mrs Mahony. How are you?' Her voice is full of meaning.

'Beth,' she says automatically. 'I'm good. How are you, Carla?'

'Oh, it's been such a terrible, terrible day. I haven't been able to take it in, really. That poor little thing.' Carla's eyes are heavy, her face slightly puffy, as if she's been unwell or crying. 'You must be finding it really difficult. You're friends with her mum, someone told me.'

'I'm sorry. I've been at work all day. I'm afraid I've no idea what you're talking about. What's happened?' Beth feels a sudden sinking, a weakening in the knees, ice racing through her veins.

'Oh, God. I'm so sorry.' The woman gives Beth's arm a squeeze. 'I didn't realise. I thought you'd have heard. We've tried to keep it from the girls, and I don't suppose her mother has had the chance . . .' She takes a breath, shakes her head as if to clear it. 'It's poor little Sophie Pennington.' Her eyes fill with tears, her voice quavers. 'She took something. Pills. An overdose. Her father's sleeping pills, they think. On the weekend.'

'And . . . is she . . . ?' Beth can barely think the word, let alone say it.

'She's alive. But she's in a coma. They can't tell yet—they don't know whether she'll pull through.' The woman is choking back sobs now. 'And there's rumours that she took them on purpose. It's not right. That poor little thing. She's only a baby . . .'

ANDI

Eventually Andi asks it aloud, cannot keep the question to herself any longer. *Why didn't we know?* She whispers the words, agonised, full of shame, to Steve as they sit waiting, one on each side of Sophie, both compelled to hold on to her in some way, clasping her hands, cupping her cheeks, only ever reluctantly breaking the connection. Both of them certain that their touch—and not the medication, the tubes and electrodes, the vigilance of the medical staff— is all that is keeping her grounded, earthbound, keeping her with them. Their touch the only thing that's stopping her from drifting away forever.

How can they have loved their girl so well, she asks, all these years, all her life, and yet not known this? Surely they've done everything they could to make her feel welcome in the world, to make her feel at home. So how is it that Sophie felt so bereft, so alone? How could she ever have felt bad enough to do this thing—to wish an end to a life they've sought to make as good and as happy as any human can reasonably expect?

Steve remains silent all through Andi's desperate questioning, his head bowed, as if in prayer, his face expressionless, distant, his jaw tight. 'Nobody ever knows, Andi.' He speaks slowly, as if the words are painful. 'That's the thing. That's the awful fucking thing. Sometimes shit happens, and there's no rhyme, there's no reason. All this pain—for nothing. There's no lesson. No meaning. Dad would tell you that it's part of God's design, that it's part of some divine plan. That there's something to be learned from all of it. But he's wrong—it's all just random. Sometimes, life's just shit.'

Andi understands that Steve is speaking from experience; this is something he knows from his work, and she's seen elements of it too, if from a different perspective. But surely what he's saying can't be true of their daughter. Surely for Sophie—beloved, talented, privileged—life wasn't shit. How could it be?

But then, how to put your finger on what your children really feel? What they're experiencing?

Andi thinks about the mystery of Gus, his infant delight in discovering the world, discovering himself—it seems so simple, so straightforward. She has watched him finding his hands, then working out that they're his to control: waving them in front of his face, shoving them in his mouth. He seems so thrilled just to be feeling himself feeling. Yet the thrill is an observer's surmise; his real feelings remain unknown, as complete a mystery as the existence of God or the extent of the universe. And his delight can turn in seconds, milliseconds even, to rage or to despair.

Sophie. That slippery, red slate-eyed infant who was placed on her chest twelve years ago, cord still attached, squalling, is the same person who lies here now. So deeply known and yet so mysterious. Nothing has changed. Everything has changed. All the potential for being who she is—this child who is at once so intense and so easy, so smart and so innocent, so focused and so uncertain, so obvious and yet so hidden—was present at that moment of birth and, Andi has to suppose, even before that. The twelve years they have been given to get to know her, and she to know herself, have barely scratched the surface of that potential. And now, when Andi tries to really think about her daughter, to fix her firmly in her mind, she seems somehow elusive, simultaneously transparent and opaque, as unfathomable as when she first arrived. We are each of us, she thinks, a miracle of solitude, unknowable to others, and surprising to ourselves.

What if, she wonders, watching the even rise and fall of her daughter's chest, what if it was there, right from the beginning? What if, right from the beginning, all the problems of Sophie's infancy—the initial months of crying, her inability to settle, her refusal to sleep without flesh-to-flesh contact, her difficulties taking the breast—what if they meant something? What if they added up to something of substance, what if they weren't, as she and Steve were constantly assured by infant nurses, doctors, parents, friends, just commonplace, temporary, infant difficulties? What if, as her parents, they'd failed to see symptoms, neglected to find a cure for some latent, but potentially fatal defect?

What if the person Sophie has become, the Sophie they thought they knew—obedient, cheerful, talented, focused, a bit shy, awkward physically, but still within the range of 'normal'—is just an act that they've accepted with relief, a mask worn to satisfy her anxious parents? What if her entire conscious life has been a desperate cover for an essential, elemental void, existential suffering, a despair that can never be eased, regardless of their infinite love?

What if?

THE GOLDEN CHILD'S TEN LESSONS FOR SUCCESS

LESSON SIX: REVENGE AGAIN

Sometimes revenge doesn't have to be about anything, really. Because why not?

It's because they're them. Because you're you. Because it feels good. Because you want to win.

Because they exist.

COMMENTS

@RANDOMREADER says:

Or because yolo? I thought that was the answer to everything.

CHARLOTTE

HER FATHER GIVES HER THE IDEA. HER MOTHER HAS MADE plans to visit Sophie the following day, but as far as she knows there's been no suggestion that Charlotte should go. Charlotte herself hasn't even considered it until she overhears her parents arguing in the kitchen as she's running back upstairs to her bedroom from the shower. She should have brought her clothes down, it's freezing in the bedrooms, and she hates the gloomy upstairs rooms at night. Hates them even more than during the day, if that is possible. Added to that, the stickiness of the grimy bedroom carpet on her bare feet, damp from the bath, makes her feel slightly ill.

'Oh, for Christ's sake, she's your friend's daughter. And she's Charlotte's friend. It *is* upsetting. There's no way you can get around it. *Life* can be upsetting. You're wrong to try and protect her from that. It's giving her a false sense of . . . everything.'

'But shouldn't we try to protect them? Isn't that our job? Sophie's unconscious. It'll be upsetting for Andi and Steve. They shouldn't have to worry about other people's kids right now. I don't understand why you think she should come too. I can't see how it will achieve anything, for either of them.'

'It's not supposed to *achieve* anything, Christ! Sometimes you really do sound like some idiotic self-help book, you know.

We're not trying to *achieve* anything, we're just talking about a really old-fashioned concept—doing the right thing. Sophie was, Sophie *is*, Charlotte's friend; Sophie is sick in hospital; Charlotte should visit her. See, it's really quite simple.'

'She's only known her for a few months, for goodness sake. Why make it all worse? It's already upsetting enough. You know they've got counsellors seeing all the girls in the class.' Her mother speaks calmly, quietly, but Charlotte can hear the anger bubbling just under the surface. 'And what if she dies? What then? Do we have to send her to the funeral? Is that another experience Charlotte really needs to have, Dan?'

Charlotte scurries away then, tiptoes up to her room, and quietly shuts the door. She's heard enough, doesn't want to hear her father's response. She stands naked in front of the speckled wardrobe mirror. Her body has a greenish cast in the tepid light, the room's timber lining seeming to soak up all the brightness. The ancient mirror somehow makes her look wider, shorter, the spotty squatness reminding her suddenly of Sophie. She gazes at her reflection, lets her jaw hang slightly, opens her eyes wide, pulls her hair back off her face, and pushes the flesh on her chest closer to make her breasts bigger. There is no way to create a real resemblance: Charlotte is tanned where Sophie is pale, and her body is bony and angular—even when she pushes her stomach out, hunches her torso down, there is not enough flesh to make her look plump. She pulls on the Dolce & Gabbana pyjamas, gingham shorts with a white poplin vest, that her mother bought her during a trip to New York. They are totally impractical for winter wear in this cold house, but she wears them whenever she needs a physical reminder of her life before here. Her *real* life.

Charlotte arranges herself carefully, lying diagonally across the bed so she can see herself in the mirror. She scoots under the blankets, pulls them up sharply, tight under her neck, then wriggles her arms free. She lifts one of her hands in the air and then lets it drop heavily, a dead weight. She clasps both hands loosely over her abdomen and lies still, eyes closed, makes herself calm and cold, her breath shallow, tries to think of nothing, to think of clouds. To be like Sophie in her comatose state, suspended somewhere between life and death. She holds her breath for a moment then sits up slowly, reaching for her iPad. She opens the camera and lies back down, this time arranging her one free arm on top of the blankets, and angles the camera properly. She closes her eyes again, slows her breathing, takes a shot. And then another. The light isn't quite right and her expression is stupid, it looks like she is about to laugh. She rearranges herself, makes her face as blank as possible, and tries once more. This time she gets it right: captures the arm, the blanket, the side of her face in repose. She looks alarmingly but interestingly absent.

Charlotte thinks she would quite like to visit Sophie, to see what she looks like. She wonders what would happen if she were to take Sophie's hand—would it be stiff or floppy? Would there be some sort of response? She would like to feel whether Sophie's skin is warm or cold, to peel back her eyelids and see what lies beneath. To see if Sophie's still in there. To find out if she's ever coming back to tell them where she's been.

The next morning, instead of taking her breakfast into the lounge room—the only room in the house that is even vaguely warm—Charlotte squeezes in beside her mother at the ridiculous little kitchen nook. Her mother is drinking tea, reading something on her iPad. She gives her daughter a sleepy smile, smoothes back her hair. 'Did you sleep well, honey?'

Charlotte shrugs. 'Not really. The mattress is *sooo* lumpy. You know, I can actually feel the springs digging into me. And I was cold in the middle of the night. I had to get up and put on a tracksuit.'

Her mother laughs. 'Poor princess. I know it's not exactly a New Jersey winter, but you can't really expect those pjs to keep you warm.'

Charlotte grins, but says nothing. She waits for a few minutes, then says casually, between mouthfuls of toast: 'Do you think it'd be okay with her parents if I visit Sophie?' She pauses, makes her face as solemn as she can, looks intently at her mother. 'It's just . . . I think it's important. We're friends, Sophie and me. Actually, I think I'm pretty much her *only* friend. I should go and see her, don't you think?'

Her mother looks surprised and vaguely worried. 'You want to go to the hospital? I don't know. I'm not sure that it would be a good idea. It might be upsetting.'

'Upsetting? You mean for her parents?'

'No. I mean for you. I'm not sure that you really need to see her. I think it might be very . . . confronting. Sophie will be wired up to monitors. She won't really look like herself.'

She tries to keep her interest hidden. 'What do you mean? Is she, will there be marks on her or something? Will she look terrible, like those ice addicts we saw on that show?'

'Oh, no.' Her mother smiles uneasily. 'I'm sure it won't be anything like that. She'll probably just look like she's sleeping, but . . . she'll have tubes attached, and, well ...' Her mother sits up straight, clears her throat. 'Darling, I'm finding it terrifying enough, going to see her. There's Andi and Steve too, they might be . . . emotional. So I'm just not sure that it's something you need to experience.'

Charlotte remembers her father's comments. 'But don't you think I should? It would be the right thing to do, wouldn't it?' She plays her trump card: 'Wouldn't her mum and dad really like it if I came? Wouldn't it be really good for Sophie to have a friend visit? I mean, who knows—maybe she can actually hear . . . Isn't that what they say when people are in a coma? That you should talk to them because they might be able to hear you?'

She can sense her mother's unwillingness, but there's really nothing she can argue with. Her mother takes a sip of tea, shakes her head, surrenders with a sigh. 'I guess you're right, darling. It is the right thing to do. I was going to go this morning, but we can call in this afternoon after school.' She pauses, surveys Charlotte for a long moment. 'You really *are* a good girl. So thoughtful. I'm afraid I underestimated you.' The smile she gives is full of pride.

Charlotte swallows her triumph, her excitement. Produces a sad smile. 'I know it's not going to be good, but if it was me, I'd like to think my friends were visiting even if I couldn't actually see them. I'd like to think they cared. Maybe we could take something for her—maybe we can call in and buy her a cupcake, even if she can't eat it.'

Then, as it occurs to her: 'Do you think Sophie will have lost weight? She's probably not all that fat anymore is she?'

ANDI

IT IS MAGICAL THINKING, SUPERSTITIOUS NONSENSE, illogical—Andi knows all that, but at first she doesn't care. Surely if she can concentrate hard enough on Sophie getting better, regaining consciousness; if she can channel her wishes and her love and, right now, her prayers in a steady stream towards her daughter, surely she'll recover. Surely the sheer immensity of Andi's love will force her daughter back to life.

But eventually it exhausts her: the endless hovering, the eternal watching of the monitors, noting every change, every slight movement—the flicker of an eyelid, the dilation of a nostril, the slightest motion of her lips, all the tiny jerky reflexive movements. She can't bear the sudden surge of hope, the crashing disappointment, a thousand times a day. She can't handle her own desperate attempts to read the faces of the nurses and doctors, though she has come to understand their inscrutability, their blankness. They are not cold, as she first thought, but considerate. Sophie's prognosis is still not entirely certain, and the staff know that they are being watched for signs, for clues. They don't want to give Andi the wrong ones, unwittingly.

She begins to look for distractions, for ways of forcing herself to look away, even if just for a moment. The initial police visits provided some sort of relief, and their questions, though painful, gave her the opportunity to think about another Sophie. Unlike the medical staff, whose concerns are only with the here and now, what the police needed was a picture of the living Sophie, not this silent mannequin-child. But their official visits were done with quickly, once they established that there was no parental negligence to investigate. That it isn't a matter for the law, but something for doctors and—God willing—psychologists to deal with. The police are still a constant presence, but they're visitors now, Steve's colleagues, and their sympathy and concern only reinforce the horror of her current reality.

But out in the real, the living world, there are distractions—countless things that need doing. For one thing, Gus needs proper maternal attention. She tries to keep him out of Sophie's room as much as she can, something she's tried to hide from Steve, half convinced now that her relationship with Gus played a part in Sophie's unhappiness. The poor baby has spent most of the last few days in exile at the hospital crèche, and though he seems content enough (cleaned, cuddled, entertained), Andi knows that some sort of maternal focus is absent. Even during the brief moments when she goes to the nursery to feed him, Andi isn't really there, she doesn't really connect with him in the way she should, in the way she ordinarily would. Something essential is missing in her response to him, and she worries that this will have an effect on him later.

So, on the fifth day of that first terrible week, torn, but knowing it is necessary, she makes herself go home for the entire afternoon, taking Gus with her. She spends some time just talking and playing, doing a fine impersonation of a normal happy mother. She croons, sings, dandles him, plays peek-a-boo—all the things she would normally do. She takes him out in the pram, walks up and down the hilly streets, pushes him through the city and along the foreshore, avoiding her usual route. She doesn't want to see anyone she knows, anyone who is likely to ask in hushed and uncertain tones after Sophie, to see their concerned expressions—desperate not to judge, but so patently glad not to be in her place.

Back from her walk, Gus soundly sleeping in his cot, there are calls that need to be made, easier somehow here than from the hospital, people who need to be kept up to date: family, friends, the school. She has had to beg her mother not to come up. Even though she would have appreciated her help with Gus, she couldn't bear to see her own grief mirrored in her mother's face. Couldn't bear her probing, either. Steve's father is too old to visit, but he phones three or four times every day. Both she and Steve find it difficult to listen to his consolations— *Whatever happens is for a purpose. This is God's will*—words spoken through tears, his old man's voice light and brittle, but still full of conviction. There have been cards, flowers, but their only visitors, other than Steve's police friends, have been Beth and Charlotte. Though there can be no real relief, Beth's warmth and concern were a balm; their company provided some sort of reassurance that things would eventually return to normal.

Before she makes the calls, she plays the messages on the home phone. There are dozens of them—so many people offering assistance, love, prayers, food—and she is barely conscious after a while of who they are and what they are saying. It's not that she doesn't appreciate the outpouring of sympathy, the support—it's that her brain doesn't seem able to process, or even really acknowledge, their sometimes very obvious distress. So puny compared to her own. But then, the last message of all, a little bit different, makes her listen.

'Andi. Steve.' There is a long pause as if the caller is thinking about disconnecting, or perhaps just waiting for someone to pick up.

'I hope . . . We all hope . . . We can't think how terrible a time this is for you right now.' She is used to the tentative nature of the calls, the quavering voices, the inability to speak coherently, but from the outset this message seems more stilted, more uncomfortable, than any of the others. In fact the woman sounds terrified. If she'd answered, Andi knows it would have been hard to resist the urge to soothe the speaker, calm her down, reassure her, regardless of the actual news.

'And I don't want to . . . none of us wants to make anything worse or to make things . . . any harder. But . . .' The voice is unfamiliar.

'If you could . . . look, if you could ring me back. There's something you should know. The girls have been telling me. I'd rather not leave a message. About what happened to Sophie. If you could ring me. Please. Any time. Sorry.' The woman leaves two numbers, a home phone and a mobile, but forgets to say who she is. Andi replays the message, but there are no clues. No names. Andi assumes she is one of the class mums. Other than a few exceptions, they are something of an amorphous mass, even though she's probably met most of them at various school dos. She tries to put the voice to a face, but it is hopeless—she can't even recall most of the girls in Sophie's class right now, let alone their mothers. The message had come through the night before, late, past nine, if the machine's clock is accurate. Andi really doesn't want to call her back. There are others whose claims are greater, whose calls she really should return first, but there is something in this woman's voice, a strange urgency, as if she needs, rather than wants, to talk to her.

215

Andi dials the house number. If there is a machine she won't leave a message. She prays for a machine: her heart is racing; she doesn't know if she can speak; she can barely breathe. But the call is picked up almost immediately.

'Anna McLachlan.' Although there is nothing tentative in the greeting—it is brisk, businesslike—it is clearly the voice from the message. Anna McLachlan. It doesn't ring any bells.

'Mrs McLachlan.' Her own voice is low, devoid of intonation. 'This is Andi Pennington. You left a message on my machine. Asking me to call.'

'Andi. Oh, God.' The woman's tone changes in an instant. 'Oh, God. I'm just so— We're all so sorry. If there's anything I—'

'Look. I don't want to be rude, but I'm not sure who this is, I mean who you are. It's all such a—'

'Oh, God. Please don't apologise. I understand. You must be . . . You probably don't actually know me as Anna McLachlan—it's my work name. My daughter, Bridie, Bridgette Stevenson, she's in Sophie's class. We've met a few times, at band camp and concerts, but I don't really do much school stuff.' Then, oddly defensive, 'I work full-time.'

Andi remembers Bridie well enough—she plays piano too— but she can't remember ever meeting her mum, let alone speaking to her.

'Oh, right. Look, I'm just home from the hospital to shower and change. I need to get—'

'There's been no change?' The woman's words sound as if they've been reluctantly dredged up, as if she is dreading the reply.

'No. She's still the same.'

'But she's stable?'

'Her heart's still beating, if that's what you mean.' She knows it is cruel, but doesn't care, already resenting having to speak to this virtual stranger.

'Look, I'm so sorry to bother you at this time.' The woman sounds embarrassed rather than hurt. 'And I won't keep you. But what I want to say . . . it's difficult, and I don't know if I should. But I've spoken to some of the other girls' parents. And my husband. He's a lawyer—well, actually we're both lawyers, but he knows a bit more about this sort of thing.'

'Anna.' She doesn't bother to mask her growing anger at the woman's rambling. 'Can you just tell me whatever it is you need to tell me? I really can't handle any more suspense.'

She hears the woman take a deep breath, as if to calm herself—or give herself the necessary momentum.

'It's about what Sophie . . . did. About everything that happened.'

'What do you mean? We already know what happened.' The story they've told everybody but a select few is that Sophie accidentally took some of her father's sleeping pills, mistaking them for headache tablets. It isn't a perfect story, far from it, but Andi is shocked that anyone, especially a virtual stranger, would dare to openly contradict it. Surely it is their right to keep their daughter's actions private?

'I know you don't want to make a big thing of it, and I understand why. But the girls . . . as you can imagine, they're all extremely upset. And there's been talk. Lots of it. About why she did it. About what's been going on at school.'

'At school? But we thought . . . Sophie hadn't said anything. We thought it was just . . . a combination of things. Nothing in particular.'

'Well, from what Bridie has told me, and her best friend, Matilda—do you know Matilda Matherson? Anyway, it doesn't really matter. What's important is what's been happening to your daughter.'

'What's been happening?'

'According to the girls, Sophie has been bullied. Very badly bullied.'

'Bullied? I don't understand. Who by?'

'It's been a few of them—a particular gang, apparently. Bridie and Matilda—they don't belong to that group—they're not allowed in apparently. Not that they care. But Sophie, she was being systematically bullied. At school. And online. On one of those social media sites they're all mad about. From what the girls say it was horrendous—almost torture.'

'And who are the girls in this group? Who was doing it?'

There is a long pause.

'Look, this is really hard, because I know . . . I know you're friends.'

'Friends? What are you talking about?'

'Your family and the Mahonys.' The woman pauses again. 'I'm talking about Charlotte Mahony. There were some other girls involved: Harriet George, Amelia Carrington, Grace Doherty, but apparently Charlotte's the main . . . perpetrator. The girls told me that she's done some dreadful things to your daughter. They're pretty sure it was Charlotte who set up that hideous website.'

'Website? What website?'

'You didn't know about it?'

'Oh my God. No. What sort of website?'

'It was . . . about Sophie. There were photos. And a film clip.'

'A film clip? I don't understand. Of what?'

'Of Sophie.' She can hear the woman take a deep breath. 'She was undressing, apparently.'

'Undressing? In front of a camera? Sophie?' It's unimaginable. Beyond Andi's comprehension, and way beyond her understanding of her daughter. 'My God. What . . . Did you see it?'

'No. I didn't. The website's gone. The girls seem to think the site was taken down as soon as she . . . when Sophie . . . But apparently someone got a screenshot. One of the other girls in the class. So there's evidence.'

'A screenshot?' Andi is having trouble understanding what the woman is telling her, what it all means. 'And what were the other things? You said they'd done other terrible things?'

'Oh,' the woman sounds flustered suddenly, 'I really don't know. Other than the online stuff. I'm not sure about the details. I imagine it was just the . . . the usual girl stuff.'

'Of course. The usual girl stuff.' Andi feels weak and suddenly sick, wondering what exactly counts as usual in this situation. Just the usual torture. She imagines the unbearable sadness and loneliness that Sophie must have felt, suffering all this in silence.

'But that's not all.' The woman is obviously warming up to something else, something bigger.

'What else?' The words have to be forced out.

She speaks in a rush. 'Apparently Charlotte told her to do it. On the website. She more or less told her to kill herself.'

Andi can't speak. She is reeling with the hugeness of it—it doesn't, can't, won't sink in. She feels hot and then cold and then hot again, but the woman hasn't finished with her, not yet.

'And that's not the worst of it.'

'Not the worst of it?' Andi almost laughs. But wait, there's more—let me drive these steak knives straight through your heart.

'No. Apparently . . .' The woman's voice drops to a whisper, as if she is in danger of being overheard. 'Apparently, it's not the first time. I don't have any details, but apparently Charlotte's done something like this before.'

DizzyLizzy.com

There's No Place Like Home

I was chuffed to be invited to write a guest post for the fabulous TrailingWife.com about the ten things I most miss about life in New Jersey. Not only an exciting moment in my blogging career, but an easy task, I hear you say.

But to be honest, I'm having trouble. Real trouble. You see, every time I come up with one thing I miss, a whole series of related memories springs up, hydra-like, and my list never gets made. For instance, whenever I think about my favourite NJ food market, I remember how long it took me to get used to shopping there. For so long the grocery stores in the US seemed foreign: the food was in the wrong aisles, all the packaging was unfamiliar, I could never get a handle on the names of things. Or the weights. Now I feel almost as alien in the local Woolworths—I could be lost in an Arab souk. I miss the paper sacks and having my groceries carried out to the car. I miss the extreme politeness of the staff and being called *ma'am.* I miss certain brands of tinned food, packaged food, the particular mayonnaise we always had on tunafish sandwiches. Oh God, I miss the tunafish sandwiches, and who says *tunafish* here?

The missing is endless in a way I hadn't imagined it would be. And it's painful. It had never occurred to me that all these seemingly inconsequential domestic things would seem so important. I had assumed that being back where the places and people are familiar would make up for it. The trouble is, I guess, that they aren't nearly as familiar as I'd hoped . . .

And that's just the first one. I've got another nine to go ☹
41 ♥

EXPATTERINGS:
@BlueSue says:
I hope it passes, Lizzy, but there are no guarantees. When we were away I always felt that I could never be my real self. I always hoped that once I got home I'd feel normal and happy again. But it wasn't to be—we'd stayed away so long I ended up feeling like a foreigner in my own country.

@OzMumInTokyo says:
Oh, yes! It's all those little things. I remember when we arrived here from Sweden. I thought I wouldn't miss any of it, but I look back fondly on so many things now: the endless summer nights, the houses, the people, the schnapps, even the cold . . . Maybe it's a case of grass is always greener? Or rose-coloured glasses?

@TrailingWife says:
Really looking forward to your post, Lizzy. Hope you find those other nine things!

    @DizzyLizzy replied:
    Almost done & dusted ☺
    @ShelaghO'D replied:
    When will the post go up @TrailingWife?
    @TrailingWife replied:
    Scheduled for first Monday of next month. And hey—I'd love one from you, too. Shoot me an email linda@TrailingWife.com

@AnchoreDownInAlaska says:
I'm *sooo* looking forward to missing things about Alaska. If I'm missing them, I won't be here. LOL.

@TrueBelieverMom says:
If you accept our Lord Jesus into your heart you will always be at home. May God bless you and all your family.

    @GirlFromIpanema replied:
    Wherever you lay your hat, eh, @truebeliever? LOL

BETH

'Mum.' It is immediately apparent from that one syllable—voiced with such breathless portentousness—that Lucy has something important to tell her.

Beth is sitting up in bed with her laptop, working on her post for TrailingWife.com and doesn't want to stop. It is past ten and she had imagined both girls to be asleep long ago; she checked on them before getting into bed herself, and though she physically tucked Charlotte in, kissing her forehead and smoothing back her hair, she hadn't entered Lucy's room, reluctant to disturb her light-sleeping daughter. Instead, she stood in the doorway and watched the slow rise and fall of Lucy's chest, assumed she was asleep. Beth guards her hour or two alone in the evenings jealously, especially on the nights that Dan is away, insisting that both girls are in bed at eight-thirty, with lights off by nine. All her non-work days are spent on the house—finishing the painting, choosing fixtures, nego-tiating with tradesmen. Nights are the only time she has to spend on her blog.

Later, it will seem remarkable, almost bizarre, that her writ-ing—in such an ephemeral here-one-minute-gone-the-next medium, unpaid and unacknowledged in the 'real' world, and practically a secret activity at that—should ever have occupied such a great deal of her time and her consciousness. Later, she will wonder whether her focus on the blog—begun as a way of satisfying her desire for something beyond her family, beyond the girls—meant that she missed certain signs. Perhaps if she hadn't been so preoccupied, with her work for Drew in addition to her online life, she'd have been aware of what was going on with Charlotte—or at least noticed certain things that in retrospect were there to be noticed.

But this particular night, she welcomes the opportunity to focus on the small stuff, to have her mind elsewhere, to not have to think about Sophie, about the uncertainty, about Andi and Steve's pain. The blogpost is trivial, but it is a welcome distraction.

'Mum?' Lucy's voice is insistent and Beth looks up at her elder daughter, who is hovering anxiously by the door. 'Can I come in and talk to you for a moment? It's really important.' She speaks quietly, looking behind her as if worried that she'll be overheard.

Beth sighs and closes her laptop, gesturing for her to come in. 'Why aren't you asleep? It's so late. Oh, come on. Come over here.' She pats the side of the bed, and Lucy sits down beside her, frowning, clearly upset. 'What's up?'

Lucy bites her lip, rubs her hand across her eyes.

'Darling? What's wrong? Is there something going on at school?'

Lucy looks towards the door then whispers, her head bent, not meeting her mother's gaze. 'It's not me. It's . . .'

She speaks so quietly that Beth has to move closer. 'I can't hear you. Lucy?'

'It's about Sophie.' Her daughter's eyes are shiny with tears, her bottom lip quivers.

'Oh, sweetie. Luce.' Her own eyes fill in response. She pulls her daughter towards her, hugs her fiercely. 'Oh God. I know it's terrifying, but I hadn't thought how scary it must be for you. But at the moment Sophie's stable and the prognosis is—'

Lucy interrupts. 'No.' Her voice is fierce. 'No.' She pushes away from her mother. 'It's not that.'

'What is it then? What's wrong?'

Lucy takes a deep breath. 'It's just . . .' She pauses, swallows. Begins again. 'It's what they're saying at school, what the girls are saying about why she did it.'

'Why she did it? You mean . . .'

'Why Sophie took those pills.'

'They just don't know, darling. Honestly. Nobody really has any idea. They're sure it wasn't deliberate, though.' It is a necessary lie, but still Beth feels guilty. She tries to speak with conviction. 'Most likely it was an accident. Sophie had a big exam coming up and then the eisteddfod, and Andi thinks she might have been having trouble sleeping. She often did. Does. She might have just wanted a good night's sleep.'

'But that's the thing.' Lucy is holding Beth's arm so hard that it hurts, her thin fingers strong, pushing into her wrist. 'Nobody at school thinks that. They all know what really happened.'

'What do they know? What's the real reason, then?'

'It was . . .' Lucy looks towards the door again. Lowers her voice. 'They were bullying her. Charlie and her friends. Her gang.'

'Charlie's gang? What do you mean? Charlotte hasn't been here long enough to have any sort of gang. I thought she was still sorting that out, playing with different girls every day.'

Lucy rolls her eyes. 'Mum. Charlie always has a gang. And eventually she's always the leader. It's just the same here as it was at Brookdale. When she says you're in, you're in. And when she says you're out, you're out.'

Beth feels her chest tighten. 'But isn't Sophie in her gang? Isn't she one of her friends? She was here just a few days before . . . before it happened. They looked to me as if they were getting on fine.'

Although, looking back, perhaps that last visit hadn't been a great success. From what she can remember, Sophie spent most of her time in front of the television with Lucy, while Charlotte did something in her room. Sophie had insisted, uncharacteristically, on a speedy exit when Andi arrived to collect her. The women barely had time to exchange two words.

'They don't hang out at school at all. I don't think that Sophie really has any friends. Anyway, it's different at school: what happens at home doesn't count.'

'So . . . what are they saying about Charlotte?'

Lucy's eyes dart across to the doorway again. 'They're saying that she's been bullying Sophie. That it was pretty bad. And they're also saying that she was bullying her online. That it was meant to be anonymous, but that they all know it was Charlotte. On ASKfm.'

'ASKfm? Is that some sort of radio station?'

'No, it's an online site. But that's not the only thing.' Lucy takes a deep breath.

Oh, Jesus. 'What else?'

'There was this website. A website that was just about Sophie. Someone sent links to practically the whole school. And they're saying it was Charlotte. That Charlotte set up the whole thing.'

'Set it up?'

'The website. It's got pictures of her. And a video. Of Sophie undressing. She's practically in the *nude*.'

'Of Sophie? But why?'

Beth takes hold of Lucy's shoulders, feeling suddenly sick.

'Why would anyone do that? Why in God's name would *Charlotte* do that?' Then, as if it's only just occurred to her: 'Where is it? Where is this site? Show me.' She feels nauseous at the thought, but she needs to see it. She grabs her laptop, pushes it over to Lucy.

Lucy recoils, pushing it back towards her mother.

'I can't find it, Mum. I've already tried Googling. It must've been a closed site or something. And it's probably been taken down now.'

'Well then, how do we know that—'

Lucy interrupts. 'But, the thing is . . . it's actually worse than that.'

She has barely been able to take in what Lucy has told her, and now asks numbly,

'How can it be any worse?'

'They're saying that Charlotte actually told her to do it—on the website . . .'

'Told her to do what?'

The child collapses into her arms, her face distorted with grief and fear.

'That Charlotte told Sophie to kill herself.'

Beth calms Lucy down, reassuring her, despite her own screeching panic, that it will all be okay, that she is sure that the whole thing is nothing but the nastiest rumours. She wipes her daughter's face with a warm flannel, the old remedy for distress, then takes her back up to bed and sits beside her, stroking her hair, until she sleeps.

Back downstairs, Beth paces the quiet house furiously, unable to settle. She wonders what she should do, what she *can* do. What she *needs* to do is find that site. To see it with her own eyes. And then to destroy it, and all the evidence that it ever existed. Should she wake Charlotte now, ask her, accuse her, interrogate her?

Should she ring Dan and tell him? But Dan will be asleep, or will still be out wining and dining, and there seems little point in worrying him with this right now. She thinks about ringing Susie, but she's so busy with her own life; Beth has made overtures since her return, but her sister has made it clear that she doesn't need or want any increased sibling intimacy. Could she call her mother? Margie? Unthinkable. She thinks about making a transatlantic call, the time would be right, but her NJ friends seem distant in every way. And what would she tell them? She wants, oh, what she really wants is to talk to Andi. To have it all cleared up before Andi hears the rumours, before the rot sets in. To reassure her that there is no way Charlotte could have done this thing, that it's all a misunderstanding, that it's nothing more than vicious rumours. And Andi, Beth is almost certain, will take her word for it, will know instinctively that she is telling the truth.

She could call Drew, he would be good to confide in, but it's too late at night. Anyway, what could he say? She imagines that he'd tell her she has nothing to worry about. That even if Charlotte has been unkind to Sophie, she is only a twelve-year-old girl, a child herself, that what's happened can't really be her fault. She can't be blamed. He would tell her to pour herself a drink, a strong one, and think about something else. He would tell her she should try to relax, get back to her blog, go to sleep. He would tell her to do something, anything, to take her mind off it.

Beth takes Drew's imaginary advice, pours herself a whisky and goes back to her laptop, opens her article. She has uploaded a photo to go with her post, a picture of the four of them standing outside the house in West Bloomfield after a heavy snowfall. They'd built a snowman, their first for the season, with a carrot nose and prunes for eyes, a glittery plastic cowboy hat from the girls' stock of dress-ups, and a terrible magenta scarf made of squeaky nylon that Margie had knitted one of them the Christmas before and that no one would wear. The girls have both grown a little since the snap was taken, but otherwise have hardly changed at all. The picture had been taken with the camera on a timer, and with all the accompanying hilarity. Their faces were glowing with happiness; Beth's own shows a contentment she knows was heartfelt and not just some trick of the camera or nostalgia. It is sad to contemplate, but she has barely experienced such uncomplicated joy since their move. It hasn't been unhappy exactly, but there's been far more stress, far more worry, than she'd expected. And they have had to make such an effort, all of them, to find a place for themselves, to fit in.

And now this.

She types furiously, adding *Snow* to her list of 'Things I miss about our life in the US'.

Right now Beth would be happy, more than happy, to go back. But she knows that it is not just the place itself that she is missing. It is the time, really, the time before now. A time when she'd known how each day would unfurl, when she'd known the contours of her own life. She'd understood her husband properly, and her children's hearts were not hidden things, but as recognisable, fathomable, familiar as her own. It might have been an illusion—maybe the seeds of all this had already been planted there and then. Perhaps all that time she had been unwittingly nurturing the monster of fate that confronted them now.

Just for a moment, she is tempted to tell her loyal readers what is going on. She can imagine their baffled responses, all of them expecting her familiar take on her experiences, her slightly blurry but definitely upbeat view of the world, and not some god-awful revelation.

She almost laughs, imagining @AnchoreDownInAlaska's cheerful response: *Oh, I'm sure it's all just a misunderstanding, Lizzy! LOL*

@GirlFromIpanema's sharp take*: There'll be something dark and dirty going on in that family, that's for sure.*

And @OzMumInTokyo's compassion: *Oh, Lizzy. I can't say how bad this makes me feel for you. You know it'll all get better. You know your baby didn't do anything wrong. Sending you hugs. Xox*

And most predictable of all, @BlueSue's inevitable Job's comfort: *What did you think, Lizzy? That life was meant to be easy? That raising children was going to be a cinch? Life is shit, motherhood is the pits, all children are a disappointment. What made you think yours would be any different?*

She goes back to her list. She prefers the rosy glow of her manufactured life to what is beginning to look like a very grim reality.

And she doesn't want to disappoint her readers.

THE GOLDEN CHILD'S TEN LESSONS FOR SUCCESS

LESSON SEVEN: HOW TO KEEP YOUR PARENTS HAPPY

Remember the time when you pushed that kid too hard on the swing, and she landed on her butt and went *wahhhhing* to the mothers, and told them that you did it deliberately? And the other mother said to her little crybaby, 'I'm sure it wasn't on purpose, darling.' And then your mother looked at you and said sternly, 'Now, sweetheart—say sorry,' without even bothering to ask you what actually happened. And so you said sorry, and the two of you kissed and made up and went back to your games. Confusing much?

It gets even more confusing when you go home and your mother says, 'Mummy knows you didn't do that deliberately, darling. It was an accident, wasn't it?' And you know she really doesn't want you to tell her that it wasn't an accident, even if it's the truth. So you go, 'Yes, of *course* it was an accident, Mummy.'

And Mummy believes you. And eventually maybe even *you* believe you.

All parents WANT to believe their children are good. Regardless of what's right before their eyes.

And you should let them believe it. That way everybody's happy.

COMMENTS

@RANDOMREADER says:
So, Goldie, was she pushed or did she fall?

ANDI

ANDI GOES TO THE VISITORS' ROOM, EMPTY AT THIS EARLY hour, to make the call. She doesn't want Sophie—she doesn't want anyone—to hear. She can only get the first few numbers punched in before her fingers begin to shake uncontrollably. She disconnects. Tries again. And again. As soon as the dial tone kicks in she feels her stomach churn, bile rising to her throat. She has written down, word for word, line by line, breath by breath, what she wants to say, what needs to be said. She even had Steve read over it. He said nothing, but he gave a brief nod before turning his attention back to Sophie, and to whatever else was going on in his head.

She last heard from Beth the evening before, a text sending love and asking how things were going, but Andi hasn't replied, and there has been no other message. She wonders now whether Beth has discovered her daughter's part in all this. Impossible to know what she might be thinking, doing. What she might be feeling.

She thinks back to that hospital visit. Steve had just gone home for a shower and a shave when they arrived. He'd left unwillingly, fearing that something, the *unthinkable* something, would happen in his absence. She'd had to force him from the room, recognising her own terror in his eyes, but knowing that other things—his personal hygiene, specifically—needed attention.

Andi was feeding Gus when the nurse, a young Irish woman with red hair, an incomprehensible accent and an irritatingly cheery manner, delivered Beth and Charlotte to the room. She poked her head around the door to announce the visitors, then left them standing awkwardly on the threshold. From the vantage point of her seat behind the embankment of monitors, Andi was able to observe the two of them unseen. Charlotte was as upright as always, but clutched her mother's hand as if she were a much younger child, her eyes wide, her mouth open, as she took in her surroundings. But she regained control of herself almost immediately, breathing deeply, pulling her hand from her mother's, stepping away. Even now, Andi is astounded by the child's monumental self-possession. How certain she was, so clearly ready for anything. Beth was another matter—obviously distressed, openly afraid. She observed her friend's stricken expression as she gazed at Sophie, wired and pale and barely alive, the way she forced herself to pull her eyes away, scan the room.

'Oh, Andi.' Beth's voice was thick. Andi could tell she was close to tears. Beth slumped against the door frame as if unable to move, her offering of flowers hanging limply, water dripping onto the floor. She breathed out on a sob, and the tears came. 'It's so terrible. I can't . . . I don't . . . Oh, poor Sophie.'

Seeing them was not as hard as Andi had expected. She had thought she would not be able to bear it, that she would be overwhelmed with envy, that she would have no way of communicating anymore with citizens from the world of the well and whole. Instead she was filled with sudden tenderness, hope. The mother and daughter—her friends—were living proof of her own former existence, a reminder of the ordinary good of the world. She pulled herself out of the chair, still nursing, and moved unhesitatingly towards them.

'Oh, God. Beth.' She embraced Beth and then Charlotte as well as she could, her own voice breaking, eyes filling. 'I'm so glad to see you both.'

The visit was brief—they stayed only twenty minutes or so—but proved to be oddly uplifting. After their emotional greeting Beth went straight to Sophie and sat by the bed, her gaze intent. She took her hand, stroked her hair, while Andi gave her the latest prognosis: the most recent MRI showed no signs of brain damage, and there was no permanent damage to her organs. Though the doctors expected her to regain consciousness, they didn't know when. There were no guarantees. Andi, of course, had consulted Doctor Google: there were cases, too many of them, where coma patients never regained consciousness, despite the doctors' expectations, despite all the signs indicating that they should.

Charlotte took a position on the other side of the bed, her eyes intent on her friend. She picked up Sophie's other hand gently. When Andi finished her report, Charlotte met her eyes, gave a small smile. 'Is there something I can do?'

Andi smiled back, pleased beyond measure by this unexpectedly natural gesture of friendship. She understood how hard it must be for a child to know what to do, what to offer in such a situation—she would have been overwhelmed at that age, unwilling to make a fool of herself, frightened to do the wrong thing, painfully self-conscious. She was glad that Sophie had such a friend.

'You can read to her if you like. The nurses say that can help.' Andi pointed to a book on the bedside table that she had been reading aloud. It was one of Sophie's favourites, *Charlotte's Web*, though Andi had just recalled the terrible sadness of the ending and decided that she would not read much further. That she would bring in something more cheerful, something funny.

'You can just talk to her, if you'd prefer. Tell her what's going on, if it doesn't feel too weird?'

Charlotte smiled. 'I'd rather read to her, I think.'

'That would be just beautiful.'

The two women sat in the plastic chairs, Beth cuddling Gus once the feed was over, and talked. Or at least Andi talked. The words gushed out as if from an unstopped bottle, her voice low to ensure that Charlotte (and Sophie, should she be somehow listening) wouldn't hear. She told Beth everything—glad to be able to open up, to tell the truth: about her despair, her guilt, about how she had not known there was anything wrong, how she'd always assumed Sophie's talent was some sort of talisman, her anxiety about Gus, her disconnection from him, her worry about the damage she was doing.

Beth was, as Andi had known she would be, calm and reassuring. 'You have to stop blaming yourself, Andi. It's not—it's not something anyone could really have known.' Beth kept her voice low too, her face turned carefully away from her daughter, although Charlotte was too busy reading from *Charlotte's Web* to bother with the women's conversation.

'The thing I don't understand is not just why, but why right now? What was going on in her life that was so hard? And then why didn't she say something? We don't think there was any particular stress—I mean, she's got eisteddfods coming up after the holidays, and exams. But Madame Abramova says she was ready months ago. She's always ready. And the situation at home—maybe it wasn't perfect, maybe things were harder with

Gus, and maybe she wasn't getting the attention she was used to, but nothing had *happened*. It doesn't make any sense. But there must have been warning signs, looking back. Things that I, that we, missed.'

'There always are, looking back. That's the thing. But you say she never gave any sign of distress. You're right—it doesn't make sense that it was about the piano, if she's always enjoyed the pressure before now. Surely she would have said something. Told you she didn't want to do it anymore. If it was the piano, then it must have come on very suddenly. Too suddenly for you to do anything. And I think, if it was to do with Gus, if she felt so miserable about it all, you'd have known.'

'But I didn't, did I? And now there's Gus, too—Christ knows what this is doing to him. He's in the crèche most of the day.'

Beth reached over and took her hand, squeezed. 'Oh, Andi, honey. He really won't remember any of this—at this stage all he needs is to be warm, to be fed, to be cuddled. Which reminds me: if you'd like me to help with him, you can bring him over anytime. We'd love to have Gus, wouldn't we, Charlotte?'

Charlotte didn't respond for a moment, and both women turned to her. The girl clearly hadn't heard the question. She had stopped reading and had Sophie's hand clutched in hers, was in the process of slowly lifting it. She pulled it right up until she was holding Sophie's arm a few inches above the sheets, when Beth repeated her question. 'We'd love to look after Gus. Wouldn't we, darling?'

Charlotte let down Sophie's hand quickly before she turned to them, her face slightly pink.

'Oh, yes.' She looked oddly uncomfortable. 'That'd be great. I love babies.' Her voice was a little overeager, breathless—she sounded suddenly like the young girl that she was.

The visit didn't last much longer. Andi thanked them both for the offer to mind Gus, but declined, and when a troop of doctors appeared in the room, ready to conduct various tests, write reports, Beth and Charlotte said their goodbyes. Both women shed tears, and the hug that Andi gave Charlotte surprised them all with its fierceness. 'You take care of yourself,' she said. 'You think you're such big girls, but you're still our babies. You just don't know how precious you are.'

It wasn't till much later, when she'd heard from the McLachlan woman about the bullying, that the odd little moment at the bedside came back to her. After their conversation Andi had showered and lain down on her bed, bone tired, her mind a quagmire, hoping for a few minutes of sweet unconsciousness. It was then that the peculiarity of Charlotte's behaviour had struck her: the furtive manipulation of her unconscious daughter's arm. She remembered the cold calculation of Charlotte's expression as she lifted Sophie's hand above the bedding—she could have been a scientist conducting an experiment—and then the look of embarrassment when she realised she'd been observed.

Andi still has no idea what the girl was doing, but now she feels her blood chill. That she was so taken in, that she left her daughter vulnerable even for a moment to whatever *evil*—there can be no other word for it—lurks in that child, horrifies her.

When she finally makes the call, Andi doesn't need her notes. The words pour out, as hot as molten lava, and just as dangerous, dissolving everything in their path.

CHARLOTTE

CHARLOTTE HEARS THE TAIL END OF THE CONVERSATION AS she's smuggling breakfast back to her room. She's woken relatively early—it's just past eight o'clock—and she has crept downstairs trying to make sure her mother doesn't hear her, or realise she's awake. She wants to take the cereal back to her room, to eat it in the relative comfort of her bed, while she watches the final episode of *Sherlock* again.

Her mother, she knows, is majorly peed off about all the time she spends in front of a screen, even though it's the holidays. She keeps going on about how unhealthy it is, telling her that she needs to get out, that it's making her irritable, tired, unfit, that she isn't connecting with her family. That she should try and be more like Lucy, who at least reads actual books sometimes, goes for the occasional walk, or spends time doing crafty things, bakes. Which is probably all true, but right now, on the days when they don't have to go to their grandmother's, all Charlotte wants to do is chill, do nothing, not even think. It's the holidays, after all.

She needn't have worried about being caught. Her mother is unlikely to hear her, she's in the study, on the phone, and is talking loudly, almost angrily. Charlotte pours the milk over her cereal, then pads back down the hall, pleased that she's been able to escape so easily. She heads up the stairs, but pauses midway when she hears her own name. She strains to hear more, but it's impossible to make anything out other than stray words and syllables. But even from here she can tell from the sound of her mother's voice, the strangled quality of her conversation, that something bad has happened. She tiptoes back down the stairs almost reluctantly, makes her way as quietly as she can along the dark hallway, stops just before she reaches the open study door.

'Andi . . .' Her mother has lowered her voice now, but it has developed a tremor that Charlotte recognises, though she has heard it only on very rare occasions, a tremor that comes just before tears. 'Andi, I don't understand where this is coming from. I know how dreadful you must be feeling. Okay—no of course I can't really know, but I can imagine . . . Oh, it sounds dreadful—but *Andi,* I think we should talk about this rationally. Not jump to conclusions.' She's speaking slowly and carefully, and her voice is blocky and stiff, as if she has a headache. 'As I said, I really have to talk to Charlotte and find out what she says. We owe her that, at the very least. You have to understand. Yes, I heard, but only late last night. And they are just rumours, remember. Of course I will talk to her, but I think it must be . . . No, of course I had no idea then that she had anything to do with it—I only knew what you'd told me, that you thought it was connected to her music . . . the pressure. I didn't know anything . . . Another incident? Who told you that?' Her voice rises in anger or distress. 'Please don't say that, Andi. It's Charlotte, it's my daughter you're talking about. She's only twelve. She's just . . . she's just a little girl.'

When she hears the phone disconnect, Charlotte turns and runs as fast as she can towards the stairwell. She is neither fast enough nor quiet enough.

'Charlotte!' Charlotte stops. Turns. There is a trail of splashed milk behind her, and at the end of it stands her mother. She isn't smiling. 'Come back here.' Her voice is like ice.

'We need to talk, Charlotte. We need to talk about Sophie.'

ANDI

BIZARRELY, THE IDEA IS INSPIRED BY A CONVERSATION WITH Steve's father, not that either of them would ever tell him that. During one of their nightly conversations, Steve gives the old man all the details of the day's progress, or lack of it, and then, uncharacteristically confiding, launches into an appalled account of their recent discovery: that Sophie was not suffering from a generalised sadness, nor broken down by excessive pressure, but was the victim of the most horrid, deliberate and sustained bullying, and that one girl—a girl they'd liked, a girl they'd trusted, a girl from a good family (*their friends!*), a girl they'd thought was Sophie's friend—was the main perpetrator. Steve doesn't tell his father about the website, the cyberbullying—that would be too much, too awful, an obscenity; there is no way the old man could cope with that sort of thing—but even so, Andi is shocked and slightly awed by his tearfully impassioned account of what they now believe to have happened. Throughout it all Steve has remained impassive as each new medical challenge has been revealed (and thankfully overcome), so frigidly distant, that Andi is almost relieved that he has finally cracked.

Steve speaks to his father from Sophie's room, and though Andi feigns distraction she is standing close enough to hear every word of the old man's reply. He is silent for a long moment, then intones in his deep, deliberate minister's voice: *Avenge not yourselves, but rather give place unto wrath: for it is written, Vengeance is mine; I will repay, saith the Lord.*

As always, his father's declamations leave Steve in a conversational no-man's-land, and he hangs up soon after. He sits, bent double, utterly motionless, holding his head in his hands. Andi pretends to busy herself by rearranging the mess on Sophie's bedside cabinet. Eventually Steve speaks, his eyes on Sophie, his voice low and infinitely weary. 'I don't know that I want to wait for the Lord's vengeance, Andi.'

'What do you mean?'

'Isn't there something else we can do? Some sort of legal action we can take?'

'But you know the police can't trace the computer—there's nothing they can do. It's a dead-end. If there's no evidence they can't even talk to them. You know how it works.'

'But can't we sue or something?'

'Sue? You mean Beth and Dan? For what?'

'For negligence. If it's true what that woman told you about Charlotte having done it before—surely they should have been keeping a stricter eye on her. They must have known she could be dangerous to other kids. Surely that's a type of negligence? Couldn't we use that to make some sort of case against them? Don't we just need balance of probability or something, rather than reasonable doubt? Surely we've got that.'

'I don't know if it is possible. I don't really know much more than you about that area of law. And I don't know that it's something I'd want to do anyway. I don't want money out of this. I just want our daughter to wake up. I want to go home. I want our lives to get back to normal. If . . . *when* Sophie recovers, I just want to forget this ever happened.'

His smile is sad. 'You know that's not ever going to happen. Even if she survives, and even if she's more or less unscathed physically, this isn't ever going to go away, is it? It'll be part of her, and part of us, forever.'

'So what would be the point? I don't understand. No amount of money's ever going to make any of this better.'

'It's not money I'm after. It's justice. Retribution. And not divine justice, meted out in the fucking afterlife, either. I want justice in the here and now. I want people to know what happened to Sophie. I want that girl—and I want her parents—punished.'

Punishment. Retribution. Once they seemed like such old-fashioned concepts, almost redundant, replaced by the modern ideas of justice that she is familiar with from work— those noble, if unattainable, ideals of truth, reconciliation, rehabilitation. But now, plunged into this new world where other alien concepts—despair, anger, fear—rule all of her waking and most of her dreaming hours, these ancient concepts are suddenly appealing. And perhaps necessary.

'Actually, maybe it's a good idea. I'll call some people. I'll look into it.' She can feel some sort of fog lifting, something clear and sharp and hard replacing it, even as the words leave her mouth. Andi looks down at Sophie, takes her hand and raises it—so still, pale, cool—to her hot cheek.

THE GOLDEN CHILD'S TEN LESSONS FOR SUCCESS

LESSON EIGHT: TELLING THE TRUTH. OR NOT.

You *could* tell them the truth.

You *could* admit that it was you who took Penny F's Dora the Explorer pencils back in kindergarten, and not poor Jonathan K who got the blame for everything that year.

You *could* confess that it was actually you who let Annie B's brand-new lop-eared bunny out of its hutch and led it to its doggy murderer, back when you were in the third grade.

You could explain that it was you who wrote those filthy letters that got Jasper O suspended back in grade school.

You could even tell them how it was you who 'misplaced' your mother's passport two weeks before you were due to fly back to Australia.

You *could.* But why would you?

They'd never believe you, anyway.

COMMENTS

@RANDOMREADER says:

That poor lil bunny. Seen Fatal Attraction, Goldie? Might be right up your alley. lol.

BETH

WHEN THE GIRLS WERE STILL IN GRADE SCHOOL, MARGIE, who worried that they were missing out on a religious (and specifically a Catholic) education—the Brookdale Academy was private, but not aligned with any church—sent them over a book of philosophical questions for children. The girls may have been slightly disappointed, but for once Beth approved of her mother-in-law's gift. The school program had an ethics component, but Beth was interested in providing some explicit parental guidance too. It was all very well to wait for an issue to come up as part of everyday life and then address it—sharing, for instance, had come up naturally when the girls were toddlers—but there were other, more complicated ethical questions that didn't arise so conveniently. The girls actually had fun with the book, which summarised what noted philosophers thought about each dilemma and gave some of the historical context; it never ceased to amaze Beth how much they enjoyed that sort of thing. The questions ranged from the basic issues of right and wrong—*Do two wrongs make a right?*—to the more existential: *Do you sometimes feel weird when you are with others?*

Then there was *Is it ever right to tell a lie?* She can remember the specific moment that they arrived at this particular question. The three of them were huddled together on the couch in front of the fire, reading. It was close to Christmas: she can recall the tree being up; the memory has a distinct rosy glow. They talked about why lying was bad, who it hurt and why. 'But is it still lying,' Lucy asked (her sweet, sweet Lucy; she remembers her back then, lisping and cuddly), 'if you don't tell the whole truth?'

Her question led, after a series of digressions, to an even trickier one. It was Charlie who asked, and she was definitely still Charlie then, smaller but essentially the same, her voice clear, her back straight, her determination already evident. 'What if you know someone has done something wrong and it's a friend? Do you have to tell on them?'

They decided eventually that, yes, in most instances you should tell on them, especially when the wrongdoing was hurting someone else.

'But what if it's someone you really love? Someone in your family? What if it was your mum or dad?' Lucy sounded genuinely anxious. 'Or your sister? What if Charlie did something terrible. Would I have to tell? What if she . . . murdered someone?'

Charlotte glared at her elder sister—*as if!*

'Well, darlings,' Beth said, and she can remember the everyday joy of pulling them closer and hugging them both hard, '*that* particular scenario is pretty unlikely. I don't really think that Charlie, that *either* of you, would ever do anything so terrible. But yes, Lucy, you probably would have to tell if anything Charlie did hurt anyone else. But don't worry, I'm pretty sure nothing like that will ever happen.'

It was unthinkable then: her Charlie hurting anyone deliberately. Her loving, smart, ethically informed daughter. If only it was unthinkable now.

So when Lucy comes to her, her sister's iPad held before her like something dangerous, a look on her face of mingled fear and disgust, along with something close to sorrow, Beth knows that there is more bad news in store. Beth understands that Lucy has no choice, that she is only doing what's right, what she's been instructed to do by her own mother no less, and this at some cost to herself—but part of her wishes that her daughter could have found some way to keep it to herself. That she could have managed to swallow some of those ethical qualms that were so faithfully, so hopefully, instilled.

'Oh, Mum.'

It is bad news for all of them.

When Dan confronts her, Charlotte denies it, of course she does. Just as she denied her mother's earlier accusations of bullying, admitting only to making a couple of nasty anonymous comments on ASKfm, and to one dubious physical encounter that someone at school told Lucy about—*Oh, that? That was* nothing, *Mum. We were just being silly. We were acting, pretending to be scary. We were practising being those angels from* Dr Who. *For Harriet's party, remember. It was a game. Nobody could call it bullying*—and the initial outrage is still burning brightly when she is presented with this further evidence of her involvement.

The outrage quickly morphs into icy scorn, despite the fact that her parents are presenting her with proof that is almost painful in its undeniability: the pictures of Sophie, the short video clip, are there in her Photo Stream—Sophie undressing, in her underwear, the close-ups of her buttocks.

'But we were just mucking around. We Photoshopped the pictures and made them look like all these weird things. I didn't even look at that recording again. I'd forgotten all about it. I don't know how any of it got on that website. I didn't send anything to anyone except Sophie. And I didn't make that website. Do you really think that if I was going to do something like this that I would make it so obvious? That I would keep these photos? A five-year-old wouldn't be so stupid.'

Listening to Charlotte, watching her daughter, her arms crossed tightly against her chest, her voice low and calm, her attitude clearly defiant, but somehow still composed, with no sign of distress or guilt or even anxiety, Beth feels something cold settle on her. Lucy displayed more emotion, surely, more compunction on her sister's behalf, more distress, when she showed her mother the compromising pictures.

'Charlotte, honey, I don't think there's any way you can keep on denying this.'

'So?' The look Charlotte gives her father is full of scorn. 'It could still have been someone else. Everything's in my Photo Stream—so it's on all my devices. Anyone could have taken whatever they wanted. It's too easy. We all use each other's stuff all the time.'

'What—so you think it was one of your friends, do you?'

She is glad that they agreed that Dan would handle the situation. Beth doesn't trust that she won't lose her composure completely. She is so close, just being here, witnessing this, seeing her daughter in this clear cold light, to breaking down. To saying or doing something she might live to regret.

'Oh God, Dad. I don't know who it was.' Charlotte shakes her head. 'I just know it wasn't me. The fact that I took the photos doesn't mean anything. Anyone could have put that website up. Maybe Sophie did it herself.'

'Charlotte. This is ridiculous. You have to stop. You're just making it worse.' Beth suspects that the look of horror on her husband's face mirrors her own.

'Actually—maybe that's it. Sophie had all the pictures, so maybe she did the whole thing. And then took the pills. Maybe she was trying to set *me* up. I wouldn't put it past her—she's so . . . passive aggro or whatever it's called.'

Beth's horror turns to nausea. The cold vehemence of her daughter's argument only emphasises its implausibility, the child's desperation.

'Oh, Charlotte.' Beth can hardly bear to look at her.

'*Oh, Charlotte,* what?' She turns on her mother. 'I've admitted that I said some mean things on ASKfm, and I've admitted that I was involved when we . . . played that joke on her.'

Dan interrupts, his face red, his breathing ragged. His anger, so rare, is shocking.

'That *joke* you played on her, those comments online, and now this disgusting website. It's not fun and it's not games: it's bullying. This is such serious stuff. Sophie tried to kill herself because she was bullied. And people are saying you were the main perpetrator. Don't try and play it down, for Christ's sake. If she dies, or if she ends up with any sort of health problems, you're going to be judged as being partly responsible. It's something you'll have to live with for the rest of your life.'

'Yeah, right: like nobody else was involved. Whatever. They were my pictures but I didn't send them to anyone except Sophie, and I didn't do the website. I did see it. But everybody saw it. There were links on Instagram. I probably should've told someone that they were mine, I guess, but I didn't see the point.' Her self-righteousness is indestructible. And intolerable.

'I mean, it's awful what Sophie did, but this stuff happens on the net all the time; it's really not such a big deal.'

'Oh, Christ. Can't you just stop? Jesus. It *is* a big deal, Charlotte. It really doesn't get any bigger. It was a big enough deal for Sophie to try and kill herself. And what if she doesn't wake up? What if she dies? You'll have to live with it if you're in any way involved. This could affect your life forever, too. You could be expelled from school. And what if the police trace this back to you? It could even mean criminal charges. Can't you see how serious this is?'

'Okay. I really can see. I can. But nobody's going to trace it back to me *because I didn't do it*. And I don't understand why you don't believe me.' Charlotte's voice wavers a little. 'I didn't write that website,' she took a deep breath, 'and I'm not ever going to say that I did. So, you can all . . .' She turns to glare at Beth, her eyes fierce. 'You can all just *fuck off*.'

Beth watches, unable to pull her eyes away, barely able to breathe, as her daughter storms out of the room, slamming the door behind her. Dan follows. She listens to the feet pounding up the timber stairs, hears more slamming, more pounding. Yelling. Screaming. She is a stranger, surely, this girl. Not her baby—her lovely Charlie. Or has she just never seen her properly before? Is this who her daughter has always been?

Beth has never thought her children perfect; what mother ever does? But she thought that they were something better than the average, both of them—special. But now, now she has to question everything. Because if Charlotte's actions are questionable, to say the least, what part has Beth played in shaping those actions?

They are good parents, she and Dan, she knows they are. They've both devoted so much of their energy not only to making things good *for* the girls, but to making *them* good. They have both tried hard to make their girls understand that being good is more than just a list of 'nots'—not lying, not cheating, not stealing, not murdering—that it is also about doing good, about being kind, about understanding that what the girls do affects others.

But now, now she must rethink everything. Because if good children are proof of good parenting, then what about bad children?

Bad children. She's known a few. She's come across them in various settings, children whose outrageous naughtiness takes your breath away. And their cunning is just as breathtaking: these are kids who pull the wool right down over their besotted parents' eyes.

There always seems to be some sort of consensus about these children; they're the ones whose reputations precede them wherever they go. They're the kids who can be guaranteed to spoil things for everyone else: the ones who throw tantrums at birthday parties, scream over a denied toy or sweet, storm off a playing field in an explosive display of bad sportsmanship. The ones who constantly induce rolled eyes, raised eyebrows, compressed lips, whispered conversations between the other parents, teachers, shop assistants, innocent bystanders.

There's generally a consensus about their parents too. It's inferred, if not said outright. Not only are these parents generally deluded about their little darlings, they've clearly done something wrong. The child's bad behaviour can always be traced back to them: they're too lax, too hard, too adoring, too one-eyed, never there.

Even in books, on television, there's a direct correlation between effort and outcome. Eva's Kevin—wasn't he meant to be a product of an ambivalence that Beth has never experienced? She loved both her children absolutely from the moment they arrived, and before—there's been no postnatal depression, no marital strife, no overzealous career orientation, no over-the-top devotion. She's tried to keep everything in perfect equilibrium, and everything that's happened since her children were born, every tiny moment of delight—first smile, first step, first word, first friend, first prize—every childhood triumph, has, until now, only validated her effort.

All that effort. For what? If her daughter is not who she thought she was, if she's not the girl they've both watched grow and bloom, then who is she?

And if Charlotte isn't Charlotte—then who is Beth?

DizzyLizzy.com

Que Sera Sera?

Oh, parenting.

So many agonising decisions.

Let's start with the birth—though sometimes that's not really a decision. Natural or caesarean? To drug or not to drug? Home birth or hospital stay?

So you've survived that one. Now, what about feeding? Breast or bottle? How long? And, should you choose to be so wicked, which formula?

Once you've made it through the minefield of sleeping (controlled crying, anyone?), it's exponential: you have to decide which toys you're going to let them play with, which (if any) TV programs they're allowed to watch, which morsels of food can pass their lips, whether or not you're going back to work, which daycare or preschool—and then, OMG, it's time to sort out schools, encourage suitable friendships . . . If you're not there yet, believe me when I tell you that it doesn't miraculously get easier when they hit five. Actually, it gets progressively more complicated.

But lately I've noticed that each of these decisions, all of them overwhelmingly important when they're made, come to seem completely insignificant. When your five-year-old walks into their kindergarten class for the first time, happy and healthy and raring to learn, you're not still thinking about whether it was a bad decision to give up breastfeeding at six months. By the time they're heading off to high school, you've probably forgotten that they didn't start reading chapter books until they were eight. And when they graduate from high school and are about to head out the door to college, my guess is you won't be worrying about whether you should have let them watch *The Hunger Games* when they were thirteen.

As my own get older, I'm beginning to think I should try and relax a little, try not to agonise over every minor decision, try to actually enjoy the kids while they're still ours.

Because, who knows, maybe we're fooling ourselves. Maybe this whole parenting caper is out of our hands, anyway. And maybe our kids are going to be who they are whatever we do.

36 ♥

EXPATTERINGS:

@BlueSue says:

I'm not so sure about this, Lizzy. I know it can be regarded these days as overparenting, but I think all the little things really do matter. Doesn't each small step add up to something? Doesn't every little bit make them who they are, shape who they become? I think our input—all of it, even when they've grown up—is crucial.

@OzMumInTokyo says:

Oh, Lizzy. You always put things so beautifully. XO

@GirlFromIpanema says:

Oh, man. I hope you're right. Just had a note home from the school: apparently my ten-year-old daughter's favourite show is *Girls*. She told the teacher that she's already up to season three. Who knew? I'm thinking a bit of overparenting wouldn't go astray around here.

> **@BlueSue** replied:
>
> Oh, dear. I couldn't bring myself to watch further than the first few episodes of *Girls*. I hate to think this is the life our lovely twenty-somethings are leading. You'll have to make your little one understand that this isn't the sort of behaviour she should be emulating—explain that there are better ways of being. I don't envy you.
>
> **@GirlFromIpanema** replied:
>
> Hmmm. Pity I can't just wash out her mind with soap, eh, @BlueSue?

ANDI

ANDI CONSULTS A COLLEAGUE FROM HER SYDNEY DAYS ABOUT the prospects of a suit. Such a course of action has never been taken here, the woman tells her, and would be unlikely to succeed—there have been cases in some US states where parents and the children themselves have been sued, but they have specific laws that make it possible. Here, it isn't as clear-cut, and liability would be almost impossible to prove. Filing any such suit would almost certainly be a waste of time and money. The school is a better bet, if it's damages Andi's after. But even there the outcome would be uncertain. Particularly, she adds carefully, if Sophie survives.

Andi snorts at the idea, explaining that she doesn't think the school is the problem, and that she doesn't actually want money—what she wants is the girl's parents to understand, to feel some of her fear, her pain. 'What if we just *threaten* some sort of legal action,' she suggests. 'It doesn't matter that it's bullshit; it'll take them a while to work it out. It'll hurt them. They'll have to see a lawyer; they'll have to tell people. They'll have to think about their fucking bullshit parenting.'

Her friend, who diplomatically ignores her outburst, reluctantly agrees; a letter is drafted and sent. But it does nothing to counter Andi's rage—her anger towards Beth and Charlotte still roils in her stomach, rises in her throat like bile, burning everything in its wake. Threatening to sue is one thing, but Andi wants to inflict something more permanent. And she wants the damage to be public. For once she wishes that it was more like the US here, that it was easier to make such things a matter of public record. She wishes that public outrage could be encouraged, that the Mahony girl—along with her parents—could be placed in virtual, if not physical, stocks.

It occurs to her that perhaps a degree of publicity is possible, even in Australia with its strictly enforced protection of minors. The press has been circling from the moment Sophie was hospitalised. Andi supposes they have some sort of contact in the emergency services, or perhaps the hospital, because even that first night, when Steve went back to the house to get things for Gus, the answering machine was blinking away. And almost all of the calls were from the media. He listened to the smooth voices, with their messages of manufactured concern, and erased them immediately. He knew two of the journos, one from the *Advocate* and the other from the local television station, and they'd seemed okay, he said, whenever they'd turned up at various jobs—crime scenes, car accidents, the occasional drunken brawl—or to court. They were irritatingly pushy; of course in that job they had to be. But once you were on the other side it was completely different—they seemed slimy and insincere, utterly opportunistic—and Steve was furious. 'Fucking parasites,' he said, 'feeding on people's misery.'

Despite Andi and Steve's refusal to participate, there was a mention early on in the *Advocate*, just a few lines reporting that a local twelve-year-old girl had been found unconscious and taken to hospital, following a suspected overdose of prescription pills. She was comatose, the article said, and grave fears were held for her life. There were no names, and no speculation about the cause. Andi only knows because someone, she doesn't know who, thoughtfully left a cutting for them. Perhaps it was one of the nurses or the cleaning staff who left the bizarre offering, anonymously. The neatly cut-out square of newsprint just appeared on top of Sophie's cluttered bedside cupboard. She read it quickly and passed it to Steve, who looked at it briefly before screwing it into a tight ball and tossing it, without comment, into the bin.

Now it seems that every day there is someone new wanting to talk to them—from newspapers, magazines, websites, television stations; all the local outlets as well as Sydney and interstate—wanting interviews, details of their *terrible tragedy*, as some of them call it, their voices hushed, tones almost reverential. *We'll make sure you remain anonymous, of course.*

A local woman who freelances for the big Sydney papers, and whose name Andi recognises vaguely, somehow gets hold of her mobile number, and Andi actually speaks to her for a few minutes, assuming she is someone from a community organisation, offering therapy or counselling, before politely trying to get rid of her.

This particular woman is persistent, however, and appears to already know more about their story than any of the others who've contacted them. Andi receives an email from her the following day, apologising for the phone call (God knows how she discovered Andi's email address) and explaining that she heard about their plight from a friend of a friend who has some sort of connection with the school, and that she would very much like to interview Andi. She is currently writing a book on cyber-crime and wants to include a chapter on child perpetrators, adolescent male hackers, mainly, but she thinks the malicious actions of teenage girls—the whole cyberbullying thing is out of control, isn't it?—might add interest and widen the audience. Bullying to the point of suicide, the woman writes in her email, might be regarded as a type of murder, mightn't it?

Andi feels her stomach clench at this, wants to write back and remind this woman that though her daughter is hovering somewhere—oh God, where is she, her beautiful girl?—in that limbo land between life and death, she isn't dead and she isn't actually a suicide. Not yet.

Andi googles the journalist's name. From her website and a number of online articles, it appears that Arabella Agostini isn't the usual true-crime writer, but a specialist in the sort of offences that don't often lead to sensational court cases, an exposer of injustice, corruption. She has written a few accounts of murders that were front-page news, but mainly her interviews focus on people who claim to have been ill-treated by faceless institutions, government departments, big business. Andi can remember reading some of them over the years, distinctly recalls being annoyed on a number of occasions by the woman's too evident sympathy with the alleged victims, with her failure to even attempt any sort of a balanced account. Her defence lawyer's instinct was insulted: she knows that always there is another side, that it is impossible to properly tell those sorts of stories, to tell the truth, without at least giving the other party the opportunity to respond to the victim's claims.

Right now her lawyer's instinct has disappeared. Andi's instinct is all maternal. This time the victim's story is the only story; there is no other story to tell.

BETH

IT ISN'T THE WAY IT HAPPENS IN FILMS OR BOOKS: THERE IS no clear demarcation, no real before and after, no particular moment, no instant when everything changes, no point of no return. No line has been drawn in the sand that Beth can look at and say: there, on one side, lies the past, all good; while in the here and now all is chaos. Instead, there's been a slow accretion of moments, a gradual dawning that things aren't what they seem.

Beth wonders sometimes whether the fact that it happened so gradually—each tiny jigsaw piece of their lives slowly building up this new picture—makes it easier or harder. Ever since she became a mother, Beth has understood the nature of the precipice that all parents anxiously skirt; one false step means sorrow. Of course she's imagined every possible scenario—what mother hasn't?—stillbirth, fatal disease, car accidents, abduction, murder. The list is endless. She's had nightmares about finding herself in the abyss, about having to face the unfaceable, the absence of hope, the emptiness of a life that's survived rather than lived. She's imagined the instantaneous nature of that fall, how it would happen just like that—an abrupt thumbs-down from an indifferent fate—unavoidable, instantly recognisable.

Instead, disaster has disguised itself. Has crept up on her.

Life has played her like a cat weaving between her legs, pretending to be tame, friendly, before sinking its claws into soft, vulnerable flesh.

For so many years Beth has been smug, imagining that everything (career, marriage, making a family) has gone well for her because on some level she deserves it. She has paid lip-service to luck; of course she has. She is aware of her great good fortune in having been born at such a time and in such a place—all those clichés of privilege. That fortune isn't quite as kind to others is always easy to explain, too—the acquaintance whose baby daughter went blind following a bout of measles after she'd refused to immunise; the woman whose daughter was hit by a car because she'd let her play outside alone. The old school friend whose son died after eating a dishwasher tablet he'd found in a low cupboard. There was *always* a reason—they had it coming, behaved irresponsibly, did something that Beth would never, in a month of Sundays, do.

She's never said it aloud, has always offered—and felt—the correct degree of sympathy or compassion or whatever is required, but on some level Beth has always secretly thought that they had it coming, that there was some balance these unlucky parents had failed to achieve, or something they had failed to do or be. And that they were, ultimately, responsible for their children's actions, their children's fate. But now, after what's happened with Charlotte, she's had to rethink her attitude. Because she and Dan just aren't those parents. She knows the work they've both put into making their family, achieving that balance, how seriously they've thought about every little thing. How they've always done their best, done more than what's expected. Surely that counts for something? Surely in this instance no one could blame them, blame her?

But Beth is wrong about this—just as she's been wrong about so many things. When the letter arrives, it's clearly official—she has to sign for it—but she opens it unsuspectingly, curiously. She reads it through with dawning horror. The document itself is like a missive from a foreign country—the language and syntax are vaguely archaic, but even so the import is clear. She and Dan are accused of negligence leading to Sophie's attempted suicide. They should be prepared to face legal action.

It is a literal reckoning of all that she has feared. The outside world has come to the same conclusion as she would have once upon a time: what Charlotte has done is her parents' fault, her parents' responsibility. And in some shape or form, she and Dan are going to pay.

The first person she tells isn't Dan, but Drew. It isn't deliberate, and it is easy to justify to herself later, but still she feels guilty, knowing that on some level she's doing something terribly wrong. When the letter arrives, she knows that Dan will be in a meeting, knows that he has a big presentation, that he doesn't need to hear the news yet.

Her first instinct is to call in sick to work—she can't face the confected portentousness of the political world, Drew's world, with this reality hanging over her. But Beth needs advice, she needs to talk to someone who might have some clue about how they should proceed. Right now. And right now Dan isn't available. She wants someone who will be understanding, non-judgemental. Someone whose support will be objective, disinterested. And when she thinks about it, perhaps that someone was never going to be Dan.

Take the previous night, for instance. She can't remember exactly what was said or by whom, but the after-dinner conversation turned sour in an instant and ended with Charlotte

charging out of the room, stamping up the stairs and slamming her bedroom door as hard as she could. Beth initially
stormed after her, determined to say her piece, but lost her
impetus halfway up and crept back down, defeated before
she'd begun. Lucy had disappeared, making herself scarce at
the first sign of confrontation. Beth should have checked on
her, she supposed, made sure her elder daughter was okay,
offered her comfort and some sort of reassurance. But she had
none to offer. Instead she slumped beside Dan on the lounge,
despairing. Exhausted. 'This is unbelievable.' She felt the tears,
almost on tap the last few days, prick at her eyelids. Dan merely
gave a resigned shrug.

'Dan, I don't know if I can cope.'

'Uh-huh.' Dan stared ahead at the television.

'And I don't know how you *can*.' She didn't even bother to
try and hide her resentment. He said nothing, continued to
look at the flickering screen.

'Dan?'

'What?' Impatiently.

'I don't know how you can function with all this going on. We
don't know if that child, if Sophie, is going to live or die.
And . . . if she dies, our daughter will be blamed. You keep going
on about Charlotte not taking it all seriously enough, but what
about you? What are we going to do? We need to protect her.'

Dan spoke quietly, without looking at her. 'What do you
mean, protect her? She's not the one on life support.'

'Sophie took those pills, nobody made her. Nobody, and not
another twelve-year-old girl, can really make anybody kill themselves. But that's not what people are saying, Dan. They're going
to blame Charlotte, however much it's Sophie's own responsibility. Or her parents'.' Beth felt slightly sick saying the words,

ashamed to be discussing the tragedy in such terms. 'This is going to ruin things for Charlotte. People will remember.'

Dan was looking at her now, his arms crossed, face impassive.

'Look,' she continued, 'what's happened to Sophie is an absolute tragedy. And I feel for Steve and Andi. But I can't—we can't condemn Charlotte to a lifetime of guilt over it. What if Sophie dies? What then? Do we tell Charlotte that she's a murderer?' Her voice was rising, getting shriller.

'Beth. You should try to calm down.'

'But we have to do something.'

'Yes. Okay. You're right. We have to do something. You've booked her in to see a counsellor, haven't you? And if things get worse, maybe she'll have to move schools . . .'

'Move schools? We can't do that to her. Where could we send her, anyway?'

'We might have to. She might need to start again . . . somewhere no one knows her. Maybe she could go and live with your mother, go to school in Sydney.'

'She's not going to Mum's!'

'She could board. Or maybe *we'll* have to move.'

'Move? But we've only just got here.'

'If it becomes . . . if it gets any bigger, or if Sophie does die, I can't see how we could possibly stay, do you? What about Lucy? It'll affect all of us. It'll be impossible.'

'Oh, God.'

'And even if things are okay with Sophie, we need to work out what we're going to do about Charlotte.'

'What do you mean, *what we're going to do about Charlotte?*'

'I've been thinking—maybe it goes deeper. You have to admit, her responses, they've been . . . well, they've been really *off.* It's got me worried. Even the stuff she's admitted to, there's no real remorse. She's not really sorry, is she? She's just upset that she's been caught. Maybe there's something wrong with her. Maybe we should be getting some sort of help for her. Serious help.'

'You know that's not true. She's confident, yes, and I know she's pretty competitive. And she's assertive—she doesn't let anyone push her around. But what's wrong with that? That's what every parent wants. And Charlotte's a *good* girl—no one's ever said anything different. Maybe there's something about the new school? Maybe the dynamic with these other girls? And her responses . . . well, the accusations—they're huge. Anyone would be defensive. Maybe she's in shock.' Beth could hear the desperation in her voice, the pleading.

'Oh, Beth. Charlotte's smart, she's a leader, she's well-behaved, she's popular. All that. But she's not . . . don't you ever think that maybe there's something missing?'

'Something missing? What are you talking about? She's always scored off the chart in every test she's ever had.'

'I don't mean intellectually. I mean . . . emotionally. I've been talking to Mum—'

'Don't bring your mother into it. Margie barely knows her. And Charlotte seems to think she doesn't like her.'

'Jesus. Mum has just noticed a few things: Charlie's emotional reactions; the way she treats us, Lucy. You know Mum only has her best interests at heart. All of our best interests. And if there is actually something wrong with her . . .' Somehow the tenderness in his voice was more painful than the anger. 'Then isn't it better that we face it? Shouldn't we try and do something about it now?'

'But there's nothing wrong with her!' Beth's chest hurt.

'She's just a *normal* twelve-year-old girl. All kids do bad things sometimes. It doesn't mean they're . . . pathological. And this is Charlotte, our, *your* daughter, that we're discussing. You can't be serious.'

'A minute ago you wanted me to take it more seriously. Now I'm telling you what I think and you're having hysterics.'

'I wanted you to think about what we could do to *help* her, but you're just saying that she's some sort of budding sociopath.'

'The two things aren't mutually exclusive.'

He sighed, looked back at the television, turned the sound up.

'I don't know what's going on with you. You're not who I thought you were.'

His smile was sad. 'You don't think that maybe that's the problem here? That none of us are?'

She goes into work as usual, waits impatiently for Drew's morning briefing with his PA, Sylvia, to finish, before knocking on his door, the letter clutched in her hand. 'Ah, Elizabeth. Come in.' He looks up briefly from his papers, then frowns, puts his pen down. She can't contain her distress; there'll be none of their usual banter today.

'This letter . . .' Her voice is barely working. 'This letter came from a solicitor this morning. They're taking legal action. Against us. Sophie's parents. They're saying it was our fault.' She sits down, legs suddenly weak.

'What? What are you talking about?'

Beth takes a breath. 'I don't know if you know, but one of Charlotte's classmates took an overdose at the end of last term.'

'Sophie Pennington? The girl who's in a coma?'

265

Of course Drew knows. He's on the school board. What had she expected?

'Yes. Sophie and Charlotte were friends. Or so I thought.'

'And?'

'Well, it turns out they weren't friends. Apparently Charlotte and a group of other girls were . . . teasing her. Or at least that's what's been said. They're also saying that the teasing is what led to Sophie's suicide attempt.'

'It sounds like some pretty heavy teasing.' Drew looks sceptical.

'If Charlotte and her friends did what they're saying, then it's more than just teasing.' She swallows. 'It's the most horrendous bullying.'

'Are you saying you don't believe it?'

'It doesn't matter what I believe. They're suing us.'

'Suing you? What the hell for?'

She begins to read the letter to him, her voice shaking, but he pulls the pages out of her hand before she's even halfway through and reads to himself, shaking his head.

'Jesus Christ. This sounds mad. I don't even know if they can take any sort of legal action.'

She tries to think of something sensible to say, but can only hear her own ragged breathing, loud in the quiet room.

'Listen. I'll see what I can find out. I don't have anything important, nothing I can't clear, anyway, for the next little while. I'll see what I can do.'

'Oh, Drew, I—'

'I know this looks awful,' his voice brims with concern, 'but honestly, I don't think it's as bad as it looks. It'll be okay. It's all going to be okay.' He sounds so certain, so definite. 'Just breathe, Bethie. Breathe.'

He sits reading over the document again for what feels like an age. She watches the way his eyes flick down the page and then up again, rereading. Finally he looks at her, raises his eyebrows, gives an uncharacteristically subdued smile. She has seen this particular smile before, the full wattage withheld. It is the smile he reserves for those of his constituents who have endured some terrible tragedy—the death of a loved one, a horrible accident. Right now, being the recipient of one of Drew Carmichael's low-beam smiles makes her feel slightly ill.

'This is bullshit, Beth. My torts law is pretty rusty, but I'm pretty sure it can't be done. Even if . . . even if the worst happens, and the kid dies, there's no way they can sue. This is about negligence, to put it simply, but it won't wash. There's nothing in our law that will allow this. I have a feeling parents have been sued in the US, and maybe even Canada. But not here. They can't actually sue you and Dan. You haven't done anything that they can sue for.'

'What about the website . . . Will they be able to trace her? Aren't we responsible for its use? We're always being told . . .'

'The police would already be talking to you if they'd been able to trace the website back to your ISP. They'd have taken all your computers. The father's a cop isn't he? I'd say they'd have done everything they could to lay charges if it was at all possible.'

'What sort of charges?'

'I'm not sure, exactly. All the cyberbullying stuff is a bit over my head. But there's the images—and the incitement to suicide. They could be pretty serious criminal charges.'

'*Criminal charges?* Against Charlotte? That's crazy. She's too young.'

'Actually she's not. *Doli incapax*, the age that children are regarded as being legally responsible for their actions, is ten. But that's not going to happen. Without any evidence that Charlotte was responsible for the site, or any instances of actual physical abuse, there's no clear criminal case to make. Charlotte didn't actually physically assault the girl, did she?'

'There was some sort of encounter, apparently, but she didn't hurt her. And it was meant to be a joke.'

'A joke. Right. Girls.' Drily. Then: 'She's a lawyer, isn't she—the girl's mother?

The girl's mother. She knows exactly how Andi must be thinking of her, but still she cannot bring herself to think of Andi, her friend, in these terms. An adversary. An enemy. The enemy. The girl's mother.

'She'll have been trying to think of ways to make you pay.'

'Pay?' Beth doesn't believe it. 'You think it's about money? No. That doesn't make any sense. I mean, they're struggling a bit, I guess, while Andi's not working, but I can't imagine they'd do this for money. They're not like that. Money isn't a priority.'

'Paying is not necessarily about money. That's not what she'll be after. It's some sort of public acknowledgement. They want your blood.'

'Our blood?'

'My darling Beth, there's nothing simpler. It's the most ancient thing in the world.' He reaches across the table and takes hold of her hand. 'It's revenge. Payback. An eye for an eye. Their daughter's future; your daughter's future.'

Drew is on the phone almost immediately, rustling up contacts, trying to work out what can be done, and, more importantly, who can be trusted to do it. He asks her nothing personal about the situation, makes no judgement, and for once she is glad of his disregard for the moral rights and wrongs, his lawyerly ability to remain disinterested.

Beth goes over the road to get them both coffee. She brushes off the concerned enquiries of Sylvia, who noticed her red-rimmed eyes and air of hysteria on her arrival. 'It's nothing,' Beth reassures her. 'Just a bit of a medical drama with my mother. You know how it is.' Beth feels guilty as she returns the sympathetic grimace; Sylvia's elderly parents have genuine problems.

While she waits for the coffee, she takes a deep breath, and rings Dan. His presentation should be over, and he needs to be told what's going on. The letter was addressed to both of them, not just her, but she finds herself almost dreading his reaction. She steps out into the street for privacy, but struggles to hear over the noise of the traffic, has almost to shout. She can barely make out his responses; even so she can sense his fury—about the letter itself, but also about the fact that she has spoken to Drew before him. That she has told Drew at all. Despite her guilt, her defence is easy: 'But I had to tell someone. And anyway, he could tell there was something wrong. What could I say?'

It isn't just Beth's choice of confidant, but her lack of discretion that has upset him. 'So what?' he says. 'You have to control yourself a bit better. You can't just go blurting this stuff out to everyone. Newcastle is a small town. Couldn't you have said you were sick or something, and just waited to tell me? Look, I expect that he's right and it's just some sort of . . . ambit claim or whatever they call it, and it probably won't go any further. But it'd be better if we could keep this to ourselves. The situation is bad enough as it is. The more people who find out what's happened, the worse it'll be.'

She tries to placate him with the fact of Drew's legal knowledge, the news that he is on the phone right now, working hard to find a solution, but that only makes things worse. 'Jesus, Beth. We don't need a Drew Carmichael solution. He'll find some dirty Liberal Party stooge and before you know it we'll be tangled up in a fucking corruption scandal.' His laughter is bitter. 'Why didn't you ring Mum? She'd know what to do, who to talk to.' His mother is the last person Beth wants to speak to. She can imagine Margie's barely concealed satisfaction at receiving more evidence of Beth's dubious character, her dark, possibly conservative, heart.

She disconnects, picks up the coffee, heads back to the office. Drew is still on the phone, very obviously on hold, tapping his fingers impatiently on the desk. When she comes in he mutters and hangs up. 'I can sort that later.' The smile he gives her is still fairly low-beam, but the fact that it is a smile reassures her.

'Well?'

'The good news is—I've asked a mate who deals with this stuff, and it's as I thought—it's just a scare tactic. There's no way it's going to get anywhere. I doubt they even intend to lodge it.'

'The bad news?'

Now the smile is completely extinguished. 'I've been talking to our Sydney office. They've just had a call from some writer who wanted to know about you, asked if she could talk to anyone here. Apparently, she's interviewing the mother for a syndicated feature. And there was something about a book, too.'

'A feature? But they can't mention names or anything . . . surely?'

'It's unlikely. Not when it's kids. But they can mention where you live, the school.' He pauses for a moment. 'And the fact that she's been in touch with our office . . . Even if they don't name names, they just have to mention that you work for a local Liberal politician. I'm afraid it won't take long to make the connection. People aren't stupid. They'll work it out.'

Her concern is all for Charlotte. 'But isn't there some way we can stop the story? What can we do? Don't you know some-one else?'

Drew ignores her questions, doesn't quite look at her as he speaks. 'The thing is, I've been talking to our people in Sydney and they're a bit worried. It's possible that it could be used as ammunition against me and against the party—the fact that you work here. I know it's ridiculous, but that's how it works. So, we're thinking it might be better for everyone if we let you go. Not necessarily permanently; just until this dies down.'

Beth looks at him blankly, his words only slowly sinking in.

'In the meantime, I'll see what I can do.' His eyes meet hers directly now, his smile's energy returning. 'You know I know *everyone*, Beth. I'm sure this can all be fixed.'

DizzyLizzy.com

Let Sleeping Friends Lie

C and I are going through a car wash, listening to the swish and batter of the brushes across the top of the car. C is entranced by the whole wax and polish show, but I have to avert my eyes, so I don't feel seasick. Going through the car wash used to be a regular and important feature of our NJ life, but we never seem to get around to it here. I've taken time off work to catch up on some important life admin stuff (including washing this incredibly filthy vehicle) so I thought I'd take the opportunity.

You see, in the quiet moments, our car wash conversations can be pretty profound. So many important things revealed (the enforced intimacy, the lack of eye contact); so many lessons given and taken. Surely these moments (and I've missed so many of them lately) are what mothering's all about?

The topic *du jour* is friendship—or more specifically, the frenzied dance that passes as friendship when you're a teenage girl. But suddenly, shockingly, C wants to know about my life.

'So, who's your best friend, Mum?'

Who's my best friend? That's not something I've thought about, lately. I'm not sure I even know what a best friend means at this stage of life.

I give the regulation answer. 'Well, I guess it's Dad.'

C looks doubtful. 'But don't you have a *real* best friend, Mum? I mean a friend who's a girl—like, someone your own age? Someone who's not family?'

'It's different when you grow up.' I don't need to see her expression to know that what I've said is lame. I'm about to qualify it with a long spiel about how once you have children, everything changes, that suddenly nothing else, not work, not friendship, seems as important anymore, but the brush intervenes.

When the noise subsides, C turns to me. 'Actually, I can see why Dad's your bestie. Life must get so boring once you get to your age. I guess there wouldn't be any point having an *actual* best friend—it's not like you ever go anywhere or do anything fun. What would you even talk about? At least if it's Dad you can both just go to sleep when you're bored of one another.'

Tedious individual that I am, I immediately take the teaching opportunity that my sweet daughter has handed me:

'That should actually be bored *with*, honey. Or *by*. Never *of*.'

Zzzzzzzzzzzzzzzzzzzzz

24 ♥

EXPATTERINGS:
@BlueSue says:

Best friends really are something you leave behind when you have kids. For women, family takes centre stage for so many years, and there's just no time left for anyone (or anything) else. And then when the kids leave home—as they do—I'm afraid we can be left high and dry. My advice is to cultivate strong support networks, ladies—wherever and whenever you can!

@GirlFromIpanema says:

From what I'm seeing go on with my little darlings, the sooner so called 'besties' are a thing of the past, the better.

@OzMumInTokyo says:

Aw, @DizzyLizzy—you know I'll always be your virtual bestie <3<3<3

ANDI

THE JOURNALIST IS DOUBTFUL ABOUT MEETING AT THE BEACH kiosk. 'It's winter,' she objects. 'Won't it be cold? Can't we meet at your place? Or, better still, the hospital?' But Andi is adamant—she doesn't want the emotion that she knows would be too close to the surface in either of those places. She wants to stay calm, stay focused, to tell the tale clearly. She wants the outlines to be harsh and stark, not fogged with a sentimentality that might bury the story were the woman to see Sophie herself, or even her bedroom, her home. The stuffed toys on the bed, the family photos, the piano that hasn't been touched for days—all the soul-shattering—and emotionally loaded— evidence of a young life that might be so tragically truncated.

No, Andi wants none of this in the article. She doesn't want it to be a tear-inducing story of a child's despair, her parents' agony; she wants a sharp, angry piece, a piece not to wrench at the heartstrings but to ignite fires. She knows that no names can be mentioned, that the most she can do is feed the rumours, that the piece will have to be phrased carefully. But she doesn't care: she wants, she *needs*, to respond in kind to the cold, wicked indifference of those children—and of that particular child.

It's revenge she's after—not consolation.

The beach is the right choice. She arrives early, finds a spot in the sun, out of the wind. The crispness of the air, the tang of the salt calm her and strengthen her resolve.

She orders a coffee, a latte. It's the first proper coffee she's had, she realises, since this all happened. Her appetite's shot, and anyway there's no real coffee in the hospital. To go out and buy a drink elsewhere seems like an indulgence, evidence of some sort of pleasure principle that's beyond her right now. And eating itself has become nothing more than an irritating necessity. There have been several deliveries of food left on their front verandah—offerings of cupcakes, brownies, chocolate slice, soup, quiche, big slabs of lasagne. Meals that can be frozen and are easy to portion and reheat in the hospital kitchen. Someone at the school must have organised a cooking bee—all those good community-minded women who volunteer to help out in times of emergency, tragedy. Steve has eaten the meals most nights, forking the food in hurriedly, but Andi can hardly bring herself to touch them. The nursing staff have chivvied her—you have to eat, you need to keep up your strength. You're a nursing mother. Think of Gus. Think of Sophie. But when she looks at the bag of pap that's keeping her daughter alive, the act of chewing and swallowing turns her stomach. She eats enough to keep alive, like Sophie, that's all she can do. When she looks in the mirror she barely recognises herself. Her hair is wild, her face is gaunt, her eyes stare out of her head like a mad woman's. She may be thinner than she has been for years, but like all the other things that once seemed important, this fact has no bearing on her happiness.

But now, sitting alone on a cold metal bench, breathing in the briny air, sipping on the too-hot, too-bitter brew, watching the other people—all immersed in their own worlds, oblivious to hers—she feels some relief. She would be content to stay here by herself for a few hours, just to be. Here, watching the seagulls, the waves, soaking up the sun, it seems almost possible to not-think.

By the time Arabella arrives, sliding in beside her, silently pushing over another cup of coffee, Andi has lost track of time altogether. 'I noticed you'd already had one, so I asked the guy at the coffee shop if he remembered what you ordered.' The journalist's voice is low, soothing. 'He didn't know about sugar, so I brought three.' She pushes sugar and a stirrer over. 'I like mine black and unsweetened. But you never know.'

Andi is surprised by the woman. Although she's seen her publicity shots, in the flesh she's not who Andi expects. And she's certainly not a typical Arabella. It's a name that Andi associates with the Monty Python version of the English upper classes. A name that seems most suited to haughty, horsey, polo-playing types. But there's nothing remotely horsey about this Arabella. She's a big lady, tall and solid. She's pale and very blonde, perhaps of Germanic or Scandinavian origin, and her face isn't beautiful, but it's striking, what would once have been referred to as handsome, Andi supposes. All of her features are large—eyes, nose, lips, chin. Her outfit is loose and layered, the fabric Eastern, hippy-ish. It's an odd choice for such a statuesque woman, but somehow suits her.

They sit and watch the waves, sipping their coffee for another ten minutes or so, barely speaking. Eventually Arabella reaches into her bag and brings out a recorder the size of a phone, and places it on the table in front of her. 'So,' she says in her measured way, 'are you ready to tell me this story?'

There is something reassuring about the woman, her bulk, her calmness, something that adds to the unexpected serenity that Andi feels just being here, away from the muted terror of the hospital room. She tells her the story, slowly, grappling with the order of events, finding it difficult to keep things chronological and coherent. But Arabella asks all the right questions, draws out memories she has all but forgotten. *Were there any early incidents of bullying when she was a very small child?* There was an incident way back when Sophie was in daycare—another child constantly pinching her. And Sophie had a hard time in kindergarten. It was one particular girl then, who claimed that Sophie was using her pencils, copying her work, but this had been easy to sort out. Sophie was teased by some dreadful girl when she first started at the college. But they thought this was all over; that particular girl had left the school.

So did you recognise that there was something wrong back then? Did anyone suggest counselling? No, it never occurred to them that it was a real problem. Sophie had bounced back as far as they could see. And made some good friends. It just seemed like one of the ordinary inevitable hardships of childhood. Girl stuff.

It hadn't seemed like a pattern then—it's only now, when Andi adds it up, when recent events are taken into account, that a pattern has begun to emerge.

She tells Arabella about the events of this year: how Sophie's only good friends had recently left the school. How when Charlotte arrived she hoped that Sophie and Charlotte would become friends and did everything in her power to encourage the relationship. Charlotte seemed to be a lovely girl—she was smart and friendly—and the two girls seemed to get on so well; Sophie adored her. Andi was friends with Charlotte's mother, and the older girl, Lucy, seemed lovely too. Andi hoped so much that a friendship would develop that she didn't notice what was going on under her nose. Until it was too late.

And so to the crux of the story. Andi tells the journalist about Charlotte's bullying, gives her all the details she has about what went on. She's compiled evidence of the virtual crime scene with the help of Bridie and Matty and their parents—links to, and printouts of, all the pages, screenshots of the now missing website, the ASKfm pages, some comments the two girls discovered on Instagram and Twitter. She's brought the disappointingly inconclusive police report: once they'd confirmed that the ISP was public, the computer untraceable, the police could take their investigations no further. She tells her what she knows about physical terrorising—incidents other classmates have reported or admitted to—cornering Sophie in the hallway, the shunning of her in the classroom and during lunch.

Andi tells her about the hospital visit, confiding that the thing that wounds is that she, too, was so taken in by this child, who on the surface is all friendly charm, but who, in reality, is manipulative and cruel, and only God knows how ruthless. She tells her about the rumours that Charlotte has done something like this before; that her bad behaviour was the real reason for the family's return from the United States. 'You need to spell it out,' Andi tells her. 'You need to warn everyone that this child is dangerous.'

It's an odd conversation; all one way. The woman remains opaque, revealing nothing about herself. When Andi tries to locate her, asking her basic things about her own life—*Where do you live? Do you have children? Are you married?*—she deflects the questions skilfully. It's a little like a conversation with a therapist, she imagines, or perhaps a priest.

Despite the therapeutic dimensions, Andi is very careful about what she reveals. After all, she doesn't want this story to be about her. So she doesn't mention her anxiety about her own role, how she didn't enjoy the initial months of motherhood the first time around, how she put Sophie in childcare and went back to work as early as she could. She doesn't mention that her first thought was that somehow, inadvertently, Sophie had been pushed too hard with her music. Or that she couldn't help wondering whether she'd neglected her emotionally during the years of IVF. She says nothing about their distance after Gus arrived and her guilt for resenting her adolescent daughter's needs.

She glosses over their family life, too—as far as she is concerned, they are a perfect little family unit, and Sophie, before all this, was happy, talented, well-adjusted. But these omissions are an effort. Part of her wants to tell the woman everything, to find out what she thinks. She is desperate to have someone, anyone, tell her what she wants to hear—to tell her that it's not her fault, that she couldn't have done anything to stop it.

But the woman is a writer, not a priest—and Andi knows her absolution would be meaningless anyway.

THE GOLDEN CHILD'S TEN LESSONS FOR SUCCESS

LESSON NINE: PLAYING FAVOURITES

Some parents, maybe most parents, have a favourite child. There's always that special one—a golden child—who's just that little bit more like them, or less like them, or kinder, or smarter, or prettier, or whatever-er. It might be unfair, but that's just how it is.

But some parents, bless them, just won't choose. It doesn't seem to matter that one kid's just about perfect and the other one's a complete ass: they just keep on going with all their lame-o unconditional love shit.

Let me tell you—these kinda parents can be hard work. But with a bit of imagination, a bit of initiative, eventually they'll come around to your way of thinking.

You can think of it as a game—it's just that nobody else knows they're playing.

COMMENTS

@SANDRADEE says:

Hi there. This might not be the right place, but I'm trying to remember the words to an old clapping game with a rhyme about a child of gold?

@HESTERIA replied:

Could it be pot of gold, not child? I remember this one:

Oh little play mate
I cannot play with you
My dolly's got the flu
And the german measles too
Slide down my rainbow
Into my pot of gold

@SANDRAD replied:

Oh, thanks heaps, @hesteria. That's the one. But I think we said sister, not dolly. ☺

@RANDOMREADER replied:

Wtf is a clapping game anyway? Russian roulette with STDs?

BETH

ONCE, THIS PARTICULAR SCENARIO WOULD HAVE BEEN HER worst nightmare. Now, even though it has been overtaken by other, more immediate horrors, the prospect of the two women—her mother and mother-in-law—spending time together, being in the same house, the same room even, still makes Beth feel highly anxious. She tries talking to Dan about it, tries to persuade him that just this once the Sunday night dinner at his mother's could be cancelled, that perhaps they should just spend time with *her* mother, whose visits are so rare . . . That surely in their current situation, the stress they are all under . . . 'Look, we don't have to tell her that Mum is coming—can't we just say that Lucy's sick?'

But Dan is simply not interested in making her life any easier. 'We need to keep things normal for the girls. We can't sit around agonising about it constantly; it's unhealthy,' he says, sounding startlingly like his mother.

And when Beth tentatively suggests that Margie instead comes to their house for dinner, the indefatigably hospitable Margie says that Beth isn't to think of it, that of course it won't be any trouble to have her mother for dinner—Francine is only one extra person, after all. 'And we've had so few occasions to get together since the wedding. What, maybe once in the last ten years? It'll be lovely to catch up. And right now,' here a solemn pause just in case Beth hasn't quite realised the gravity of her predicament, 'right now, I think your mother and I should be putting our heads together to work out ways to help you both.'

'Oh, yes,' Beth chirps. 'So generous. Thank you. Mum will be thrilled.' She can see her mother's polite shudder at the thought of putting her head anywhere near Margie's, can already picture the thinly veiled hostility between the two women: her mother haughty and superior; Margie concerned to the point of caricature. It is going to be bad. She knows that before the event. She just doesn't know how bad.

Her mother promises to come early in the morning to watch the girls play in a holiday hockey carnival, but doesn't arrive until almost five o'clock. In the event, only Lucy plays anyway. Charlotte hears that morning that a number of the team's mothers are refusing to let their daughters play if she is on the field, and the coach—an old girl, only in her early twenties, who played State during her time at the school—calls Beth to let her know what's going on. 'Look, I think what they're doing is really wrong,' she says. 'But I really don't know what to do. Charlotte's one of our best players, but if the other four don't come we'll have to forfeit. I can't get on to Mrs Pollux, the sports mistress, she's away.' Beth doesn't discuss it with Dan or the girls, but quietly responds in the way she knows the coach wants her to. 'It's okay,' she says, 'Charlotte has a bit of a cold anyway. It won't hurt to sit this one out.' She breaks the news to Charlotte, who is sitting in her room, watching reruns of *Supernatural* on her iPad. She shrugs, barely looks up. 'Whatever. It's no biggie.'

'Charlotte.' She looks at her mother reluctantly. 'It's not okay. It's awful. I'll be talking to the headmistress when you go back. This isn't right.'

Charlotte rolls her eyes. 'Whatever. Honestly, Mum, it's just those idiots from the bottom class, so like, who cares? You know, Zelda Lamprati and Tegan Maxwell. Tegan is the one who got suspended for throwing her bra at the substitute art teacher. She actually took it off in class. I guess their mothers are just making some lame point.'

Beth stays at the hockey centre to watch a few of Lucy's games, but finds it difficult to maintain her composure, faced with the curious glances and the occasional frosty silence of the other hockey mothers. Lucy is her usual unflappably cheerful self, and even manages to deflect a pointed question about recent events from one of her less diplomatic team mates: 'Hey, is it true that your little sister put that girl in a coma?' The girl speaks loudly enough for all the players, and their parents, to hear.

Lucy smiles and shakes her head, looking vague. 'I heard she took some pills. The poor thing,' she says, before turning away. Beth admires her daughter's calm answer; if anyone had dared to ask her, she's not sure how she would have responded.

Dan and Lucy have already left for Margie's by the time her mother arrives. Beth watches from an upstairs window as her mother gets out of her car. Francine gazes at the house, her face inscrutable, but her thoughts are as clear to Beth as if she's had them broadcast: she would be marvelling that the house still looks like a dump—an eyesore in this otherwise salubrious neighbourhood despite months of work. She would be wondering, as she has from the moment that Beth met Dan, really, what Beth has got herself into. She would be looking for faults to point out: *Doesn't the car need washing? Actually, doesn't the car need replacing? Why don't you have someone in to mow that little square of lawn if Dan doesn't have time? Why don't you pave it? Do you think that old settee on the verandah is really worth keeping?* So many things would irk her that Francine would find it hard to know where to begin. Beth is just glad she and Dan have agreed to keep the details of her absence from work to themselves, telling everyone that she's on leave.

But it isn't quite as bad as she imagined. They are running so late that there isn't time for her mother to give the house any more than the most cursory inspection, and her only mildly critical comment is about how long the renovations are taking—*Beth must be absolutely desperate to get new furniture, the old stuff is so depressing, how can she bear the smell?* Perhaps her mother is more concerned with finding a way to bring up what she refers to as the *Charlotte situation* to bother with the house situation. Now, Beth hurries her mother and Charlotte, who has livened up markedly in the company of her maternal grandmother, down to her car. 'Sorry to rush you, Mum, but you know Margie.'

'Well, the thing is, I don't actually know her at all, Beth darling. We've probably only spent an hour or two in one another's company since the wedding.'

'Well, I can tell you that Nan is a *stickler for punctuality.*' Charlotte's mimicry of Margie's voice, the slight pursing of the lips, the conjuring of her ever-present air of disapproval, is so spot on that Beth can't help laughing. 'Oh, you're being naughty, Charlotte,' she says. 'Stop it.' Francine gives a little smirk, raises one perfectly maintained eyebrow. She pats Charlotte on the head. 'Hmm. Glad to see it isn't all sweetness and light around here. A little bit of goodness goes a long way, sometimes.'

Beth winces but Charlotte giggles, oblivious.

Dinner is on the verge of being served when they arrive. Margie pauses in her stirring of gravy—home-made of course, no Gravox here—and welcomes Francine with a warmth and solicitude that seem genuine, ignoring her air kiss and enveloping her in a bosomy hug. 'Francine. It's so lovely to see you! We really should do this more often. How silly that these two have been married for so long and we're still virtually strangers to one another.'

Ah. She never disappoints. There it is, the slight barb, so neatly slipped in that a stranger to her techniques (or the deliberately obtuse Dan) might not notice the carefully coiled aggression nestled in the warm and fuzzy heart of Margie's most innocuous comment. Francine, on the other hand, is looking slightly affronted by the unsolicited hug, the warm ooze.

Beth offers to help with the final preparations of the meal, but Margie predictably shoos both her and her mother into the living room, where Dan sits watching the news. 'Lucy's just setting the table, so it won't be long.'

Dan gets somewhat reluctantly to his feet, gives his mother-in-law an awkward squeeze and offers her a drink.

'Just a small one. I think I might head back after dinner, after all.' She waves away their half-hearted protests. 'I have a charity do in the morning and I'd rather not be rushed. At my age I really need my beauty sleep.' Her mother's charity dos were a joke during Beth's childhood, she and her sister coming to the excruciating realisation during their adolescence that they were Francine's code for meeting up with a man, and always entailed her arriving home, dishevelled and uncharacteristically merry, in the early hours of the morning. They never knew the names of either the charities or the men. But now, with Francine in her late seventies, Beth suspects that the charities are genuine, and feels momentarily sad about her mother's solitary life.

Dinner itself is pleasant enough, with both women behaving impeccably—Francine offering all the right compliments; Margie accepting them graciously. The girls' table manners are not dreadful enough to excite comment from either grandmother and Margie says nothing when Charlotte boasts about getting top marks in an end-of-term maths exam. 'It was geometry that we already did in grade school at Brookdale. I can't believe that everyone here thinks this stuff is hard.'

'Well, they're not all engineers' daughters, are they?' Dan's tone is slightly repressive. Lucy looks at her father and pouts. 'Well, I'm totally hopeless at math, and I'm an engineer's daughter too.'

'Ah, I'm afraid you may have inherited that from me, Lucy dear.' Margie gives her a sunny smile. 'I've no idea where your father got his maths brain from. It certainly wasn't from his father, and as for me . . .'

When they discuss it later, Dan and Beth disagree on the origin of the argument, Dan insisting, naturally, that it was Francine's fault, that Margie was—as always—blameless. That Francine had totally misread her meaning. That Margie had said one thing and she did not mean another.

It begins innocuously enough. They are finishing dessert, a chocolate tart that Lucy has helped make. When Francine compliments Margie on the meal, she makes particular mention of the dessert. 'It's the sort of thing I never usually eat, but this is something special.'

'Well, it was actually Lucy who made it.' Margie gives a proud smile. 'She's a clever girl in the kitchen, our Luce.' Francine's answering smile is exaggerated. 'I'm such a terrible cook, though I suppose I've no real interest in food. This talent must come from you, Margie.'

'Well, I'm really just a good plain cook—and that's all I'll ever be. But Lucy's got a bit of magic in her hands. The pastry— it's so light. Don't you think it's a beautiful experience,' she says, addressing Francine with a gravity that Beth knows her mother will find absurd, 'watching your grandchildren grow up? It's like watching your children all over again: they develop all sorts of skills and talents that you never had yourself. It always amazes me how children can be so different to their parents.'

Her mother, clearly bored, and hoping to move on to a subject more closely connected to the world of adults, murmurs, 'Oh, yes indeed.' But Margie has more to say.

'And it's sometimes so difficult for parents to acknowledge this. In all my years of teaching it's been one of the things I've found most difficult to deal with—that parents are so fixated on their children being who they want them to be that they see only what they want to see. Good and bad.'

Beth can sense that Margie has already plotted her conversational destination. She might be weaving subtly towards her ultimate target, but her mother-in-law is, without doubt, in missile-lock. Beth tries to change the subject, in an attempt to deflect her, but Francine's unerring sense of combat has picked up on it too.

'Now that's an interesting observation. I would've thought that these days parents were the opposite. That they take far too much notice of their offspring's individual tendencies. Look at Beth. I'm sure by the time my girls were Lucy and Charlotte's age, I more or less left them to sort things out themselves. I don't think it worked out too badly. But Beth—and her sister, Susie, too—they never stop probing and worrying and arranging things and asking their children how they feel. They're basically stage-managing their lives.'

'Oh, I don't disagree. Compared to this generation I think our mothering was a bit more in the direction of benign neglect. No, it's not that . . . My concern is that so many parents really have no clue about *who* their children are. And they don't seem to care. It's as if they want a particular sort of child and they expect that if, as you pointed out, they choreograph their children's lives entirely—orchestrate everything for them, ensure that every moment of their life is filled with some sort of activity or enrichment, arrange their friendships, pick the right schools—that everything will automatically fall into place. That they'll become the people they expect them to be—regardless of their own personalities or interests. So many parents seem to feel that after all this they actually deserve a proper *return* on their *investment*—because that's the language they're using. They really can't believe, after all the hours of violin and ballet and rugby and art or whatever, plus the classes in self-esteem and the visits to the psychologist, that their little Johnny isn't actually perfect. They feel that he ought to be perfect, because he ought to represent the sum total of all their years of effort.

'Even at our school, which isn't exactly full of well-off families, we have such a hard time convincing parents when their children have done something wrong. Even when we show them the evidence, they just can't see how it could be possible. Not after all their hard work; all the money they've spent. It makes effective discipline almost impossible—if you can't convince the parents that their kids have done something wrong, you've got no hope with the children themselves.'

Margie's gaze settles briefly on Charlotte and then quickly moves away. But Francine hasn't missed it.

'Goodness!' Francine is frighteningly direct. 'Does this have something to do with what's happened to Charlotte's classmate? Are you implying that this mess is somehow Dan and Beth's fault?'

'No, of course I'm not! This is entirely theoretical. Dan and Beth are . . . exemplary parents.' Margie looks so shocked, either by the thought or by Francine's outrageous bluntness, that Beth almost laughs. Dan, however, is clearly offended on his mother's behalf.

'Francine.' He frowns at her across the table. 'You're way off track here. Of course Mum wasn't talking about Charlotte. Or us, for that matter.'

'Oh, I think perhaps she was. And I think it's quite an interesting perspective for her to take.'

At that, the girls, who have been too busy scoffing tart to bother listening to the adult conversation, both look up, as if suddenly conscious of the tension. Beth recognises only too well the look on her mother's face, the rising colour, the narrowed eyes, the superior smile; can sense her building up to something big.

'Mum, I think you might leave it now. I don't think the children need to hear—'

But her mother interrupts. 'No, I think this is exactly the sort of thing that the children ought to hear, Beth. It might undo some of the terrible damage done by their pushy, entitled parents.'

Margie stands, her lips tight, and moves around the table collecting the dirty plates. 'Of course I wasn't talking about my own family, Francine. Lucy and Charlotte are both lovely girls, and Dan and Beth have done a wonderful job. What has happened to that poor little girl is a tragedy, but I don't think it's really our place to discuss the whys and wherefores.' Her voice is bright, but to Beth's ears somehow lacks sincerity.

Lucy looks over at Margie, frowning. 'But Nan, when you were talking to me before, you said that you thought we really need to talk about what happened to Sophie, and that our not talking about it properly was a . . . symptom? . . . of parenting today.'

'Symptomatic.' Her grandmother's schoolteacherly habits kick in automatically.

'Symptomatic. And then you said that our generation had everything provided for us except a moral compass—'

'Thanks, Luce. We've got the picture.' Dan's voice is firm. 'I think you girls can go in and watch television now. You can finish your dessert in there.' Lucy's face reddens, she gives her mother a bewildered, apologetic look, picks up her plate and follows her sister, whose face has remained stony throughout the conversation, into the living room.

Francine picks up her wine glass and empties it in a single gulp. 'I don't know that it's a lack of . . . how did you put it? . . . a *moral compass* that's the problem. You don't think that there's some sort of media hysteria about bullying? Don't you think that it's wrong that a child of that age should think it's a reasonable response to *kill* herself because some other silly girls are saying nasty things? You don't think that might be an issue? I don't think it's our granddaughter who has the problem, Margie. I think she's a strong, clever girl, and that she'll develop as much of a conscience as she needs to get by in this world.'

Margie is clearly offended. 'It's one thing to be strong and clever, Francine,' she huffs, 'but surely we want more than that from our young people. It might be old-fashioned, but don't we want kindness and humility as well . . . and more conscience than you need just to *get by*?'

Francine gives a snort. 'Oh, Margie dear. Your Dan hasn't got where he is by being kind and humble, or by overtaxing his conscience, whatever you might like to think. The world's not really how we'd like it to be, is it? The good don't get ahead by being good, they get ahead *despite* being good. And on that note,' Francine smiles benignly at the shocked company, 'I think it might be time for me to leave.'

ANDI

SHE IS SURPRISED WHEN SOON AFTER BREAKFAST THE WARD nurse ushers in Dr Holding, the school headmistress. It isn't the official visiting hour yet, and ordinarily visitors would be asked to wait until the doctors have done their rounds, but Dr Holding obviously has some sort of authority even in the hospital. The young nurse, Laura, seems nervous, anxious to escape, stays only to announce the woman's arrival and then rushes off.

Dr Holding watches her retreat, shakes her head. 'Laura McMahon. She's an old girl. A nice enough lass, if not one of our high achievers. There's only so much even the best school can do. Nursing's an excellent career choice for her. I know it might be old-fashioned, but I still maintain that nursing's a good career for a woman.'

The headmistress bestows a regal smile on Andi. Andi is still in her pyjamas, too tired to even stand up, to greet her properly. The woman stands just inside the doorway for a moment, gazing steadily at the patient, taking in the formidable bank of machinery, the stark room with no illusions of comfort. 'My eldest son almost died of meningitis when he was seventeen. He was in a critical condition for almost a week—we really thought we'd lose him. That's almost twenty years ago now, and it's still painful to think about. I'm sure he was in this very room. This place is so frightening. So . . . sterile. You know they're doing everything they can, but all this just adds to the nightmare.'

Andi is not sure what she's meant to say; her instinct once would have been to ask after her son's current state of health, seize on whatever sense of shared experience and camaraderie the woman is offering, but right now she doesn't have the inclination, let alone the energy. She's only just able to manage common courtesy. Empathy and curiosity are beyond her.

Dr Holding walks over to the bed and looks down at Sophie. 'You forget just what babies they are at this age. In a year or so it all changes, they seem to become women very rapidly, but she's not there yet.' She touches Sophie's cheek gently.

'We just really hope she's going to get the opportunity to make that change, Dr Holding.' The statement is bald, but the woman isn't fazed. The smile she turns on Andi is gentle, her eyes are full of compassion.

'I understand how worried you must be—and nothing the doctors say is going to mean anything until she comes out of this. But I know Dr Cominos well; I think you can trust whatever she's telling you.'

It's a question as much as a statement, and Andi responds automatically. 'Dr Cominos says the prognosis is good. That it might only be a matter of days. There have been some signs, some responses.'

Dr Holding's smile widens. 'Sophie's a very lucky girl.'

'I guess it depends on your definition of *luck*.' There's no disguising the bitterness in Andi's voice.

'I know that from where you are now it must all be very bleak. But believe me, things will get better. Believe it or not, in a few months' time, things will be back to normal.'

'That's the thing, though. I don't even know what normal is anymore.' The confidence is wrenched from Andi almost unwillingly. 'What was going on when I thought things were just going along normally? Obviously for Sophie, some kind of nightmare had become normal. How am I meant to trust my own perceptions? I obviously don't have a clue.'

'Oh, my dear.' Dr Holding moves over to Andi, takes her hand. 'Do you know, I've been working with teenage girls for more than forty years. I've raised two of my own. I have three adolescent granddaughters. My God, I believe I may have been a teenage girl myself, once upon a time.' Her laugh is surprisingly merry. 'But I still can't, with any honesty, say I understand what's going on in their minds. And nor, believe me, can they. That's the trouble. They're the most horrendous little bitches one minute, utterly vulnerable the next. And then, something like this—what Sophie's done—it seems like such a significant, such a calculated, act. But you'll probably find that once she's safely on the other side of it, it'll be just as inexplicable to her as it is to us.'

'From what I've heard—and from what I've seen—it's not entirely *inexplicable*.' Andi's tiredness is evaporating, replaced by a dull, angry energy.

'You mean that repulsive website. And the online taunting. I agree—it's hideous. It couldn't be worse. But you have to get it into some sort of perspective.'

'Into some sort of perspective? How can we have any sort of perspective on something like this?' Andi can't believe what she's hearing. 'Our daughter tried to kill herself because of that website. That girl told her to kill herself.'

'It has to be put aside. Forgotten. For Sophie's sake.' She pauses, then says slowly, deliberately, 'And for the other child.'

'We don't need to do anything for the other child. Charlotte Mahony,' she says the name loudly, deliberately, 'needs to be punished. She should be—'

'What? Burnt at the stake? I know you don't want to hear this, but the thing is, Charlotte Mahony is a child too. Her actions—whether she denies them or not—are, like Sophie's, probably beyond her conscious understanding. She'll wake up one day, maybe she already has, and be horrified by what she's done. Truly, she will. And she should be given the opportunity to do that as privately as possible. Believe me, Andi, nothing you can say or do to her, or her parents, will make that happen any faster. She's essentially a good child, from a decent family, and I believe—and my instinct is rarely wrong—that she'll find her way. But if you go ahead and publicly shame her, whether it's through the media or through legal action, you're not going to . . . advance matters. It won't be of benefit to anyone.'

'Advance matters? What do we care about advancing matters?' Andi laughs, can feel the hysteria bubbling up. 'And anyway, how do you know about that . . . we haven't told . . . ?'

'Let's just say that there are a number of people worried about the school's reputation.'

'The *school's* reputation?'

'Andi,' Dr Holding speaks gently, 'I'm assuming you want Sophie to come back to school when she's better?'

'I honestly don't know. We really haven't thought about it. We haven't got that far. But maybe not, if that's the sort of thing that goes on. If that's the sort of school you run, the type of girl you attract. Maybe it's just not the place for Sophie.'

'I can assure you that the college doesn't have a premium on *any* particular type of girl. You'll find that the same sort of thing goes on in every school—regardless of their PR. But

I would suggest, and I suspect that her doctors will suggest this also, that the best plan for Sophie is to get her life back to normal as quickly as possible. To get her back to school, get her back to her music, get her back to everything that's familiar. We can do a considerable amount of damage control. You'd be surprised. There are some girls in that year whom I can rely on to look after Sophie, to befriend her, if you like.'

'If you can do that, why didn't you do it earlier?'

'I'm afraid we just weren't aware of the extent of Sophie's isolation, until it was too late. But now that we are, I think a bit of discreet social manipulation might work wonders.'

'And what about the Mahony girl? Will she be coming back next term?'

'As far as I know there are no plans by her parents to pull her out. I suppose we could ask her to leave the school—and I suspect that's what you think we should do—but we don't really have grounds for doing that. We've spoken to a couple of the girls in the class, just informally, as well as to the police, and there's really no evidence that Charlotte masterminded all this. There's only rumour. We have to consider whether she's likely to be a further danger, and whether the school can help her to . . . get beyond this. We might look at some sort of disciplinary action, or perhaps compulsory community service for the four girls we believe were involved in some form of physical bullying, but without any firm evidence, we can't do more. And we certainly can't single out Charlotte.'

'I don't see why not.'

'We're not the police, or a court of law, we're a school—we have no way of proving her culpability definitively—and our job is to *educate* children, not punish them. We will most certainly be implementing further anti-bullying programs school-wide.' She waits for a response, but Andi only shrugs. 'If Sophie comes back, we can rearrange the classes so that the girls are rarely together until this all dies down.'

Andi looks up at the headmistress. 'It's not likely to die down, though, is it? Once the story's . . . out there. I mean, we've kept it anonymous, but still—people will know.'

'Everybody at school knows that *something* has happened—there's no way of shutting down that sort of gossip completely. And a number of girls in Sophie's year will know quite a lot. But they don't know everything. As it is, we have the opportunity to control the situation considerably, to put a certain slant on events, if you like. We can say the rumours are untrue, suggest that Sophie had an accident. And left to their own devices, people forget so quickly—you'd be surprised. But once the "official" story's in the media, and if any sort of legal action goes ahead, damage control will be far more difficult.'

'I suppose so.'

'It's going to be difficult to make this go away even if things are kept quiet. But once you make it public it's another matter. Your story—Sophie's story—won't just be hers anymore. It'll be public property. And it'll never ever go away. It might be the thing that defines your daughter forever. And I don't know if that's what you—or anybody—really wants.'

PART FOUR

SOPHIE

IT IS THE LOVELIEST OF LOVELY DREAMS. THE SORT OF DREAM she always wanted to have; the sort of dream she's tried to conjure up herself. 'If you think of all the things you love most, Soph,' her dad once told her, 'just before you go to sleep, you'll dream about them.' Every night she thought hard, pictured all the things that made her happy, but it never really worked. Her dreams were just the same mishmash of real life and fantasy—sometimes good, sometimes frightening—regardless of her efforts.

But this dream—this dream *is* everything she thought so hard about all those years ago—things she's practically forgotten. There are clouds like marshmallows: soft white clouds like the ones you see beneath the wings of a plane and wish that you could jump right into and tumble about in like a magical jumping castle in the middle of space. And there are unicorns; of course there are unicorns! Hundreds of them, all different colours, floating about with their gossamer wings and glittering horns. And there are sugar-coated sour-strap rainbows that can be climbed and eaten. There are tiny creatures like fairies, whizzing about busily. And then there are the characters from all the books she read as a kid, and the movies she loves—the BFG and Matilda, Miss Honey, Charlotte and the pig, Charlie and Willie Wonka. Dorothy and her crew are there too, and Harry, Hermione and Ron, playing quidditch and casting spells.

Every now and then real people appear in her dream. Her mother and father, of course, though they don't actually do anything, just speak endlessly to one another, their voices too low for her to make out what they're saying, their faces always very serious and worried. Every now and then Gus makes an appearance, dressed only in a nappy and looking like one of those old-fashioned angel-babies with a bow and arrow. He has tiny white wings that he flaps sporadically, giggling madly as if he can't quite control what he's doing. Madame Abramova is there, looking years younger and almost pretty, conducting a choir that Sophie can't see. There are people she hasn't seen for ages, like Ruby Sussex, who was her best friend in Scone. Dad's mum, Grandma Jess, who died when he was young, and who she only knows from photographs, is there too, smiling gently and telling her that everything is going to be okay . . .

Of course there's a musical soundtrack to this dream—it's that piece from the *Nutcracker Suite* that her old ballerina jewellery box plays when she opens it. In the dream the song plays over and over without ever slowing down the way it does in real life, and it's not the tinkly mechanical sound that comes out of the real box, but the deeper, more resonant—and oh so familiar—sound of the piano.

The most interesting thing about the dream is that Sophie isn't actually in it. Instead, it unravels just like a movie—as if she is there watching it, rather than participating.

But then, as always, the dream comes to an end and she has to wake up. There are no more unicorns or rainbows, no more cherubs or quidditch or Matilda . . .

Just bright lights in a white room and the sound of her own heart beating.

And somehow, here, she, Sophie, is the centre of the story . . .

ANDI

'CAN I HAVE A PARTY, MUM?'

Andi is surprised by the request, but pleased. They are due to leave the hospital only a few days before Sophie turns thirteen, and she's been wondering how to mark the occasion. It needs to be celebrated, but she isn't quite sure what Sophie, what any of them, will have the appetite for. Sophie seems fine—more than fine, she seems amazing, really—but her psychologist has warned them that this equilibrium might be transient, that they need to be careful, that their daughter might be vulnerable forever.

A small family party would be perfect, she thinks, just the four of them and the grandparents, perhaps one or two of her siblings and their younger kids . . . but Sophie laughs when she makes the suggestion.

'No way. That would be totally lame, Mum.' Sophie is sitting cross-legged on her hospital bed, painting her fingernails a particularly vile shade of blue—the polish a gift from one of the nurses.

'Lame. Right.' Andi looks over at Steve but he's busy amusing Gus.

'Family isn't a *party*, Mum. Family is just normal life. Don't you think I deserve a proper birthday party after missing all of the school holidays? I can't believe I've been in hospital for three whole weeks. That's lame too.'

Andi snorts. 'Oh, like, totally lame. My feelings exactly. So, back to this party. Who do you want to come?'

'Of course, you can invite all the family if you like.' Sophie pauses, perhaps waiting for her mother to thank her for her generosity, but when a response isn't forthcoming, goes on. 'I think we should invite the neighbours, Geoff and Liz, and the people across the road. The ones with the Irish wolfhound— Mari and Michael. I really like them.' Andi wasn't aware that Sophie even knew any of their neighbours, who are all young-ish childless professionals, but she murmurs her assent.

'And I think the nurses, the three nice ones anyway, and maybe Dr Cominos should come. And,' on a run now, not wait-ing for her mother's response, 'how about Dr Holding—you said she came to see me—and Madame Abramova and maybe some of the teachers. Miss Foley? Mrs Hinchcliffe? And then there's my friends . . .' Andi holds her breath, waits.

'So do you think Ruby's parents would bring her? She could stay overnight, couldn't she? And there's Tess, I'm sure they'll let her out of school for a party. And Maya could fly up. Her parents can afford that, can't they? Or we could pay?' Sophie pauses again, thinking hard. 'And I've been trying to make a list of my friends from school, but I *really* think it'd be easiest if we just invite the whole class—I know that's heaps of girls, but I *really* don't want to leave anyone out.' She gives a small sigh, looks at her mother enquiringly.

'The whole class, Sophie? *Everyone?*' Sophie was over the moon when she realised that most of the flowers and cards in her room had been sent by her classmates. As Dr Holding had predicted, she was adamant that she wanted to go back to HLC, and as soon as possible, pooh-poohing any sugges-tion that she should consider changing schools. Even so, the thought of inviting the entire class to her birthday party seems a little over the top to Andi. 'I don't know that that's such a good idea.'

'I know it might be a bit expensive. It's a lot of people. A lot of friends. But if it's too much we can always ask them all to bring something, can't we?'

Andi says nothing for a moment. She looks across the room to Steve, who despite the wriggly baby has caught the tail end of the conversation. He appears to be laughing and crying simultaneously. She looks back at her daughter, who is now admiring her handiwork: ten garish fingers spread out across the pristine white of the sheets. 'So Mum? Is that okay? If we tell everyone to bring something to eat?'

'It's okay, Sophie,' Andi says. 'It's more than okay. It's brilliant.'

CHARLOTTE

THE FIRST DAY BACK AT SCHOOL IS NOTHING SHORT OF surreal.

There's the news that greets her, that greets everyone, on arrival, initially whispered as rumour and then made official by the headmistress during morning assembly.

'Girls, I would like to share the wonderful news that Sophie Pennington, whom I'm sure you're all aware has been in a coma after falling seriously ill, has recently regained consciousness. According to her doctors, she has suffered no ill effects and is likely to be back at school in just a few weeks. Let us all bow our heads in prayer and give thanks . . .'

There are heartfelt sighs of relief, tears are shed, and there's even a little bit of sobbing from some of the more emotional girls. Charlotte's eyes stay dry, but she keeps her head down during the prayer and is careful not to look at anyone for the remainder of the assembly. But when they're filing out, and the whispered conversations start up again, she's surprised to find that there's no one seeking her out, or glaring at her; no one's looking her way at all.

Then, when she's called up to the office during first period, Mrs Caress, the mostly grumpy school secretary, is weirdly warm and chatty, asking her how her holidays went, even offering a Mintie from her hidden supply while Charlotte waits to see Dr Holding. And when she's finally ushered into the head's office, her knees trembling, her throat dry despite the mint, Charlotte is surprised by the friendliness of Dr Holding herself. Oh, she's stern enough, but Charlotte can sense that under the surface severity she's all caring concern and motherly kindness.

Dr Holding gives her the talk, of course she does, basically saying the same things that both her mother and father have said about what it means to be a good and compassionate person, about never being cruel, about looking after the weak. She brings God into it too, which she has to, Charlotte supposes, as HLC is a churchy school.

The headmistress says that she knows that Charlotte is a good girl at heart, a bright girl, that she has so much potential—real leadership potential—and that she doesn't think she should be made to suffer for one childish, thoughtless but serious error of judgement. Dr Holding expects that she has already been punished, perhaps *most* severely by her own conscience, and is certain that she has learned a great deal from this mistake, that it is one she will never repeat. Even so, there is a need to provide some corrective action: she and the Head of Academics and the school counsellor will be meeting later in the week to devise something appropriate, most likely a community service program, but in the meantime Charlotte should offer up thanks that Sophie has recovered, and should make an effort to reflect on what the Gospels, what Jesus, says about forgiveness.

She even asks Charlotte whether she wants to say anything, and when Charlotte explains, for the thousandth time, that she is really sorry about being mean at school and on that stupid ASKfm, but that she didn't, she *truly* didn't, have anything to do with that website, that she didn't tell Sophie to kill herself, that she would never do anything that awful, Dr Holding just nods and pats her hand. 'I'm afraid that's something that you're never going to be able to prove, Charlotte. And whether or not you did it, many people, including Sophie and a number of your peers, believe it was you. That's something you're going to have to live with—or live down. But you're a strong girl, and a smart girl,' she gives a small smile, 'and I'm sure you'll find a way. Now, off you go—back to class. And you can send Amelia Carrington to see me next. I realise you're being blamed for this, but I *will* be talking to the other girls who were involved— and I'll be saying just what I've said to you.' Dr Holding looks grave. 'I don't want any of my girls being bullied—but nor do I want them to *be* bullies.'

Charlotte is almost overpowered by relief: she hasn't been expelled or even suspended. She might have to do some sort of community service, but she hasn't been given an actual detention. She hasn't even received a single demerit. And once back in class she has the unexpected pleasure of instilling a degree of terror in the others, Amelia, Harriet and Grace, who have somehow managed to distance themselves from the whole affair.

By lunchtime each of the girls has seen Dr Holding, but none of them is keen to share what's been said. It seems as if nothing much has changed, as far as their friendship goes. The gang of four is still intact—Charlotte, Amelia, Harriet and Grace—they're still pretty tight, and there's a new girl, Esther, who's just moved from South Africa, who sits with them at lunch and promises to show them how to make the sweet plaited friendship bracelets she's wearing beneath her long sleeves.

All of the other girls are just doing their usual thing—giggling or arguing, eating or not eating, gossiping about who's in or out, who's been dumped or who's a slut, who's put on weight or lost it. Other than the brief outpouring of emotion that had followed the morning's announcement, there's been barely any mention of Sophie. Charlotte had expected the suicide attempt, the bullying, the website, to still be the talk of the school; had assumed she'd be the subject of fevered whispering, the recipient of dirty looks. But apart from the odd cold shoulder and a few pointed comments from Matty Matherson and Bridie Stevenson, who seem to have appointed themselves Sophie's personal champions, there's been nothing she can't handle. And there's been no obvious change in the year dynamics. With the news of Sophie's recovery, it's almost as if the events of last term never happened.

And right at the end of the day, most bizarrely of all, Charlotte receives what amounts to a public pardon. Dr Holding herself comes to the class to make the announcement: Sophie Pennington is having a thirteenth birthday party and she wants them all to come. A blanket invitation has been issued to the entire class. *No exceptions.*

BETH

THE NIGHT BEFORE SCHOOL IS DUE TO GO BACK, BETH AND Dan sit the two girls down and tell them what's going on. They explain as simply as they can about the letter from the Penningtons' lawyer, the article that's due to come out, the ramifications of the whole thing being made public. They talk to them about what is likely to happen at school. There is no way to shield either of the girls completely—certain things are bound to be said; apparently the journalist has phoned a number of families, teachers, even the college headmistress. As far as they know, nobody's agreed to speak to her, and there are laws against naming minors, but that doesn't mean there won't be some sort of backlash at school. They warn the girls to stay calm. 'There's no need,' Dan tells them, his words chosen carefully, 'to respond to anything that anyone says. Whatever you do, don't react. And if it gets even the slightest bit nasty, we've spoken to Dr Holding and she says you're to go straight to her office and she'll deal with it. And,' he adds, addressing Charlotte specifically, 'she's told me that she's going to be talking to you first off, in the morning. So be prepared.'

The girls are surprisingly calm about the whole thing, though Beth has no clue as to what's going on in Charlotte's head. She's become so guarded—in her words, her expressions, her actions—that it's impossible to know what she's thinking, how she's actually feeling.

The only thing that seems to have remained constant in all this, the only one of them to have come out of the whole thing intact, and in some ways stronger—is Lucy. In those moments when Beth is capable of finding the good in what is happening (there are other things to be glad about, of course: she is still married, Dan has his job, her children are healthy, no one at Dan's work knows what's going on, the kitchen installation is due to begin in the next few weeks), she marvels at Lucy's remarkable resilience. Charlotte is booked in to see a counsellor, and she's considered making an appointment for Lucy too, imagining all sorts of damage from the trauma that's been inflicted over the past weeks, but whenever she asks her how she is, and whether she needs to talk to someone, Lucy reassures her. She's fine. *Truly.*

'And your friends,' Beth asks, 'is everyone being okay to you? There's not too much gossip? No online nastiness? You haven't been . . . dumped or anything?'

Lucy gives her a slightly pitying look. 'It's actually not about me, you know. One or two girls have mentioned it. But I don't hang with those mean-girl types like Charlie. You know that. The popular girls barely even know I exist.'

She says this with an odd air of satisfaction. Once upon a time Beth would have tried to draw out of her exactly what she meant by that remark, and whether she was really okay with her status. Once upon a time, Beth would have worried that Lucy was deliberately short-circuiting her own social success: that she wasn't ambitious enough in her friendships or that she was somehow narrow-minded, or worse, self-satisfied (Margie's genes); that she might be missing out on other possibilities, friendship-wise. She would have worried that it was a sign of poor self-esteem and tried to do something to compensate. But now she's happy to accept Lucy's reassurance at face value, is simply relieved. Despite everything that's happened, their elder daughter is okay. Lucy—who may not be a Queen Bee, Alpha Female or even one of the school's Leaders of the Future—is clearly a rock.

Lucy's relationship with her younger sister doesn't seem to have suffered either. In fact, since all this happened, the girls seem to have become closer than ever, closer than they have been for years. With Charlotte's usually frenetic social life at a virtual standstill, they have had more time to spend together. They cuddle up on the lounge watching movies, or swing together, one each end of the hammock, reading. There are even some half-funny, half-exasperating moments of ganging up against their parents, the girls siding with one another in ways they wouldn't usually. It's not that they've ever really fought, but for the past few years, as Charlotte has inexorably caught up to her elder sister in so many areas, overtaking her in some, there has been a certain cooling between them.

Beth has never been able to put her finger on what exactly happened: it's not as blatant as hostility, but a definite distance had been developing, perhaps connected to the shift in the elder–younger dynamic that had made them almost equals. Now, with all the shit that's going on, Beth is pleased to see Lucy regain a little of her former primacy. Charlotte is slightly more humble, deferring in small ways, and even seems to find some comfort in being the younger sister again, no longer pushing against some perceived older-sibling authority. She wonders whether advice, or even protection, has been sought and given.

Despite Dr Holding's reassurances, Beth stays close to home their first day back, cleaning sporadically, hanging out washing, trying to write a new post for her much neglected blog, worrying that she's going to be called up to the school, that there'll be dramas. At half past nine she gets a call from Drew.

'Have you heard?'

'What? Is it bad news?' Her first thought is that the article has come out, her second, shamefully, that Sophie has died.

'Oh God, sorry. No, it's good news. I've had a call from Dr Holding. Sophie Pennington regained consciousness over the weekend. She's still under observation, but it looks like she's going to make a full recovery, and they expect she'll be able to go home in a few days.'

It is good news, of course, but there's still the twin blades of the article and the legal action hanging over their heads. She tries to articulate her relief, but Drew interrupts, second-guessing her response. 'It's great news, but I know it could be better. Apparently Dr Holding spoke to the mother last week; she actually visited the hospital, tried to make her see reason. I'll make some calls, see what I can find out. Maybe they'll feel differently now that she's out of danger. Maybe they'll pull the pin.'

'Thanks, Drew. I'm really grateful. For everything.'

'I'm just sorry about how this panned out work-wise. I really wish things could have been different. But politics, hey? When this is all over—well, we can take another look at it then.'

She tries to call Dan a couple of times, but he is with clients and doesn't return her calls. His PA's voice gives nothing away: even on Beth's third attempt there are no chinks in her cool politeness. 'I'm so sorry, Mrs Mahony. Mr Mahony's still in a meeting. I'll make sure he gets the messages.'

When the girls arrive home, the three of them cram into the kitchen nook to eat the afternoon tea Beth has prepared as a special treat—pikelets with jam and cream—and though they both seem slightly subdued, there is no indication that it's been anything more than an ordinary day. Beth asks, but carefully, trying not to appear too worried, 'So, was it okay? Did anybody say anything?' Neither girl answers for a moment, but only, Beth realises, because they are unwilling to interrupt their feasting.

Charlotte is first to respond. 'It was fine, Mum.' She gives a slight roll of her eyes, the dismissive shrug that is fast becoming her signature response. 'It's not that big a deal. I mean, everyone's been worried about poor Sophie, but they told us she's like totally better, and nobody's said anything to me. I had to go and see Dr Holding, but so did Amelia and Grace and Harriet. And she says we really have to move on. I mean, it was terrible and obviously the situation got a bit out of control, but she knows that it was really nobody's fault. Dr H says that everyone makes mistakes and that I have a heap of potential and *blah blah blah,* so that's all cool. She said me and Grace and Harriet and Amelia might have to do community service or something. But that's probably going to be fun, don't you think?'

Beth doubts that the school community's response has been as blasé as Charlotte maintains, and wonders if this is the crux of what Dr Holding said to her daughter, or just the part she's chosen to remember. Part of her is glad that Charlotte has made her peace with herself so easily, that the events aren't going to haunt her, scar her somehow, but another part of her is chilled by her daughter's glib recital, her easy acceptance, her clear lack of remorse. It's what she wants, what she's always aimed for—evidence of self-esteem, resilience, emotional maturity. The irony doesn't escape her.

When Lucy gives her account of the day, her emphasis is slightly different. 'It was so amazing when they announced that Sophie was going to be okay. It was like, it was like a *miracle*.' But she isn't quite as complacent about the reactions of the other girls. 'It wasn't anything awful, like, nobody actually said anything mean,' she hurries to reassure her mother, 'but I'm sure a few of the girls were talking about what happened. And the teachers. Some of them were just . . . *funny*. You know, you can tell. I thought Miss Foley seemed a bit awkward or something.'

Charlotte listens to her sister, frowning slightly. 'You know, Lucy, you'll just make things harder for both of us if you imagine people are still talking about this. And anyway, it doesn't really affect you, does it? It isn't about *you*.' She slathers a pikelet with jam and cream and shoves it into her mouth, glaring at them both. She chews slowly, and then her face changes suddenly, her eyes lighting up. 'Actually, I *do* have something amazing to tell you. I can't believe I forgot!'

Beth's phone is buzzing—Drew. 'Hold on a sec.' She answers it distractedly, her eyes on Charlotte, who's clearly bursting to share her news.

Drew doesn't bother with any niceties. 'It's all good, Beth. I spoke with the Penningtons' solicitor, and apparently they've decided to drop the case.'

'Oh, thank God.'

'And, even better, I've heard from a contact at the *Herald*; the story's been rewritten. There's nothing that's even remotely connected to the Pennington girl or you. Right at the last min-ute, so a bit of high drama, apparently. I think the Penningtons got cold feet. Perhaps the article didn't go the way they expected, and of course the girl's recovery changes things. Fortunately for you, good news is no news.'

Beth lets Charlotte tell her amazing story before imparting Drew's update, though, child-like, she finds it hard to supress her relief, her joy.

'So, you'll never guess what, Mum? Not only is Sophie all better, but she's having a thirteenth birthday party next week. Dr Holding told us last period.'

She notes her mother's look of surprise with satisfaction, goes on. 'But that's not all. The invitation was to everyone in the class. And Dr Holding came up to me especially to make sure I understood that I was definitely invited, and said that I really should go. She said that it would be an important gesture of . . . *reconstruction* or something.'

'Goodness!' Beth is stunned. 'This is . . . miraculous! I've just had a call from Drew saying that the Penningtons have decided that they're not going to sue. And apparently the article doesn't say anything about . . . this.' Just like that, the nightmare has ended—and now it's to be as if nothing ever happened.

'Wow. It's all a bit mad, isn't it?' Charlotte is looking almost smug. 'I guess it would've been different if Sophie had died, but.' She says the words almost indifferently, scooping cream onto another pikelet. 'And someone told me it's going to be a crazy party—unicorn themed or something. She's going to have all those little kid games, like Mummies and Pin the Tail on the Donkey. I'm not sure what we're meant to wear, though. Are we meant to dress up or just wear ordinary clothes? Do you know, Luce?'

But her sister is beyond answering. She is weeping silently, her head bowed, her hands covering her face. Beth, shocked, moves to her side. 'Lucy. Lucy, honey. What's wrong? Has something happened?'

'I'm sure you're invited too, if that's the problem. I mean, you know Sophie likes you much more than—'

Lucy interrupts her sister. 'There's nothing wrong.' A shaky smile breaks through her tears. 'It's just that I've been so scared. I've been so worried about everything. That something bad was going to happen . . . That Sophie would die, and Charlotte, that Charlotte would be in trouble . . . It was so awful. It's just . . . I'm just so happy. I almost can't believe it's all over. And now the invitation. It's . . . amazing.'

Beth takes her elder daughter in her arms, holds her as hard as she can. 'It's just too amazing. I know. I'm with you there, honey.' She feels the answering tears well in her own eyes. 'I'm with you there.'

RANDOM FACT No 2

HOW TO INDUCE VOMITING

The internet suggests a heap of ways to do it. We all know about fingers down throats and jiggling that wobbly bit, but this can be difficult to pull off in public. And then there's mustard and warm water—but that might be a bit awkward too. I mean, mustard, it's bound to bring everything up, but . . . erk. Then there's something called Ipecac—but where the fuck would you get that shit?

So, it looks like the simplest, and most easy to disguise, is the salt-water method. Just add a few teaspoons of salt to water (or even juice, or lemonade), shake vigorously and *voilà*!

Or do I mean *blargh!*

COMMENTS

@DrPat says:

Hi, Golden Child. Vomiting is definitely not the answer to any body image problems you might be experiencing. Do you have any caring adults or older friends who can help? If not, please feel free to reach out: DrPat@syracuseclinic.com

SOPHIE

SHE DOESN'T PLAN ANY OF IT. IN FACT, THE INVITATION IS made genuinely in the spirit, as Dr Holding puts it, of reconciliation. Sophie wakes from her long dream completely and utterly tranquil, as if the unicorns and rainbows have magically cancelled out all the bad memories. She wants to draw a thick black texta line beneath the past, dividing it from the now. And she wants everyone to see it. She wants to go back to school—because when she thinks about it there are so many aspects of HLC that she loves—and go on as if nothing has happened.

But as the time for the party (which is to be slightly smaller than Sophie's original grand conception) draws closer, she begins to worry a little about the weirdness of the situation. She wonders whether it will be completely weird. How will she greet Charlotte? What will she say to her? And what if Charlotte says something about what happened; what if she wants to apologise? The prospect is just too horrible to contemplate. Her mother and father, she knows, are worried too—she's overheard them discussing it. And it isn't the awkwardness, it isn't even Sophie's well-being they're concerned about. They aren't sure they'll be able to disguise their rage, behave civilly. They actually come very close to contacting the Mahonys and uninviting Charlotte on the eve of the party, but Sophie's paternal grandfather, visiting for the occasion, somewhat surprisingly intervenes. 'It's important that you let the girl come,' he says. 'It's a public show of Sophie's strength of character. If she's brave enough to face up to her worst enemy, and big enough to want to forgive her, then you should support her. Whatever the cost to your pride.'

The thing is, when she's actually face to face with Charlotte, Sophie suddenly realises that she hasn't really forgiven her. Up until now she's had no particular feelings towards her, save the same warm fuzziness that she feels about almost everything, but at the sight of Charlotte, waiting at the front door with her mother and sister, her face uncharacteristically solemn, the fuzzy feeling evaporates. It's replaced by a sharp feeling of anger, which, though as unfamiliar as it is unexpected, isn't entirely unpleasant. But Sophie manages to greet her, to greet the three of them, calmly, to thank them politely for their gift—a silver charm bracelet—and lead them into the kitchen where all the other girls and a few mothers are already congregated.

Even Sophie notices that the conversation pauses momentarily when the Mahonys enter, and there's a communal shuffling, subtle, like herd animals moving closer for comfort. Conversation quickly resumes; no one looks at them—neither girls nor parents—or greets them. Her mother, who manages to dredge up a strange thin-lipped smile, offers some polite words of welcome. There are none of the heartfelt hugs that other girls and their mothers have offered, just a stilted hello. Charlotte's mum thanks them for the invitation, her smile a little too friendly, her voice shaky and high. She makes her excuses quickly, gives a general wave, and Andi leads her back down the hallway. Charlotte stares after her mother for a long moment, then turns to Sophie. 'Hey,' she says, not quite meeting Sophie's eyes, 'this looks really cool.' She smiles, but her bottom lip trembles.

Sophie can't help grinning. 'I don't know that it's cool, exactly. But it *is* pretty awesome.'

The family room has been decorated exactly the way she wanted it, with rainbow streamers strung across the ceiling and unicorns of various size, colour and design swinging between multicoloured paper lanterns. There are unicorn-horn party hats and the food is themed—crème horns, rainbow cakes and clouds of fairy floss. There's nothing healthy in sight. It's like the ultimate little-kid party. Six months ago the girls would have sneered at it—in fact six months ago Sophie wouldn't have dared to hold such a party, and even if she had, no one would have come. But now her entire class is here, full of good cheer, and apparently genuinely glad to see her, glad to be here—and all prepared to join in, to make it fun.

Sophie can see that Charlotte is anxious, that she really wants to say something else to her. 'Hey, Sophie, it's really good that you're okay,' she begins, but Lucy interrupts, her voice quietly authoritative. 'Charlotte. Remember what Mum said? You know she said you weren't to—'

Sophie would like to hear Lucy's reminder to her suddenly red-faced sister, but just then Matilda Matherson arrives with her two sisters, and Sophie can't help giving a happy squeal as she skips off to greet them, Charlotte forgotten in the excitement.

She tries hard not to take too much notice of Charlotte's movements during the party, and there are so many girls, all of them vying for Sophie's attention simultaneously, clamouring to stand near her, share sweets, cake, food, to be her partner in all the silly games, that it's easy to get swept up in the fun of it. She's vaguely aware that Charlotte is far quieter than usual, that she sticks close to her sister and remains at the edge rather than the centre of things. She notices, too, that the other girls, while not exactly avoiding her, aren't necessarily including Charlotte. For once, even Harriet, Amelia and Grace have dispersed into the group, aren't hanging with one another; all the traditional divisions have dissolved.

She has a brief and slightly awkward conversation with Lucy, who she meets in the kitchen, filling a cup at the sink. 'I was just getting some tap water,' Lucy explains. 'Sugar overdose. It's an awesome party, though. Really fun,' she says, swirling the water in the plastic cup as she speaks. 'And I think you were really, really kind to invite us—you know, after everything.'

'Oh, well, I just thought it would be good to . . . you know, to have everyone.' Sophie shrugs. She likes Lucy well enough, but isn't sure that she wants to have this conversation with her, or with anyone else, for that matter.

'Yeah, well, you probably don't want to talk about it right now, but I just want you to know that I'm really sorry about what happened. And about what they did—Charlotte and the others, I mean. I'm so glad you're okay. And don't worry, Charlie won't get away with it.' Lucy takes an absentminded sip from the cup, grimaces, keeps swirling. 'You know—karma. It'll catch up with her eventually. She might be my sister, but sometimes . . .' She gives a meaningful smile and heads back into the melee before Sophie can respond.

Sophie, who's forgotten what she came for, hovers in the kitchen doorway. She watches as Lucy goes to the food table, where she tops up her cup with lemonade and piles a plate with assorted party food before heading over to her sister, who is standing alone. Charlotte's forlorn expression brightens a little when her sister approaches bearing food and drink. She takes a long sip from the cup, makes a face, bites into a sausage roll. That was it! Amelia and Elinor wanted more crème horns. Sophie goes back into the kitchen to find them.

The final game—Uni-Horns—is really just the promised Pin the Tail on the Donkey with a unicorn twist. Instead of a donkey they have a rather wobbly outline of a unicorn, drawn by her granddad and coloured in by Sophie. Golden horns, which have been printed from the internet and pasted onto cardboard, are given to each player. At thirteen, the girls are really too old for the game, and for all the kiddie party games they've been playing, but they enter into the contest just as enthusiastically as they would have when they were six, jostling to go next, giggling hysterically at each other's efforts, the horns pinned in all sorts of ridiculous positions, Matty's best of all, the one that leaves them clutching their stomachs—dead centre on the unicorn's butt.

Sophie's mother does the turning and pointing of the first blindfolded girl, but then Lucy, who looks less than excited by the prospect of being spun herself, volunteers. The older girl is way better at the whole spinning thing than Andi, getting right into the spirit of the game, spinning each girl hard and fast and then giving her a gentle push in the right direction. A few of the girls claim dizziness after they're spun and have to be guided to the unicorn, their steps hilariously hesitant, some of them buckling at the knees, almost as if they're drunk.

When it comes to her sister's turn, Lucy tightens the blindfold with a flourish, then, despite Charlotte's squealing protests, turns her even more rapidly and for far longer than she has turned any of the other girls. Before anyone can offer to guide her, Lucy gives her sister a firm push in the middle of the back. Charlotte takes a single slow step, then another, and then pauses, swaying dangerously. She shuffles forward a step or two and stops again, clutching her stomach. She stands still for another long moment, and they all wait, mesmerised, as a slow shudder moves up her torso. She gives an agonised yelping retch and then vomits, a thick pink surge across the floor. Still nobody moves to help. Charlotte sobs, her body wracked by another spasm. This time her legs give out and she falls heavily, blindly, knees first and then hands, into the foul puddle.

Sophie, stricken, sees Lucy at the edge of the stunned crowd, watching her sister intently. There's an odd look on her face, but it's gone immediately, replaced by an expression of embarrassment. Sophie searches for her mother, who is moving, but not fast enough, to the scene. Before she can do anything, Charlotte gives another shameful yelp and vomits again, the mess globbing slowly down the front of her party clothes.

The giggles are surreptitious, quickly muffled. Sophie puts her hands to her mouth, trying hard not to follow suit. And then Matilda Matherson, loud, pitiless: 'Oh, dear. That's so gross. Poor Charlotte. Has anyone got an iPhone? We should totally make sure everyone sees this.'

BETH

SHE IS SO PLEASED THAT CHARLOTTE, AND THEN LUCY, HAVE been invited to the party that she doesn't even consider the extreme awkwardness, the painfulness, of her and Andi's meeting. She worries about Charlotte, of course, primes her, warns her not to say too much—to Sophie or anyone else. It would be best to let things settle, she tells her; left alone it will all calm down and eventually even be forgotten.

Charlotte looks at her scornfully. 'I'm not going to start apologising for something I didn't do, if that's what you're worried about.' Beth's stomach clenches, but she stays calm, giving a dismissive wave of her hand. 'Okay, Charlotte. All I'm saying is that this is an opportunity to smooth things over. The Penningtons have been very generous and made the first move, so let's keep it going.'

She hasn't thought past Charlotte's response, and so her own anxiety comes as a surprise. Waiting at the door, hearing the cheery hubbub inside, she begins to shake, her heart pounding so loudly she can barely hear, and when a smiling Sophie runs out to greet them, her manner so unselfconsciously friendly, it takes her a moment to find her voice. If it didn't mean leaving Charlotte to her fate, she would have hightailed it out of there. But the moment passes, the words come, and she follows Sophie and the girls into the house. She notices—how can she not?—the sudden quiet, like a collectively indrawn breath, as the three of them enter but she forces herself to keep moving.

She manages to greet Andi, whose feelings are masked behind a polite smile and a perfunctory greeting. 'Thanks for bringing them, Beth,' she says stiffly. 'It was important to Sophie that the whole class be invited.' So much can be read between these particular lines, but mercifully there's no opening for Beth to add anything meaningful. She says nothing more than what's expected, what's polite, but even that's strangled, almost incoherent, and then Andi is leading her back down the hallway, opening the door to usher her out. 'We'll be done by two-thirty,' she says, closing and locking the screen door, as if making sure that Beth has no opportunity to say anything, to *offer* anything. 'I'll have the girls ready at the door, so there's no need for you to come in to get them.' In other circumstances this would be a kindness, offered for convenience—no need to leave the car. But here, now—Beth knows the gesture's not designed to make things easier for her.

Dan is spending the afternoon in his office, and she had intended to go home and write up a new blogpost; but she's lost heart. And what can she possibly say, right now—what observations, what reflections can she possibly offer? Her kids, her job, her marriage, even her house—however she looks at her life, there's just no suitable straw to be spun, and no possibility of fashioning gold. She hasn't posted for almost two weeks, the concerned messages are piling up in her inbox, but other than sending a breezy, *I'm fine, just busy! Thanks so much for asking. Miss you too Xxx*, to her most loyal readers, she's largely ignoring them. She still hasn't finished her blog for TrailingWife.com—and the guest post date is looming. Beth can feel the whole thing winding down, her motivation as much as anything. What's the point?

She feels so unsettled after the visit to the Penningtons'. Her nerves are jangling and there's a dull pain in her head. She walks upstairs to the bedroom wearily, each step an effort, and lies down on the bed. She tries to read but it's no good. Plays an audiobook but the narrator's accent grates. She tries a basic meditation technique that sometimes works for her: count backwards from one hundred, breathe in, breathe out, starting again whenever she loses track. She has finally reached three— on her fifth try—when her mobile rings. It's Andi. 'Charlotte's been sick,' she says, her voice brisk. There's no give in it, no warmth. 'You need to come and pick her up.'

It's a mess—in more ways than one. When she arrives, Charlotte and Lucy are waiting outside, standing by the front gate, with a vaguely familiar woman—another of the class mums, Beth assumes, although she has no idea of her name, or her daughter's. Charlotte's face is red, her eyes puffy, her hair is a tangled mess, and although there's been some attempt to clean her up, the front of her jersey and the knees of her trousers are stained and damp. Lucy is standing supportively close, obviously trying to comfort her, but is just as obviously being brushed off. When they see her, Beth contemplates gesturing for them to come straight over, but does the right thing, reluctantly exiting the car and heading over to the waiting trio.

Charlotte hurtles past her without a word and disappears into the back seat, slamming the door closed, while Lucy hangs back politely. The woman speaks in a rush, before Beth has time to ask her anything. 'She wanted to wait outside, poor thing. She's a bit . . . whiffy. Andi's cleaning up, so I thought I'd wait out here with them. It was a bit of a disaster, I'm afraid.

Charlotte had an accident during a game. She didn't quite make it to the bathroom. It's a timber floor, so I don't think there'll be any permanent damage, do you, Lucy?'

But Lucy is clearly not concerned about the state of the Penningtons' flooring. 'It was actually my fault, Mum. I was in charge of spinning all the girls, and I totally didn't think. I feel really awf—'

'Oh, no, it wasn't *anyone's* fault, sweetheart,' the woman interrupts, keen to reassure her. 'She'd probably just eaten too much. It happens all the time. Fizzy drink, lollies, cake. All the excitement.' She gives a little shrug, winces.

'It doesn't matter.' Beth grabs Lucy's hand. 'We'll just get her home and clean her up. Can you . . . can you thank Andi and Steve?' Then, before she can stop herself, 'And can you tell them we're sorry. She's sorry. Tell them Charlotte is very sorry for whatever mess she's made.'

Charlotte is silent during the short ride home, and once there she still refuses to speak, heads straight to the bathroom and locks herself in. Beth gathers clean clothes and leaves them in a neat pile outside the door. Lucy is waiting for her in the kitchen, clearly prepared for the inevitable interrogation.

'So what happened, Lucy?'

'It was nothing, really. I mean, it was awful, but it wasn't anything Charlotte did. She just vomited—she really couldn't help it.' Lucy is so transparent, her anxiety so evident; Beth knows there's something she's *not* saying.

'And did anything else happen?'

'That's all. Really.'

'I can tell there's something you're not saying. Whatever it is, you need to tell me.'

'Well . . . okay.' Lucy takes a deep breath. 'It's just that everyone laughed when Charlotte vomited. And then when she fell over in it, they . . .' She pauses.

'What? What happened?'

'Well, one of the girls said something really horrible—about it being a pity that they didn't have it on film. You know, so they could Instagram it, or whatever—show everyone.'

'Oh, God.'

'And then . . . it was so awful. It seemed to take ages for anyone to help her and Charlotte was just sort of lying there, vomiting and vomiting, and her hair was all over her face, and she couldn't see, and everyone started laughing. Even some of the parents.' Lucy's eyes are wide and shiny with tears. 'And Mum, it was really my fault. I spun her pretty hard, but it was just for fun. I didn't mean to make her sick.' She gives a little sob.

'Of course you didn't mean to, darling. It was an accident.'

Beth tries to comfort her daughter, hugs her, but the sobs only grow louder. Lucy wraps her arms around Beth's middle, hiding her face, her shoulders shaking; the weeping increasingly intense. The sobs veer alarmingly into what sounds like hysterical laughter, and just for a moment, Beth is tempted to join in.

RANDOM FACT No 3

HOW TO BREAK A BONE

There are so many crazy ways to do this. The one I like the best is the potato method. You just put potatoes on the bone you want to break overnight, and in the morning you tap it with a spoon. And then—just like that—*snap*!

If this method fails, which it will, because it's fucking stupid, here's the hardcore advice: why not hit the limb with a hammer or crush it under a heavy piece of furniture? Yup. I reckon that might do the trick.

This is going to be difficult to pull off AND it's going to hurt like a goddamn bitch. But it's *so* going to be worth it.

COMMENTS

@RANDOMREADER says:

Potato method! Are you serious?

BETH

By early evening Charlotte still hasn't emerged from her room. Beth is just about to start on the dinner—what they call a Margie meal: sausages and mashed potatoes, carrots and peas—when she hears angry shouting coming from upstairs. She can make out Charlotte's voice, shrill and accusatory, though the words aren't clear. She calls up the stairway for them to stop, but there's no point, she knows that neither of them will hear, and is wondering whether to intervene, when she hears a loud crash. There's the sharp sound of breaking glass and then a heavy slam, powerful enough to shake the ceiling, the walls. There's more yelling, high-pitched, frightened, and then a long wounded howl. She races up the stairs, not stopping to think.

In Lucy's bedroom, the antique wardrobe, solid mahogany, huge and apparently immovable, has been knocked onto its side. Lucy has been knocked down too, and is lying alongside it, screaming horribly. Her forearm and hand are pinned beneath the cupboard, the rest of her arm and shoulder are impossibly twisted. Shards of glass from a light fitting litter the carpet. Charlotte is crouched beside her sister, pushing desperately, unable to move the wardrobe even a fraction. 'Mum! Mum!' She too is shrieking, hysterical. 'Lucy's arm. It's stuck. I can't move it. I can't get it out.' There is no time for words now, or even for thinking. Just the tasks, done methodically, as if in a trance, of somehow levering the weight off her daughter, of getting her to her feet, half carrying her down the stairs, settling her in the car, driving her to the hospital, calling Dan.

'So what happened?'

Lucy has been anaesthetised, plastered—luckily it is a clean break and doesn't require surgery—and is lying propped on a hospital bed, waiting for the specialist. It's only Beth and Lucy; Dan has taken Charlotte home, but he's heading back shortly, and will wait with Lucy until she's released.

Beth has avoided asking the question until now, isn't sure that she actually wants it answered. But there's no way of putting it off any longer: Beth knows, they all know, that there's no possibility that the wardrobe fell over by itself.

At first, Lucy is resolute in her denial. 'I can't remember.' She shrugs; her face and voice are devoid of expression.

'Oh, come on. That cupboard couldn't have fallen on you without some sort of . . . assistance. Were you climbing on it for some reason? We've told you never to.' Even as she says it, Beth knows that this solution, however attractive, is highly unlikely.

'I don't know. Honestly. The last thing I remember I was just opening it, and the next thing it was on top of me. It was always really wobbly.'

'It's not the slightest bit wobbly. You and Charlotte saw Dad and me trying to move it out. And we couldn't.' When they first moved in, Dan and Beth had wanted the large cupboard for their own room, but they hadn't been able to move it more than a few feet. 'It would take—deliberate force—to make it pitch forward like that. It couldn't happen just by opening it.'

332

Beth moves closer, leans down so her face is level with Lucy's. 'Lucy, if your sister did this somehow, you need to tell me. We need to know.' She has to whisper, the words are almost impossible to think, let alone say. 'If there's something wrong with her, we have to do something. Charlotte needs our help.'

Her daughter's reply is sharper than the serpent's tooth, the poison deadlier.

It's after midnight when Dan gets home. Beth is sitting in the kitchen, her laptop out, trying to distract herself. She cooked the sausages, but Charlotte refused to come out of her bedroom to eat. Dan walks straight into the kitchen, heads to the fridge. He opens a bottle of beer and takes a swig. He doesn't look at Beth, doesn't say a word.

Eventually Beth speaks. 'I think you're overreacting. I know it's bloody awful. And I know we have to do something. But I don't understand why you've taken Lucy to your mother's. She should be here. With her mother, not her grandmother. And you shouldn't have told Margie it was Charlotte's fault. It's just playing into your mother's hands.'

He looks at her now, incredulous. 'Playing into *my mother's* hands? What the fuck? None of this has anything to do with my mother. What are you talking about? I just thought it was the best thing to do, the *safest* thing. For *Lucy*.'

'You know as well as I do that it's more than that. Your mother has had it in for Charlotte since we got here. She's . . . you know, I think Margie's pleased about what's happened—it's giving her the excuse she needs.' She knows, even as she says the words that she's being irrational, avoiding what's really at stake, attacking the wrong target.

'The excuse she needs for what? What exactly is it that my mother wants?' He sounds less angry now, more concerned. 'Oh, Bethie. My *mother* is not the villain here.'

'I can't believe you don't see it. All this. It means she's won. She'll have been right about everything. About the school. About Charlotte. About me. It's just going to confirm everything she already thinks.' It's a relief to actually say it aloud at last, to have all the vague stirrings of the past months finally coalesce into a firm idea, even if it's not the one she should be focusing on.

'Oh, for fuck's sake. You've lost the plot.'

'Mum's right, Dad. Nanny doesn't like me. Actually, I think she probably *hates* me.'

Charlotte is leaning against the kitchen doorjamb, her arms crossed, her face pale, her eyes red from weeping. But she's composed, speaks calmly.

'Oh, darling.' Beth feels her heart contract. 'Of course Nanny loves you. Everybody loves you. That isn't the issue.'

'She doesn't. But I don't care about that. There's something else. Something even worse. It's Lucy. She's doing all this: her broken arm, the website. She must be. I've been trying to work it out, but I don't understand why she's doing it. Why she keeps trying to get me into trouble. It's like she hates me. It's like she's gone crazy. '

'Oh, Charlotte. Your sister hasn't done anything. Lucy loves you. I don't know why you can't just tell the truth. It's . . . I don't know if you're sick or what the hell is going on. But this lying— it has to stop.' Dan is shaking, his voice is shrill.

'I *am* telling the truth. I've been telling you the truth from the beginning. I said I was mean to Sophie a few times, at school and on stupid ASKfm, but that's it. I *did* take those photos, I told you that. But that was just a game we were both playing, and I didn't put them on that website. I don't know how they got there. Somebody got them off my iPad. And I didn't, I promise, I didn't break Lucy's arm. I wasn't even in her room when it happened. I was in my bedroom. I swear.'

'How could she make a wardrobe fall on top of her? It's impossible.'

'We worked out how to push it over ages ago. Don't you remember? We found that old book about pulleys and levers and moved all our bedroom furniture. It's simple.'

'But why would she want to hurt herself? It doesn't make sense.'

'There's no reason.' Charlotte's voice quakes. 'I told you— she just hates me. I don't know why.'

'Oh, honey, stop it. Just stop. Nobody hates you. We all love you. Lucy loves you and we love you. You're our child—we'll always love you.' Beth tries to put her arms around her daughter but she pushes her away.

'I don't want you to *love* me.' Charlotte is crying now, great heaving sobs. 'What good is that? I want you to *believe* me.' She looks straight at her mother, her eyes tragic, her mouth trembling; takes a deep breath. 'And if you can't believe me, what sort of parents are you?'

What sort of parents are they? Once, when she thought she understood who her children were, Beth had known the answer to that. Now, it doesn't bear thinking about.

If You've Got an Itch

I remember when we first announced that we were heading back to Australia, an expat friend of mine laughed at my excitement and told me that it wouldn't last. 'You've been away too long; you're used to the expat life. You'll be sick of being home in no time at all,' she said. 'I give you six months, a year max, and you'll be itching to move again.'

I laughed. I didn't believe her. We were back to stay. It was time to settle down, to give our girls the chance to grow up close to family, to experience Aussie life, to stretch a little under that vast southern sky . . .

But it looks like my friend was right. It hasn't even been a year and we're on the move again. It's not that we don't love it here—we do! It's lived up to our expectations in every way: being close to family, experiencing all the sights and sounds of our birth country, giving our girls some of those same opportunities and experiences that we had.

But. Somehow it's not enough. It looks like we're hooked, you see. Hooked on change, hooked on adventure, hooked on experiencing new places, new people.

Chicago, here we come.

COMMENTS CLOSED

THE GOLDEN CHILD'S TEN LESSONS FOR SUCCESS

LESSON TEN: END GAME

Just say you have two children, equally beloved. One comes in screaming with a broken arm, saying that her sister's to blame—that she pushed a wardrobe onto her, that she could even have been killed.

These children don't usually fight, and neither of them has ever done anything really bad to the other—not publicly anyway. But one of them has been in quite a lot of trouble lately. Maybe she's in a whole heap of shit. The other one—she's never been in any sort of trouble. Not ever. She isn't as clever or talented or pretty or as popular as the other sister, or so they assume, but right now, as far as behaviour goes, *she's* the good guy. When this child tells her parents that the other sister broke her arm *deliberately*, they're going to believe her.

And the more the other child protests, the worse she makes it. Her parents have already lost respect for her. And now—why, they're actually scared of her. Funny, right? They might still love her, who knows? But they sure as hell don't trust her. Hey, maybe they don't even want her around anymore. There are special places for kids like her, after all.

But that other one. She's destined for greatness. They've made their choice: she's the one.

The Golden Child.

COMMENTS

@RANDOMREADER says:

You are one sick sistah, Goldie. Glad you aint mine.

@CHARLOTTEMAH says:

Hey, Lucy. Cool blog. Wow—the things that come up when you google 'oleander poisoning'! So why'd you stop at lesson ten? I'll bet you've got more of that really awesome advice to give out to your non-existent readers. Maybe you're too busy having fun in Chicago—now you're an only child 'n' all . . .

So, yeah—I've met some pretty interesting folks here at my 'special' school. It's not that bad, in fact it probably isn't all that different to a regular boarding school. Though I guess it'd be different if we were all bad kids from bad homes—not that they're allowed to call us bad. Lol. They prefer to call us 'troubled'. And hey, it's awesome to be back home in the US. Still, all things considered, I'd really rather be in the windy city with my beloved family.

Oh, and here's some news that might interest you. My old buddy Sophie P sent me a message a couple of weeks ago. Apparently, she's been thinking about that whole birthday vomit disaster. She thinks that maybe you had something to do with it, and now she's all worried that maybe I didn't set her up after all . . . It got me wondering too. Salt water! Who knew?

Anyway, I've taken a heap of screenshots, so don't bother pulling this shit down, or changing it. I'm sending them to Mum and Dad right now. They're gonna be thrilled.

Lmao. See y'all real soon XXX

They Carry Your Heart

What would it take to stop loving them? You know, don't you, that you never will. You know that mother love doesn't depend on them being easy to rear, doesn't depend on them always being good or kind or sweet or easy. If you can love a newborn, those relentlessly crying, always hungry, devourers of sleep, destroyers of all things orderly—you know there's no choice.

The moment they're born, that's it. You've given them your heart and there's no way you can ever get it back.

Even if you want to.

COMMENTS CLOSED

ACKNOWLEDGMENTS

THANKS ARE OWED TO MANY PEOPLE.

To my agent, Alexis Hurley, for her faith that *The Golden Child* would eventually get there—and for getting it there. To William Callahan and Liz Parker at Inkwell Management, whose critiques of the not-quite-there-yet book were incredibly helpful.

To Mary Rennie, publisher and editor extraordinaire, whose gentle insistence that I could do it better has meant that I've done it better. I think Mary has read this book almost as many times as I have—and she still likes it! I'm struggling to find the right words to express the extent of my gratitude, Mary—but will get a better paragraph to you asap.

To my brilliant editor Amanda O'Connell, to whom I solemnly swear that I will never again write a first draft that alternates between past and present tense.

To the remarkable team at HarperCollins Australia—Shona Martyn, James Kellow, Alice Wood, Jaki Arthur, Anna Valdinger, Sarah Barrett, Graeme Jones and Hazel Lam—for their enthusiasm and all-round excellence. It's been such a pleasure to work with you all.

To the wonderful team at Skyhorse who've brought the novel to an American audience: Alexandra Hess, whose early enthusiasm will always be appreciated; Kirsten Kim who has some stellar publicity skills as well as a keen editorial eye, and to Erin for the spine tingling cover design.

To the lovely Addison Duffy at United Talent Agency for reading when she should have been partying—and for making some dreams come true. To my early readers—Marie Battisti, Jaye Ford, Susan Francis, Shari Kocher, Sophie Masson, Sharon Noble and Abi Shepherd—who assured me that the book was worth reading, and rewriting. To my sister Rebecca James, who has read and reread, and can always be relied upon to provide a sharp eye—and an endlessly patient ear. And to my smug literary friend Linda Martin, whose editorial advice was, as ever, priceless.

To Richard Hardy, whose lucid explanation of civil law helped untangle some knotty plot ideas. To Detective Acting Inspector Julian Thornton from the NSW Police Fraud and Cybercrime Squad who provided helpful specialist advice on legal issues surrounding cybercrime. And to former Senior Constable Darren Shepherd who once again provided information on police procedure, as well as some good advice on bad sentences.

To my specialists in contemporary adolescence, Maddi Battisti and Nell Shepherd, who told me when I was being lame, and provided a few choice phrases. Sometimes inadvertently.

To the amazing Creative Word Shop writers, for making me think hard about the how of writing again—and to Ed Wright, who helped make that happen.

To Jeffrey Braithwaite, Kristiana Ludlow and the rest of the CHRIS team at the Australian Institute of Health Innovation, for keeping me sane.

To the friends and family who've shared their stories of parenting over the past two and a half and a bit decades—I couldn't have done it without you (and by 'it' I mean both raised children and written this book). You've been inspiring in every sense of the word.

To my extended and ever-extending family: as ever, your love and support are what keep me going. To Darren, Sam, Abi, Nell and Will—as ever, you're the why.

And lastly, to my father, Tony, whose devil's advocate dissing of Jane Austen when I was a teenager set the whole thing in motion. I'm just sorry you missed this one, Dad.

Wendy James is the mother of two sets of siblings born eight years apart, in the digital and pre-digital ages. She is the author of seven novels, including the bestselling *The Mistake*. Her debut novel, *Out of the Silence*, won the 2006 Ned Kelly Award for first crime novel, and was shortlisted for the Nita May Dobbie award for women's writing. She works as an editor at the Australian Institute of Health Innovation.